ADVENTURES IN MANIC DEPRESSION

TALES IN FINE MADNESS

ADVENTURES IN MANIC DEPRESSION

TALES IN FINE MADNESS

Stuart Goldman

Shaker Square Press

Published in the United States by Shaker Square Press
P.O. Box 8268, Calabasas, CA, 91372.

Front and rear cover art by Ray Troll
Cover design by Stuart Goldman, Heather Anne Cheney.
Book interior design by Daniel Barrozo, the Ink Studio.

Adventures In Manic Depression: Tales In Fine Madness/Stuart Goldman
ISBN 978-0-9899174-1-4
1. Goldman, Stuart 2. Literature-Fiction/Non-fiction/Authorship I. Title

Shaker Square Press email address:
info@shakersquarepress.com
info@stuartgoldmanadventures.com
website: www.stuartgoldmanadventures.com
wikipedia.org: Stuart Goldman

First Edition

This book is dedicated—with
great love and affection—to my parents,
Maurice Goldman and Ethel Mann Goldman.

I must soon quit the scene.
—Benjamin Franklin

Ah, they must be seen—the masks people wear under our great opalescent skies. And when they walk and move, daubed with cruel colors, wretched and pitiful under the rain, bowing and fawning... terrified figures at once insolent and timid, growling or yapping, with shrill falsetto voices or loud metallic voices, with the heads of macabre beasts and the unexpected, unsubdued gestures of irritated animals.

Repulsive humanity—ever on the move...in cast-off clothes, shimmering with spangles torn from the mask of the moon. Then I saw things in a big way, and my heartbeat quickened and my bones trembled, and I divined the enormity of these distortions and anticipated the modern spirit. A new world loomed up before me.
—James Ensor

We are not told of things that happened to specific people exactly as they happened; but in the beginning is when there are good things and bad things...things that happen in this life which one never tires of seeing and hearing about—things which one cannot bear not to tell of and must pass on for all generations. If the storyteller wishes to speak well, then he chooses the good things...and if he wishes to hold the reader's attention, he chooses the bad things. Good things and bad things alike; they are the things of this world and no other.
—Murasaki Shikibu

HONEST VOICE

To the editors:

It is my understanding that Mr. Stuart Goldman's writing for our publication elicits largely negative mail. Therefore, I must cast my vote very much in favor of his continued presence in the *Reader*.

Mr. Goldman is a thoroughly refreshing throwback to the crabby but stirring era of H.L. Menckenesqe journalism. Whatever his problems—mostly within the realm of "good taste—he is an HONEST voice who frightens people due to his very integrity. This does not mean he is a "nice" man. But reading his latest commentary, "Coitus Interruptus," (*Reader*, July 11), convinces me he is a brutally truthful one.

I suppose that extreme feminists and similar axe-grinders will heap abuse upon Mr. Goldman once again for his "insensitive remarks." Such a reaction only demonstrates the accuracy of his views—that sex is the most coercive, inherently fascistic area of human activity. Mr. Goldman's resolution not to allow his cock to enslave him is a courageous position (and one not so different than taken by the ancient Gnostic Christians and modern Buddhists). If he steps on a few toes, he is only doing so in the process of recoiling from the shocking creatures we call the Human Race (yes, ladies included).

Mr. Goldman is not at fault for exercising his choice of not "fucking" and saying so. I applaud his resolute nature and uncompromising position

—*The Los Angeles Reader*

YER AVERAGE JOES

To the Editors:

Undoubtedly you will receive countless letters from outraged gays, feminists, and every other kind of special-interest group regarding Stuart Goldman's "Final Cut," ("Elvis, Dylan, Ali and Me," *Reader*, June 28).

I would like to speak for the non-extremists—the men in the middle. Not the trend-mongering, West L.A. snot wipes, but just your average Joes. We're guys just trying to get by, guys with pot bellies, clothes that never seem to fit right, and looks that don't get many in return. We suffer silently, while the more obnoxious of the species—the whining yuppies—complain and get the attention...making the whole world look to be wimped-out clones of Prince, or cardboard Springsteen hunkers.

Stuart Goldman is a rare breed of writer. He carries the torch ignited by Hunter S. Thompson, and is more focused than Charles Bukowski. The amount of mail Goldman's articles stir up is solid evidence that a lot of people don't like to hear the truth.

I'm an often lonely writer and sometimes feel ready to throw in the towel. But when I read Goldman, I wanna get up and write my ass off. I wanna scream for the rights of normal individuals with antiquated belief systems where men are men, women are women, and the role reversals haven't become so terribly suffocating.

Hemingway isn't dead; he's still living in Stuart Goldman—a chauvinist pig with enough guts and talent to fill every empty beer can I've ever tossed.

—*The Los Angeles Reader*

CONTENTS

CONTENTS

CONTENTS

A WORD ABOUT STUART GOLDMAN

Stuart Goldman has been a working journalist for 42 years. I remember reading some of his early articles in the *L.A. Weekly* and thinking—*this* guy's got balls. There was no subject too remote, too off the beaten path, or too taboo for him. He tackled anything that captured his imagination, and put it into tangible form so the reader had a fresh understanding and insight into the subject he was presenting.

Stu's new book—*Adventures In Manic Depression*—provides a very special brand of insight. He tackles a variety of mindboggling subjects. Whether he's writing about taxi dancers, lovers discovering secrets about each other, or childhood haunts—he always gives you a visual so compelling that you can't look away. When I read his work, I can see into the walled courtyards, lighted windows, secret rooms and hidden places of the heart. Being a writer and musician myself, I know that creating anything engaging is no easy task. It's not something you learn at journalism school. But because Stu is also a musician, he knows all about rhythms, pacing and space—and it comes out in his writing. In a sense, this book is a "symphony" of sorts.

When I asked Stu how he was going to put together a single book containing such a disparate variety of subjects (he goes from writing straight newspaper-style crime reportage, to heartrending recollections of many of his family members, to fairy tale like fantasies) he said he took the cue from his father, a well-known composer of classical music. "I grew up in a musical home," he told me. "I watched and listened to my father sit at the piano for hours at time, composing cantatas and symphonies. I learned that it was not so much about the note on the page, as it was the rhythm...the timing—when to make use of a crescendo, or when to let the music become so quiet that you can *barely* hear it. When I write a story—I do it as if I'm composing a piece of music. There's no great mystery to it. It's in my blood—that's all.

I've known Stu for over 15 years and he can be crusty and uncompromising at times, but he always looks beyond the obvious and finds the things about his characters that makes them tick. He forces you to see the world from their point of view. He writes from "the inside."

Stu is not just a "writer." He's an artist. Coupled with a life experience that's found him working on stories about serial killers, to pouring over children's books, *Adventures In Manic Depression* is a compilation of forty-plus years of Stu's life's work. It contains everything from true crime reportage to Hemingwayesque short fiction.

Like Norman Mailer, Stu is a slice-of-life writer. When I first read Mailer's *Last Exit to Brooklyn*, I was totally captured, shocked, curious and awestruck—wondering how a writer could fire up my imagination, manipulate my mind and entertain me all at the same time. Stu knows how to do this—and he's a pro at it. At times, Stu reminds me of Mailer. However, he confessed to me that his biggest influence is writer John Fante—a man who lived in and wrote about the city of Los Angeles like no other. Stu also uses L.A. as a backdrop for many of his stories. As a columnist for so many L.A papers (he moved to L.A. from Cleveland, OH in 1957) Stu has absorbed every inch of territory in the City Of The Angels.

Stu likes to make use disguises. He's like Clark Kent in "Superman."

When Stu decided to infiltrate a UFO cult, he posed as someone who'd been abducted by aliens. When he wanted to interview skid row bums, he lived on the streets of downtown L.A., taking his meals at the Midnight Mission. When he decided to do a piece on a little known phenomenon called Taxi Dance Halls (dime-a dance-halls), he adopted an assortment of disguises so that he could enter these timeless places as a customer, rather than a reporter. He admitted to me that—as a dyed-in-the-wool obsessive-compulsive—he got so addicted to the dance halls that he wound up spending six months researching his piece (falling in love with one of the dance hall girls while writing his story). "I have a very classic case of manic depression," Stu admits. "But instead of considering it a handicap, I turned it into a lifestyle. Anyhow, the keyword in the title of this book isn't 'manic depression,' but rather—'adventure.' If I hadn't considered my life to be one nonstop adventure, I'd have blown my brains out years ago."

I've just finished reading Stu's book. I read it from cover to cover. It was *that* compelling. So now, I know all about taxi dancers: where they work, how they engage their customers and what their motives are in doing what they do. That's what a good writer gives you. He's takes you on the ride along with him.

Adventures In Manic Depression is a mix of investigative journalism and fiction. A series of short stories and essays that not only entertain, but that give the reader an insider's look at people you never dreamed existed. I was so enthralled with Stu's beautiful taxi dance hall piece (I've got a little bit of Stu's yen for the dark side of life), that I asked him if he'd take me to downtown L.A. one night and give me a guided tour of these ghostly, secret places. He turned me down flat. "Once I decide to do a piece, I guess I'm a bit like a method actor. I give up my personality and become someone else. After I do a piece that demands that kind of 'inner shift'—I always have to de-tox afterwards. Once the job is finished, I can never go back."

So I guess I'll just have to go settle on just being what I've always been—his best friend and companion. Stu is like a brother to me. We bonded instantly. Ever since we first met (and made music together), we've had one of those special relationships that you know is there forever.

So I invite you to get a glimpse (and it's only a *tiny little slice*) into Stu's world when you pick up *Adventures In Manic Depression.* I guarantee you that after you enter the world that Stu presents, you won't emerge the same person as when you opened the book. And, as happened to me, I'll bet that you'll be reading and re-reading it for a long time to come.

—*Jane Getz*

INTRODUCTION

First, let me prattle on a bit about what this book is *not.* This is not a book "about" manic-depression—that is, the subject is rarely dealt with directly, except in a few entries. Nor is it a book that is intended to give you any particular intellectual insight into this condition.

On the other hand, if you have somehow gotten the notion that this book is going to be a barrel of laughs, you're dead wrong. It's pretty dark stuff. Death seems always to be hiding somewhere in the background. Madness skitters in and out of corners.

The keyword in the title of this book is "adventure." Adventure is really a child's word. At least for me, it conjures up images of knights in gleaming armor, Robin Hood flying over castle walls, fierce pirates with knives in their teeth, and Superman leaping over tall buildings in a single bound.

Of course, adventures can often be pretty scary. In fact, to be *true* adventures, a story must—at least for a time—take you into depths of the pit.

A word about stylistic unity. There isn't any. In addition to the fact that these pieces are a collection of writing done over a forty-plus year period, they consist of a mélange of material—essays, fiction, letters, interviews—even a wee bit of poetry.

At first, I made an attempt to separate the fiction from the non-fiction, but ultimately wound up banging my head against the wall. Clearly, there are pieces which are straight reportage; yet there are other pieces (*A Dimestore Tale, Sleepwalker*) in which I truly don't remember if they are partially or wholly invented.

As regards the state-of-mind which produces such work, I offer this quote from the writer, William Maxwell.

> *"What we, or at any rate, what I refer to confidently as memory—meaning, a moment, a scene, a fact that has been rescued from oblivion—is really a form of storytelling that goes on continually*

in the mind and often changes with the telling. Too many conflicting emotional interests are involved for life to ever be wholly acceptable, and possibly it is the work of the storyteller to rearrange things so that they work to this end. In any case, we lie with every breath we take."

On the upside, this is not a book that necessarily has to be read from front to back. (I happen to read books from back to front, but that's another story). My intention is that the book be something that the reader can dip into at anytime—a box of candy (some sweet, some bitter), which you can munch on for a bit, then come back to at your whim.

I put this collection together more as I would a musical composition. Rhythm, timing...and room to let the notes (words) breathe—*these* are the key ingredients. In fact, as I was compiling the pieces, each story came to have its own soundtrack. Would that I had enough computer knowledge to put a soundtrack to run in tandem with each piece.

If what I've said makes you feel a bit queasy—not quite certain of what you're getting yourself into—that's good. Though I truly do want this to be an "enjoyable read," I warn you in advance that I intend to take you down some dark tunnels, into pits that may seem bottomless, and to claustrophobic places from which you'll find yourself running...gasping for air. If that doesn't appeal to you, then I suggest you close this thing right now and find something better to do with your time. There's certainly plenty of stuff out there today, all of it constructed to both amuse or entertain you. And if it's one thing I'm *not* interested in doing—it's providing entertainment.

Lastly—this collection contains articles and stories written between the years 1970 and the present. I have made no attempt to "update" any of the pieces or put them in any sort of chronological order—so if you feel kind of like you're in some kind of time machine—it's not *you*—that's the nature of the beast you're dealing with.

There. That's enough. From here on in, you're on your own.

—December, 2013

GROTESQUERIES

GROTESQUERIES

A DEATH IN ISLA VISTA

I killed this guy once. It was weird. I was driving back up to school at UCSB late on a Sunday night. Right after you get outside of Oxnard, the freeway turns into Pacific Coast Highway.

It was real foggy outside, so you could barely see two feet in front of you. I was kind of nervous, so I turned up my car radio to help calm me down. I can still remember the song that was playing—*Seven and Seven Is*—by Love. Then all of a sudden, I felt this kind of *thump* on my car; it wasn't a great big thump or anything like that. Just a *normal* thump. Then my front windshield cracked down the middle.

I pulled over to the side of the highway and got out of my car. In the middle of the road I saw what looked like a pile of gray rags. My first thought was that I'd hit a dog or something. Then, before I had a chance to do anything, several other cars ran over the thing. I saw pieces of red stuff fly away from the object. It was only then that it struck me that I'd hit someone.

Things get a bit hazy after that. I remember a cop car pulling up, and a moment later, an ambulance. It all went really fast. The cop got my name, my registration and stuff, then he said they'd be contacting me. That was it, really.

I got in my car and drove back to Isla Vista, where I was sharing an apartment with a couple of old high-school pals.

When I got there, my roommates were standing in the living room, listening to *Rubber Soul.* I told them that I had just hit some guy on PCH, and I was pretty sure the guy was dead. For a minute or so, nobody said anything. Then we all started laughing. Not because it was funny or anything, but because it was so—well, *weird.* Then I started crying.

That was the only time I ever cried about what had happened. In fact, that was the only time I ever really felt anything at all about it.

I was in therapy at the time. My therapist was this real nice German lady named Mrs. Guteroff. I told her about what had happened and all. I asked her how come I didn't have any emotions about it. At the time, I had a problem having emotions about *anything.* I was kind of like this walking dead man. Still, it seemed to me that when something like this happened, you ought to have *some* kind of feelings about it.

Mrs. Guteroff was very supportive of me. She explained that since I knew nothing about the person I'd hit, he effectively had no identity, and therefore it was perfectly normal that I didn't have a lot of feelings about it.

"But I just *killed* a guy!" I exclaimed. "Shouldn't I be feeling *something?!"*

"First of all," she said, "you *are* feeling something. The very fact that you're concerned that you *don't* feel anything, means that you *are* feeling something."

"But...I don't *feel* like I feel anything," I retorted.

"It's quite possible, "Mrs. Guteroff explained, "that you're in a state shock. If that's that case, you'll probably experience a delayed reaction at some point in the future.

She wrote out a prescription for Librium and told me my time was up.

After that, I tried to find out something about the guy I'd hit, so that at least I'd know who he was. After contacting the Ventura police department, I finally got some information.

His name was William Travers Holben. He was 35 years old; the officer I spoke with described him as "a transient." Apparently, he'd been drunk and was trying to run across PCH when I'd hit him. The officer I spoke with told me that the accident was clearly Travers' fault and not mine.

Even before they told me that it wasn't my fault, I'd already thought of other ways to get out of it…like maybe I'd just hit him but he wasn't actually *dead*. Or: It was the cars that ran over him *after* he was lying there that killed him—not *me*.

But in my heart I knew that was bullshit. I'd dealt the death blow. I knew it in my gut. And even if the guy was a transient and all, he hadn't *always* been one. He had been something else once. He had a *mom* and a *dad*. He'd once been *in love* with someone. He had a *past*. I mean, people just aren't *born* bums—something *makes* them that way!

It really bugged me that the police would just write him off like that. Anyway, who ever heard of a bum with a pretty name like William Travers Holben? *Nobody*—that's who!

I thought all kinds of stuff about the guy for awhile, but finally I guess I sort of just forgot about the whole thing. The only two real bad things about the whole incident, were that the next day, I was washing my car off, and I saw that there were pieces of hair, and what looked like part of the guy's skull stuck in my grille. I remember washing them into the gutter real quick.

The other thing that still sticks in my mind was this weird thing that happened after I'd pulled away from the accident. I was driving along—just sort of numb. Finally I came to a stoplight in Summerland, which is right outside Santa Barbara.

I was stopped at a signal, when this car pulled up next to me. Then, I saw that the man driving the car was trying to signal to me. I didn't really want to acknowledge the guy, but he seemed real frantic about getting my attention, so finally I reached over and rolled down my passenger side window.

I can still see the guy. I remember thinking that he looked exactly like Robert Mitchum. Not just *any* Robert Mitchum, though. I specifically remember that he looked like Robert Mitchum in that movie, *The Night Of The Hunter*. I half expected the guy to have the words LOVE and HATE tattooed on his knuckles—just like old Mitchum did in the movie.

Anyhow, after I rolled down my window, the guy rolls down his window.

"Do you want to go to confession?" he said.

"What?" I blanched.

The guy looked at me; then he kind of half-smiled. It wasn't a very nice smile.

"I saw what happened back there, and I want to know if you would like to ask God's forgiveness," the guy said. "I'm a priest, and I thought I might be of help."

I just sat there looking at the guy. The next second, this huge black bubble of anger welled up in my gut. For a second, I imagined pulling the guy out of his car and beating his fucking face into the pavement until it was nothing but a bloody pulp.

"No, thank you," I said. "I don't believe I'd care to do that."

I rolled up my window and drove off. But then the *really* weird part happened. The guy started following me! He followed me almost the entire way back to campus.

I remember thinking all these crazy thoughts—like maybe the preacher guy was some kind of maniac or something. I thought *all kinds* of weird stuff. Then I thought maybe I'd gone into shock and I was just hallucinating the whole thing.

Finally, when I got to Goleta, the guy pulled off the freeway. I watched his lights in my rearview mirror as they disappeared into the fog rolling in from the ocean. I remember my hands were shaking real bad. They didn't stop shaking until I got back to my apartment.

Like I said, the whole thing is pretty hazy. Sometimes I think I might actually have invented it. You know how if you tell yourself something so many times, sometimes you don't know whether it really happened or if you just made it up?

Anyhow, I never forgot that guy; in fact, I still think about him. Sometimes when I'm driving, I feel like some crazy preacher who looks just like Robert Mitchum in *The Night Of The Hunter* is following me. I wish I wouldn't think that stuff…but I just can't seem to help myself.

DANCING WITH MR. D.

So I'm walking down the street the other day, minding my own business, when I feel this tug on my shoulder. I look over to find this very degenerate guy looking at me with those, you know... *searching* eyes. But before I can brush him off with some clever remark like, "Get the fuck away from me, you filthy swine," the guy says, "God bless you, brother," and hands me this little card.

I keep walking. Now generally I just chuck these things in the gutter, but for some reason, this time, I don't. Some little voice inside me just says... *keep it.*

Hold on a sec. A brief aside is necessary before I continue this little tale. There's something I've gotta tell you that can't wait. It's nothing really. No biggie. I simply want to remind you of the fact that *you are going to die*.

Ah, excuse me?

You heard me. I said—you're going to die, that's all.

Look, I'm sorry for the subterfuge, but I needed to get down into the paragraph far enough so that wouldn't be the first thing you'd see when you began reading. I know it was sneaky, but I had my reasons, OK? Trust me. Now, if you don't mind, I just want to run it by you one more time, because like the *EST* followers say, you gotta "get it." So, here we go. Ah-one, ah-two, ah-threeeeeee...

YOU ARE GOING TO DIE.

Just a minute, goddamnit. Don't run away so fast. Stay there a second. Chew on it a little. Soak it up. Absorb it.

Now—what's your reaction? Are you bugged? Are you thinking, "So, I'm gonna die, big goddamn deal," or, "What the fuck *is* this anyhow"...or, "*Goldman's really gone off the deep end now.*" But the deal is—*whatever* your reaction—in fact, if you are reacting at *all*—you aren't looking at it. I want you to *look at it*, dig?

OK, let's try it once more. It's really quite simple. I want you to stop what you are doing—put everything out of your mind—and just realize that the one unalterable fact of your life is that someday (and probably sooner than you think) you simply aren't gonna be here anymore. That's right. You're just going to be gone off the face of the earth—and everything is going to go on without you.

Are you getting it a little bit?

Good.

See, we all spend tons of energy avoiding that one ugly fact. But my contention is that all the other stuff—all the junk that you go through your little daily dramas about—your stupid job, the fact that you defrauded the IRS or that you hate your wife...that's nothing. That's *shit.*

No, there is one and only one problem that confronts each and every one of us, and that is the simple and terrible truth that...*we want to live, and yet we must die.*

But instead of looking at it, we try to escape it. I'm not just talking about movies or sports or video games. That's too obvious. I'm talking about the escape of politics, the escape of religion, the escape of relationships, the escape of having ideas, *opinions* about things. The escape of talking and arguing endlessly—on and on and on about *nothing*. That's what we do day in and day out—we make all this noise, so we don't have to *look*.

The problem is—it'll sneak up on you. Like at 3:00 in the morning, when you wake up in a cold sweat. Yeah, you know that one, don't you? Or perhaps you're in a crowd of people having a swell time, when all of a sudden, for no reason, you'll feel utterly alone. Completely cut off from everyone else. Horrible, isn't it?

The reason that happens is simple. You've been avoiding the fact that you *are* all alone. *Totally* alone. You can't actually relate to anybody—not really. Because you're locked inside this…this sack of skin, inside this bag of memories and opinions and ideas. You can't escape it. No matter how close you get—even in that glorious moment of almost-unity, the much-vaunted orgasm—you don't *quite* get outside of yourself. There's always a wall there. And that wall—that terrible black hole—is always one thing and one thing only. Don't let the shrink fool you by calling it an anxiety attack. That's bullshit. No, that bottomless pit that you don't want to look into—that's *death*, baby.

Go ahead. Say I'm morbid. Say I'm obsessed with death. What the hell is that supposed to mean? Of *course* I'm obsessed with death! Why the hell *shouldn't* I be? I mean, here you have the most incredibly crazy, idiotic...the most *insane* thing in the world—the fact that we have to die—and we don't fucking wanna *know* about it!

Wake up assholes! Do you realize how great the chances of your death are right this very second? There are a million...zillion ways you can go.

Let's take diseases for starters.

Cancer. That's the big daddy these days, right? It gets one out of four people—that's what they say. Then you've got your basic heart attack—tons of people wipe from those everyday. AIDS—a real up and comer. Don't like that one? How 'bout a nice blood clot in the old brainpan? Or maybe a coronary occlusion? I could go on.

In fact, I *will*. Let's see… We've got TB, Alzheimer's disease, blood poisoning, multiple sclerosis, Parkinson's disease, diabetes, leukemia, rheumatic fever, anorexia, cirrhosis of the liver, rickets, pneumonia (isn't this fun?), Marfan's Syndrome, neurofibromatosis, cystic fibrosis, sickle-cell anemia, meningloma, medulloblastoma, pituitary tumor, malignant neoplasm, cerebral thrombosis…

Had enough? Ah, but we mustn't forget natural disasters—fire, earthquakes, floods. Or your common household accidents, such as drowning, strangulation, poisoning, asphyxiation, and electrocution. Anyone for a brain concussion from falling in the shower?

Car crashes!

Plane crashes!

Then, of course, there are the slightly more unusual (and unpleasant) occurrences. For example: A maniac could break into your house and disembowel you. Or—a *group* of maniacs could break into your house and disembowel you. You could be killed by a bomb, run over by a garbage truck, given the wrong operation, sacrificed by devil worshippers!

You get the idea, I'm quite sure.

The point I'm making is quite simple. Every second we are alive is a fucking miracle.

A brief aside. True Confessions time here. I want to share a little experience I had last week. It'll just take a moment, so bear with me.

OK, I had decided to write a column on the Big D, right? So there I am at the old typer, cranking up a pretty good storm—feeling real cool. Even a little bit cocky, if you wanna know the truth. Like... *I'm gonna lay some heavy stuff on 'em this week*, right? So I'm rolling along, when all of a sudden I feel kind of this warm rush in my nose. And I think, "*That's* interesting." The next second I look down and I see that the front of my shirt is covered with blood.

Right, a stupid nosebleed, that's *exactly* what I thought. So I sit down, pinching the old nostrils between the thumb and forefinger like they tell you to do...but after ten minutes, the fucking thing isn't stopping. In fact now it's *pouring* blood—it's all over me, the sink, the floor, everything. The next second, this funny little idea pops into my head.

I have a brain tumor (or at least something very major).

Totally irrational—but that's what I thought.

Ten minutes later I'm sitting in the emergency room at Kaiser Permanente. I must look like I just came off the set of *Texas Chainsaw Massacre*, because when the nurse comes out and sees me, she freaks. She rushes me into a room...where I *wait* (still pouring blood) for about twenty minutes.

Finally, this nice lady doctor comes in and says, "What's the problem?" And I tell her I'm sure I'm hemorrhaging internally or something. She wipes me clean, looks up the old nostrils, puts some stuff in there to cauterize the spot and tells me everything's OK, it's just a nosebleed and I should go home and take it easy.

Fine. Great. I'm cool...I'm gonna *live*.

But there's one little problem. When I get back home I notice that I feel very...peculiar—sort of like I've just had the shit beat out of me by 47 Hell's Angels. At first I don't know what to make of it. Then it's obvious. I'm in *shock*. It's like…all of a sudden my body is this… *thing*, which can, you know, break. Which can erupt. Which can gush. Which can—if it so decides—just *quit* on me.

In the martial arts there is a particularly devastating blow that (when translated into English) means "the heart-stealing punch." It's a psychological blow, not a physical blow. But if this blow is delivered correctly, what you do to your opponent is—you take away his spirit—his *heart*. Every fighter knows that this is the best way to beat a man. Because once you've destroyed your opponent's will, he's all yours. And that's what happened to me. A dumb little nosebleed had delivered the heart-stealing punch to me.

Direct hit.

After I realized that had happened I sat down and thought about the piece I'd been writing on the Big D. What was immediately clear was that I was totally full of shit. The only thing I could really and truly say about death was that I was scared like a motherfucker of it.

But I noticed something curious happening to me over the next few days. A change in attitude. For example, I noticed that I didn't want to punch every stupid jerk that pissed me off, like I usually do. I took more care when I drove—slowing down, not honking my horn and cursing at everyone like a maniac. I was more aware of what I ate, how I spoke, what my reactions were. Somehow everything looked different—more fragile...*delicate*.

I don't mean to sound like some cosmic muffin, but things just seemed more cohesive, more rhythmic. In fact, I had the most curious sensation like I was…yeah, like I was *dancing*—that was it! And it didn't take me long to realize who my dancing partner was. That's right, he was the cat who'd delivered the heart-stealing punch to me—my old nemesis (yours too)—good old Mr. D.

See, the deal is, we *all* have to do the death dance. But the trick is to do it while we're alive—not when we're lying in some goddamn hospital bed, rotting away from cancer. See, every day he holds out his hand and asks us to dance with him, but we turn him down.

Ah, sorry—think I'll just sit this one out.

Forget it. You gotta do the dance, my friends.

I have encountered a fair amount of death during my life. Not that that makes me any kind of an expert on anything. But what I've learned is that if you're open, death can be a great teacher.

The lessons aren't necessarily always profound. Many times death can simply be mundane—even boring. Other times it'll tear your guts out and spread 'em all over the floor. At others it'll have a sense of humor.

Yeah—death is weird. Like a lot of times we might hate somebody and then they die…and suddenly you realize they weren't so bad after all. In fact, you even kind of miss them.

Take Tommy Thompson, who recently kicked the bucket. One of the world's biggest assholes, Tommy. A guy who didn't give a flying fuck about anybody but himself. Oh, but you should've heard 'em after the funeral. *What a great guy…blah blah blah…he was so wonderful blah blah blah…*and on and on and on. Oh man, it was priceless.

Hey, I'm not putting it down. Those people *meant* it. Me, I kinda miss the schmuck too. He was one of a kind, old Tommy, and none of us are ever gonna see him again.

But you gotta watch it when you're thinking stuff like that, 'cause pretty soon you start patting yourself on the back for being such a great human being. Besides, the flip side of the coin is—"*Phhhewwww!* I'm glad it was *him* and not me. He was really a great guy and all, but thank you, Lord—thank you for making it *him* that's buried in the fucking ground while I'm still here where I can feel the sun on my back and taste this great cup of coffee and look out the window and see that incredible girl with those big beautiful titties."

What it all comes down to is—*you gotta do the dance.* 'Cause if you don't—if you reject him, or ditch out every time he makes an appearance—he'll come up behind you just when you're least expecting it, and he'll knock you to your fucking knees. Oh yeah, he'll make you get humble *real* quick, I guarantee you.

Take that nosebleed. Don't tell me that was an accident. No way Jose. I was sitting there feeling real high and mighty and *lickety-whap!*—I got put down on my fucking ass.

So the choice is yours. You can sit it out, or you can get out on the floor. I say get out there and *shake* it! Get crazy! Get nuts! Be wild…

be awkward...be stupid...be romantic. Be silly, be timid...be great...be terrible...be schmaltzy—I don't care. Make a goddamn fool of yourself if you feel like it. Get out there like Brando in *Last Tango*—pull your pants down, bare your ass at the world and wiggle that baby in their faces.

Just *do* it. It's easy, really. Sometimes it'll be a fast one, other times it'll be a waltz. Sometimes you'll lead, sometimes he'll lead. But soon you'll find you can adapt to all of it. And after awhile, you'll see that you're even getting pretty damn graceful. After that, well—it's kinda nice. Yeah, kinda *sweet.*

Oh yeah. That little card I was telling you about—the one the religious fanatic gave me? I figured I'd share it with you, because when I finally looked at it, I decided it was pretty cool. In fact, I even went back to the guy and asked him if I could have a bunch more, which pleased the old fucker all to hell. And now every so often—if I get the notion—I give one to somebody. Oh, they don't always like it, and I can understand that, I guess. But it's silly if you ask me, because the message is a real good one.

It's a simple card. On it there's a drawing of this big, black hearse. And right underneath, in bright red letters, the inscription reads: YOU MAY TIE YOUR SHOESTRINGS IN THE MORNING, BUT THE UNDERTAKER MIGHT UNTIE THEM BEOFRE NIGHT. ARE YOU READY TO MEET YOUR MAKER?

Think about it, darlin'.

CHUCK AND JUDY

Judy sat in her kitchen and stared into her cup of coffee. It was too black. She poured more Cremora into it. On the table in front of her sat the *L.A. Times*. She glanced through the Metro section. The usual stuff—car crashes, crimes of every imaginable sort. Nonetheless, Judy always turned to this section first.

After draining her cup of coffee, Judy lit up a smoke. She French inhaled, though she wasn't aware of this. She'd been doing it since high school. Somehow it made her feel younger. Not so conscious of the years slipping by.

The morning paper lay on the table. Judy read a story about two 14-year old girls who'd been murdered the previous day. The girls had been tortured before they were finally killed. Nipple clamps, ice picks in the brain—the whole bit. A bullet to the head had finished each of them off. A shudder went through Judy's body as she imagined how it would have felt to watch yourself die. Then she let it go.

Underneath the story was a photograph of the man who'd been arrested. Judy looked at the picture for a long while. The man looked, well...he looked so *normal.*

How horrible, Judy thought, absently puffing on her cig. Still, she found herself unable to stop staring at the photo. The caption said that the man's name was Charles Bagley, Jr.

Somehow the name was perfect, Judy thought to herself.

Judy got up and absently began doing last night's dishes. As she scoured the crockpot, she felt something dull inside her skull. A kind of pulling thing. *I must be depressed*, she thought to herself. *Better be careful. Don't let it get to you.*

Judy's thoughts wandered back to the murder of the two girls. So much violence out there. But it wasn't just the violence. Death seemed to be everywhere—lurking darkly about the edges of everything. Just yesterday morning, Emma, her next-door neighbor, had been diagnosed with bone cancer.

"Six months—that's what they gave me," Emma had laughed bitterly. Then she went home to pack lunch for the kids.

After Emma had gone, Judy choked down bitter tears. But she knew she wasn't really crying for Emma. No, it was more for herself. For her own sad little life, and more—for the fear of her own death. Judy pictured Emma wasting away. Then she pictured *herself* wasting away. Now the tears really began to come. They felt dark brown.

For some reason, Judy drifted off to a scene from her childhood.

She would have been perhaps 11 or so. In her room, she'd had an aquarium. It was supposed to be for tropical fish, but Judy had stocked it with goldfish instead. The goldfish looked so pretty, she thought. She could sit for hours just watching them swim around, making those curious little O things with their mouths.

Judy recalled how she'd stare into the cool blue of the tank for hours—her mind drifting off to the sound of the pump. Her thoughts would go *pop, pop, pop* inside her head—just like the bubbles in the tank.

Oh, how Judy loved her aquarium! One of the things she liked best was to leave the light on at night. It was so comforting—that light. Sometimes she even imagined that she were one of the fish, swimming around in there. Ah, what a life *that* would be!

After a bit, Judy drifted off into a long-forgotten memory. One day she'd come home from school and gone to look at her fish. But as soon as she got into her room, she knew something was wrong.

Judy looked inside the tank.

There it was!

A snail had gotten hold of one of the goldfish, and was eating it. The fish was sticking halfway out of the snail's mouth. It was trying to wriggle free, but the snail had swallowed too much of it already.

Judy wanted to reach in and pull the fish out of the snail's mouth, but for some reason she didn't. She just sat there on the edge of her bed watching the fish being consumed.

Judy continued to watch. For some strange reason, she felt a stirring in her loins.

The fish continued to disappear. It seemed very noncommittal about the whole thing. Soon, the tip of the fish's head disappeared inside the snail. After the snail had swallowed the fish, it just sat there, attached to the aquarium wall.

Judy watched the snail for a bit. Then she put her hand into the tank. Slowly, she peeled the snail off the wall. It didn't want to come off, but Judy kept on pulling. After she'd removed the snail, she sat there holding it in her hand. The next instant, she put the snail on the floor, then stomped down on it with the thick heel of her shoe. There was a loud popping sound as the snail's insides shot out against the wall.

Funny, Judy thought. She could still hear that popping sound—still feel the snail underfoot—28 years later. As she thought back on the incident, Judy's hand traveled down to her crotch. To her surprise she found that she was wet.

The morning mail clunked inside the front-door mailbox. Judy took it and spread it on the kitchen table.

Junk.

Judy chucked the pile aside and lit another smoke. She felt blank. *I feel so tired,* she thought. That was Judy's problem. She felt so tired lately. She used to enjoy just sitting around in her bathrobe, maybe just watching a little TV. But lately, she'd lost interest even in that.

Joanie, Judy's daughter, had suggested that she see a psychiatrist. "It's silly," Judy had told her daughter. "I just need a hobby. You know—something to keep me busy."

But Joanie had insisted. So Judy had driven to Brentwood, where she entered a neat red brick building. Inside, she sat in the waiting room of someone named Dr. Pulaski.

Across from Judy sat a woman who was fiddling with her hands. The woman kept wringing her hands and picking frantically at her skin. Judy watched the woman, but the woman didn't look back. She just kept picking away.

Judy continued to watch. The woman kept looking at the floor, wringing her hands and picking at her skin. Judy could tell that the woman must have been pretty at one time. But now she'd gone soft. The features of her face seemed to have melted into one another. Nothing looked distinct. The effect was very disquieting.

She's finished, Judy thought to herself.

The door opened. In the doorway stood a tall, lean man. Judy didn't really take in the man's face. She just noticed that he was wearing a pair of light-brown tweed slacks and a yellow button-down shirt. There were flecks of gray at his temples.

Perfect—Judy thought to herself.

"Mrs. Dansch?" the man said.

Judy looked up.

"Won't you come in?"

Once inside the office, the doctor asked Judy to sit down. She noticed that his voice was very kind. Kind and gentle. Listening to it made her feel safe and kind of drowsy.

During her allotted 50 minutes, Judy talked about lots of things. She talked about the year since her husband's death. She talked about her problems with Joanie. She talked about the agoraphobia and the panic attacks that had kept her trapped inside her house. She talked and talked and talked.

Judy didn't mind talking. She kind of liked it, actually. It was as if she were telling a story about someone else. Nothing of it touched her.

Judy noticed the doctor looking at his watch. At the same time, she found herself wondering what he'd be like in bed.

"We'll have to stop now," the doctor said. Still, that same quiet tone. Judy noticed that he didn't look at her when he spoke. She hoped he hadn't picked up on the little sexual fantasy she'd indulged in. But no—how could he?

As she got to the door, the doctor handed her a slip of paper.

"Lamictal," he said. "It'll help the depression. You might feel a slight dryness of the mouth...perhaps some dizziness, but it'll pass in a couple of days."

Judy thanked him and left. As she walked down the hallway, she enjoyed the feel of her heels on the soft pile carpeting.

By the second day, the medication had begun to take effect. The fear was still there, but the edges of it had softened somewhat. Also, when she slept, Judy didn't feel like she was going to fall down that horrible black hole anymore. Nor was she waking up in the middle of the night with the cold sweats. Things felt lighter. Or maybe softer. Somehow, everything seemed to have the texture of Velveeta cheese.

Still, nothing interested her. Judy noticed it as she leafed through the morning paper. None of it was related to her. She poured a fresh cup of coffee and lit a cigarette, letting the smoke drift up to her nostrils.

She thought about going next door to talk to Emma, but right now she wasn't in the mood. Finally, she got up and sat on the couch, flipping the television set around until she finally settled on *The Price Is Right.*

Judy watched the people on the show. Everyone looked unreal to her. All those people—jumping up and down and clapping like a bunch of chimpanzees just because they'd won some stupid prize.

The world is crazy! Judy thought. *Completely crazy.*

The next second, she was fast asleep.

Something jolted Judy awake. A hand on her shoulder. Judy looked up to find a man standing over her. The first thought that came into her mind was that it was her husband. But no—it couldn't be. Her husband was dead.

Judy looked up at the man. She thought she should be afraid, but somehow she wasn't. It was then that she saw the shiny kitchen knife in the man's hand. Judy watched curiously as the man slowly raised his hand and held it high over his head. Oddly, she made no effort to do anything.

The man held the knife like that for another moment. Then he plunged it down, sinking it deeply into the bone just above Judy's sternum. She put her hand up to ward off the blow, but the knife simply cut through it like butter. She felt something hot and spurting—then everything was red.

The man raised his arm and brought the knife down again. This time it punctured her throat.

Again and again the man brought the knife down.

It was odd. Judy still felt detached. All she could think was, "My God, I'm being *killed!* This is *absurd!*"

Judy tried to make some noise now, but no sound came out of her mouth. Just a sort of croak. She watched in fascination as the crimson ran down her arms.

Judy's life was draining from her body. She knew this, and yet she did not know. The whole thing was peculiar—so very peculiar.

The man simply stood over her—watching. Though her vision was growing hazy, Judy got a good look at him now. Yes, he *did* look like her husband. The square set of the shoulders, the strong jaw. He's kind of pretty, Judy thought to herself. Just as she thought this, the man looked down at her.

He had a strange look on his face. Judy thought that he looked almost sad. As she was losing consciousness, Judy thought about her life. She didn't think any particular thing about it—she just thought of it all together. It was like a blob of some kind. A shape—or maybe even the *sound* of a shape. She could feel it, but she didn't know what it was—this life that was draining out of her.

Everything was hazy now. The man was looking down at her with a curious, childlike expression on his face. *My God*, Judy thought—*he's standing there—watching me die!* Still, even as she thought this, she had an odd feeling—almost like she wanted to comfort him.

The edges of things were melting into one another now. Judy knew it was finishing. She whispered something, but only a gurgling sound came out of her mouth.

She tried once more.

Finally the man leaned his ear down close to her mouth.

"What's your name?" Judy croaked.

The man looked down at her, unblinking. He seemed to be thinking hard. Still, he said nothing.

Judy reached up and tugged at the man's collar. She was desperate now. Really desperate.

"Your *name!*" she pleaded.

Now the man leaned close to Judy. He put his mouth up to her ear. And then he whispered something. He whispered it in a tone so gentle and soft that a great peace came over her and wrapped itself around her, like a father's loving arms.

"It's Chuck," the man said. "My name is Chuck."

TEENAGE TALES

TEENAGE TALES

TRUE LOVE

I've had crushes on lots of different girls in my life, but I don't think I've ever been quite as crazy for anybody as I was over Cheryl White. I first met Cheryl in junior high, and we went all through high school together. How can I describe her?

Blonde hair—almost white blonde—perfect, smooth skin, clear blue eyes, wonderful oval teeth, a little dimple in the chin. I mean, I know it probably doesn't *sound* all that incredible, but it *was*. But see, it wasn't really any of these qualities that made Cheryl so special. It was something much less tangible. She simply had, well—some kind of *magic*.

Sometimes I didn't think she was quite human. It was almost as if she'd been made from some other stuff than regular people are made of—fresh cream, perhaps. She always kind of sparkled—as if Tinker Bell had sprinkled some of that magic faerie dust on her.

Besides, unlike most really pretty girls, Cheryl wasn't the least bit mean or snotty. She was actually a genuinely nice person. So naturally I was in love with her—I mean, *come on*—what the heck do you *expect?*

Of course, so was everybody *else*.

Cheryl never seemed to have one boyfriend though. She didn't go steady with the captain of the football team or anything like that.

In fact, she always liked more quiet, sensitive, intelligent guys. Guys like me.

Somehow, though, I knew that she'd never be mine—though God knows, I spent enough hours dreaming about us running off together and getting married and maybe living in a cabin somewhere in the mountains, or in a tiny flat in Paris. You know—all the usual sort of stuff you dream about when you're crazy for someone.

Still, Cheryl and I did have this—ah, sort of affair—a brief but wonderful time together that I will never *ever* forget.

It took place in Biology class one afternoon. On this particular day, our teacher, Mr. Hanks, told us we were going to see a movie. Of course we all loved movies—because then it was really like you weren't in school anymore. I particularly loved them because I sat right next to Cheryl, and it was dark and it was almost like being in a *real* movie with her—though of course I never would have tried anything tacky, like grabbing her tit or any of the other stuff that you tried with *normal* girls.

No, just to sit next to Cheryl White in the dark—*that* was enough.

So, the lights darkened and the movie came on and the projector went *clackety clackety clack*—and there I was, sitting next to Cheryl White...in the dark. I remember that particular day it was real hot and sticky, and naturally the air conditioner in the room was busted, so everybody was kind of sweaty and stinky. And as I sat there next to Cheryl, I could actually *smell* her.

Now don't get me wrong—she didn't smell bad or anything. No, she smelled absolutely *wonderful!*

I can still remember—she was wearing this yellow, sleeveless summer dress, and I glanced over—just at her shoulder. I can still see it—round and smooth and brown. An absolutely *perfect* shoulder. I could see that she was a little bit sweaty...and with that wonderful smell coming off her, oh *man*—I just wanted to lick the sweat off her body.

I sat there awhile more. I was *dying* inside.

Soon, I couldn't stand it any longer. And then I did something real brave. I don't know—I just *had* to, you see?

So—ever so gently—I slipped my hand over Cheryl's lap, and lightly put it on top of hers.

Oh, God—was I terrified! But you know what? To my surprise, she didn't flinch or pull away. Nothing.

Then the next second, she did something truly amazing. She turned her palm upwards and clasped my hand in her own.

It's funny—even the way Cheryl White held your hand was perfect. She didn't squeeze too tight, or move her thumb all over the place like some girls do—you know—to try and show you how affectionate they are and stuff.

God, there's nothing worse than somebody who makes a big deal over *hand holding*. But like I said, Cheryl didn't *do* that.

What she'd do is, every so often she'd squeeze my hand—just a little bit—sort of to let me know she liked me, I guess.

I squeezed back, being very careful to apply just the right pressure, so I wouldn't seem like some creep who didn't know the finer points of hand holding and all.

What's more, even though it was hot as hell in that room, Cheryl's palm never got sweaty. I'll bet if it'd have been anyone else, that hand would've been slipping and sliding all *over* the place in about two seconds!

The only torturous element of the whole thing was that I was painfully aware of every second that went by.

Oh, I know! I should've just let time stop, and—you know—basked in the Ever Present Now...the timeless eternal glory of True Love. But I just *couldn't*. Because somehow I knew that when that movie was over and those lights went back on...whatever meeting of the souls Cheryl White and I were having would vanish forever.

And so we sat like that. Me, half in heaven, half in hell—and Cheryl, who seemed, as always, perfectly at ease and content. And when, at that dreadful moment when the last frame of the film clacked through the projector, Cheryl squeezed my hand one more time... maybe just a *little* bit harder than before—yeah, I'm pretty sure of it. Sort of saying goodbye. And then, well—I can't really remember if *she* took her hand away first, or if I did. Knowing me, *I* probably did, because, like I said, I didn't want to be one of those guys that hung on past when you were supposed to.

I guess I'll never know that if it really was me who took my hand away first that day. And who knows? Maybe if I hadn't, Cheryl would've looked over at me with a new light in her eyes—you know, she'd have felt my Divine And Glorious presence—and then we would've walked out of class, our hands and souls firmly entwined...down the hall and out the school gates and off into the sunset together.

Maybe.

I mean, who the heck knows *that* kind of stuff?

Anyhow, it didn't happen that way. No, what happened was that the bell clanged and it was 2:45 and our hands unclasped, and Cheryl and I both got up and walked out of the classroom.

I remember I walked just a little bit ahead of her...and as I started down the hall on my way to 5th period, I thought about saying something—but I knew it was too late. Behind me, I could hear Cheryl laughing and talking with a bunch of her girlfriends. And she went her way and I went mine and that was it.

It was over.

Now I know what you're wondering. You're wondering: *did he wash his hand?*

Well, to tell you the truth, I don't remember.

I mean, I'm sure I didn't wash it for *awhile*—but I don't think I got all neurotic about not washing it for the rest of the week or anything like that. Because I knew instinctively that whatever had taken place between Cheryl White and me was enough. Somehow it was meant to last *forever*. Which I guess it did—because—right this very second, I can *still* feel what it was like to have Cheryl sitting there, right next to me in that darkened classroom.

In fact, I can *still* smell her—right this very second.

And you know, I guess maybe Cheryl White truly *was* some kind of magical faerie princess. In fact, I'm absolutely *sure* of it, because, well—if *that's* not magic...then I don't know what the hell is.

TEENAGE TALES

THE GIRL WITH THE TEN-POUND TITS

When I was in the 10th grade, I had this girlfriend named Bobbi Sobieski. Bobbi was real pretty, but the trouble was, she had no tits to speak of. All she had were these sad little nipples. But it was OK though. I mean, what the heck—it was sure better than sitting in your stupid room with a stack of jackoff books under your bed.

My mom always caught me with those jackoff books anyhow. I mean, just when I'd get a real good rhythm going, she'd barge right in. I'd try to get my hand out of my pants real quick, but I never quite made it. Oh man, it was *awful.* Of course, she'd always pretend like it was an accident, but I knew better. Moms are sneaky like that. They really are.

Anyway, Bobbi went away to school the next year, so I didn't see her for awhile. But when she came back the next summer, something truly *amazing* had happened to her. She had sprouted these incredible melons on her chest! They were stupendous, wonderful, and absolutely fascinating.

"How did you get *those?*" I asked happily.

"I *grew* them, silly!" she replied matter-of-factly.

Yessir, Bobbi was quite a gal. And fortunately, she was very happy to let me inspect her new zoobers. I spent hours checking them—pulling, probing and tweaking them to my heart's delight. Truly, I felt I could have done it for the rest of my life. I could simply imagine no better way of spending my time.

Anyhow, one night I took old Bobbi to the drive-in. We saw *The Ten Commandments*. I'll never forget it. I especially loved the part when Charlton Heston parted the Red Sea. It really looked fake—but old Charlton was such a ham, you had to love the guy, with his big old phony *basso profundo* voice and all.

Anyway, Bobbi and I fooled around a little during the first movie, and during the second one, I finally got her bra off.

Christ, what a bra! I'd never seen anything like it in my entire life! It was this monstrous Cross-Your-Heart number, and it had all of these goddamn straps on it. It looked kind of like a gigantic corset. It took me a million years to get the damn thing off—but it was worth it.

There were those tits again!

"Hi," I exclaimed.

"Hello there," they replied.

I swear, every time I got those tits in my hand, they seemed to have grown bigger.

"Jesus," I said to Bobbi, "These things must weigh ten pounds each!"

Bobbi didn't seem too amused by this statement.

"I'm gonna go get me some popcorn," she said, buckling up the gigantic bra.

"OK," I said, "Get me some Juju Bees while you're at it." (Bobbi always paid for the candy when we went the movies. That's another reason I liked her).

Pretty soon she came back with the goods. We put the popcorn between us and started eating. I was thinking of doing that old trick where you put your dick through the bottom of the popcorn box, but I couldn't figure out how to get it in there without Bobbi seeing me.

At any rate, after twenty minutes or so, I had her bra off again, and soon I got my head in between those wonderful tits of hers. One time I looked up and all I could see was this gigantic nipple staring me right in the eye. God, that nipple was as big as my whole head!

The problem was, for some reason, it reminded me of that scene in *20,000 Leagues Under The Sea* when Kirk Douglas was getting pulled into the mouth of the giant squid, and all you cam see is a close-up of the squid with his one old goggle eye staring at you. I didn't *want* to think of it, but I couldn't help myself for some reason.

Pretty soon I started laughing like crazy.

It was awful.

And before I knew it, Bobbi had that goddamn bra back on again.

Boy, was she *mad!* I told her a million stupid times that I was sorry, but she wasn't having any of it.

I told her she was being silly, but she said she wanted to go home.

I told her I wanted to see the movie.

"Take me home."

"No."

"I said...*take me home!*"

"*No!!*"

"*Yes!!*"

"*No!!!*"

It certainly wasn't a particularly intelligent conversation.

Anyway, finally, Bobbi got all huffy and got out of the car—to get some Milk Duds, she said.

Bobbi was sort of a pig, to be perfectly honest with you.

Anyhow, after she'd gone, I started thinking about her up there at the snack bar with her big old dumb tits and all. Right now she was probably standing in line with a bunch of those stupid Canoga Park people—*you* know, the kind of jerks who wear undershirts and have a million tattoos all over their backs and stuff. It was a pretty depressing thought, to tell you the truth.

But then I had this flash of inspiration!

The next second I started my car—then I proceeded to leave the drive-in.

I felt good driving home—even though I knew it was kind of a crummy thing I'd done. But it wasn't *that* crummy if you stop and think about it. I mean, heck—we were at the *Canoga Park* drive in and Bobbi only lived in *Reseda*...so even if she didn't get picked up by one of those stupid undershirt morons—even if she had to *walk* home—it wouldn't be such a bad deal. Actually, she sort of needed the exercise.

Anyhow, I figured that *I'd* gotten the rotten end of the deal. After all, I had just lost the greatest pair of tits I'd ever have probably in my *entire life!*

I never quite figured out why I left Bobbi at the drive-in like that. It just seemed like the proper thing to do at the time. The only thing I regret is that I didn't get her to give me a Polaroid photograph of her tits. If she had, I would have asked her to autograph it for me. I really would have. And later in life—you know, when she had a bunch of stupid kids and some crummy husband that worked as a car mechanic or something—I'd even have let her *borrow* it if she wanted to. Probably by then, she'd have been tripping over the goddamn things—so what could have been nicer than to show her kids than a picture of her tits when they were still firm and attractive and everything? But see, girls don't think of stuff like taking Polaroid pictures of their tits to keep for posterity. They *should*, but they just don't. That's what I mean about girls. They're *funny*.

See, the actual deal is, I don't think that men and women can ever *truly* understand each other. It's just not in the cards.

Like for example, you can be married to a woman for years...and she'll *never* really understand you. But you can go down to the local bar, or the Greyhound Bus depot and sit down next to a *total stranger* and tell him your whole goddamn life story in ten minutes...and the guy'll know *exactly* what you're talking about.

But listen, I'm not complaining—about women I mean. I *love* women—I really do. But *understand* em? Nah—forget it.

Not in a million stupid years.

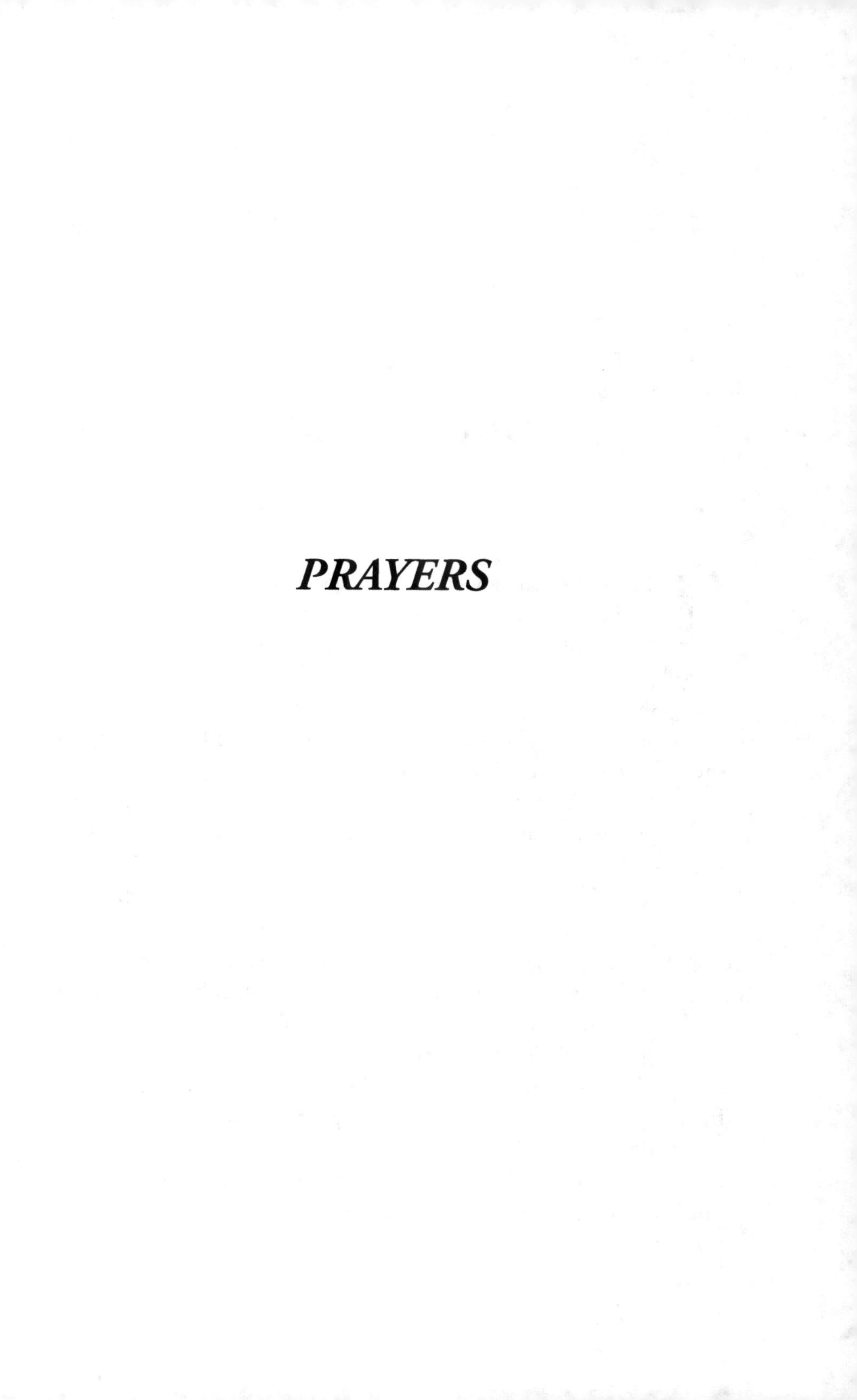

PRAYERS

PRAYERS

DOING THE MELT

The bookstore I work at is called Borders. It is located in Agoura, California. I work there three days a week. I work on what is called IPT—the inventory process team—which basically means that I shelve books all day long. This is the third Borders store I've worked at.

I like shelving books. It gives me a sense of order, and it helps shut off the storm that is usually going on in my head.

Most of the people I work with are very nice. I don't know any of their names, because they aren't real people. They are just Version People—people I've seen before a million times.

The only thing I can tell you, is that practically everybody at Borders has tattoos. Some of them even have pins in their lips and rings in their noses, and a lot of them have these those stupid haircuts where the hair goes into a giant point on top of their head, or else it's bald on one side and long on the other.

I really can't figure out why people would do this to themselves. I mean, I know there's a lot of peer pressure to be like the rest of your friends when you're a teenager...but I promise you, no matter how much peer pressure there was...*I'd* never put a stupid ring in my nose or stick pins in my lips and eyebrows. I guess it's really not much fun being a teenager, always having to look *cool* so that people will like you.

Besides the pierced tattoo people, there are usually one or two old ladies working at any Borders. At my last store (located in Palm Springs) there were about four of them, and they were all really fat and had gigantic butts.

At this particular Borders, there aren't any old ladies, but there are a couple of really old guys who make me extremely nervous. They look like old guys who probably live in some crummy little apartment all alone, and have nothing to do all day except wonder when they're going to die, so they take a crummy job at Borders in order to make them feel like their life has some meaning even though it really doesn't.

I feel sorry for the old guys. The one at this store has a real red face and a very bad wig and he always sits alone in the break room drinking his tea and nobody ever talks to him (those young kids can be real snotty when they want to). Of course, I'm sort of an old guy too—but the thing is, I don't *look* like an old guy and I *certainly* don't *act* like one.

Even though I don't know the names of the Replaceable People who I work with, I do have a rather intimate relationship with some of the people who come in the store. These people who I have this connection with aren't just normal customers; they're what I call the Regulars—people come into the store on a regular basis and do exactly the same thing every time they come in. Which means they generally take a pile of books or magazines and sit there for hours reading them—or else they sit in the coffee shop with their computers and pretend they're working, when really they're just hanging out, or sleeping...or maybe eyeballing some of the cute girls who work behind the counter.

I said I was intimate with the Regulars, but that's not because I talk to them or anything. These aren't the kind of people you'd ever want to talk to. No, they serve a completely different purpose for me. They're there for me to *observe* them, which is my favorite thing in the whole world (besides hiding under the bed covers).

When I observe people, I do this...thing. I call it The Melt. The only way I can explain it, is that when I do The Melt, I make myself go all soft and mooshy inside—I kind of *disappear* myself—and after that, I can go inside other people's bodies, and I can find out everything I need to know about them without them even saying one single word!

I mean, I can find out *everything*—what they think about, who they love and who they hate, what they're scared of and what they dream of. It's *all* there for the taking! It might sound complicated, but actually it's quite simple.

I learned to do The Melt when I was really young—maybe six or seven—and I've perfected the technique over the years. If you're a journalist—which I guess I am—it's a really good thing to be able to do.

There is one problem, though. Sometimes, you don't *want* to know a lot of the stuff you find out when you do The Melt. You find out stuff that makes you real sick...stuff that makes you feel like you're going to throw up or something. When *that* happens, you have to hurry up and get back *out* of the people real quick, and then you have to use a *different* technique in order to disappear *them* (which is a little bit harder than doing The Melt).

So far, my favorite Regulars are—the Girl With No Face, the Angry Belching Guy With Big Zits On His Neck, and the Ear Picking Troll (this guy really and truly looks exactly like the troll in that book—*you* know—the one about the Three Billy Goats Gruff...where the troll is hiding under the bridge waiting to eat the billy goats. (I certainly don't want to get eaten by a troll—I don't know about you!) Oh yeah, I almost forgot the guy who never changes his clothes, and who comes in every day with his sack lunch and sits there reading those Japanese comic books all day (I think they're called *Manga*; they're drawn real badly and they're very popular these days).

At first I hated this guy, but later on I began to like him, because I knew he was homeless and didn't have anywhere to go—but instead of being out in the street, panhandling with all the other homeless people, he'd elected to hang out in a bookstore and just read all day long (even if he reads junk instead of real books). Now what harm is there in *that?*

In my old store in Palm Springs, there was this one Regular we called the Newspaper Lady. She was a black woman of indeterminate age. She came in the store every single day. It was sort of her home.

A lot of times she fell asleep in one of the big comfortable chairs. She'd sleep until somebody would wake her up. You aren't allowed to *sleep* in Borders. That kills me. They can't kick you out if you stay in the store all day reading things and never buying them, but if you fall *asleep*, they can tell you that there's no sleeping allowed.

What a bunch of idiots.

Anyhow, what was different about the Newspaper Lady was that she had all these bags with her, like a lot of homeless people do... but instead of having the bags stuffed with all her crummy personal belongings, every single one of her bags was filled with *newspapers!*

At first, this was a total mystery to me. But then I understood. What she'd do was, wherever she sat—whether it was in the coffee shop or in one of the big, comfortable chairs—before she'd sit down, she'd cover the *entire chair* with newspapers. She'd cover it so that absolutely no part of her body would actually make contact with the chair. If she went to the coffee shop and bought a Coke or something (she always had enough money for Cokes, which are pretty expensive), she'd never take the drink with her bare hand. No, first she'd cover her hand with newspapers, so that the glass wouldn't touch her fingers. I guess she had a phobia about things touching her body.

One day when I came in, I saw her in the Music Section. I couldn't believe my eyes. She was standing there, bopping around in time with the music (she was in the black music section of the store), listening to some gospel music through the earphones. But the thing is, she had her *entire head* covered with newspapers...plus she had *extra* newspapers wadded around her ears so that the earphones wouldn't touch them.

Obviously she was either unaware of how crazy she looked, or she simply didn't care. In any case, she was having a big old time listening to the music and bopping around the aisles, getting all twisted in the earphone cords, all the while singing *real* loud (she actually had a pretty good voice). Of course, she'd scared away everybody who was around her, so she pretty much had the whole aisle to herself.

I thought to myself that this was one of the most wonderful things I'd ever seen! She had revealed a whole other aspect of her personality. Normally, she was very quiet, and she kind of walked around real sneaky like.

Also, when she was in the coffee shop, she stole every single packet of sugar from the little sugar bowl. After she'd stolen the sugar, she'd go sit at a table (she always sat with her back facing you, so you couldn't really ever see her face), and she'd pour all the sugar onto a napkin. Then, came the best part. After she made sure nobody was watching her, she'd stick out her big old pink tongue, and she'd lick all the sugar off the napkin!

Every time she did this, she'd wind up with her face completely covered with powdered sugar. She looked just like Al Jolson or maybe Marcel Marceau—*one* of those guys. Either she didn't know how weird she looked...or else she simply didn't care.

One day I was sitting in the coffee shop eating my lunch when I felt a tap on my shoulder. I looked up, and lo and behold—it was the Newspaper Lady!

"Sir," she said to me. "I was wondering if you had the correct time. You see, I seem to have lost my watch."

I was in shock...not just because she'd actually talked to me, but because her diction was so good. Also, she had this really nice voice... kind of soft and real low. Clearly, I now had to change my whole opinion of her. Damn, this was going to take some *work!*

I told her the time.

"Thank you very much, sir," she said, turning and rapidly walking away.

That was when I smelled her. I don't know why I hadn't smelled her before—probably because I always watched her from a distance, so she wouldn't see me.

Obviously, she had taken a dump in her pants. In fact, you could actually *see* it—this big old bulge in the back of her shorts.

I had to go outside and gulp a bunch of air, because the smell was so horrible. But there was absolutely no doubt about it—she was walking around with a huge load of crap in her pants. Maybe she *was* real intelligent, but she was also *crazy* as a friggin' loon! I mean, this baby needed to be locked up—and *quick!*

The last time I ever saw the Newspaper Lady was the day before I quit the store to move to L.A. to live in the house that I never come out of because I'm too scared.

I had parked my car across the street in the Bank of America parking lot because there were generally no spaces left in the Borders parking lot and the Nazis who ran the mall said they'd give a parking ticket to any store employees who parked in their stupid lot.

Anyhow, the sun was just going down and it was beginning to get dark...and as I crossed the street, I saw her. She'd put down a whole bunch of newspapers on the grass and she was lying on them—flat on her back—just staring up at the sky.

Soon it would be dark and cold (the desert gets really cold at night), and she'd undoubtedly try to cover herself up with more newspapers.

I thought to myself how crazy she was. Nothing she did added up. I mean, for someone who doesn't want anybody looking at her, she'd opted to make her bed right in the middle of *everything!* She didn't even have the sense to go and hunch down in a doorway or something, like normal homeless people do. What in God's name was *wrong* with her?!

Usually when I leave a place, I never think about any of the Regulars anymore. There are too many new strange and wonderful people you can do The Melt with. But for some reason, after I left that Borders, from time-to-time I'd think about the Newspaper Lady. Whenever I'd think of her, I'd smell that smell again, and I'd have to go outside and gulp a bunch of air to keep from throwing up.

I told you that I don't usually get involved with the regulars, but recently, I actually did get involved (sort of) with the Girl With No Face.

As far as I could tell, she was probably 18 or thereabouts. She always wore the same thing—jeans, T-shirt, hooded sweatshirt, and a pair of those black and white tennis shoes, either with no laces, or with the laces untied. She had this really pretty blonde hair that she wore in one of those curly, Stevie Nicks type of hairdos that managed to cover up most of her face.

When I say she didn't have a face, what I mean is...she *had* one—but none of her features were distinguishable from one another. It wasn't one of those faces that deformed people sometimes have, where one eye is up and one is down, or their mouth is kind of sideways. No, this was *way* beyond that. I mean, she had eyes, a nose and a mouth, but you couldn't really distinguish them as separate from each other—they were all sort of smooshed together.

The only thing I could think of is that she might have been one of those people who had tried to kill themselves by putting a shotgun in their mouth, but they screwed up and managed to live. Only *now* they were going to look like the Elephant Man or Quasimodo for the rest of their lives!

I watched the Girl With No Face a lot. She usually hung out in the Music Section...and she'd just *be* there, kind of bopping around while listening to her favorite CDs. I liked the fact that she hung out in the Music Section. That meant that whatever else she might have felt—I mean, about not having a face and all—at *least* she was comfortable enough to hang out and listen to music that made her happy.

She also liked books. When she wasn't in the Music Section, I'd find her sitting somewhere on the floor, with a huge pile of books stacked up right next to her. So now I knew that she liked reading and that she liked music. That meant that she had a world that she lived in—a world furnished with things she loved.

Cool.

Oh, yeah: she'd always drink the same thing—an extra large latte with a lot of whipped cream on top. What I'm trying to say is that she had a *routine*.

She also limped a little bit, but not real bad or anything. In a way, it kind of made her more attractive.

I don't know why, but I couldn't stop thinking about the Girl With No Face. I thought about her while driving home from work, and I thought about her while watching TV at night (which is normally my time for expelling all the people who I had made contact with during the day from my brain. I mean, I didn't want any of those people's vibes polluting *my* house!)

I was reading the Bible a lot during that time. I was trying to figure out if The Girl With No Face was a Christian. But how could I possibly know—since I didn't really even know for sure if *I* was a Christian. I mean, half the time I believed in *something;* the other half, I felt like there was no possible reason for existence.

I mean, if there really *is* a God, how could He possibly explain the Girl With No Face!? What could she have possibly done to deserve a life of eternal pain, humiliation and damnation? A life in which she'd never have a boyfriend...in which nobody would ever kiss her on the lips (or even the cheeks or the eyelids). A world where other people would avoid looking at her wherever she went. Why would anybody create a wonderful teenage girl like this, then relegate her to living her life in the pit of hell!?

Why why why why why why why? C'mon, you bastard...give me an answer!!!

I tried to imagine the Girl With No Face's life. Even though she always wore the same clothes, she wasn't poor. She didn't reek of poverty. She might have even had a lot of money, but she just chose to wear old T-shirts and tennis shoes so she could look like other kids her age. Whenever she came in the store, she was always alone. I could only assume that she didn't have any friends.

She probably lived with her mother (for some reason, I knew there was no father) in a small apartment or condo that was near the bookstore; that was why she came in so often.

I pictured her bedroom. It'd be a typical teenage girl's bedroom, with maybe pink wallpaper and a matching bedspread. She'd have a desk, a mirror, a computer, an iPod, lots of books and CD's—all the *good* stuff. And the walls of her room would be covered with pictures of her favorite rock groups—Green Day or whoever was popular these days. I thought she might even have a Teddy Bear on her bed (I got even more pissed at God when I thought of that Teddy Bear).

Soon I came to a decision. Somehow, some way...I was going to make contact with the Girl With No Face. It wasn't going to be easy—but I just *had* to do it.

I tried to figure out what I'd say to her. I couldn't tell her that she was beautiful, or that it didn't matter that she had no face—she'd just know I was lying, and that would hurt her even more. I thought about telling her about Jesus...but how could I do *that*, when half the time I didn't believe in the guy myself? Besides, she'd probably just think I was a fanatic of some kind.

All I knew was that *somehow*, I had to tell her that I *cared* about her. After I'd broken the ice, I pictured us having coffee together, discussing the travails of the world. Just two old pals, hangin' out.

A few days later I spotted her. I turned and walked in her direction, so we'd have to pass one another. When I got up close, I couldn't think of anything clever to say, so I just said, "Hi!"

She didn't even look at me. She passed me by without so much as acknowledging my presence. I wasn't surprised. She'd probably spent her whole life perfecting ways of avoiding people.

On the way home, I was torn. My heart ached for her. I thought that maybe at least she had created a beautiful world inside her head...a world that was pink and blue and Christmassy—a world where she could turn the music up as loud as she wanted and dance, flying *waaaay* up high...*up in the sky...up to the moon*—

A few days later, I saw her sitting on the floor of the Music Department. She had her usual pile of books stacked alongside her. I turned around for a moment, but when I turned back, she was gone (she would always disappear real fast, like that). Fortunately, she hadn't put away any of her books.

I immediately went to examine her pile, so I could see what she'd been reading. Left open was a book on the history of the Beatles, plus a bunch of other books on various musical groups. One of them was *No One Gets Out Of Here Alive—the* story of the Doors' lead singer, Jim Morrison.

A couple of days passed where she didn't come in. Then one Saturday afternoon, I spotted her. This time, she was in the Photography Department, and there she was, sitting on the floor next to her pile of books. She had her face buried in a book and her hood pulled way up over her face—which was the style she'd developed so as not to let people see her.

It was now or never.

Without thinking, I walked right up to her and stood there...but she didn't look up at me.

"Excuse me," I said, "But I have a problem. I have this niece about your age, and she loves music. Actually, she *really* likes the Beatles. But see, I have no idea which Beatles' records are good, and I was wondering if, ah...if maybe you could help me out."

There was a pregnant silence. She pulled back her hood and looked up at me. I'd promised myself that if she would just *look* at me,

I'd look her right in the eyes, and that even if I was shocked by her face, I wouldn't show it.

She thought for a moment, then she said, "*Rubber Soul*—that's the *best!* And maybe after that—*Revolver*. Those two are *really great!*"

Her voice sounded like it was coming out of her neck instead of what should have been her mouth...but her words were clear and understandable. There was no giant speech impediment or anything.

"Cool!" I said.

"Oh yeah, what about the Doors? She also likes the Doors... *Sheesh*, can you believe it? Fifteen years old...and she's a throwback to the Love Generation!" I laughed. "I mean, that's *my* era."

She thought for a moment, but she didn't turn her face—her wreck of a face—away. Then she said, "Probably their first album is the best—the one with *Light My Fire* on it. There are some others," she continued, "but I don't really know them very well. But the first one is *really cool!*"

"Hey, thanks...thanks a *lot*, man," I said (I call everybody *man*). Then I turned on my heel and left.

Thank you, God. I *did* it! I had made *contact*. And she'd actually *looked* at me.

We had looked into one another's eyes!

I promised that I wouldn't expect anything after that. I knew that maybe the next time I saw her, she wouldn't look at me again, but it didn't matter.

I had gotten to her.

For some reason, I didn't see her for a while after that. I began to wonder if maybe she'd moved, or if she was sick or something.

Then one day, she was back. There she was, coming down the steps, holding her extra large latte. I turned and walked in her direction. She always walked with her head down...but when I got right next to her, I caught her eyes, and said, "Hey, man...what's happening?" I raised two fingers and waved hello.

"Not much." she said, raising her two fingers—waving back at me.

Then she was gone.

I had to walk outside real fast because I didn't want anybody to see me crying.

I stayed out there for a pretty long time.

After that day, I didn't think about her so much, and I stopped having fantasies about us becoming best friends or soul mates and all that kind of stuff. But there was a new lightness in my heart. I could actually believe in God—or something *like* God—at least for awhile.

FOR MY MOTHER

Ethel Mann Goldman (1916-2000)

Now that I am an old man, I cannot look back upon my old works without losing my way in the past. Sometimes, lying in bed at night, a phrase or a paragraph or a character from an early work will mesmerize me, and in a half dream, I will entwine it in phrases and draw from it a kind of melodious memory...of an old bedroom in Colorado, or my mother, or my father or my brothers and sister. I cannot imagine that what I wrote so long ago will soothe me as does this half dream, and yet I cannot bring myself to look back...I am fearful; I cannot bear being exposed by my own work. I am sure I shall never read these books again. But of this I am sure: all of the people of my writing life, all of my characters are to be found in the early work. Nothing of myself is there any more, only the memory of an old bedroom... and the sound of my mother's slippers walking to the kitchen.
—John Fante

People get real uncomfortable when they're confronted with a grown man crying. I know. I've been crying a lot lately. I have no idea when it's going to come upon me. I see something... hear something...and *boom*—I'm gone.

At first when it started happening—like if I were in my car—I'd try to hide it...then I'd drive home as fast as I could so that I could get inside the front door. Then I'd let go.

But then I figured—wait a minute! This is *stupid!* Why do I have to hide my feelings? Why am I embarrassed? Am I making somebody uncomfortable? And if I am—who cares?

So now I just let it happen. I mean, I don't making huge scenes in public places or anything. If I'm really going to howl—to pound the walls—I do that inside the confines of my own house.

Oh, before I forget...the reason I'm doing all this crying lately is that my mother died last month. According to the experts, I'm in the "shock" phase of bereavement—which is probably accurate. I mean, half the time I walk around totally numb—then all of a sudden, I'll just fall apart.

Ultimately, what struck me as a result of not being able to control my emotions is how much energy we all put into putting on a proper "face" for the world.

And for *what?*

You know, you get some guy talking to himself in a public place...people look at him like he's nuts. I wonder...if I really started crying and screaming like I do when I'm within the confines of my house, whether somebody would call the cops on me? Hmmm. Yes, I'm quite sure they would

Well, fuck them.

I'm getting off the subject here, which is my *mom*. I've had a lot of loss in my life...many good friends, almost my entire family...but I've got to tell you that there is absolutely *nothing* that equals the pain of losing a parent. And if both your parents are gone, well—that's a whole different ballgame.

You know what? I really don't *get* people—I'm talking about people my age—who talk about how they have become "relegated" to losing their parents. You know—they say stuff like, "Well, this is the age when that happens...so *sure* it hurts—but it's *okay*."

For my money, these people are full of shit. What the hell do they mean, "*It's okay*"? I feel like punching them senseless when I hear them spewing this crap. Losing a parent is the most horrible—*the worst thing ever*—that you'll deal with in your entire life. It is a wound that will *never* heal. It's like getting all of your limbs sawed off, and you know that they're never going to grow back.

So those people who blabber about "going through the grieving process" or give you advice about how to "cope" with your loss—well, I think that those people are insane. There's no "coping" with this one, my friend.

Of everyone in your life—your spouse, your children—there is nobody who loves you like your parents and, I think, *especially* the person out of whose womb you sprang—*your mother*. I can't speak for anyone else, but in my case, that's the bottom-line, bone-hard truth. You are not bonded to your father in the same way that you are to your mother. And there's *nobody* who loves you as absolutely, as *finally*—as *unconditionally*—as your mother. No matter *what* you do...no matter *how* much pain you may cause her...no matter how many terrible, heinous acts you commit, your mother *continues* to love you.

Always and forever.

When your mother dies, all that is gone. Nobody will ever be there for you like that again.

By the same token—and this is something I realized only during the last months of my mother's life—I loved her in the same way. Absolutely...unconditionally. No matter how angry with her I might have been (and I was angry at my mother much of my life), I loved her so deeply that I simply cannot find words to describe this.

My mother and I really didn't "get along" during much of my (adult) life. She was the ultimate nudge. Every single cliché about Jewish mothers—my mother had all those qualities in spades. I can say with a good degree of accuracy that my mother helped to destroy both of my marriages. She was so positive that neither of my spouses was "right" for me (she was absolutely correct, by the way) that she put her curse on those two relationships. And though I can't blame her for my marriages ending (I did that all by myself), I *can* say that she most certainly helped drive the knife in. For that—and for countless other times she inserted herself in my life and made herself the center of things in which she had no business being involved—I was often *furious* with her. My rage was deep-seated, and soon metastasized throughout my being. I spent countless hours and tens of thousands of dollars in therapy trying to work my way through *that* mountain of ager and resentment.

But you know what? Once I realized my mother was dying, all of that anger vanished—*poof!*—without a trace. God revealed to me that none of it was of any consequence whatsoever. And then—just like that—He removed it. And so, during the last year or so of her life, I was able to love my mother as unconditionally as she had loved me during her *entire* life.

I thank the Lord for this most miraculous change of heart...for this great gift. Only He could have bestowed it upon me.

I think my mom was a bit taken aback when I "changed." She seemed almost embarrassed by my show of emotions. Where before I had been cold and distant, now I held her hand; I brushed her hair... put cream on her face, or chapstick on her parched lips. I told her a hundred times a day how much I loved her.

It was hard for her to express herself. She rarely spoke directly of her love for me. Rather, she just "showed" it. She would not drown me in "words of love," yet daily, she would show how much she loved me in a thousand ways.

Toward the end, when the dementia had rendered meaningful conversation almost nonexistent, she would continue to "tell me" of her love. Just a look...a touch of the hand...

It was unbearably painful for me to hear this bright, articulate former schoolteacher unable to speak her mind—and I know it was equally painful for her.

One time as we sat together on the couch, she looked over at me, and—knowing I was ashamed of having gained weight, she said—"You're still a very handsome man." Dementia or no dementia, she spoke directly to my heart. No—a mother's love overcomes even the most heinous...the most demonic of brain diseases; it cuts to the bone. Dementia, be damned!

My love for my mother grew like a wild bush during those last months. It was so powerful that it physically hurt. My heart was rent asunder. I would have traded places with her—given my life for her in the blink of an eye—had I been able to. I asked God many times to allow us switch places, but He didn't see fit to grant me my desire. I wish I could say that I'm not angry with God—not so much for taking her from me—but for allowing her to suffer the humiliation that comes with dementia. There are no words to describe my fury. My anger is boundless.

I miss my mom so bad. No—I'm going to say it properly. I'm going to say it like I *feel* it.

I miss my *mommy*.

I'm five years old again. My mommy is gone, and I'm frightened and I'm scared and she's not here and she's never going to come back—

I walk through the day in a fog; I wake up in the middle of the night covered in sweat. I grab my pillow and hang onto it for dear life. I leave her bedroom light on, and sometimes—if I can muster the courage—I go in and fluff up her pillow. I lie in her bed, inhaling her smell into my nostrils...

I guess this "phase" will trail off sooner or later...I have no idea when. But I know that the wound itself will never scar over. And I don't *want* it to. I don't *ever* want to learn to "cope." I would consider that a curse. I *need* to feel this pain—the pain helps me to survive.

I think I've said enough here. All I really want to say to each of you is this: if your parents are still alive, do me a favor—just go *talk* to them. You don't have to get all mushy or tell them how much you love them (though that's a good start). I know how hard this is to do. Do it...no matter how painful it is for you. Talk to them...and more importantly—*listen* to them. They have *stories* to tell you. And you *need* to hear their stories. Trust me—you *do*.

If your parents are already gone, I suggest you talk to them anyhow. You have things to *tell* them. Things that have remained hidden in your hearts for many, many years.

Stop making excuses! *Do* it! And just because they aren't here physically, doesn't mean they can't talk to you, as well! No, I'm not intimating some kind of psychic hogwash. I'm just saying—you *can* speak to them. And, if you listen, they will speak to you as well.

Try it. See if I'm not right. Once you begin to engage in these conversations, you will find, I think, that it is truly the most important "work" you have to do during this lifetime.

Stop wasting time. Your days are growing short, and your time will soon be at hand. So do it now.

If you don't...your soul will never find rest.

PRAYERS

FOR MY FATHER

Maurice Goldman (1910-1984)

I never knew my father. I knew his presence; I knew his music—it resounded throughout our house during the entirety of my lifetime—but I never knew *him*. To me, he was a ghost.

During countless years, my father and I would pass each other in the hallway. I'd say "Hi, Dad," and he'd say, "Hi,"—but we never looked one another other in the eyes.

I certainly never hated him, nor even truly disliked him. But I *was* scared of him. He was a man with a tremendous amount of rage inside him, and though he never hit me, just one *look* from him would leave me shaking.

In 1983, when my father found he had cancer, we began to connect.

It wasn't a verbal connection, but it was there all the same. I took care of him; I went to the hospital and got his medicines. When he could no longer walk, I bought him a cane.

I sat next to him on the couch and we watched a boxing match on television.

"They're bums!" he said with disgust, as the two fighters waltzed around the ring. It struck me that he'd used a term from his era—the '40s and '50s—not mine.

Nonetheless, he was right. They *were* bums.

One time, I overheard him say to my mother, "I guess it's a good thing that Stuart is in the house." (I was living at home again for the millionth time in my life).

Soon thereafter, I sat in the hospital and watched him as he lay dying. I put ice chips on his mouth when his lips would parch; I held his hand. He was in a delirium. He kept saying, "Sam...Sam..." (Sam was his older brother—whom he hadn't seen in years).

The moment finally came. I put my head on his chest and then looked up at him.

"I love you, Dad," I said.

"I love you, son," he replied, looking into my eyes.

That was the first time in my life my father had ever called me "son."

He died shortly thereafter. My mother and a few family members were by his bedside. I was asleep in a motel room I'd rented a few blocks from the hospital. When my cousin came and knocked on my door early in the morning, I knew that he was gone.

I rushed to the hospital, but by the time I got there, everybody had left the room. The nurses wouldn't let me go inside. Several minutes later, I heard a distinct sound. It went *"zip!"* I knew exactly what it was.

A few moments later, two men in white carried my father's body, now encased in a blue leather bag, down the hallway. I wanted to yell at them to stop...but nothing would come out of my mouth.

I remember driving back home as if in a dream. Oddly, I was not crying.

Today, if I ever accidentally drive by that hospital, I have to cover my eyes with my hand so I that I don't see it.

I remember absolutely nothing about his funeral. Not a single image remains. He was cremated—per his wishes—and his ashes put on a shelf in some hallway. The actor David Janssen—who had played the lead on *The Fugitive*—was right around the corner. For some reason, I liked that.

And that was it, really. He was gone. To be honest, I didn't mourn. I didn't grieve. I didn't know the person whom I was supposed to grieve for.

And so I went on with my life. I rarely thought of him, or truly missed him. When I'd see my mom go through her ritual of lighting a candle for him on his birthday, or on their anniversary, I'd feel a pang in my heart...but it was more for her than for him.

Twenty-three years pass. And then, something strange happens.

God steps in. And God does what he does best. He works a miracle.

When I tell you this, I mean it, absolutely. There is simply no other way to describe what's happened; I know that nobody but the Lord could have engineered the manner in which this story has evolved.

In my closet sits a box. This box contains every single letter that I've ever received during my lifetime. For the most part, they are letters from friends. They began arriving shortly after I moved away from home to attend San Francisco State College in the fall of 1963.

I loved getting letters—but what I really loved was *writing* letters. That's all I ever *did* that year was write letters. It was the beginning of another life, though I didn't realize it at the time. The more letters I wrote, the more I'd get back. Every day I'd open my mailbox, and the letters would tumble out. I'd read them over and over, savoring every word—especially the ones from girls I had crushes on—(and there were plenty of those). Sometimes I'd swear that I could actually *smell* the writer of a particular letter on the paper.

Somewhere around 1985, the letters stopped coming. It was the advent of the Internet. It was the end of an era—an era in which people shared stories with one another in letters. Emails can contain thoughts (usually in incomplete sentences), but rarely, if ever, do they contain *stories*. But because I never threw out any of the letters I received—today, the entire top of my closet is filled with file boxes full of letters.

I love my boxes of letters. I believe I can say that they may well be my most treasured keepsake. The letters don't contain simply facts. They contain a road map of history. *My* history. Each one of these letters—even if the writer had not been terribly significant in my life—contained a piece of *me*...a piece which I could now bring back into the foreground of my mind and replay, scene-by-scene, as many times as I cared to.

But the facts—the day-to-day "stuff" which people talked about—were strictly secondary to the real prize of these letters—the *secrets* that they held. *That's* why they were so powerful! Because no matter how many times I'd re-read a particular letter, every time I'd re-read one, more and more of these secrets would reveal themselves to me.

Whenever I move (and I've moved many times over the years), my boxes of letters are the first thing I pack. They never travel in a moving van. They travel in my car, where I can keep an eye on them.

Recently, for some reason, I started "sorting" the letters. I began a rudimentary filing system. At first I filed them by the year in which they were written. Then the system became more elaborate (and much more fun). I was filling up manila folders titled, "College Letters," "Letters From the Road," (these came from the years during which I traveled the world as a musician), "Letters From Girls I Was In Love With," "Letters From Girls I Didn't Care About..."

You get the idea, I'm sure.

I have two full boxes labeled "Letters From Mom and Dad." As I was filing, I'd often stop and read particular letters, but—for some reason—I rarely re-read any of the letters that I'd received from my parents. I don't know if it was because I was disinterested, or because I was afraid of what I might find.

About a month ago, for some reason, I was ready to start another filing session. Before I knew what I was doing, I went straight to the boxes containing all the letters from my parents. For the next 24 hours, I read without stopping. When I was done, I began re-reading them again.

Most of the letters are from my mother. My mother was an incessant letter writer. She was such a *nudge*. Even though I was miles from home, she kept on taking care of me, as she always had. I was still her "little boy." I was *always* her little boy (and thus I have remained a boy).

On the other hand, the letters from my father were clearly *not* written to a little boy. They were written to a person who my father hoped would someday grow to be a man.

My father's letters were typically short, and curt. I could feel his anger—his rage—in these letters. Worst of all, I could feel his sense of disappointment. I knew that his disappointment wasn't just with me, but with the way his own life had turned out.

In one letter he actually wrote, "More than anything else, Stuart" (he always called me by my first name—never "son")—"you must break the curse, the curse which was handed down from my father to me, and now to you. The reason I've been so angry with you, Stuart, is that I saw that as you grew up, you came to be more and more like me. I wanted to tell you that beyond anything else you do, you *must* break this pattern. I failed. I didn't know how to help you. I was not a good father, and I'm sorry for that..."

When I finished reading that sentence, all the distance that had existed between my father and I during the course of our lives simply vanished. Something else had replaced it. A door—one which had remained closed for years—had opened.

I sat there on the floor, and read that one letter over and over and over.

I can see it now...the shape of his handwriting (he had beautiful handwriting; he always wrote with an ink pen, never a ballpoint).

That particular letter was written perhaps 35-years ago. Now, as I reread it these many years later, something happened. A flame began to burn inside me.

At first, I didn't know what was happening. Then the thing revealed itself. I now had a *mission*—to bring to life a man whom I knew nothing about.

I began to hunt through the file cabinets and boxes stored in the garage for anything I could find that might reveal things about my father. Other than a small suitcase full of photos, a few letters, and some old home movies, little remained. I searched the Internet for information. Though my father was a well-known and highly respected musician, there was precious little about him on the Net. He'd been a private man all his life. And the trail he left was—even for an investigative reporter—a difficult one to follow.

I felt lost. The task remained beyond my grasp. How would I ever find out who he was? Most of my relatives—especially from his side of the family—were long gone.

I called my sister and asked her if she had anything. The following day, she turned up carrying a gigantic suitcase. When she opened it, I saw that it was filled to the brim with scrapbooks (my mother was a great scrapbook keeper...I should've figured!). The scrapbooks contained literally hundreds of articles about my father; they covered the time from when he began his musical career in the '30s, to his death in 1984. Besides the newspaper articles, there were letters—written both by him and *to* him—as well as many recordings of him—some on reel-to-reel tapes, some on cassettes, some on 78 RPM records. My father was a prolific writer. He's written hundreds of cantatas, operas, and pieces of "religious" music (much of which was in Yiddish). A real find was several records of his scores from movie soundtracks he'd made when we'd first moved to Hollywood. I had no idea that my father had scored the noir classic *Lady In The Lake,* as well as dozens of soundtracks for cowboy movies—including two of my boyhood heroes, Roy Rogers and Gene Autry.

Though my father's original stardom (and he really was that... he was a *star!*) had diminished later in life, he never stopped writing. He finished his last cantata ("Echoes Of Yiddish Life") shortly before his death. Because he was too weak to go to the opening night's performance, he was relegated to watching it on videotape from his hospital bed.

I don't mean to brag (yes, I do!), but my father was not simply a multi-talented musician. That is far too pale a description. No, the proper word is *genius.*

His love of music appeared early on. At age five, he was already composing original music. At 24, he became the youngest man to conduct a symphony at Cleveland's famed Severance Hall. Shortly thereafter, he won a scholarship to study at Tanglewood, Massachusetts, where he worked alongside two of his heroes, Ernest Bloch and Aaron Copeland. Like those men, my father's work broke the boundaries of traditional classical music—employing melodies and harmonies that combined classical and contemporary music—thus creating a "new" form that was decidedly *avant garde.*

He came to Hollywood in the '40s and scored films, but Hollywood was not his *métier.* He returned to Cleveland to work in the area he knew and loved—the world of Yiddish music. Back home, he headed up the Opera Department at the Cleveland Institute of Music and the Vocal Department at the Cleveland Music School Settlement. He served as the cantor at both the Temple on the Heights, Euclid Avenue Temple, and later—after returning to Los Angeles in the '50s—at University Synagogue in Westwood.

Over the course of his life, my father composed and arranged hundreds of songs, cantatas, operas, and choral pieces—both liturgical and secular.

To my amazement, I found that many of his compositions were inspired by original Biblical texts. The most well known of these is his choral work "Al Naharos Bovel" (*By the Waters of Babylon*), which is based upon the 137th Psalm.

Over the next several weeks, as I read through the articles and letters, I began to uncover my father's history (his *story*)—the jobs he'd held, the inside story on many of his more famous compositions (many of which are still played and performed today). But more important than the accolades—and they were many—I began to know *him*. The ghostly figure whom I'd passed so many times in the hallway finally began to materialize. After all these years, the mystery of the man began to reveal itself to me.

After I'd read everything in that suitcase, I knew it was time to listen to the music. I'd been avoiding it until now. There were a few cassettes, and 78's, but most of the music was on reel-to-reel tapes. I purchased an old reel-to-reel machine on eBay and waited—biting my nails to the quick—for it to arrive.

Of course when it the tape player arrived, it didn't work. After an eternity of tinkering, the bloody thing came to life. I put on the first tape—a cantata my father had written with famed radio biographer Norman Corwin in 1954, entitled "The Golden Door." It was a piece commemorating the 300th anniversary of Jewish settlement in the United States (the American Jewish Tercentenary).

Upon hearing the first notes, I recalled hearing bits and pieces of the cantata as my father hummed them while composing at the piano. As I listened (and this is the magic and the power of music), the composition began to trigger scenes from my boyhood that I'd unconsciously buried.

The next tape I played was labeled, "Maurice Goldman Sings Songs Of Hanukah." After hearing the first note, and the sound of that gorgeous baritone voice, I was on the floor. I wasn't just crying—I was *shrieking*—wailing like a wounded beast who'd had a knife plunged into his heart.

How many times had I heard that voice, singing the *broucha* as we lit the Hanukah candles each year? Each note, each breath, caused me *unbelievable* pain. And as the wound bled out, I could feel the broken pieces of myself coming together again...like magnetic particles striving to reach one another...to make themselves into a whole.

So you see, I now have the tools. Through the articles and the music, I am now piecing together my father's life story. And my *own* life story as well. As I said, the articles were wonderful, but it was the *music* that lit the lamp which now illuminated that once dark room.

My God, what *spirit*...what a vibrant, elegant presence was within that music. That quiet, remote man who'd sit hour after hour at the piano, frantically scribbling notes on paper while ignoring the din of his son playing Link Wray's "Rumble," (the first tune learned by every fledgling guitar player) in the next room—that man had now become a living presence.

And a mighty presence it was! How could I have passed that presence in the hallway so many times and not felt its power? But of course I *had*. That's why I had avoided him all my life. I didn't want to be touched by that presence; it would have destroyed the path I was on—the path of my own pleasure and satisfaction at the cost of all else.

And so, as this new obsession—the obsession to bring my father back to life—began to overtake me, I surrendered myself to it. And soon that thing called the "real" world, and everything in it, vanished.

During these past weeks, I have been letting that empty hole that's always been at the very center of my life, fill up. Don't get me wrong. It's not necessarily a joyful experience (though it can be). But mostly it is *pain*—pain the likes of which I have never known before. I'm literally on the operating table, where the doctor—who for some reason has denied me the use of anesthesia—is cutting open my carcass. My entrails spill out of the open wound, as the surgeon's knife digs deeper.

I don't care. I am no longer on this earth. I am a stranger from another galaxy. I go for days without food or sleep. I wander around the house in a stupor, mumbling, babbling incoherently, pounding the walls—crying, yelling...*screaming* at the top of my lungs.

Occasionally I wonder if the neighbors or the people who walk past my house can hear the shrieks—literally the sounds made by a wounded beast—that are coming from inside my house.

I know that my mom would be angry at me for staining her new carpeting. For my tears are not tears. They are blood. I am wounded... gutted. My blood stains the carpet and spatters the walls like a scene out of *Night of the Living Dead.* I am leaking like a sieve, reddening everything I touch.

The blood that I'm spewing in is not just my blood; it is the blood of Maurice Goldman—a man who has come to live inside me—a man who tells me stories—a man who wakes me in the middle of the night and speaks to me in a language that only I can understand.

His spirit and my spirit do a strange dance. It is the dance of life. It is the dance of death. I don't know what it is, and it matters not a whit.

Sometimes I ask God why he waited so long to allow this encounter to take place. Yet somehow I know that it had to be like this. This is the story that I had been waiting until now—in the sixty-first year of my life—to write.

Along with the articles in the scrapbooks, I found an envelope containing a poem. It is a very short poem, written by a little-known writer named Mary Lee Hall. It is entitled "Turn Again To Life." As I read it, I recalled that my father had read this poem at the graveside, when my mother's sister—my Aunt Charlotte—died in 1982.

Whenever I read this poem (and I read it often, since it is now Scotch-taped to my bedroom wall), my father is alive once again. He is speaking to me, though I'm sure that wasn't his intention at the time he first read it at Charlotte's funeral.

Yet I know beyond a shadow of a doubt that my father uttered these lines so that I could read them now, at a time when my life—before embarking upon this journey—seemed unbearably bleak and without purpose.

Thanks to my father, that time is over.

If I should die and leave you for awhile,
Be not like others sore undone, who keep

Long vigil by the silent dust and sweep.
For my sake, turn again to life and smile,
Nerving thy heart and trembling hand
To do that which will comfort other souls than thine.
Complete these dear unfinished tasks of mine,
And I perchance may therein comfort you.

MEMOIRS

MEMOIRS

A MEMO TO BARBARA

Lord, what is man, that Thou hast regard for him?
Or the son of man, that Thou takest account of him?

Man is like a breath, his days are as a fleeting shadow.
In the morning he flourishes and grows up like grass
In the evening he is cut down and withers.

So teach us to number our days,
That we may get us a heart of wisdom.

—Prayer adapted from Psalms 144 and 90.

They're packing up the boxes now. Soon the house will be empty. Your things...*your* life—stuffed in cardboard boxes. Somehow it just doesn't seem right.

Surely that's one of the worst things about death—the packing away of things. Hell, my dad's clothes sat in the closet for three years before I was finally able to convince my mother to give them away.

So, how long has it been, little cousin? Funny, though you were nine years my senior, I always thought of you as younger than I.

Two months. Two months now that I've been living alone in the house where you lived for the past 20 years. Drinking my morning coffee at the kitchen table where you drank yours...writing at your desk...sleeping in your bed.

Do you know that I didn't change the sheets for the first three weeks I was here, Barb? No, I needed to sleep in those sheets...to feel the places that your skin had touched—to smell you—to *absorb* you.

So there I lay in your monstrous bed, looking at the stacks of books on the night table, wondering which ones you read before falling asleep. But I couldn't figure anything out. All I could see was the image of you during those last weeks of your life—tiny and frightened—lying there, laboring for breath. Sucking on that goddamned oxygen lung.

I know...I know, little cousin. I know that you were scared. Scared of falling asleep...scared that you might not wake up.

During those last days, I'd sit at the edge of your bed, aware that there was nothing I could do but fluff your pillow or freshen your water...maybe rub your back a little. And though I did my best not to let you see it, I was furious. Furious that I couldn't simply *will* the health that was in my own body into yours. It's in moments like these that you realize what puny, powerless things we humans truly are.

We didn't see each other much during those last years, Barb. But whenever we did, it would instantly be *right there*. That special connection. How I loved those long talks we'd have, because they were always "core" stuff. Stuff that *mattered*. I always marveled at how you'd tune right into where I was at. Highly sensitive—those antennae of yours.

But I know I wasn't special in that regard. You did that with everybody, didn't you? It didn't matter whether it was a friend, a colleague, your kids, or the gardener. You always had a way of making whomever you were talking with, feel that they were the absolute center of the universe. That was your gift, Barb. That was why people would instantly find themselves telling you their story.

And now I've had a chance to listen to yours. The house—it told me *everything*. All I had to do was to be quiet and listen.

I remember staying in your old house on Landale Street in Studio City, where we stayed when our family first moved to California in the '50s. I slept in your room, Barb.

Remember? Sometimes we'd stay up all night talking. Sometimes, I'd fall asleep, only to wake up later and find you reading.

Always reading...

Listen, Barb...there's something I've got to get off my chest. One night you came home late from a date, and you began to get undressed for bed. I was still up, but I pretended I was asleep so that I could watch you. It was so dark in the room that I couldn't really see anything—just your silhouette. Still, I've always felt guilty about spying on you like that.

Well, now you know.

Here in your hallway, I look at the framed photos that line the walls. Everyone is here—your mom and dad, my parents, Grandma and Grandpa...assorted uncles, aunts and cousins.

Hey! There you are in your ballet tutu at age 13. Pretty cute stuff! And later, in high school—your hair in a bob. You look just like Betty, in *Father Knows Best*.

And look! There's Grandpa Jake in his grocery store back in Cleveland. Must've been around 1948. God, will you *look* at that place! All that *stuff!*

I especially love this one—Uncle Norm (your dad), lounging in the hammock of his back yard in Studio City. Exactly as I remember him—a clean, freshly pressed white shirt, a cigar clutched between his teeth.

You know, those old photos always get to me for some reason. I don't know Barb, but I just can't believe that we—we who are now flesh and blood—will someday turn into those old photos! We'll be gone—and people will look at us and remark how funny we looked "back then."

Which reminds me of something you said in a letter you'd written to your husband, Lee, back when he was stationed in Germany. I found it in a stack of letters out in the garage. I guess maybe you were depressed or something that day, because at the end of the letter, you said this really awful thing. You said, "You know, Lee, one of the things I can't bear is that someday we'll just be gone. We won't be here anymore, and the world will go on without us."

Good God, Barb! You must've been about 18 when you wrote that! What the hell were you doing, thinking those thoughts at that age? But the worst part is that I can't argue with you. Because the truth is that everything really *does* go on without us. And that just seems *wrong*. See, when I was a kid, I always had this feeling that when somebody died, things should just *stop*. At least just for a moment. But it *doesn't*—does it?

Nothing stops. Everything just keeps right on going. It's horrible.

So tell me, Barb—what of death? Tell me, oh great teacher, great mystic—why couldn't you beat it? Why couldn't you lick the demon? You—who knew the secrets. *You*, who were supposed to be the warrior.

You see, I'm not about to let you off the hook. Not *yet*. Because I don't believe that you were supposed to go like that. Sorry, but nobody's going to convince me that it was "your time." And please, don't give me any of that crap about *karma* and *reincarnation*, or *everlasting peace*. Sorry, I don't want to hear it.

I remember once we were talking about Hoshi—the lovely Oriental wife of our cousin Gerry—who died in that swimming pool accident. As her houseguests made party conversation, she slipped beneath the water. She couldn't swim. No one noticed a thing, so quietly did she drown.

"She died of courtesy," you told me. "Any Jew would know that."

As always, you were right, Barb. Because surely, any of our people would have *shrieked* with rage. They would have shouted and screamed and made a terrible din—because Jews don't *believe* in silence. No Buddhas, they. Rather they use *sound*—words, chatter, noise—to battle the only real enemy—*the hardening of the heart*.

So I will not let you go quietly, Barb. No, I will make a stink and a scene. I will scream and shout and raise the rafters! I *must*—don't you *see?*

Sorry for the melodrama. I know you would have hated it. But, *damnit*—it's no small task living in your old digs. You left so much of yourself here. I can feel your presence most strongly here in this room—the study—where you wrote. And you're in the doll house, too—"the spirit house," you called it. For you, that miniature house—with all its wonderful detail—was a place you built to house the souls of the many departed loved ones in your life. A place where they could finally find rest.

We've had a lot of death in our family, haven't we, Barb? More than our share, I sometimes think. Both your parents, my Mother and Father, Aunt Charlotte, Aunt

Adeline, Uncle Norm, Aunt Flo, Grandpa and Grandma—not to mention the many friends.

All gone.

And now you. You know what, Barb? For the first time in my life, I understand your need for ritual...your insistence that the family get together every year for Passover and Rosh Hashanah. Now, as the clan shrinks, I understand.

But despite your insistence on ritual, Barb, I will not light the *yahrzeit* candle for you. No, I refuse to light one of those hideous "reminders" that Malinow/Silverman insists on sending out each year. I prefer to do my own ritual—here at the typewriter—or perhaps at 3:00 a.m.—the hour when I find myself sitting straight up in bed—fully awake. The hour when I can feel something...*someone*... whispering to me. Trying to tell me—tell me *what?*

You see, this is *my* ritual, Barb.

To listen.

To find out.

Soon it begins. Soon the house and everything in it—the walls, the books, the artifacts you collected from your many trips around the world—almost seem to conspire to make their personal histories known to me. I don't have to do a thing. Just be quiet.

Like the night I opened the book next to your bed (Jung's *Memories, Dreams and Reflections*) to a passage you'd bookmarked. And read this: *"I feel very strongly that I am under the influence of things...questions which were left incomplete and unanswered by my parents and my grandparents, or perhaps more distant ancestors. As if I've had to complete or perhaps to continue things which previous ages had left unfinished."*

And then, amongst your papers, I found an incredible remembrance of our Grandmother, Sophie. It was about a lesson that she taught you as a child, back in the old Taylor Road house in Cleveland, where our family grew up.

It was such a simple lesson. And yet it held the secret—the *key*.

It was one of those days when you'd stayed home from school, pretending to be sick. One of those cold winter days when the windows were opaque with frost. There you were—you and Grandma Sophie—in the kitchen. The kitchen was the room you loved best, for there you and Grandma would cavort and talk and while away the hours.

She'd flip the radio on to "The Polish Hour," and soon she'd start to dance about...grabbing you and doing a crazy polka—right there in the midst of the blood and the feathers of the chicken she was cutting up for dinner!

Then she did something *special.* She showed you how to warm a coin and press it to the frost-covered window. And afterwards, you'd look through the glass, past the yard, to the big houses up on the hill. And as you peered through the tiny hole that the warm coin had made, Grandma told you that each one of those houses held *people...* and more—that each one of those people had a *story.* And so, each day you would peer into one of those houses, and Grandma Sophie would tell you stories about the people inside them.

And that was the *secret*, Barb—that every house had a life of its own—a life which could be *penetrated.* And inside the houses were *people*—each with their own story. A world within a world within a world...each different and wondrous...each to be discovered...if only one opened one's eyes. If one simply took the trouble to *look* and *listen.*

And the best thing about the secret, Barb, is that once it's yours, you can never lose it. It's yours *forever!* As you wrote in your journal: *"Even now, as I walk along a street in my own neighborhood or in Istanbul, and the lights are left on and the shades are drawn, I look into the houses. I look into the faces, greedily, gratefully, and I am in that place...that life. I own what I behold..."*

So that's the secret, Barb. The miraculous gift passed on by our Grandma Sophie. Our uneducated, illiterate, Russian, peasant Grandmother. The gift of *storytelling.* And now that I know, I see that I, too, have the gift.

Now the boxes are almost gone. Your things...carried out to the waiting cars to be given away—spread amongst those who loved you. I don't want anything, Barb. I have everything I need. Here—inside me.

Yes, you are *in* me now. Now I understand. I have listened. I have heard the story. And if I have truly understood...if the seed has taken root, then I will—as you did with such grace and skill during your lifetime—make certain that I, too, pass it on.

MEMOIRS

REQUIEM FOR A VALLEY GUY

Item: A man shot his wife to death in a crowded parking lot of Topanga Plaza in Canoga Park, CA, on Saturday. The man was then fatally shot when he pointed the weapon at an off-duty Los Angeles police officer working as a security guard in the shopping mall, authorities said. The identities of the couple, who were pronounced dead at the scene, were not immediately disclosed by police.

It was just a small item at the bottom of page three of the *L.A. Times*. Nothing particularly unusual. Hell, there's at least one of these in the paper just about every day. Still, it got to me for some reason. I sat back and tried to figure out why. It didn't take me long.

Though I'm a native Ohioan, I have, for the better part of my life, lived in the San Fernando Valley—a suburb of Los Angeles. Most people simply refer to it as "The Valley." Sometimes I even think of myself as (God help me) a *Valley Guy*.

I remember when Topanga Plaza first opened. I'd just graduated high school. It was the first real mall in the Valley. It was a source of pride. *Our* mall. Today, the place looks undeniably tacky—a cheesy version of the gaudier (but no less repugnant) malls that have become our Global Villages of sorts. Nonetheless, I have undoubtedly imbued

Topanga Plaza with some sort of spiritual quality. Sort of an "exempt" status from the ugly realities of the "real" world. A status resulting from the innocence which one associates with one's teen-age years. Which is why, no doubt, that news clipping got to me.

However, I must confess that despite these somewhat soppy sentiments, the other part of me—the spoiled, well-bred, undeniably snobby kid from Cleveland—has always regarded the Valley (of which Topanga Plaza serves as the quintessential symbol) with a certain horror. When we first moved here, I could never quite accept the fact that my neighbors included people who drove pickup trucks and RV's, went bowling on Saturday mornings, and shopped at god-awful places like Kmart. It was all so…uncouth.

As a kid, I guess I found my new surroundings somewhat amusing. It was sort of like I'd just landed a role in a *Ma and Pa Kettle* movie. However, as the years passed, my antipathy for the Valley blossomed into what can only be described as a profound sense of repulsion. (This, despite the fact that today the Valley is considered one of the more "chic" spots in Los Angeles). Sorry, I don't care how they try to disguise it…the Valley has a heart and soul that can never be altered.

Turn a wrong corner in the Valley, and suddenly you're in Tijuana!

I can think of nothing more depressing than driving down a street like Sherman Way (only one of the many Valley streets which I detest) and seeing mile after mile of hideously nondescript apartment buildings with names like The Tiki Gardens, The Outrigger and The El Cortez (they always have 5-year-old "Grand Opening' signs plastered on them). You know the kind of apartments I'm talking about…the ones where tinfoil serves as window covering and shopping carts litter the ugly weed patches that are supposed to pass for front lawns. Sure, I realize that there are apartments like these all over L.A.—but there is a certain extra tawdriness about the ones located in the Valley.

Okay, let's get down to brass tacks. You wanna know what the Valley is? I'll tell you: The Valley is, well…it's 7-11, Big Gulp, Abba Zabba, Bazooka Joe, Supercuts, *The National Enquirer*, Kung Fu video games, red licorice (not black), dice hanging from the rear-view mirror of '68 Chevys, pot-bellied men in tank tops, polyester shirts, and/or T-shirts bearing beer emblems on the back.

The Valley is fat ladies in floral print mumus, cops that look like they just got out of high school (these guys inevitably have those infuriating neatly cut moustaches and stone-dead eyes), drive-in movies, do-it-yourself car washes, sunglasses with those little strings that you wear around your neck, see-through t-shirts, beer nuts, lava lamps, red plastic purses, exercycles, skate boards, landau tops, sheepskin seat covers, beat up old cars with bondo on the side and a bunch of empty Coke cans and crumpled up newspapers all over the floor. Oh yeah. And donut shops. *Lots* of donut shops.

The Valley is Bob's Big Boy, Midas Muffler, Sears, Walmart, Thrifty Drugs, (not Save-On), Penny's, Montgomery Ward, Kinney Shoes, Taco Bell, Jack In The Box, Naugles, Taco Bell, Earl Scheib, Pep Boys and Lees Bars, Stools and Dinettes. It is the Corbin Bowling Alley, The Rocket Bowling Alley and the Canoga Park Bowling Alley. In fact, every bowling alley in the world is *actually* located in the Valley.

The Valley is parks. Not very nice parks. Parks where the drinking fountains either don't work or the water is real hot, and the grass is half-dead. The Valley is pickup trucks, campers, RV's, jeeps, mobile homes and vans with those stupid oversize tires and Western murals stenciled on the back windows. It is bad oil paintings of Elvis, Telly Savalas, Sylvester Stallone, Liberace, Barbara Streisand, Wayne Newton and Jesus that hang in people's dens (all Valley dens have wood paneling). It is cigarettes. Everyone in the Valley smokes cigarettes (primarily Marlboro, Winston and Kool filtered) And they *never* dump the ashtrays. Oddly, people who live in the Valley (even the ones that don't smoke) smell like cigarettes. Come to think of it, they actually *look* like cigarettes!

The Valley is the ugly brown and orange plastic chairs that adorn the waiting rooms at Kaiser Permanente Hospital—the ones littered with year-old issues of *Reader's Digest, Ladies Home Journal* and other magazines that nobody wants to read. And the mother with her hair in rollers, a dead cigarette dangling from her lips, and a million screaming brats climbing all over her (which she never bothers to tell to shut up, even though they're driving everyone else in the place nuts). And the old man with the cane sitting quietly in the corner, smiling for no reason.

There are no black people in the Valley. And any that are here are not *real* blacks—or at the very least they are very insecure about being blacks. Also no Jews. All the Jews live in *Encino*—and Encino (despite the fact that it is physically located here) is *not* the Valley. Studio City (also allegedly in the Valley) is not *truly* part of the Valley. Neither is North Hollywood. North Hollywood is *Mexico*. Spiritually, the Valley is Canoga Park, Reseda, Van Nuys, Simi, San Fernando, Panorama City, and any place with an 818 area code. If you've got an 818 area code—you're dead meat, Jack. If you've managed to maintain a 213 number, you're safe (at least for the time being).

Men that live in the Valley work tarring roofs, in lumberyards, auto body shops or hardware stores—and they all sell real estate on the side. (Come to think of it, *everybody* in the Valley sells real estate). These men have names like Chuck and Leroy, or maybe even Dirk. Their wives are those bone-skinny women with little hairs growing out of their chins who stay home during the day and watch soap operas and clip coupons out of the *Daily News And Green Sheet.* Many of these wives have tiny, ugly dogs (poodles, schnauzers, and the like). Dogs that they walk real early in the morning that leave huge, glistening piles of crap on your lawn.

It is no accident that the Valley is the capital of the Porn Industry. Many Valley people are into swinging, S&M and kiddie porn, as well as being members of assorted cults...witchcraft and satanism being the most popular. (Charlie Manson's bunch got its start in the Valley). And everybody here—bar none—is on drugs—primarily reds (speed) and 'ludes (downers). Cocaine is more Santa Monica, Beverly Hills-ish.

Another curious thing about people in the Valley is that they don't really grow up (yours truly included). They just become old teenagers. Many Valley men look like those guys that you used to see at Elvis concerts. You know—guys that wear white belts and white shoes. Guys who have '50s hairdos that they've actually had *since* the '50s. Also many Valley men favor flattops. Inevitably, the

Valley flattop men have those kind of stick-out ears which seem to be growing out of their necks.

Valley people tend to be either very skinny or very fat. There are very few middle-sized people here. Not only this, but Valley women seem to like to *flaunt* their fat. I swear—you find a fat woman in the Valley, and nine times out of ten she'll be prancing around in some skimpy little tennis outfit, or even a bathing suit! It's *amazing* (not to mention highly repugnant).

As for the thin Valley women, they tend to have that *Auschwitz demeanor*. You know—their skin has that sort of yellowish tint that comes from smoking five packs of cigarettes and drinking 20 cups of coffee every day for the last 10 years. In fact, Valley people (women in particular) have a very distinctive look which the practiced viewer can instantly recognize. It's sort of like they've gotten dried out—like some old piece of beef jerky.

Some things that are *not* Valley include chocolate phosphates, Italians, grand pianos (people who play keyboards in the Valley all play organs or synthesizers), dill pickles, black cherry soda, Halvah, Marcel Proust, Leonard Bernstein, Picasso, James Thurber, Beethoven's Fifth Symphony, Eiderdown quilts, Greek olives, bouillabaisse, Gefilte fish, Challah bread, herringbone sports jackets, and books on German humor. Fireplaces are *not* Valley (unless they are those gas kind with the fake logs). Red knee sox are *definitely* not Valley. Green…*maybe*.

Turkey sandwiches (on white bread) are Valley. So is diet salad dressing (Thousand Island, not Roquefort). Orange Crush is Valley. Anything orange is Valley. Also, those decals that reflect different colors that people plaster on their rear bumpers are *very* Valley. Blonde hair is Valley. Dark hair is not. Curly hair—nix. Hair on the chest is not really Valley. It's more *Fairfaxy* (the Borscht Belt).

Tastee Freeze is Valley. Kool Aid. Also, those wax coke bottles you used to chew when you were a kid. Pez is not Valley. Anything Jewish is not Valley. Example: Vernors ginger ale is Jewish, not Valley. Root beer is definitely *not* Valley. Night school is Valley, and so are all trade schools. PC computers are Valley. Macintoshes are not! Divorces are *very* Valley. Seascapes. Prozac. Juju Bees. Zorries. Unleaded gas.

Cremora. Oh and that most maddening of all phrases—"Have A Great Day!" Started right here—I promise you.

Cunnilingus is Valley. Vaginal sex is not. The Three Little Pigs are Valley. The Big Bad Wolf isn't. Cheating on your wife is extremely Valley. Lime jello is Valley. Yellow is Valley. Brown is Valley. Radio Shack. Q-tips. The May Company is Valley. Robinson's is *not*. Neither is Nordstrom. Sears—absolutely 100 percent pure Valley!

Despite rumors to the contrary, Bill Gates actually lives in the Valley. Jimmy Conners (remember him?) is from the Valley, and Chuck Connors too, for that matter (he's also dead). John McEnroe is a stone cold Valley dude. All the Elvis imitators in the entire world live in the Valley. Michael Jackson was *raised* in the Valley. John Voight is Valley, despite the fact that he's a longtime member of Chabad House (sorry to have to rat you out John). Chuck Norris is pure 818 area code. Jack Nicholson—though he did a great imitation of a Valley guy in *Five Easy Pieces*—has never been in the Valley in his entire life! Wayne Newton *ought* to live in the Valley. However, it's OK that he lives in Las Vegas, because Las Vegas *is* the Valley.

Other Valley residents include Frank Sinatra, Jr., Tonya Harding, William Shatner, Jean Claude Van Damme, Pauly Shore, Steven (I wanna be a mercenary) Seagal, Dr. Deepak Chopra, Criss Angel, Mary Tyler Moore, Cal Worthington, Oprah Winfrey, Tori Spelling, Lee Majors, Vanna White, the stupid lead singer from Poison (sorry, I forget his name), Priscilla Presley, Eddie Murphy, Neil With The Deal, the guy that used to play Eddie Haskell on *Leave It To Beaver*, (presently working for the L.A.P.D.), Julio Iglasias, Dr. Joyce Brothers, Mr. Ed, Harry Connick Jr., Earl Scheib, Hulk Hogan, all of the ex-Mouskeeters (the ones who aren't dead or in jail), Farah Fawcett, Garth Brooks, Art Garfunkel, Ann Landers, Gene Simmons, Nora Ephron, Donny Osmond, Ed McMahon, Squeaky Fromme, Bob Eubanks, Rin Tin Tin, Chubby Checker, Slim Whitman, Billy Barty...a lot of aging child-stars who have kicked drugs and turned to God, as well as many game show hosts. Also all the plumbers and electricians in the world live in the Valley.

Do you begin to get what I'm saying here? No matter how you cut it, the Valley is still a hick town with aspirations of being something else. But there's no way to disguise it. I don't care how many billion-dollar malls or cute little French bistros or Cappuccino joints they put up. This Valley is—and always will be—Beverly Hillbillies-land. And even if you've never seen this place, it doesn't matter. There's a "Valley" somewhere not far from you. Because the Valley *is* America.

Thinking about all this stuff got me a little nostalgic, so I hopped in my car and began aimlessly driving around. Before I knew it, I found myself at Topanga Plaza. The first thing I did was to snoop around the parking lot. I guess I was looking for the smell of death—some sign of the cancer that had invaded this sacred teenage haven of mine. But it wasn't there. Nothing. Just a vast sea of cars with personalized license plates and those stupid sunglass things on the windshields.

I ventured inside the mall, got a cup of coffee and sat in the "Food Court," whereupon I engaged in approximately an hour of anthropological research (i.e. people watching). It was really quite amazing. Despite the requisite costume changes, the Mall People still looked exactly the same as they had 30 years ago! Now if you could have magically transported this bunch across town to the Beverly Center, they would have immediately been tossed out for being impostors.

I could feel a good-sized depression coming on, so I decided I'd better split. I wanted to find this one old high school hangout of ours, which happened to be a freeway underpass. We spent a lot of time there, hatching plans, telling stupid jokes, smoking cigarettes—all the stuff that teenagers normally do.

Actually, what I wanted to see was if this one particular piece of graffiti that we'd spray-painted on the underpass wall was still there. I don't know why, but it'd stuck in my mind for some reason. What it said was: FREDDIE BLOWS DEAD GOATS...

The statement referred to this guy named Freddie Moskowitz. And while, if I recall correctly, Freddie had several strange habits, this particular one was not amongst them. Somehow, though (I never could quite figure out why) poor Freddie had been branded by this cruel piece of slander. We just never treated him quite the same after it had appeared (in bright red spray paint) on the underpass wall. Nobody ever copped to the actual deed. Sometimes I think maybe ol' Freddie wrote it himself!

It didn't take me long to find the spot. I parked my car, got out, and headed into the underpass. There was plenty of graffiti all right—including the names of various gangs, rock bands, couples declaring their eternal love, pentagrams—all the usual stuff. But nothing that said "Freddie Blows Dead Goats."

Somehow, this made me even *more* depressed.

As I exited the underpass, I encountered a little kid, maybe 10 or so. He was hawking flowers. They weren't particularly *nice* flowers. It looked like he'd probably stolen them from various people's lawns.

"How's business?" I asked the kid.

"Not so hot," he replied.

"So, why don't you move to another corner?"

The kid eyed me warily. "Dunno," he squinted.

I could think of no retort.

"How much for a bouquet?" I finally asked.

"Dollar-fifty."

I dug into my pocket and yanked out a couple of bucks, whereupon he handed me a rather wilted bunch of flowers. I took them and walked back into the underpass. I stood there for a long time, perusing the names scrawled on the wall.

It was awful. I didn't recognize even one of them.

Somehow I didn't want to leave. I guess I was listening for…for what? A *sound?* A *hint?* A *whisper* maybe—from one the old ghosts? I wasn't really sure. Whatever it was, it was not forthcoming.

Finally, I set the flowers down on the sidewalk, right underneath the spot where the infamous Freddie Moskowitz graffiti had once anointed the wall.

"So long Freddie," I said. "Hope everything turned out OK for you."

When I got back to the corner, the kid's flowers were there, but he was nowhere in sight. I stuck around for a couple of minutes, but he seemed to have disappeared. Either he'd gone off in search of a new spot, or else he'd just gotten fed up with the whole deal and bailed out. Then again, maybe he'd been kidnapped!

Good Lord! Maybe I'd pick up the paper tomorrow morning only to be confronted with a grisly article about some poor kid who'd been supporting his sick mother by selling flowers. And now they'd found his lifeless body chucked in some garbage dumpster!

I could feel my blood beginning to boil.

Those filthy scumbags!

I'd track those murderous scoundrels down if it was the last thing…

But then I cut it out. I knew what was going on. It was just the dramatist in me working overtime. Anyhow, this wasn't *my* movie any longer. I'd just written FADE OUT on the final scene moments earlier, beneath the freeway underpass.

Sorry kid, but I'm afraid it's gonna be up to somebody else to write you a role in *their* story. Hey, quit complaining! You got a walk on...and that ain't bad when you stop and think about it. Hell, it took Freddie nearly 30 years to get his first shot. And guess what?

It wasn't even a speaking role.

MEMOIRS

SQUAREHEAD

When I was a kid, there was this guy in our neighborhood named Wahee Troger. There was something wrong with Wahee. He had one of those real big heads—you know... the kind of head that's way too big for your body and it has those little stick-out ears like a lot of guys in the Navy have—the kind of ears that if you were sitting behind the guy in a movie it'd be real hard not to flick them real fast with your finger. Anyway, us kids invented a name for Wahee—it wasn't a very nice name, actually.

We called him Squarehead.

Squarehead didn't do much of anything. It was hard to tell how old he was. I guess he was around 40 or so, but he still lived with his mother in a kind of crummy house in a not-very-nice neighborhood.

Sometimes when we were out for recess, we'd see Squarehead hanging around the schoolyard...just sort of watching us. At other times, we'd see him walking along the street, carrying a shopping bag. He always had that shopping bag with him wherever he went. Nobody ever really knew what was in that bag, and we never wanted to ask.

Sometimes he'd be walking down the street, and a bunch of us would walk behind him going, *"Hey, Squarehead! Hey, Squarehead!"*

Sometimes we'd even bonk big fat stones off his back. Well, actually *I* didn't do it, but I *watched* while the other guys did it.

I was sort of a coward, I guess.

Kids are shitty—they really are. Sometimes, the shitty ones change and get okay later in life, but mostly they just stay shitty. They grow up to be very crummy people.

I don't know—I guess in some funny way, I used to think about old Squarehead, and I figured that in a way, maybe he really might have it better than the rest of us. He seemed happy just being by himself. Him and his bag. I guess maybe I was wrong though.

One day a bunch of us went to the movie. Saturday afternoon matinee—*The Creature From the Black Lagoon.* When we got to the theatre, there was Squarehead out front on his tricycle, just pedaling around. He was much too large for a tricycle, naturally, and he looked quite silly.

Just as we were going into the theater, he wheeled over and said, "Hey, can I go to the movies with you guys?" I was kind of shocked, because it was the first time he ever talked to any of us.

He'd been planning to do it, too—you could tell.

"Beat it, you stupid freak," said my friend John Lowinski.

John Lowinski was one of those guys I was telling you about who no doubt grew up to be a very crummy person. He once took a shit in this guy's car and blamed it on me. I sort of hated him, and I never could figure out why he was my friend.

Anyway, we went into the movie and left Squarehead out there. It made me feel real funny or something—I don't know. I kept trying to watch the movie, but I couldn't stop thinking about him out there all alone on that terrible tricycle of his.

It was awful.

Finally I got up to go up to the lobby—like I was getting some popcorn or something. When I got up there, I walked out front and looked around for Squarehead. I was hoping he might still be hanging around, I guess—but he wasn't there.

I looked out at the streets. They looked so empty and sad.

I was feeling real peculiar to tell you the truth.

I stuck around for a while more, then I went back into the movie. I sat down next to Judy Fosdick.

Later, during the second picture, I tried to put my hand on her tit, but she wouldn't let me.

Well, that's about it. Oh, yeah, a couple of weeks later, John Lowinski's father died. When I went over to his house, he was sitting underneath the piano, crying.

The next month we moved away from the neighborhood. It was the last time I'd ever see John Lowinski or Judy Fosdick or Squarehead or any of the rest of the kids ever again.

MEMOIRS

CAULIFLOWER ALLEY

D*ing!...ding! Ding! Ding!* The sounding of the bell indicates that the meeting is to come to order. But most of the 75 or so people in the room—all engrossed in small talk—don't seem to hear.

"SHAAAADUP!" comes a voice from in back.

The talkers quiet down and shift around in their chairs until they're all facing an American flag that's posted in front of the room. They rise to deliver the Pledge of Allegiance, and the room fills with the sound of their voices chanting in unison.

To a casual observer, the scene might not look out of the ordinary. Given that the average age appears to be around 60, perhaps it's a meeting of a local Elks Club or Moose Lodge. But a closer look at the group reveals that there's more to the story. There's an abundance of strange-looking attire—lots of dark, pin-striped suits, black homburg hats, even a pair or two of spats. And those *faces*—the squashed noses, scar tissue, eyes slightly off kilter, ears bent and twisted into odd shapes.

No sir—this is no ordinary bunch.

What this is, in fact, is a meeting of the Cauliflower Alley Club, an organization of former boxers and wrestlers. Every Wednesday, for the past 15 years, the motley crew has been meeting at various places in and around Los Angeles.

Today, the luncheon is taking place in a private room at the Old Spaghetti Factory in Hollywood. "Frankly, I'm not sure how long we'll last here," says club president Mike Mazurki. "The boys can get a little rowdy. We don't always last too long in one spot."

Since its inception, the Cauliflower Alley Club has grown from a mere handful of members to around 600. It includes many of pugilism's greats—Henry Armstrong, Jack Sharkey, Mushy Callahan, Lou Nova, Jack Dempsey, Archie Moore, Freddie Blassie, Carl "Bobo" Olson, Kid Chocolate, Gene Fullmer—the list goes on and on.

The club also boasts honorary members from the film world—George Raft, Jimmy Cagney, Jack Palance, Robert Conrad, Sylvester Stallone, and Kirk Douglas, as well as a host of other members who are all famous something-or-others. There's Jack Pepper, who married Ginger Rogers when she was thirteen; Kirk Allyn, the original movie "Superman;" Doc Levin, who invented the first mouthpiece; the guy who glued the hair on the original King Kong; another guy who quotes the Bible backwards (God knows why)...plus one whole hell of a lot of war heroes.

Though the Alley has chapters all over the globe, the real action still takes place right here. After all, Hollywood and the fight game are nearly synonymous. Most of the luncheon talk revolves around the great days of Hollywood Legion Stadium—one of the West Coast's largest fight spots in the '20s, '30s, and '40s. During that era, a Friday night at the Legion would find the ringside seats filled with stars like Charlie Chaplin, Rudolph Valentino, Al Jolson, Clark Gable, Humphrey Bogart, Errol Flynn—all fight fans.

Sadly, the Legion Stadium was razed in 1959. A bowling alley stands in its place today. And the great era of boxing and wrestling—according to most Alley members—is gone forever. But the memories aren't gone. They're right here in this room—in the faces and in the tales of the men gathered at the Old Spaghetti Factory.

At 88 "Young" Abe Attell isn't quite sure whether he's really the oldest Alley member, but everyone agrees that he's got the most stories to tell.

"Yeah, I seen 'em come an' go," Attell says proudly. "I was *there* Charlie!"

Attell grew up on New York's Lower East Side and started his boxing career in 1903 by protecting the corner where he sold newspapers. "There was another kid on my corner one day," Attell remembers, "an' I told him that it was *my* spot. We got into it, an' I beat the hell out of him."

When the fight was over, a stranger walked up and delivered the classic line: "Hey kid, ya wanna learn how to box?"

Attell turned out to be a natural. On his first day in the gym, one of the pros training there offered Attell a buck if he could make his nose bleed. "Two minutes later, I'd earned my first dollar."

Running away from home at age 14, Attell hopped trains all over the country, picking up fights wherever he could. "I was cocky, an' I was good. I got off a train in Oakland, and I beat up the toughest guy in town."

When Attell boxed, the days of 75-round fights had already passed, but he recalls some 25 and 30 round bouts. Boxing was still illegal in many states, and Attell fought whenever and wherever he could—on barges, in stockyards, barns, back rooms, and on the Vaudeville stage.

It was around this time that he met one of his boyhood idols—the great John L. Sullivan—who gave the young boxer some pointers. "He told me if I was serious about boxing, I had to train all the time, an' also not to mess around with booze or broads.

"Actually, I was kinda shy, an' I didn't like drinkin' all that much, but I did have a weakness…three cushion billiards. When the fights were over, you'd find me down at the local pool hall."

At 16, Attell suffered a torn retina of the left eye; it has left him partially blind ever since. But that didn't stop him. He fought until losing to "Wop" Flynn in 1922, beating some of the best in the world along the way.

How does Attell see the fight game today?

"Ah Jeesus…it's just *awful*. I was at the amateurs last night, an' I didn't see five good punches thrown all evening. Those guys don't know the basics. Ya gotta keep your hands up, then ya stick…stick—like this—see?"

Attell is up shadowboxing all over the room.

"Yeah, I can still wing a punch, but I wouldn't wanna hurt nobody. Like, the other day in the supermarket, I bumped shopping carts with this little old man, an' the guy says to me"—Attell adopts a thick Yiddish accent—"'*So ya vant I should give you a punch inna nose?* An' I says, '*Please don't hit me…I'm a sick man.*'"

Attell stifles a laugh. "Hell, I coulda blown on the guy, an' he would've fallen down."

Only a couple of years back, Attell happened to be in a restaurant when a robbery took place. "I saw this guy pull a rod, an' before he knew it, *bam!…*I hit him with the most beautiful left hook you ever saw. Left him out cold for 15 minutes."

Attell stops to savor the memory. "Yeah, I don't pick on no little guys, but any hanky-panky like that, an' I can *still* put some sucker's lights out!"

The Cauliflower Alley Club calls itself a nonpartisan organization—amenable to both males and females—but that's not quite the case. Aside from the obvious fact that there are more male than female fighters, club members couldn't give a hoot in hell for Women's Lib. You'd be surprised if they did. After all, these men grew up in an era where women were *babes*, *dolls* and *broads*.

On the other hand, Alley members do hold women up on a pedestal. "We don't really go for women boxers," says a longtime clubber." "Women—ladies that is—shouldn't be banging each other in the tits."

Double standard notwithstanding, Maria Bernardi—club secretary, bouncer, and former World Women's Wrestling Champ—has the distinction of being "one of the guys." This must owe, in part, to Bernardi's demeanor while she was on the wrestling circuit from 1937 to 1963.

Nicknamed "The Tigress," Bernardi was the quintessential villain. "I took a worse beating from the fans than I did in the ring," she recalls. "I've been hit on the head with chairs, cut with knives, and I've had my hair pulled out by the roots. The fans really *hated* me—an' I *loved* every minute of it. If they cheered me, I'd get hoppin' mad."

Bernardi was "a shooter," which basically means that she didn't take any shit from anybody. "If they tried to hurt me, I'd warn 'em once—then I'd just tear 'em apart. I've broken more 'n' a few legs in my day, mostly with a stepover toehold. Yep, I'd just bust them damn legs right off."

She also took her share of punishment. "I've had my arms, my legs, an' my back busted, my nose broken three times, an' my ears cauliflowered."

Bernardi pulls back her hair to reveal an ear that does, in fact, resemble the vegetable it's named for.

"Feel it," she says.

I reach over and finger the ear just above the lobe. It's hard as a rock.

Bernardi answers the next question before I can get to it. "You know, a lot of men get their kicks watchin' women fight, or fightin' us themselves."

On occasion, Bernardi has wrestled men "privately" for money. "It's a *business*," she says. "If havin' a woman beat you up gets them off, fine, but I don't want nothin' to do with those creeps outside of a business situation."

One evening, while eating dinner with another female wrestler, she was propositioned. "This guy walks up to us an' says, 'Which one of you girls wants to fuck?' I got up, batted my lashes, an' kicked him square in the balls. Hell, I was a married woman at the time."

Bernardi's first marriage ended after she dropkicked her husband down a flight of stairs.

"I say love 'em an' leave 'em."

During her career, the 55-year-old Bernardi fought in every conceivable arrangement—tag teams, Battle Royales, mud matches, and against both women and men.

"I remember fighting this black guy once, an' he didn't want to hit a lady, so I had to rile him up. I kept saying, 'Whatsa matter, nigger…afraid to take a swing at me?' He got mad and let one go, an' I tackled him and *boom!*—down he went. He got up, swung, an' down he went again. Finally, I got him in an Indian Death Lock, an' that's all she wrote."

Bernardi's favorite move was a hair throw followed by a body slam. "Once I got 'em on the mat, I'd jump up in the air and come down on 'em with all my weight. The fans would go nuts. They wanted to *kill* me. But, hell, that was the *idea*. I made my living from the boos."

A shiny, new, cream-colored Cadillac and a silver Jaguar are parked in the garage of Count Billy Varga's hillside home in Toluca Lake. Unlike many Alley members who've wound up on welfare, Varga estimates that he's earned more than $3 million during his 30-year wrestling career.

"One of the saddest memories I have," Varga says, "is of my friend Gorgeous George, who died alone and broke in some flophouse down on Western Avenue. My father, who taught me how to wrestle, also taught me something equally important: it's not making the money—it's *keeping* it."

Varga, who owns property in Beverly Hills, as well as a silver mine in Nevada, evidently learned the lesson well.

Varga remembers his father—the late great wrestler Count Joseph Varga—with a mixture of pride and awe. "The man was ruthless. I think the only real beating I ever took in my life was from him. He was *amazing*. He had a neck like steel. If you grabbed him around it, he'd just toss you off like a fly."

Varga himself has a bull neck, massive arms, and a barrel chest, all of which give the impression that he's much shorter than his 6'1" height. "Fortunately, I inherited my father's body, which had a constitution that didn't break up. Lots of wrestlers wind up crippled in later life, but I'm still in great shape."

Varga declines to reveal his age. "I'd just lie to you. Let's just say I won't see 50 again."

Varga turned pro in 1942, and kept up a steady pace, sometimes working as often as six nights a week, until he retired with the World Heavyweight Crown in 1972. Along the way, he also captured the Junior and Light-Heavyweight wrestling titles, beating such foes as "Dangerous" Danny McShain, "Wild Red" Berry, and 450-pound Haystack Calhoun.

In the beginning,Varga was the fair-haired boy of wrestling. That lasted until 1957, when fans unexpectedly started booing him. Rather than fight the reaction, Varga went with it. "I got pretty rough...pretty mean...after that."

He recalls a match in which the opponent kept digging his fingers into Varga's eyes. "Finally I got him in an arm bar, and then—CRRRRUUUUNNNKKK! You could hear that arm snap through the whole arena."

Varga bristles at the suggestion that wrestling is nothing more than a sideshow. "Maybe now, but not in *my* day!" And fake blood capsules? "Absolutely wrong! That blood was *real*, brother—I *know*. I shed plenty of it."

Then I ask Varga the same question I've asked several other Alley members. Which of the fighting arts would work best in a street fight? Unfortunately, I'd made the mistake of telling Varga that I'd studied martial arts.

"Let's see…just for fun," he says, getting up off the sofa. "Don't worry..."

As soon as I stand up, Varga comes at me, and as he does, I throw a side-thrust kick at his midsection. The next second I find myself on the floor, my leg twisted into a ridiculous-looking pretzel.

"Now," Varga says, "all I have to do is apply a little pressure… like *this...* "

"Yeah, jeez," I gasp, "that's really *something...*"

Back in my chair, I resume a safer line of questioning. We talk about the old times, and Varga sadly recounts the heyday of wrestling in L.A. In those days, matches could be found every night in places like Ocean Park (where Steve Allen was the commentator), the Venice Arena, and the Red Barn—to name a few. "All gone, except for the Olympic (Auditorium)," Varga says. "It's a shame. Luckily, I'd always planned for the end of my career. Even when I was champ, wrestling was never my whole life because they forget you so quickly. When you're the champ, you can't breathe, you've got so many people around you. But just *don't* be champ, and you've got *all* the breathing room in the world."

At 74, Jimmy McLarnin is still a dapper, little Irishman who loves nothing better than to talk about "the great science of boxing." The former two-time Welterweight Boxing Champion eases back in his chair and begins telling me about his ring career.

"I got a dollar for my first fight, and $60,000 for my last one. I made good money in the game. Yessir, boxing's been *real good* to me."

McLarnin smiles a huge smile, that causes his eyes to disappear into a sea of wrinkles.

McLarnin started off as a flyweight, and worked his way up through the bantamweight, featherweight, and lightweight ranks, finally winning the welterweight title from Young Corbett III in 1933. He later lost it to Barney Ross—but McLarnin came back to beat Ross and regain the title a year later, in 1935.

Some of his buddies at the Alley remember McLarnin as a fighter who came to punish you. "I don't know about that, but I certainly wasn't one of the Joes that'd carry you for five rounds. I went in there to take the other guy out. Hell, it was dog eat dog, as far as I was concerned."

Unlike most Alley members, McLarnin's face is unmarked, though he has the dubious honor of receiving an award for having the worst hands. And it's true—McLarnin's knuckles appear to be pushed back nearly to the wrist. Knuckles notwithstanding, he looks as if he might have made his living as a bank teller.

"Pop Foster, my manager, taught me the art of hitting and *not* getting hit. I learned fighting from the ground up—no shortcuts. Hell, he had me working on my jab for two years!

"My strength was that I had two good hands, and I could take you out with either one of them. I was a boxer *and* a puncher. And that's the secret—you box a fighter, and you fight a boxer."

Does McLarnin recall his toughest fight?

"Sure, it was against Tony Canzoneri, in 1929. He hit me on the temple in the second round, and for the rest of the fight I didn't know where I was. Got the holy hell beat out of me. The worst part was that I'd just gotten married, and it was the first time my wife had ever seen me fight. My face was such a mess that she could barely look at me.

"After I recovered, I told my manager, 'Pop, I want Canzoneri again.' It was the only time in my career that I'd ever wanted revenge. Well, we got the match, and I just *destroyed* him. He was in a coma for three days. Thank God he recovered. But he never fought a good fight again."

This time McLarnin isn't smiling.

What does McLarnin think of today's crop of fighters? "The day of the great fighter is over," he says flatly. "They talk about Holmes or Ali. Hell, Dempsey, Louis—they would have run those guys right out of the ring. I wouldn't let any of 'em carry my jockstrap. It's a *disgrace.*

Plus, today all the fight clubs are gone. The game is controlled by a few people."

Who? Don King? Or is McLarnin talking about the Mafia? Now he looks uncomfortable. "Lemme put it this way—I can't name any names. And, as for the Mafia, if they were around in my day, I wasn't in contact with them. I wasn't aware of it."

Dropping the matter, McLarnin carries on. "For me, it was an honorable sport—a great art. *Yessir!* And I'm damn proud to have been a part of it!"

McLarnin's reticence to discuss organized crime is typical of Alley members. With the mere mention of the word "Mafia," lips automatically button up—a response that would seem to indicate that most of these guys *have* had contact with the underworld. Be that as it may, nobody is talking.

Well, *almost* nobody. The exception to the rule is one Mr. Vince Barbi, former prizefighter, actor, producer, writer, philanthropist...*and* one-time friend of the Syndicate.

"*Please*," Barbi admonishes, "*don't* say Mafia. It's not accurate. The only *real* Mafia is in Sicily."

A big, gregarious 68-year-old, Barbi will talk your head off in an Italian accent so thick you have to strain to catch all his words. After listening to his tales, you suspect he's stretching the truth at times... except for one small detail: Barbi insists on backing up every single statement he makes with letters, documents, books, and a veritable ton of photographs.

The first picture he shows me is of himself attired in boxing gear. It was taken in 1932, and Barbi—a member of the Italian National Boxing Team—had come to the States to fight in the Olympics. Even then, the coarse features and heavy-lidded eyes made him look just a wee bit shady. And luckily so. Barbi's mug promptly landed him steady employment in films, playing—what else?—a hood.

"Looka this," he says. "Here's me an' Ernie Borgnine. I love the man...an' there's me an' Brando, see? Now here's me with Bob Mitchum—a beautiful pal of mine...ah, and there's me escorting Anita Ekberg. Had an affair with her...she had a cunt that you love to kiss, *mmmmm, mmmmm.* Now she weighs 250 pounds...eats macaroni three times a day. Oh! Here's me an' the Chief Of Police in Naples…married to my sister…how you like that, eh?"

The banter continues until we come across a photo that I'd been hoping to see. It's of Barbi and another "beautiful pal"—one Salvatore Luciano—otherwise known as "Lucky" Luciano. "He was the boss of all bosses," says Barbi with more than a hint of pride.

Barbi met Luciano in Manhattan's Vesuvius Restaurant in 1932, and the two *paisanos* hit it off immediately. Later, Luciano, owner of several New York nightclubs, put Barbi in charge of them.

"Now lemme make one thing clear. I was never *in* the Syndicate. I had an acting career to pursue. But these guys, well, they were all beautiful pals of mine…"

A trifle disappointed, I go for a "bottom-line" question. Has Barbi ever seen anyone bumped off?

"Oh, sure," he says casually. "One night in the Nineteenth Hole—one of my places. These two guys come in an' pull out pieces. I thought it was all over for me, but it was the guy standing next to me they were after. Blew him away. Half his head came off on my suit. *Tsk, Tsk.* Poor fella…"

Luciano was deported to Italy in 1935, and later Barbi went over to Naples to meet him. There, he became involved in a march on Rome, the purpose of which was to promote the establishment of a pension fund for hoods.

"Sounds crazy, right? But it was really bad for them over there. Everything had become illegal—even prostitution—and these guys were all going broke." Barbi has recently completed a screenplay entitled *Heaven for Black Sheep*, which uses the Neapolitan scenario as the backdrop for his story.

When Luciano died in Naples in 1962, Barbi was there to bid his old friend farewell. "I really miss the bastard. He always said to me, 'Vinny, keep up your acting…an' I never wanna see you carrying no fuckin' piece!'"

Barbi took the words to heart. Any killing he's done has been on the big screen. "I've bumped off 665½ people in pictures so far," Barbi says, brightening up. "The half was a midget. I been looking for another midget for awhile now—so I can make it an even number. Hey, if you know one, lemme know, willya? I'll make him an offer he can't refuse."

Old fighters never die—they just go to Hollywood. The adage seems tailor-made for Alley members. These guys are the mugs, the muscleheads, the mobsters of a thousand films. During their careers they've pounded and pulled each other to death, and in the process have created some of the cinema's most unforgettable images. Their faces have come to be a part of our collective consciousness. They are, perhaps, the true sculptors. Undoubtedly, the most notable example is club President, Mike Mazurki.

That face—a beleaguered visage—a virtual roadmap of lines, crevices, secret nooks and crannies. How many people has it scared the hell out of? It's been seen in films like *Nightmare Alley, Donovan's Reef, Some Like It Hot, Night and the City, Dick Tracy,* and countless others. Mazurki's most famous role, though, is that of Moose Malloy in the 1944 version of Raymond Chandler's novel, *Farewell, My Lovely,* which was titled *Murder, My Sweet* for the screen. That film launched a career as a heavy who'd strike terror in to the hearts of millions.

And yet here's Mazurki sitting in his modest Burbank apartment, flanked by two toy poodles that occasionally nip at his feet. Somehow it just doesn't seem right.

"I started wrasslin'"—he doesn't say *wrestling*—"pro in '34," Mazurki rasps. "My first picture was in '12. I played a Russian wrassler."

His voice sounds like he's been gargling with gravel since his wrestling career began.

Austrian director Josef Von Sternberg spotted Mazurki in the ring and tapped him for the wrestler's role in *The Shanghai Gesture* (1932). In that film he got to say "da" and "nyet," later graduating to lines like "Yas, boss" and "Stick 'em up." Even though acting offers kept coming in, Mazurki continued wrestling until 1965, when he finally hung up his tights at the age of 55.

The dual career worked well for him. The more movies he was in, the greater his draw in the ring. The more he wrestled, the more marred and battered his face became, resulting in more film roles.

"I love the picture business, but I always loved the sport too, y'unnerstan'?"

"I've had every bone in my body broken during my career. Plus, I was blinded twice...an' of course I got *this.*" He points at a huge, cauliflowered ear.

Mazurki's ear served as the model for the Golden Cauliflower Ear Award that's given to newly inducted members. Mazurki seems particularly proud of that. If necessary, he has a plastic ear to put over the real one, but most of the time it sits in the bottom of a dresser drawer.

"The way I look got me into pictures," he says. "I was big an' ugly, an' I did real well on account of it. Of course, the fact that I could, you know, threaten people—an' make it believable—helped, too."

Mazurki recently saw *Farewell, My Lovely* (the remake of *Murder, My Sweet* starring Robert Mitchum) but he didn't much care for it.

"The guy who played Moose Malloy—he was just too stiff. When he said, 'Where's my Velma?' (the classic line in the film) there was nothing behind it. You gotta say it like—" Mazurki contorts his face into a mask of rage—"'WHERE DA HELL'S MY VELMA?"

Both of the poodles hightail it under the couch for cover.

Then the face relaxes and Mazurki resumes recounting the tales of Hollywood's Golden Era. Despite the coarse features, and the gravel voice, there's a tremendous grace...an uncanny gentleness about the man.

It doesn't take long to see that—in his case, anyway—there really *is* a big softie underneath the tough guy exterior.

When I tell Mazurki this, he looks slightly taken aback. The next second, a huge meathook of a hand is waving in my face.

"Lissen, pal—don't spoil my image, *unnerstannn'?"*

I nod my head.

"Thassright," he says with a wink, "you just tell 'em I'm one real mean son of a bitch."

I'm back at the Old Spaghetti Factory, attending my sixth weekly luncheon with the Alley. It seems more like six years have passed. I feel like I've been living inside of a Damon Runyon novel or through one long, late-night movie. This will be my last meeting—at least for a while, and to tell you the truth, I'm feeling kind of sad. These boys (Alley members are all called "boys") have a way of opening their hearts to you—perhaps just a little too quickly.

They are a proud bunch of individuals who are aware, but not disdainful, of the fact that, by and large, they've been forgotten by society. Many are lonely. For them, the weekly meeting, the recounting of old tales, the constant giving of plaques, awards, and trophies (God, how many trophies have I seen given out?)—*the ritual*—are of prime importance. It's all they have. Each of them has known what it was like, at some point in his or her life, to have been cheered—to have been a star. And that experience, when it's over, leaves a permanent vacuum.

And then there's death. "We look at each other each week," Mazurki says, "and we wonder which one of us is going to go next. We've carried more guys to the grave than I can remember, but I'll tell you one thing—we do it with dignity. For these guys, *that's* what's important."

Àpropos of the statement, on this particular day, Dick Mastro, the club's master of ceremonies, is going to deliver a eulogy for a member who's recently passed away.

The bell is rung ten times—standard procedure when there's a death in the "family"—and then Mastro begins his speech. But death or no, the Alley members never lose their own special brand of cool.

"Our old friend isn't really gone," Mastro says in summation. "He's just sleeping."

From a side table comes the retort:

"I'll lay you eight to five against that!"

And the meeting goes on. Introductions are made, as they are each week. When I attended my first lunch, I was introduced by name only—but now, I'm that *famous* writer from that *famous* L.A. paper.

Everybody at the Alley is famous, you see.

The introductions continue.

Young Abe gets up and sings a few verses of "When My Baby Smiles at Me." Tiger Joe Marsh receives a resounding round of boos, and another guy tells a joke that nobody gets but which receives much applause.

When the introductions are done, the entire clan—as it has each week for the last 15 years—launches into the Cauliflower Alley Club Song. It's an awkward little ditty, and their parched voices are terribly off key as they sing. But on this day, and to these *famous* ears, well—it sounds sweet as hell:

Bless us all, bless us all,
The heavy, the light, and the small.
Bless our flat noses and cauliflower ears,
For we are the ones whom they stood up and cheered
Now we're saying 'So long,' to us all,
May God keep us busy
We'll see you next Wednesday
Stay cheered, guys and dolls,
Bless us all.

ROMANCE

ROMANCE

MY DATE WITH ANNETTE

I'm 44, and what I'm about to reveal is one of my deepest darkest secrets. *For the past 35 years I've been in love with Annette Funicello!* There, I've said it!

Cleveland, 1955: Each afternoon at 5:00 p.m., I'd be glued to my TV set watching *The Mickey Mouse Club*. Did I care about Mousecartoons and Mousekasongs? You gotta be kiddin'! I cared about one thing and one thing only—*Annette!* I was barely ten years old, and I was stone-cold, head-over-heels, crazy in love with a Mouseketeer.

In 1958, my family moved from Ohio to Studio City, California. I went to North Hollywood Junior High. Well, you'll never guess who was in my seventh grade homeroom. Joey Funicello—that's right, Annette's kid brother. I followed him home from school one afternoon, which is how I learned that Annette lived only two streets over from my house on Sarah Street. At night I'd lie awake, caught up in nonstop Annette reveries. The fact that she was alive, breathing—only a few blocks from me—was *torture!*

Flash forward to 1989. My friend, Jim Dawson—editor at *Sh-Boom* (a teen magazine)—calls me up. "Stu, can you find Annette Funicello and interview her for a cover story?"

Can *I* find *Annette?* Is the Pope Catholic?

After umpteen phone calls and dead ends, I get hold of a lady at Disney who knows Annette. I babble like an idiot, and she says she'll see what she can do.

And so this middle-aged teenager sits at home waiting for a phone call. And he realizes that nothing that's happened over the last quarter-century—marriages, divorces, therapy, career changes—none of it has touched this *thing*. He is still head-over-heels in love with a now-grown-up Mousketeer.

A week later my phone rings. "Mr. Goldman, you have an interview with Annette next Saturday at noon. Let me just give you her address…"

"You mean her, ah...*home address?*" My heart is pounding like a jackhammer. "Uh, sure—that'd be just fine," I say casually.

Next Saturday morning—feeling exactly like a teenager on his first date—I drive up a hill and park across the street from a single-story California modern affair on a cul-de-sac. I walk to the door, my knees knocking.

Ding dong.

"Just a minute..."

Be cool, man, just be cool.

Footsteps. *God, she's coming…*

And then—there she is! And for the first time we are standing face to face—Annette and me—and God—she's gorgeous beyond belief, and—oh, man, I can't believe *this! After all these years, it's really, truly, actually* her!

Cool as can be, I shake hands. She ushers me into the house.

Inside, I realize that in my attempt to be cool, I'm being aloof. *The hell with it; spit it out, man.* "Listen," I say to her. "I have to tell you something. If I don't, I'm never going to be able to get through this interview. I, ah, you see, well…I've had this terrible crush on you all my life and…"

And as I'm saying this I'm thinking, how many times has she heard this before? She probably thinks it's just some stupid line and I'm…but wait a minute. She's…she's *blushing*.

I made Annette Funicello *blush!*

When we sit down and start the interview, I'm doing my level best to sound reportorial, but all I can think is *I'm sitting only a few inches from her!* For the record, there's nothing remotely lustful in all this. What I'm feeling is pure, simple, '50s, movie-magazine, fairy-tale love! *Walt Disney love!*

But ten minutes, later my nervousness is gone...and I feel like I've known her all my life. Talking to Annette is like talking to an old friend. And so we talk about the '50s, about Elvis and Frankie, our first boyfriends and girlfriends, the old neighborhood, growing up, having kids, freeway traffic, how the beach makes your hair frizz up, our parents…we talk about *everything!* Just shootin' the breeze—Annette and me.

Three hours later we're still yakking when, without warning, I feel odd again. It's like, after all these years, I'm sitting in Annette's kitchen. I can see it all—the little notes on the icebox, the dishes waiting to be put away. There are no more secrets. And suddenly I feel terribly sad.

I can't put it off any longer. It's time to go. I get up to leave, and Annette and her husband Glen—a big, friendly, down-to-earth guy—walk me to the door. For a moment, I wonder if I should dare to *kiss* her goodbye (only on the cheek, natch), but, finally, we shake hands and I say goodbye and she waves and shuts the door and… and…and...it's *over*—

Driving home, I realize that I'm depressed. I have to say goodbye to the dream I've carried with me for 35 years. The past really *is* over. The love of my life is now a middle-aged woman sitting in a kitchen in Encino, smoking cigarettes, with three kids and a husband and dishes in the sink. She's all grown up. But what's worse, is that a boy who fell in love with a girl back in those wonderful, innocent '50s has to grow up too. And it hurts.

Two days later I'm still feeling blue when the phone rings. I recognize the voice immediately. "Hi, Stuart—it's Annette. Listen, Glen and I were wondering if you'd like to have dinner with us. We really both enjoyed talking with you so much, and well—we'd just like to get to know you better. Be friends."

I stammer a yes and hang up the phone. Can it really *be?* Yes, by God, it *can!* Annette Funicello just asked *me* out to dinner! I can't *believe* it...and I'm whooping and shouting my head off and I run to the front door and yell at the top of my lungs and the guy across the street watering his lawn stares at me like I'm some whacked-out loony, and the truth is—I guess I *am*.

Hey, Annette! Annette Funicello! I love you!

Article from *Sh-Boom* Magazine provided by LFP Publishing Group, LLC.

ROMANCE

B-GIRLS

I don't know what's wrong with me. I just can't seem to find a normal girlfriend. I mean, here I am pushing the big 4-0, so you think I'd be trying to find me a good woman to settle down with. It's not that I don't think about it. I *do*...I really do. It's just that I keep getting sidetracked, so to speak.

Take right now for instance. I'm head over heels, crazy in love with this lady boxer. I'm not talking about some aerobics bimbo or anything. Uh-uh. I'm talking about a lean, mean, tough-as-nails, street-wise pro-*fessional* fighter—a girl that can kick *your* ass, *my* ass, and just about any other guy's ass I know. On top of that, she happens to be one incredibly beautiful, sexy hunk (*hunk!* How do you feminist yo-yos like *that* one?) of a woman. Not only do I love the way she looks, the way she walks, the way she talks...I love the way she sweats, the way she *stinks* after a workout. I love everything *about* her, to tell you the God's honest truth.

This is nothing new, by the way. Even back in college, I never much cared for "normal" girls. You know—girls who lived in dorms...girls who studied drama or psychology. Those girls were all so...*boring*. You know—they'd talk about how many units they were taking, or how many miles-a-gallon they got in their stupid cars, or about the frog they'd just hacked up in biology, or their mother's tumor…shit like that. After a while it got so you'd know what they were gonna say before they'd ever open their mouths. They put me to sleep in about two seconds. In fact, in some weird way, they were all sort of versions of one another. The Doppelganger Women.

But this all ended the summer I split with my student loan money and hotfooted it over to Paris. There, I promptly fell head over heels in love with my *first* French Girl, a lovely young thing named Monique. God, she was so…*French.* The way she pursed her lips when she talked. The way she said "*zees*," and "*zem*" and "*zose.*" Oh, man… it just *killed* me.

Monique and I mostly ran around holding hands and making goo-goo eyes at one another. But by the end of summer, we were talking of getting married. I bought her a copy (in French) of *Sons and Lovers* (I was big on old D.H. at that time) and she blushed and batted her French eyelashes and I was even more crazy about her than ever. We made plans for her to come to L.A. the following year. And sure enough, the next summer, Monique arrived—suitcase in hand—at the L.A. airport.

But something was *different.* Monique still batted her French eyelashes. She still said "*zees*" and "*zem*" and "*zose,*"—but somehow it just wasn't quite as...special.

Soon I began to notice little flaws—things I'd somehow missed before. It was awful. I hated myself, but I couldn't help it.

And soon I knew the terrible truth.

Somehow, the magic had disappeared.

The story gets blacker still. Monique wound up running off with a rather slovenly fellow who was a roadie for a not-especially-good rock 'n' roll band. Soon, they got married, and Monique went to work as a waitress at a Burger King on Van Nuys Boulevard.

Somehow I just couldn't reconcile the notion that the love of my life—my wonderful little French girl—could have turned into a Van Nuys burger slinger right before my very eyes! It just didn't seem right. But that's life, eh?

However, something else happened to me during this period. I saw the film *Five Easy Pieces,* which had a strange and very powerful effect on my life. Shortly after seeing the film, I dropped out of college. I'd decided to become a country-and-western musician. This had some vague connection with Jack Nicholson's bowling-alley, beer-drinking lifestyle, but that was about as much explanation as I had.

The film also affected me in another way.

I became totally obsessed with waitresses.

Soon I'd made my dream into a reality. I was travelling around the country in a big old Greyhound Scenicruiser, playing steel guitar for Doug Kershaw (a fiddle player known as "The Rajun' Cajun.")

I liked the gig, but mostly I liked the fringe benefits, which included, of course, innumerable opportunities to meet waitresses.

Oh, all those sweet young waitresses! The way they poured that coffee! The way they sashayed right up to you and said, "Warm it up, mister?" It drove me right out of my mind.

I wrote them letters on napkins—short clever letters to let them know I wasn't your average stupid musician. Usually this did the trick. I composed poetry, sent flowers, bought gifts. Even proposed marriage. You think I'm *kidding?* I'll have you know—you cynical sonsofbitches—that I actually went whole hog and *married* one of them li'l waitresses. Swear t'God, friends and neighbors. Found her in L.A. where she was waiting on tables in the Palomino Club—one of L.A.'s primo country nightclubs.

It was love at first sight. And what'd I do? Why, hell—I dragged her outta that club, threw her in my car and drove straight through—90 m.p.h. all the way—to Las Vegas, where we got hitched at 3:00 a.m. in one of those crazy off-the-strip wedding chapels.

Look, I know what you're thinking. And you're right—because even as I stood there, saying my vows, a little voice inside my head went—"too far, ol' buddy. This time you took it *too far…*"

Oh dear, oh dear—the power our fantasies have in shaping our lives. Still, with one marriage on the rocks, you'd think I'd learn, huh? You'd think I'd wise up.

No way, José.

In fact, over the last decade or so, I've gone through an amazing variety of what I can only term "B-Girls." Girls whose lives one might tend to think of as...ah—sort of…shabby. Girls your parents wouldn't approve of.

Oh, my poor parents! That their son—their bright, talented, oh-so-well-educated son—their *genius* of a son—should be cavorting with such…such dummies! *Bimbos!…*You'd think he'd have some *respect!* But what does he do? How does he repay us for all the money we spent putting him through college…through analysis?

He brings home a topless dancer!!

That's right, dear friends—a topless dancer.

A topless dancer named Wanda.

I met Wanda when I was playing steel guitar in this dump in Northridge called Ryan's Roundup. Ryan's happened to be situated next door to an even trashier dump called the Pink Pussycat. During our breaks, me and the boys would go over there to have a beer and ogle the girls.

I had my eye on Wanda from the start.

And one warm summer night she took me home with her.

I don't quite know how else to put it; she fucked my brains out, plain and simple. The girl simply could not get *enough*. And what did I do in response? Me—the budding steel guitar genius?

I fell crazy in love with her—*that's* what.

I pictured me and Wanda getting hitched…maybe we'd live in a mobile home in Agoura—y'know…someplace with an abundance of 7-Elevens. Wanda would dance at night…I'd be playing steel in some little joint down the road. And on Saturday afternoons we'd go shopping at Kmart. You know, we'd have a shitload of screaming kids with boogers hanging out of their noses and ketchup all over the front of their shirts, and we'd stop and have lunch—chili dogs and sodas and potato chips—right there in *Kmart!* Man, it'd be *great!*

I'm telling you, I was totally *serious* about this gal.

It wasn't long before I'd invited her over to my folks' house for dinner.

My mom was totally cool about the whole thing. She made a great dinner—set the dining room table with the best silverware—the whole shebang. There was Schubert on the stereo. And there we sat—me, Wanda, my little sis and my mom and dad. And you know what? It was *exactly* like the scene in *Five Easy Pieces*—the one where Jack Nicholson brings Karen Black home to dinner.

To put it gently, let's say that there was a certain lack of ah—communication—at the table. Oh, my folks were extremely pleasant to Wanda and all, but still—the atmosphere was rather *thick* on that night. Every so often my dad would just give me one of those *looks*.

To make matters worse, old Wanda indulged a bit too heavily in the dinner wine...which apparently didn't mix too well with the pot roast. Pretty soon she excused herself to go outside and get some fresh air.

It was a few moments before we heard the retching. It was quite loud. Concerned, my mother ran out into the backyard where she found Wanda puking into the swimming pool. Caring soul that she is, my mom tried to help her to the bathroom. For her concern, she was rewarded with a load of vomit all over the front of her dress.

I decided that the best thing was to get Wanda home. She tried to grab my dick as we were saying goodbye at the door, but I don't think my mom saw this, as she was busy cleaning herself up.

By the time we got to Wanda's place, she was feeling pretty frisky. Fact is, she was hot to trot! But for some reason I wasn't much in the mood. I kissed her (on the cheek) and said goodnight.

I felt sad. Even a fantasy junkie like me can't be blinded to the truth forever.

No, Wanda and I would not walk down the aisle to a George Jones song. There would be no little Stu and Wanda babies—no long, blissful afternoons spent shopping at the Kmart. Ah me, ah me. Reality had reared its ugly head.

At least for awhile. After the Wanda episode, I seemed to cool out for a bit. And then—as if the dry spell had only served to whet my appetites—I began to roll again...this time with a full head of steam.

I went through quite an interesting succession of B-girls during the following months. These included a call girl (she came to my house one cold and lonely night, but we never, ah, *consummated* things. Instead we wound up sitting on my bed discussing Krishnamurti!); a 16-year-old-runaway from Atlanta who robbed liquor stores and read Proust; the lead singer in a rock 'n' roll band whose primary gift was that she could fart 72 times in a row (*I know*—she did her performance for me); a nymphomaniac female cantor; three born-again Christian sisters from Texas who sang gospel songs and loved to "share men." Also one belly dancer, two taxi dancers, one foxy boxer, a mud wrestler, and a female security guard.

Now mind you…none of these gals were sought out for their physical assets—gifted as they were in those areas. No, I was interested in *them*—each and every one—as *human beings*. I wanted to probe their minds. I wanted to study their customs, their mores, their habits. I—the budding B-girl anthropologist.

Though serious study often proved difficult, I wasn't to be dissuaded from my mission. No, sir! Besides, it was a million times better than spending an evening with some songwriter who wanted to play me her terrible original material, or some lame-brained UCLA co-ed who wanted to babble about how her trip to Europe that summer had broadened her horizons. Or, God forbid, some whacked-out, whale-saving, vegetable-eating Scientologist. No, *sir*—it was strictly salt-of-the-earth gals for *this* boy.

And as time goes on, I'm forced to admit I'm hopelessly hooked. I *must* be. I don't know why else I wound up in Las Vegas last month in the apartment of a stripper named Gee Gee. I'd gone there on assignment from the *L.A. Times* to do a piece on the art of striptease, but heck—I could've done the gig and flown home...right?

Wrong.

So there I sat in Gee Gee's one-bedroom apartment. We lay on the couch, watching an old black and white movie on TV.

I looked around the room. At the tinfoil on the windows. At the terrible seascape on the wall. At the glow-in-the-dark poster of Keith Richards.

Pretty soon I began to get depressed.

Gee Gee's kid started squalling in the next room. She got up and went in to quiet him. There I sat, staring at the TV. I tried to concentrate on the movie, in which a giant bald-headed man was destroying a town. He was pulling up palm trees by the roots and flinging them at the townspeople, who ran hither and thither, screaming at the top of their lungs.

Then I recognized the picture. It was *The Amazing Colossal Man.* Ironically, the town that the Amazing Colossal Man was destroying happened to be *Las Vegas!* Somehow the symbolism was not lost upon me.

When Gee Gee emerged from quieting her kid, I told her I wasn't feeling so hot, and that I needed to go back to my hotel and get some sleep. She seemed disappointed, but she didn't question me.

Nice gal.

Back at my hotel, I sat in the coffee shop. Everyone around me looked like a cartoon. A group of fat women with blue bowling league shirts sitting behind me were talking real loud. In the booth directly next to mine sat an old man and woman. The woman was wearing a Mickey Mouse T-shirt. Both of the old farts were talking in these monotone voices and smoking cigarettes to beat the band. They appeared to be totally disinterested in everything except for their cigarettes—which they sucked on right down to the filters.

Watching this depressed me even more.

Then a voice above me said, "Coffee, sir?"

I looked up.

She was beautiful.

Blond pony tail...a smattering of freckles. A tiny overbite.

The nametag on her uniform read "Suzzy."

God—*Suzzy*.

It was perfect.

"Can I get you anything, sir?" she asked, brushing a strand of hair from her face.

I was transfixed. She was absolutely *wonderful.*

"Sir?"

"Oh, yeah…I'll, ah…I'll just have coffee."

Suzzy turned and walked away.

I watched her from behind.

Nice walk—a little masculine—but nice.

Great ass.

I watched her pour the coffee.

My heart was pounding a mile-a-minute.

I took a pen out of my shirt pocket and began to compose a note on my napkin.

It would be short, but extremely clever, I knew.

Yep. Things were looking up.

It was going to be a fine night after all.

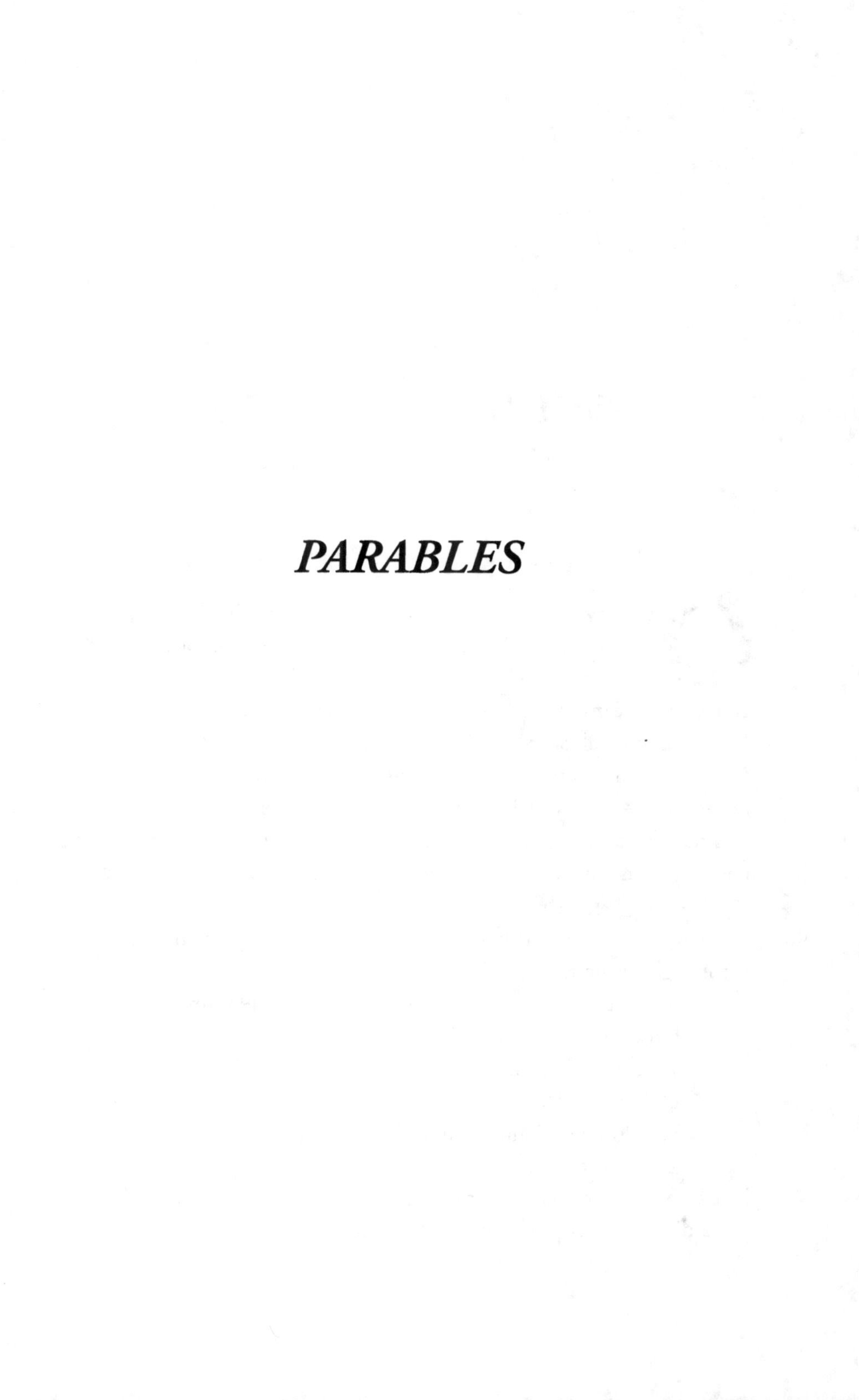

PARABLES

PARABLES

THE BUM WITH THE PERFECT HAIR

One day the devil took a walk down Main Street. He saw many people there, many sad and lonely people. He didn't really want to bother with them, as they weren't prime meat. But then he came to a doorway and saw an old bum sitting in there. He was a typical bum, all dirty and smelly and disheveled. But one thing about this bum struck the devil immediately. He had absolutely *perfect* hair—the most beautiful hair that the devil had ever seen. It was jet black, with little flecks of grey in it. It was combed straight back, and just barely touched the bum's collar. It was sparkling clean, shiny—and it was shaped just *perfectly*.

As the devil was thinking this, the bum took out a comb and ran it through his hair.

Now the devil stepped directly in front of the bum.

"How ya doin', pardner?" the devil said.

The bum looked up at him.

"Doing okay, brother…how 'bout yourself?" said the bum.

"Fine, thanks," said the devil.

The bum regarded the devil for a minute, stopping to take in his black-checked sports coat and freshly polished shoes. "Say, pal—you got a dime for a cup of coffee?" the bum asked.

Yep, thought the devil—just like all the rest. The devil pulled out a shiny new quarter and handed it to the bum.

"Thanks, pardner," said the bum.

Now the devil looked at the bum, then said to him, "My friend, what would you say if I told you that you could have *anything* in this life that you wanted?"

The bum looked up at the devil kind of funny.

"Now, why would I *want* anything?" the bum said. "I've got everything I want right here…my smokes, a nice doorway to crouch in, a blanket Father Flotsky down at the mission gave me to keep warm… Naw, I don't need *nothin'*."

The devil looked perplexed.

"But, son," he said, "Wouldn't you like to be in a nice house with a fireplace—maybe a little woman at your side…?"

Now the bum let out a hearty laugh. "Heck, no!" he said. "I *had* all that stuff. Why do you think I'm down here? I'm *happy*, man! I'm *mighty* happy!"

"You just *think* you're happy," smirked the devil.

"No," said the bum, "I really *am* happy."

The devil just shook his head. Boy, these guys sure could be difficult at times. The devil looked at his watch. It was getting late and he had business to do.

"Well, my friend," he said, "If you change your mind, you let me know."

He turned and started to walk away, but then he stopped.

"By the way," he said, "You've got very nice hair."

The bum stayed silent for a long moment, regarding the devil.

"I know," he finally replied. Then, as if on cue, he pulled out his comb and ran it through his sleek black mane.

The devil watched the bum with great admiration. Then he turned on his heel and began walking down Main Street.

He sighed a little as he walked.

Sometimes his job could be a real pain in the ass, and this, he could tell, was going to be one of those days.

INVESTIGATIVE JOURNALISM

INVESTIGATIVE JOURNALISM

MURDER AS THERAPY

"I prosecute child abuse. Only the parents are dead when I do it."
--Attorney Paul Mones

It may seem callous to refer to a murder trial as entertainment, but the fact is that the case of the Menendez brothers—on trial for the shotgun slaying of their wealthy Beverly Hills parents in August of 1989—has become the media event of the year. Recently Jay Leno spent an entire week reeling off Menendez jokes. Not to be topped, *Saturday Night Live's* mock news anchor, Kevin Nealon noted that basketball player Larry Johnson had recently signed an $84-million contract. "To give you an idea of much $84 million is," Nealon deadpanned, "the Menendez brothers would have had to kill six sets of parents for that kind of money."

Each day, the tiny Van Nuys courtroom where the trial has been going on since July 20, is besieged by scores of reporters, screenwriters, true-crime chroniclers, voyeurs, and a smattering of Menendez groupies, who often begin camping out at 2 a.m. in hopes of getting one of the few available seats in the courtroom.

It's no secret that the public loves murder trials; but when I find myself wrestling with some strange Menendez minutiae at 3 a.m.

rather than peacefully snoozing, I'm forced to stop and wonder why this particular case has grabbed us by our collective libido.

Jose and Kitty Menendez were ambushed while eating berries and cream in front of their family-room TV set. Mrs. Menendez was filling out the application for her younger son, Erik, to attend UCLA. At approximately 10:00 p.m., the brothers burst into the room and emptied their shotguns into their parents—more than 15 shots in all. After blowing off the back of his father's skull, Lyle Menendez reloaded his gun and issued the *coup de grace* to his mother's left cheek.

Following the killings, the brothers went on a spending spree, dropping nearly $1 million (the Menendez estate was estimated at $14 million) on Rolex watches, Porsches, condominiums and a restaurant, while the Beverly Hills police ran around chasing sundry leads (some of which were provided by the brothers) that purported to link the killings to the mob. It would be seven months before the brothers were arrested.

Throughout three years of legal wrangling over the admissibility of tapes made by their therapist, Dr. Jerome Oziel (in which the brothers allegedly confessed to the crimes), they maintained their innocence. It was only ten days before the trial commenced, that the brothers admitted to the murders, claiming that they shot their parents in self-defense. After years of sexual and other abuse, they said, they now believed that their own lives were in jeopardy.

Part of the seductiveness of a capital trial is the juxtaposition of the maddeningly civilized court procedure and the life-and-death struggle going on just beneath the surface. A trial is warfare—nothing more, nothing less. Often in death-penalty cases, a curious role reversal takes place, wherein the defendant becomes the victim and the prosecutors are transformed into bloodthirsty assassins. In this case, the stalkers are Pamela Bozanich, a strikingly attractive young attorney who, with her habit of wearing over-sized bows affixed to her braided ponytail, resembles a schoolgirl; and a small, pleasant-looking Japanese-American man, Lester Kuriyama. Their prey are two baby-faced boys in their early twenties.

The defense has done a marvelous job of assisting the brothers in playing up their victim roles. Dressed each day in fuzzy crew-neck sweaters and neat '50s haircuts, they look like something straight out of *Ozzie and Harriet*. The outfits are carefully chosen—down to the colors of the boys' shirts...most often soft pinks and baby blues. Both Leslie Abramson (Erik's attorney) and Jill Lansing (Lyle's attorney)—the brothers have separate juries and counsel—play classic mother figures. Miss Abramson is the quintessential Yiddishe mamma, alternately strict and dotingly maternal.

Sitting next to her client at the defense table, Miss Abramson often picks a stray piece of lint off Erik's sweater or smooths his hair. Miss Lansing plays the gentle docent—sort of a combination hospital nurse and schoolmarm. There is a lot of touching between the women and the brothers; the attorneys often sit with their shoulders rubbing up against the boys, or with their arms draped around them. Much of this is obviously for the juries' sake; nonetheless, one gets the sense that the women—particularly Miss Abramson (who calls the brothers "adorable")—truly care for their clients.

The prosecution has been openly derisive of the defense posture. Miss Bozanich referred to the trial as "a cheap version of divorce court," and compared Lyle Menendez's tearful recollections of child abuse to a "performance by Laurence Olivier which rapidly degenerated into Sylvester Stallone."

The prosecution has chosen not to attempt to refute the abuse claims, instead focusing on the murders themselves, as well as the elaborate cover-up constructed by the brothers. Miss Bozanich characterizes the case as "an ordinary domestic murder with a bit of extra glitz." The motives, she says, are simple: hatred and greed.

But fascinating as the case is, there's something more off-putting about the trial itself. It has the look of a bad TV movie. The brothers' testimony—despite its tearfulness—seems hollow. We all know that defendants are scripted to some degree, but in this case, one gets the sense that we're seeing not simply a script, but an artfully crafted melodrama. This is baffling—that is, until you learn about an unseen member of the Menendez defense team—a man named Paul Mones.

An attorney, Mones is the author of the best-selling book *When a Child Kills: Abused Children Who Kill Their Parents*. The book puts forth the theory that abused children are akin to victims of battered-women's syndrome, which, in some states, has been afforded the status of a legal defense in cases of murder. Mones clearly would like to see the Menendez case set a similar precedent for abused children. (It seems worth mentioning that at the time they killed their parents, the brothers—aged 18 and 21—were legally adults.)

According to proponents of this defense—most of them from the feminist legal community—victims of battered-women's/battered-children's syndrome have been so badly damaged that they can no longer distinguish fantasy from reality. Thus, their perception of "imminent danger"—which is necessary in order to plead self-defense—may be skewed. Victims of the "syndrome" (the use of the term *syndrome* is one of the many attempts to elevate it to the status of a biological disease) are said to suffer from PTSD (Post Traumatic Stress Disorder), which afflicts Vietnam vets and Holocaust survivors.

Mones' practice currently consists entirely of hiring himself out as a consultant on parricide cases. He has even come up with what he describes as "a comprehensive manual" that guides other lawyers in preparing and trying their cases. Among other things, the packet includes a protocol for identifying witnesses and readying them for testimony; suggestions for uncovering hidden clues of abuse; a 'how to' on picking the jury, and sample opening and closing arguments."

Given the current popularity of charges of abuse, it has been a good move. Mones says he has more cases than he can handle. In the Menendez case—certainly his most noted to date—Mones has been in court almost every day. Some courtroom observers have noted that during the brothers' two weeks on the witness stand, Mones appeared to be guiding them through their testimony by the use of hand and facial signals.

Mones's book is a kind of combination true-crime, self-help book. Throughout, Mones portrays himself as a sort of Lone Ranger—a hero whose research has forced him to walk through "some of the most grotesque and dismal quarters of the human landscape" in the effort to rescue victimized children from the hideous misdeeds of their evil parents. In Mones' view, the murdered parent is responsible for his *own* death. Mones' condescending attitude toward "abusive" parents (what actually constitutes *abuse* is something he never bothers to tell us) is revealed when he states, "My first reaction to the dead parent is most often disdain and hatred. But as the facts unfold...my anger diminishes and is replaced by pity."

Mones' book includes no information as to how many of these youthful killers lie about having been abused (research indicates a high percentage of the tales are invented). Nor does Mones ever mention that in nine out of ten cases, the killers come up with elaborately designed cover-ups for the murders (one would think that if the killing had such a cathartic purpose, they'd readily admit their acts). Nor does Mones ever bother to mention the survivors of the parental "holocaust"—the many children of abusive parents who *don't* kill their parents, but whose natural coping mechanisms enable them to lead normal lives.

Adhering to Mones' advice, the Menendez defense team has succeeded in putting the dead parents on trial. With the constantly demagoguing Leslie Abramson at the helm, the attorneys have pulled no punches in portraying Jose Menendez as a tyrannical, sadistic deviant who used his sons as sex slaves, torturing them with toothbrushes (toothbrushes?), pins, needles, and "Rambo knives." They've even managed to drop the suggestion that the father's alleged molestation was part of a satanic ritual. The role assigned to the mother, meanwhile, is that of a whacked-out, pill-popping co-conspirator.

What the defense lawyers hope, of course, is that by painting the parents in as horrific a fashion as possible, they will persuade the jury to ignore the letter of the law and in effect say, "They were such horrible people, they *deserved* to die." This time-honored legal tactic is known as "jury nullification."

In order to shore up this convenient bit of casting, the defense has called in a parade of "experts" including Doctors Ann Tyler, Ann Burgess, Stuart Hart, and Jon Conte. In over a week's worth of testimony that often had the jury snoozing, each of the smug, pontificating hired guns attested to his or her belief in the brothers' tales of abuse and a life of terrorization by their parents.

Some of the most disingenuous moments in the brothers' testimony seem to reflect Mones' influence. At one point, Erik Menendez actually likened himself to a concentration-camp victim. In this case, however, the concentration camp was a $5 million Beverly Hills mansion—complete with tennis courts, coaches, maids, and an unlimited supply of cash and credit cards. This concentration camp had no locks on its gates, no armed guards. Though Mones derides the oft-asked question about children who killed their parents—"Why didn't they just leave home?"—as a "knee-jerk" reaction, that question remains to be answered.

In the cosmology of the self-help movement, all human failure stems from our lack of ability to love ourselves and the worst thing a person can have is a bad case of low self-esteem. In the Menendez family, where approval was rarely forthcoming from the boys' perfectionist father, self-esteem was, at best, difficult to maintain. In the end, though, the brothers seem to feel they would have ultimately gotten the approval they sought all their lives.

Lyle Menendez (who, only days after he'd blown his parents to smithereens, gave a moving, thirty-minute eulogy testifying to what a great man his father was) stated in court, "I think my father would have been proud of me (for murdering him)." When the stupefied prosecutor asked if he really meant that, Lyle answered unblinkingly that he believed his father would have admired the fact that he had finally stood up to him—not to mention that he'd done it in such a convincing fashion.

But the most dumfounding testimony came from Erik, who ultimately confessed the murders to his therapist, Jerome Oziel, and later to his friend Craig Cignarelli. When asked why he had confessed, Erik—who admitted he was wracked with guilt after the murders—said, *"I needed someone to tell me that I was really a good person."*

If guilt is indeed a response to our God-given knowledge of right and wrong, good and evil, then this statement is particularly repugnant. The young man who had just blown away his parents wanted to be told, "I'm OK, you're OK."

Whether the Menendez brothers go to prison (it seems unlikely that they will receive the death penalty) or whether they return to their Beverly Hills mansion and their tennis courts, they must live forever with the fact of their evil deed. But in a world where morality is dictated by therapists rather than God, where evil is discounted as myth, where *feeling good* is the end-all and be-all, they can be comforted by the thought that murdering an "abusive" parent is not only permissible—it's *healthy.*

Increasingly, this cut-price nihilism pervades the moral climate of modern America—its schoolrooms, law offices, television studios, welfare offices, mainline liberal churches and temples, and wherever two or three Ivy League Ph.D's are gathered together in Freud's name. We have known for some time that it was this climate which produced ghetto kids who would kill for a sneaker; we now know that it also shapes rich kids who will kill for a swimming pool, two tennis courts, and a Porsche.

For believers in this cheap, ersatz ethical system, remorse has been replaced by self-pity and self-righteousness, truth has been traded for moral relativism, and the only thing one can ever be guilty of is bad judgment. Of all the ugliness we've had to witness in the Menendez case, this fact is perhaps the most shameful.

INVESTIGATIVE JOURNALISM

SEARCHING FOR NATALEE:

CONFESSIONS OF AN OBSESSIVE-COMPULSIVE TABLOID NEWS JUNKIE

I admit it—I'm hooked. I'm a junkie.

For the past month and a half, every day at precisely 5:00 p.m. I flip on the TV and watch the following newscasters: Bill O'Reilly, Greta Van Susteren (does anyone else think there's something wrong with Greta's face?) Joe Scarborough and (much as it pains me to admit it) the always noxious Nancy Grace.

I don't watch these shows in order to get the news. No, the fact is, I engage in this daily ritual for one reason, and one reason only. For tidbits—no matter how small or how insignificant—of the latest findings in (as Greta is fond of referring to it) "the frantic search for Natalee Holloway."

Frantic, my ass.

We all know the story. On May 30, 2005, 18-year-old Natalee Holloway—on vacation in Aruba with classmates to celebrate their high school graduation—failed to show up for her return flight to the States. Holloway was declared missing; her parents (along with several relatives) hopped on the next plane to Aruba.

The game was on.

Over the course of the coming days, three young men who'd been with Natalee on that final night—Joran Van Der Sloot and brothers Deepak and Sateesh Kalpoe—were questioned by the police, but never detained or arrested.

Several days later, two black security guards were hauled off to jail, the result of testimony by the boys that they'd dropped Natalee off at her hotel, where she'd been ushered inside by two men attired in security guard uniforms.

The two guards had been incarcerated for over a week, when one of the Kalpoe brothers admitted that they'd made up the story. The police promptly released the guards and took the Kalpoes, as well as Joran Van Der Sloot (who'd reportedly been "making out" with Natalee in the back seat of the car) into custody. The problem was, some ten days had elapsed since Holloway's disappearance, giving the youths ample time to dispose of any evidence.

Several days later, Van der Sloot's father, Paulus (who is some kind of political mucky-muck on the island, but is definitely *not* a judge) was also arrested, but was released almost immediately. Allegedly, the elder Van der Sloot had told the boys not to worry. "If there's no body, there's no case," he advised.

Over the coming weeks, between the younger Van der Sloot and the Kalpoe brothers, there circulated some twenty-three different versions as to what took place on Holloway's last night in Aruba.

The world watched while the Aruban police conducted an error-laden investigation that would have embarrassed any Crime 101 student. Some three weeks after the fact, the authorities finally got around to taking DNA samples from Van Der Sloot and the Kalpoes (who'd been freed from jail).

The FBI came and went. The Dutch Marines came and went. A search group from Texas came, and most of *them* went.

Nightly, one or more of Natalee's relatives (primarily her mother Beth and her stepfather "Jug") appeared on TV to discuss the case. As the investigation wore on, the parents looked more wan and more desperate with each passing day.

Nearly two months into the case, the chief prosecutor decided she needed a two-week vacation; meanwhile, the Aruban Chief Of Police resigned. Though "hope" remained the operative word, the fact was that authorities were no closer to finding out what happened to Holloway than they had been on day one.

From a journalist's point of view, the story had "legs"—albeit weak ones.

Countless kids go missing every day. Moreover, the truth of the matter was that, aside from the media circus, the Holloway case had nothing in particular to distinguish it from countless other kidnapping/homicide cases which are on the books every single day.

So. The emergent question—for this writer at least—is simple: why is it that every evening, bar none, I find myself plonked down in front of the TV, waiting to see if there are any new twists and turns in this bloody thing? Why is it that each night, I spend hours before going to sleep running through possible scenarios as to what happened to Natalee Holloway?

Was there—I asked myself—a hole in my soul? A hole that'd formerly been filled by the Michael Jackson trial, the Scott Petersen case, and the Robert (yawn) Blake case?

Oh, sure, I had a legitimate excuse. As an investigative journalist—one who'd worked primarily on criminal cases for the past five years, I could make the argument that I had good reason to be following the Holloway debacle. It was, after all, newsworthy—was it not?

My writings included both celebrity and non-celebrity cases. I'd covered the O.J. Simpson case for *Penthouse* magazine. I'd reported on the Menendez Brothers murder trial for *Los Angeles* magazine. I'd exposed a UFO abduction cult. Following that case—which took up six months of my life—I was dispatched by the *L.A. Times* to go to Louisiana to cover what turned out to be the largest mass murder in that placid Southern state.

My writings had garnered me a certain amount of notoriety. The mainstay of my journalistic reputation was that when I worked on a story, it was never just casual. Rather, I was *smitten*. Let's be honest. I was stone-cold *obsessed* by each and every one of them. I loved it all—the drama, the chase, the spin, the leaks, the cover-ups, the trials.

I never worked on just a single project. Rather, I'd work on several stories at a time. That way, if one fizzled out, there would be another waiting in the wings. We're talking obsessive-compulsive syndrome*…big time.*

Stored in my already overcrowded office, were umpteen boxes full of projects...some resolved, others still ongoing I had a massive file on Charles Manson, including some never-before-published letters written by the famed '60s killer. There was a box for Richard Ramirez (the Night Stalker), and another for Ed Gein (whose handiwork had inspired the film "Texas Chain Saw Massacre"). Another file box was occupied by research on a little-known serial murderer known as "the Torso Killer." The Torso had killed and dismembered some 38 victims in and around Cleveland during the '30s and '40s, all the while taunting the police with cryptic letters and postcards.

The Torso's nemesis was none other than Elliot Ness, of *The Untouchables* fame. When the case was at its zenith, Ness had bee appointed as the Crime Commissioner in Cleveland. Reportedly, the ex G-man became completely obsessed with capturing the Torso Killer...and though he came close on several occasions, he was never able to land his prey. When Ness retired in 1944, some opined it was his failure to catch the Torso Killer that had ended his career.

Fast forward. Last night at around 10:00 p.m., I found myself online, searching for a cheap flight to Aruba.

It was time to jump into the fray.

I didn't care if there were a million other yahoos down there working on this story. To hell with them. I *knew* I could solve this thing—even if I had to kidnap Joran Van Der Sloot, along with that smarmy father of his, and interrogate the two of them at gunpoint. Government cover-up be damned! Hell, I'd taken on satanic cults and lived to tell the tale... This thing was going to be piece of *cake*.

Thankfully of late, I'd been taking my meds. Clearly I was in the throes of a full-blown manic episode. Fortunately, when I found myself getting all hopped up like this, I'd learned how to step aside, take a deep breath, and consider the wisdom (or lack thereof) of my actions.

I reminded myself that the Holloway case was quite simply, not all that interesting. On a slightly more somber note, I knew that barring the uncovering of new evidence (so far there was virtually none), on September 6—the end of his 60-day period of detention—Joran Van Der Sloot would walk out of jail, a free man. And that would pretty much be that. Oh, there'd be a little fuss, but eventually the case would dry up and disappear. No, there was no movie or book deal waiting at the end of this lurid little tale. Only an empty wallet and another box full of clippings and notes, which would make my already overcrowded office even more claustrophobic than it already was.

There was always a certain amount of depression accompanying this kind of "reality testing." My manics were cruel mistresses, and they went down hard. Still, I knew I'd be okay. After all, there were, at any point in time, countless new and even more horrid crimes to which one could, with relative ease, become addicted.

Moreover, there were some interesting "offshoots" to this case which, in and of themselves, made for good story material.

It had been pointed out by several media pundits, that the only reason the Holloway case had garnered the kind of attention that it had, was because it fit a certain profile. Which is to say that, in order for a missing person case to be deemed media-worthy, the victim, of necessity, had to be young, Caucasian, pretty and blonde. It also helped if they came from affluent parents. Make that affluent, *God-fearing* parents. (If the victim's family professed a belief in the Gospel of Jesus, as the Holloways had, they could add millions of "believers" to their loyal legion of supporters). No doubt about it; invoking the name of the Lord was always a wise move—both emotionally and financially.

I had to concur with my more savvy media colleagues. The Holloway case had made the big time because Natalee fit the profile to a T. Had she been fat, had she been ugly, had she hailed from a poor black or Chicano family, the closest Natalee would ever get to fame would be on the side of a milk carton.

My mind wandered back to the cases of Laci Peterson, JonBenet Ramsey, Polly Klass, and Elizabeth Smart. I thought of all the kids that'd been killed during the Columbine High School Massacre. Though I'd been smitten with each one of these stories, they were now nothing more than distant memories.

If *my* memory was short, the public's was far shorter. Over the past ten years, the media had created a new breed of news glutton. They had a hellacious appetite, these folks, but it was an appetite that was fueled by titillation, rather than an actual interest in knowledge or truth.

These cases came and went. As an audience, we'd been conditioned to latch onto a kidnapping, a child molestation, or a nice, juicy murder to get involved with. Yammering on about whatever the latest tragedy was gave us something to *do*. More importantly, it helped us to forget the emptiness of our own humdrum little lives.

With the anti-climactic ending of the Michael Jackson case, the media pundits found themselves frantically searching for something titillating that they could sell.

Unfortunately, of late, the pickins' had been pretty slim. Let's see—there'd been a little bit of heat on Jennifer Wilbanks, the bug-eyed "Runaway Bride," though for my money, it should've been Kim Tran (a 38-year old Alaskan woman who'd chopped off her husband's penis when he'd refused to end an affair with a younger woman) who deserved the airtime and the ink.

For their misdeeds, both Wilbanks and Tran received community service. Wilbanks landed a paltry half-million dollar book deal from publisher Judith Regan.

Ho-hum.

We'd also seen the capture of Dennis Rader, the famed BTK Killer (bind, torture, kill). During a 30-year period, during which he committed at least ten murders—Rader had hidden in plain sight, residing in the same house (along with his wife and children), holding the same job and serving his community, both as a Cub Scout leader and president of the Christ Lutheran Church congregation in his hometown of Wichita, Kansas. Following Rader's arrest, the most oft repeated quote, was (three guesses): *"But he seemed like such a normal guy!"*

Rader confided to an interviewer that he blamed the murders on "a demon" that had gotten inside him during his childhood. He then proceeded to describe the killings—in all their gory detail—all the while speaking in the unaffected manner of your run-of-the-mill sociopath.

Rader may have been insane, but he was no dummy. He'd recently launched his own website, where he currently hawks various and sundry of his belongings, including personal journals—even the clothes he'd worn while he strangled and mutilated his victims.

On July 6, police arrested Edward Duncan III, a convicted child molester, at a Denny's restaurant in Coeur d'Alene, Idaho. Six weeks earlier, Duncan had kidnapped 8-year-old Shasta Groene, along with her older brother, Dylan (who was later found dead). Duncan also murdered Shasta's mother, her boyfriend, and another brother. Shasta was spared, though she told police that Duncan had molested her numerous times during the weeks in which he'd held her captive.

Unfortunately, Duncan himself wasn't much good for any salacious sound bytes, though Nancy Grace and her cohorts managed to get a wee bit of mileage out of a page culled from Duncan's internet blog, titled "Blogging the Fifth Nail" (referring to the nails used to crucify Jesus).

And so the murders and kidnappings went on, and the news yokels, with their store-bought tans and frozen hairdos, yammered on, doing their damndest to sound indignant whenever they talked about the plight of the victims and their families.

"*In courtrooms, classrooms, operating rooms, boardrooms, churches, airplanes, people no longer talk to each other; they entertain each other. They do not exchange ideas; they exchange images. They do not argue with proposition; they argue with good looks, celebrities and commercials.*"

So wrote Neil Postman in *Amusing Ourselves To Death*, a book that (thank God) has remained on the shelves since its publication in 1985. In that book, Postman cautioned that a world dominated by television—as opposed to print—would result in an "Orwellian nightmare."

Unfortunately, Postman was correct. Over the years, we've seen a subtle, but all-important shift in the manner in which we take in the news. Today, news and "tabloid news" have become virtually indistinguishable. Which is to say that there is no longer any line of demarcation between news and sensationalism. Second, since we watch the news much as we would watch any other piece of entertainment, we have sucked it dry of vitality...of essence. There is no longer any real grappling with issues, no genuine interest in the subtleties of the case at hand.

What with the proliferation of blogs and websites, news has become available to us in real time. When critics point out that neither the blogs nor the websites have any built-in fact-checking system, bloggers respond by pointing out that you aren't any more likely to get the "facts" from reading a daily paper or watching the 6:00 p.m. news. Sorry, Bill, they say, but there *ain't* no "no spin" zone.

Further complicating the issue, is the popularity of reality TV. These shows have created an entire subculture unto themselves. It's truly incredible what's taken place on television since MTV debuted *The Real World* in 1989. Today, there are hundreds of reality shows vying for your attention. Whatever your particular pleasure, you can find a reality show that'll be right up your alley.

Let's see—we've got Celebrity Reality (*The Osbornes, Hogan Knows Best, Meet the Barkers*), Courtroom Reality (*Judge Judy, Celebrity Justice*), Dating and Relationships Reality (*Cheaters, Elimidate*), Hidden Camera Reality (*Girls Behaving Badly, Scare Tactics*), Prankster Reality (*Jackass, Punk'd*), Fashion Reality (*Extreme Makeover*), Movie Biz Wannabe Reality (*Project Green Light*), Law Enforcement Reality (*Cops, America's Most Wanted*), Mystery Reality (*Cold Case Files, Unsolved Mysteries*) and of course the ever-popular Talent Reality (*American Idol, Rock Star: INXS*). Let's see—have we forgotten anything? Well, never mind, you can be sure someone will create it in fairly short order.

As opposed to film, TV is considered to be a "cold medium." We watch it in our living room, not in a darkened theatre on a massive screen. TV creates in us a certain sense of intimacy, while at the same time allowing us to freely move between "real world" activities (going to the kitchen) and the hypnotic state of mind that is necessary in order to become involved with the characters who we're watching onscreen. The result is that while a film may be more emotionally "moving," we tend to *believe* what we see on TV without questioning it.

Everyone knows that the reality shows aren't "real." That is, we know that there's a camera crew and iceboxes full of food and a first-aid kit readily available on the desolate islands where *Survivor* takes place. We know that, no matter how freaked out the poor victim on *Fear Factor* may appear to be, he's not going to wind up in the ER, or locked away in a mental institution.

Reality TV is built upon deception, but its not the same kind of deception of say, *The $64,000 Question*—the famed '50s quiz show in which contestants were provided with answers to the questions prior to the airing of the program.

Reality TV treats the audience as a sort of co-conspirator, as someone who's "in on the joke,"—someone who's willing to suspend, for the time being, his disbelief.

Reality TV appeals to the voyeur in each of us. We *like* to lurk, we *like* to watch without giving others the opportunity to watch us. Thus, the popularity of reality TV has gone hand-in-hand with the ever-growing number of Internet voyeur or "spycam" sites. On the Net, you can watch without being watched...*or* you can become involved. For a mere pittance, you can tell the girl on the webcam which particular sexual acts to perform, while you lie back and take it all in.

As TV viewers, we can vacillate between our urge to spy, and our desire for intimacy and involvement (without actually being involved). By involvement, we mean simply that because Jay Leno and David Letterman appear in our living room each night, we've somehow come to feel that we "know" them...that they are our "friends." This misperception has resulted in major increases in cases of celebrity stalking, the numbers of which grow frighteningly larger each year.

In 1987, a 19-year old Tucson, Arizona, man name John Robert Bardo had become obsessed with actress Rebecca Schaeffer, star of the then–popular sitcom, *My Sister, Sam*. After repeatedly watching the show, Bardo came to feel that he and Schaeffer were "meant to be together." Bardo then wrote a fan letter to Schaeffer; unfortunately, she made the mistake of replying to it.

Bardo, who had erected a virtual shrine to Schaeffer in his bedroom, decided to make the trip to Los Angeles. He easily obtained Schaeffer's home address from a private investigator, and was able to use computer databases to find out whom she called, where she ate, and where she shopped. Having this information made Bardo feel "close" to Schaeffer.

When Bardo saw Schaeffer in a movie scene in which she was in bed with another actor, he decided that she must be punished for her "misdeeds." On the morning of July 18, 1989, Bardo went to Schaeffer's Hollywood apartment and began to pace, watching for any sign of her. In his knapsack was a copy of J.D. Salinger's *Catcher in the Rye*. And a gun.

Bardo decided on a "direct" approach. After a courier had delivered scripts to someone in the building, he decided to go ahead and ring the buzzer.

When Schaeffer appeared at her doorstep, Bardo pulled out a photo that she had sent to him. He told her that he was her biggest fan. Schafeffer asked him to leave and closed the door. Bardo went away, but—moment's later—returned in a fury. He buzzed again, but remained hidden when Schaeffer opened the door. That brought her across the threshold, whereupon Bardo burst out of his hiding place and shot her point-blank in the chest. Calmly, he walked away. Schaeffer fell to the ground, dead.

Bardo later recalled that she had screamed, "Why? Why?"

Because we are all on information overload, this new reality-based TV/internet news medium has created a kind of blurring affect in our perception. The result, after ingesting even small doses, is a disturbing kind of brain fuzziness. Sometimes when you see something take place in real life, it seems as if you're watching TV. And vice versa.

Steven Spielberg used this reverse-reality effect in making his hit film *War of the Worlds*. What the film actually served up, underneath its skimpy plot, was an immediate trigger to cause images of 9/11 to emerge in the viewers' brains. If the film gave us PTSD symptoms, we have Mr. Spielberg to thank.

Lest we forget that ratings are the name of the game—be it film or television—all we need do is to check out the evening news. Need we point out that on every station, bar none, the lead items are always disasters, no matter how many more important stories are taking place in the world?

It's no accident that TV will interrupt real programming to focus on a freeway chase or a robbery in progress. If we're lucky enough, we might even get to see the cops kill somebody while we sit there and munch our Fritos.

We are not simply engaging in the tired old bugaboo that sex and crime always sells. That's old news. We're discussing, rather, the manner in which the "news" is dressed up. Are we deluged with disaster after disaster in order to keep us informed? Or to heighten our awareness so as to dissuade further acts of a) child molestation, b) serial murders c) terrorism?

Sorry, folks, it's not awareness that is being sold. The subliminal message of this terror-laden newspeak is that we're *helpless*—that we must live in a constant state of paranoia and fear. It's the same methodology that cults use when brainwashing their members. The first step is to overload the new member's brain with (dis)information, then to make him so fearful that he cannot live without the cult. Once those tasks are accomplished, it's quite easy to program the person in question.

If you don't agree that you're currently brainwashed, try going for a few days without watching any TV, reading the newspaper or going on the Net. Try seeing what life feels like *without* your daily fix. (And have your bottle of Valium ready when you attempt this little experiment.)

Perhaps it would have been better for Natalee Holloway if her parents had engaged in a few scare tactics before letting their daughter travel to an island halfway around the world, sans any real chaperones, and without any built-in code-of-conduct which might have allowed Natalee to avoid whatever dark misdeed took her life.

Natalee and her friends were there in Aruba for one reason only. To *party*. That term doesn't mean what it did ten years ago. Rather, it's synonymous with taking drugs, exposing yourself, acting stupid, having sex with people you'll never see again…in short, indulging in massive doses of anything and everything that *feels* good. That is the ethos. That is the goal.

What we need to understand, is that what happened to Natalee was not an accident, but rather, a direct result of the cultural climate in which we've come to live.

That climate has had its appetites shaped by the popularity of *Girls Gone Wild* and the countless other *Spring Break*-type shows that clog the airwaves and the Net. As the cover of *National Review* recently announced, "Pornography Is Everywhere."

Disagree? Just take a look around. You can't turn on your TV, or go to a movie, or drive for one mile without your titillation-sensors being tickled. Indeed, pornography *is* everywhere—at the video shop, the grocery store, in your newspaper and in your mailbox. And although American society grows increasingly accepting of this state of affairs, porn is unmistakably dangerous: it presents a warped image of sex and self-satisfaction that mangles the values of faith, (true) friendship, marriage and family.

Another interesting twist in the behavior of teenagers today is that there's been an odd kind of role reversal. Today it is *not* okay for a girl to be prudish, let alone want to prize her virginity. In fact, today it's the *women* who are often the sexual aggressors. It's the women who are pulling up their shirts, and baring their heinies in public. It's the women who are leading the charge into the ever-growing sexual Neverland.

You can see this male-female role reversal at work in a show like *Elimidate*, (which might as well be called *The Biggest Whore*). On this show, several girls vie for the attention of a single male. As the show goes on, the girls get drunker, show more skin, and love bomb the contestant in order to win the prize. There's only one way to win this little deal—that's to let the guy know that he's going to get laid at the end of the show. Surprise!

In *Amusing Ourselves To Death*, Neil Postman pointed out the differences in the nightmarish visions of the future as predicted by George Orwell and that of Aldous Huxley in *Brave New World*:

"Orwell warns that we will be overcome by an externally imposed oppression. But in Huxley's vision, no Big Brother is required to deprive people of their autonomy, maturity and history. As he saw it, people will come to love their oppression, to adore the technologies that undo their capacities to think. Orwell feared that the truth would be concealed from us. Huxley feared the truth would be drowned in a sea of irrelevance. Orwell feared we would become a captive culture. Huxley feared we would become a trivial culture. The civil libertarians and rationalists who are ever on the alert to oppose tyranny have failed to take into account man's almost infinite appetite for distraction."

Last night, I happened to flip on the TV just in time to catch a rerun of Greta Van Susteren's nightly report from Aruba. With a lack of any new footage to show us, Greta teased her audience by offering up some "exclusive, never-before-seen" footage of Natalee Holloway.

Throughout the course of the next half-hour, the clip was run over and over again. What this "exclusive footage" turned out to be were some old home movies shot by Natalee's mother during a dance/cheerleading rehearsal at her high school. The grainy, occasionally overexposed footage features a smiling Natalee, attired in a sequined cheerleader-type costume–complete with a top hat and baton—performing a routine along with the rest of her dance troupe.

I wasn't quite sure why, but there was something oddly disconcerting about the footage. No doubt, some of it had to do with the fact that there was no soundtrack, thus giving it the quality of an old silent film.

But there was something else.

When you look at Natalee Holloway, you feel like you *know* her—that you've seen her before. And the fact is, you *have.*

If asked to describe Natalee Holloway, the first thing you'd probably say is that she's pretty. And she is. But Holloway's prettiness is that of a Barbie doll. Natalee is pretty in the same way a million other girls her age are pretty. All the elements are there—the blonde hair, the big blue eyes, the smile, the cute figure. But in the end, there is absolutely nothing remarkable about the girl in the videotape. She is every teen Writ Large.

And so as Van Susteren prattled on, reassuring Mrs. Holloway—as she does every night—that "Natalee is in all of our hearts and prayers," the girl in the video swirled and twirled, dipped and swayed—all the while holding that tight little smile—the smile that we've seen in every one of her "missing" photos—the smile that makes us feel like we know her...even though we *don't* know her and will *never* know her.

At the end of the video, Natalie turned to hug a teammate. Then, still smiling, she bowed to the audience.

The credits rolled.

INVESTIGATIVE JOURNALISM

ONE-ON-ONE WITH A TAXI DANCER

Loni Bendix is a taxi dancer. If that term doesn't mean much to you, they used to call them dime-a-dance girls. Except, the price for "renting" Loni today is 30 cents a minute, or $18 an hour.

Every city has taxi dance halls. Los Angeles has 12 of them, all located within a one-mile square radius of one another. Taxi dance halls haven't changed much over the years. A man will pick the girl of his choice, buy dance tickets, stamp his time-card for a certain amount of time—and for that time, she's his. He can buy her coffee or a non-alcoholic beverage. Every dance hall has a TV room to which the couple can retire, and where the action gets a little heavier.

Loni's been working as a taxi dancer since she was 17. She just turned 21, though she looks considerably older. Taxi dancing was Loni's first job in Los Angeles, where she's moved to from her hometown of Muskogee, Oklahoma. Loni was escaping not only small-town life, but an abusive father—a man who'd molested her throughout her childhood. When she was 17, Loni was impregnated by her father, and bore him a child. She declined to elaborate on this incident during the interview, except to say that she loves her son.

Since moving to L.A., Loni has rarely ventured outside of the downtown area where she shares an apartment with four other taxi dancers. She's never seen the ocean. She's never been out with a man whom she didn't meet in the clubs. Despite the fact that she expresses distaste for the world of the dance halls, she says she's comfortable there. Asked what she'll do with her future, she just shrugs. For Loni, the dance halls are both the beginning and the end of the line.

SG: *Loni, how long have you worked the dance hall circuit?*

LB: Almost four years, I guess. I sorta lose track of time. I quit for a while, tried some other gigs. Waitressed a little. Made beds in the Holiday Inn. Worked in a sweat shop, sewin' clothes. Actually, I've quit lotsa times, but I always end up back in the clubs.

SG: *How many clubs have you worked?*

LB: I've worked all of 'em except for the Savoy, which is a shit hole. Just in the last two months, I've switched clubs three times.

SG: *Why do you change clubs so often?*

LB: You gotta go where the business is. Take this club. The customers are mostly Oriental businessmen. They're a lot better than white guys. In fact, lately, I have been dancing almost exclusively with Orientals. That is, except for Flips. They're a waste of time.

SG: *Flips?*

LB: Filipinos. I don't like them much. They don't spend the dough like the Chinese or the Japanese do.

SG: *What have you got against Caucasians?*

LB: White men are fucked! They don't respect women, for one. A typical white male is a guy who beats his wife all day and loves to say, "Hey, baby, I'm 12-inches." Orientals are a lot nicer. They know how to treat a woman. And they really know how to spend the dough. *That's* what's important.

SG: *What kinds of things have they bought you?*

LB: Oh, I've gotten jewelry, furs, trips to Vegas, Hawaii. You name it. I almost never pay my own rent.

SG: *Do these men want you to sleep with them in return for these…gifts?*

LB: Well, sometimes, yeah. Other times they just want you to go shopping with them. Orientals get off on having a white chick hanging on their arm. It's a status symbol for them.

SG: *Do you ever sleep with them?*

LB: Sure. But only if I like 'em. And if I do, they're gonna pay for it—*believe* me.

SG: *Would you consider yourself a prostitute?*

LB: No, I'm not for rent. I'm just sleeping with somebody I like for money. I don't see anything wrong with that.

SG: *Do you like what you're doing?*

LB: Are you kidding?! This job sucks!

SG: *Could you elaborate on that?*

LB: Well, lemme put it this way. How would you feel if some guy with the most horrible body odor, bad breath, spit coming out of his mouth and a hard on was grinding you all over the floor? Do you think that sounds like fun? Well, lemme clue you in. It's not. And that's the name of the game here most of the time. No, this is a horrible, disgusting job. I hate it.

SG: *It does sound pretty awful.*

LB: Like I said, it sucks. Still, in a way, it's better than going to a regular nightclub. I mean, the guys treat you terrible there, too. At least here, you're getting paid.

SG: *Why don't you get out of the dance halls altogether if you hate them so much?*

LB: The thing is, the longer you stay here, the harder it is to quit. I guess I'm stuck. I guess maybe I'm addicted. I hate to admit it, but that's the truth. Working at the dance clubs is like a drug. You hate it, but at the same time, you need more of it.

SG: *But surely you could do something else. There must be some reason that you keep coming back to work in these places.*

LB: Maybe it's that…here I'm not alone. Here I have friends. Like when a new girl comes in, I'll teach her the ropes. I'll show her how to work the room, how to get rid of the creeps. How to deal with the owners and the floor managers. I like to do that…help out a new kid. Makes me feel good about myself.

SG: *What are the men like who frequent the dance halls?*

LB: The men? Mostly pigs. Pigs and losers. It's a real sad bunch, believe you me.

SG: *What happens in the TV rooms?*

LB: Hand jobs mostly. Most of these guys just want you to diddle them. Of course, some of 'em want more, but they don't get it. If you want to sleep with a guy, you set it up for after you get off work.

SG: *Are these clubs basically just disguised brothels?*

LB: Well, I don't want to get nobody in trouble, but I guess you might say that, yeah. Depending on the club, the girl will either work for herself, or the club will take a piece of the action. In that case, the floor manager will set up the deal.

SG: *How does that work?*

LB: What happens is, a guy goes to the floor manager and says, "Who can I get what I want from?" The floor manager asks him what type of girl he wants. He'll describe her. Then, the floor manager will introduce him to a girl that looks like what he wants. The guy dances with her, buys her a drink maybe. He's already dropping money on her. Then, after the club closes, he'll take her "out to breakfast." That's when the real business gets taken care of.

SG: *What kinds of girls work the taxi dance halls?*

LB: You name 'em, we got 'em. Some girls are bad. Some are everyday people. Some of 'em work day jobs. Some hook. Some are here to make their coke connection. Some are just plain crazy. There's all kinds. One of my roommates is 45-years old. She works here at night, and in the days she works at a factory. She came here from Seattle just to find her a man, but so far she ain't had no luck.

SG: *What reasons do girls have for working in the dance halls? Surely the money is not that good.*

LB: All kinds of reasons. Some are lonely. Some think they're gonna meet a man. Others are just tryin' to pay the rent.

SG: *You mean some girls actually think they'll meet the man of their dreams in the dance halls?*

LB: Oh, yeah. You'd be surprised how many of the girls working in these places are just waitin' to be swept off their feet. The Cinderella deal—y'know? I used to feel that way myself.

SG: *Isn't that unrealistic, considering the type of men who frequent these places?*

LB: Yeah, but you gotta dream, right? There's always that slight possibility that Mr. Wonderful's gonna come in and—you know—you're gonna pay him to sleep with *you!*

SG: *What was it like for you when you started working?*

LB: When you first come here it's horrible. Your checks are tiny. They bullshit you when they tell you that you're going to make $500 a week. That's only if you get good tips, and in the beginning, you don't.

They tell you they'll teach you the ropes, but they don't. They don't tell you the most important thing, which is what to do if the guy gets a hard on. They don't give a shit about you. You're just a piece of meat.

SG: *What happens to a girl when she works these clubs?*

LB: You get hard. A girl will change physically in six months. Also, once you start working here, your relationships are finished. I had a boyfriend for a while, but no more. I don't want a boyfriend now. All they do is hassle you. It's like…you dance with a buncha jerks all night, then you come home and you have this guy putting his hands all over you. You don't want that when you get home. You just want to be left alone.

SG: *What about the men who own the clubs? What are they like?*

LB: They're a buncha pimps. They think they own you. If they get a hot chick, they work her 'till she's used up. Me, I don't go for that. I'm my own boss and I let the owners know it. They like me 'cause I'm good for business. I'm still young and fairly good-looking. Let's face it…a lot of the chicks that work these places are dogs.

SG: *Is the world inside the dance halls different from the outside world?*

LB: Well, it works two ways. As far as men go, yeah. Only creeps come into these places. Creeps and losers. I'm speaking of the white clubs now. Like I said, Orientals are different. They've got more class. But as far as white guys—what's great in the dance hall, I wouldn't look at out in the street. So in a way, it's two different worlds. In another way, it's all the same.

SG: *How do you mean?*

LB: It's all a gigantic hustle. The world outside the clubs...the world inside. It's all the same. That's why I stay. In here, *I'm* the one doing the hustling. *I'm* in control. Out there, everybody's a victim. In here, the *men* are the victims…and that's just the way I like it.

SG: *Why are the men victims?*

LB: Because…what you do here is what they call the "dry hustle." You make a guy think you're going to go to bed with him—but you never do. You keep him dropping his money. I mean, if you wanna go to bed with him, and he'll pay good money for it, that's up to you. But the name of the game is that you just keep him horny, and he keeps coming back night after night and dropping more money on you.

SG: *Don't you ever feel guilty that you are conning these men?*

LB: No. It's all part of the game. *They* know that it's a game. They might not act like they know it, but somewhere inside they know. And like I said, if a guy makes the right moves, or says the right thing or catches me on the right night, maybe I'll go to bed with him. I just want it to be *my* choice, that's all. So, no, I don't feel guilty. There's a lotta things worse you can do to a man than to dry hustle him.

SG: *What have you found is the best technique for working a customer?*

LB: Sympathy. You tell 'em a sob story. Tell 'em you can't pay the rent, or that your mom's in the hospital. You just use stuff from movies you've seen. It's amazing how good it works. That's why I like movies. They give me ideas.

SG: *What other methods are there for keeping a man on the line?*

LB: If you get a hot one—a guy that comes in and spends a lotta dough—you get his phone number. Then you call them up periodically and let them know you're thinking about them. That always keeps them hooked.

SG: *Do you ever bring somebody back home with you?*

LB: Well, I live with five other girls, and so we try not to bring business home. But every so often, one of us will. But if my roommates started bringing home different guys every night, I would say, "Hey, man… this ain't no motel!" I really try to keep my business and my home life separate.

SG: *Don't you ever want to have a committed relationship?*

LB: I don't make commitments because I don't keep 'em. Hey, I'm 21 years old and you know what? Nothin' is gonna last forever. Why should I get my feelings built up when I know it's gonna be over?

SG: *You seem awfully bitter for someone your age. Don't you have dreams?*

LB: I used to have lotsa fantasies about how wonderful my life would be—but no more. My last real fantasy was with my ex-boyfriend. But that was the last real dream I had, and it ended when he beat the crap out of me and then tried to stab me. I don't *have* dreams anymore. I figure this is about as good as it's gonna get.

SG: *Do you hate men?*

LB: Of *course* I hate men! Why else would I be working here?

SG: *Do you ever think about getting out of this world altogether?*

LB: I think about it, yeah. But here I am. That's reality. That's just the way it is, I guess.

THE SWEET SCIENCE

THE SWEET SCIENCE

THE BADDEST DUDE IN THE WORLD

The Urquidez Brothers' Studio—looking somewhat squashed—sits between a self-service laundry and a Thai restaurant in one of the San Fernando Valley's countless look-alike shopping centers. Inside the building this evening, a group of about 15 students, dressed in starched white uniforms and different colored belts is going through a regimen of exercises.

At the front of the class, a stocky sharp-eyed man, wearing a slightly rumpled outfit held together by a black belt barks commands at the students. As the youngsters go through the various kick-punch combinations, the instructor—with a short bamboo staff in hand—prowls the room. Whenever it appears one of the pupils isn't giving his all to the workout, the dawdler receives a resounding whack on his butt or the back of the legs. The actual pain involved is probably less than the sound would indicate, but it's enough to please a group of moms-and-dads sitting, scrunched together on a wooden bench in the back of the studio. Not only are their kids being taught self-defense—they're learning the art of discipline as well.

At 8:30 p.m. the class breaks up, and the kids and their parents head home. Benny Urquidez, one of the brothers who own the karate school, looks tired as he takes off his top and chucks the sweat-soaked garment in a corner. But rather than shower and call it a night, Benny dons a pair of six-ounce boxing gloves, goes over to the heavy bag hanging in the corner and begins methodically banging away at it.

A minute or so later a bell rings, but Benny doesn't seem to hear it as he continues pummeling the bag. Moments later, a stubble-faced man wearing a red sweatshirt sticks his head out of an office door. "Three minutes, champ. Remember what I told you. You *rest* when that bell rings. Then you go two more rounds with the hands...then three with the legs."

Benny nods, and when the bell rings again, he resumes punching—bobbing and weaving, sticking the bag with short jabs, looking more like a boxer than a martial artist. At the end of three rounds, Benny takes off the gloves and begins kicking at the bag. He starts somewhat tentatively, kicking lightly—just flicking the leg outward—almost as if it were a jab. But as the minutes pass, the kicks get harder and harder...and soon the bag is swinging back and forth in time with Benny's flying feet. The *pop! pop!* sound echoes through the room.

The stubble-faced man has now emerged from the office. He stands watching, his arms folded and brows knitted. "Don't just put that kick out there, brother—*snap* it!" he orders.

Arnold Urquidez is Benny's older brother. He's also his trainer and manager, and the reason for the solemnity here, is that Benny isn't simply another martial arts practitioner. He's a professional full-contact karate fighter, who at 26, holds the title of World Lightweight Full Contact Karate Champion. Of the five brothers and one sister in the Urquidez family—all of whom hold black belts not only in karate but also in judo, aikido and kendo—Benny is the only one to have turned pro. And now that he's earning upwards of $10,000 per fight, the workout this evening is serious business.

"OK champ, that's it," says Arnold. "You've got ten miles to run, then you get your ass home and get some sleep. You've got a fight next week."

Benny nods at his brother. Then, without looking at the bag behind him, he jumps straight up, turning 180-degrees in midair. At the completion of the half-circle—with the full impetus of the turn behind the motion—he whacks the bag with the heel of his foot, sending it flying almost off its chain. When he turns back toward Arnold, there is the slightest trace of a grin on his face.

"Nice one bro'," Arnold says. "But better not use that jump-spin kick in the ring, or somebody's liable to take your head off."

The only sound in the studio is the squeaking of the bag as it rocks back and forth on its chain.

"OK. You might as well get that run over with," says Arnold, breaking the momentary silence. "Now *move* it!"

The next instant Benny is out the front door and into the streets of the San Fernando Valley.

Full-contact karate has little to do with the sort of histrionics one sees in a Bruce Lee movie—or even with what is taught in a conventional martial arts class. It is, in fact, an outgrowth of Thailand's oldest and most popular sport, known as Muay-Thai, or kickboxing.

Today, while kickboxing is still popular in Thailand, it's even more popular in Japan. And the Japanese kickboxers have taken over the Thais' reputation as being the most brutal fighters in the world.

In a kickboxing match, two fighters square off in a ring approximately the size of an American boxing ring. Each fighter wears eight-ounce gloves. But there, the comparison with boxing ends. In kickboxing, opponents go at each other with fists, feet, knees, elbows and head-butts. The only prohibitions are choking, biting and spitting. A match consists of nine two-minute rounds, and the victor wins by decision or knockout. Rarely does a fight go the distance.

Still, if kickboxing looks like an any-thing goes free-for all, it's come a long way from the days when combatants fought bare-fisted and without rules. It was customary then to bind the hands with strips of horsehide soaked in glue, so as to inflict maximum damage on one's opponent. For some matches, ground glass was mixed in with the glue. Fighters fought until one was unable to continue because of injury or death.

In the U.S., full-contact karate—the equivalent of kickboxing—is only a little more than five years old, but it's rapidly gaining popularity. Like Muay-Thai fighters, full-contact karate fighters make use of the standard front and side kicks, but they also employ the more colorful jumping, spinning and flying kicks. The resulting matches are more exciting and spectacular then boxing. This—along with the blood and guts of the sport—seems to provide an unbeatable combination.

Rudolf Nureyev, the celebrated ballet dancer, after seeing his first match, commented on the similarity between the moves of the martial artists and those of people in his profession. He called full-contact "the most beautiful and awful of sports."

Not surprisingly, the main critics of full-contact are the traditional karate practitioners, who feel that the sport is undermining the "true spirit" of traditional karate. The Urquidez brothers regard this as so much doubletalk.

"In the first place, full-contact is completely different from traditional," says Benny, who has spent years practicing both. "In traditional karate, you learn how to break ribs, joints—or even to jerk the other guy's eyeballs out of his head. It's the art of maiming and killing in its purest form. So what you've got is a sport versus a method of self-defense. But I'll tell you something," he continues. "I've been in both traditional and full-contact, and as far as I'm concerned, at least 50-percent of what they teach you in regular karate is total bullshit.

"The whole martial-arts world is shrouded in mysticism. But most of it is just hype. It's easy to see why people are attracted to it. You know—everyone wants to feel they've got the inside dope on some mysterious Oriental art. But see, my brothers and I were all street fighters before any of us ever got into martial arts. So naturally, we were a bit suspicious of the whole so-called spiritual side.

"For us, fighting was no joke. A lot of times, our lives depended on it. When we fought, it was for *real.* We didn't believe in leaving the other guy standing, because he might come back and cave our skull in with a two-by-four.

"Now don't get me wrong," Benny adds. "I love karate...but it's important to separate martial arts—which is an 'art form'—just like dancing or painting—from fighting.

"Take kata (the study of form) for example, which is the most beautiful discipline imaginable. It's got nothing whatsoever to do with *real* fighting. You get out on the street after training at most of the traditional schools, and you're gonna get your ass kicked. And then, there's all that other shit—the so-called secret killing techniques—like the *Palm Of Death.*" (The technique Benny is referring to is one by which a trained martial artist can cause massive internal injuries, or even kill an opponent, simply by touching him, while sending negative vibrations to a designated area of the body).

Inside the Urquidez's school, the rest of the brothers break up into fits of laughter at the mention of *Palm Of Death*. Ruben, a bulky ex-Army sergeant, whose specialty is judo, seems to find the notion highly amusing.

"Martial artists are really just a bunch of babies," Ruben scoffs. "They always come in here and ask us the same stuff. Can a kung fu man beat a karate man? Is judo better than aikido? Could a good boxer take a kickboxer? How would Benny do against Muhammad Ali? It's the same old shit...just like in the old cowboy movies. Everyone wants to know who's the toughest, the meanest...the baddest dude in the world.

"As a result, we've got all these guys who've studied various styles of martial arts wanting to challenge us. We've had 'em all—Tae Kwon Do, Kung Fu, Shotokan, Tang Soo Do...you name it.

"The last one that came in was in full drag. Some Oriental guy, dressed in an all-black kung fu outfit. He said he would take on our best fighter. Well, we put one of our beginning full-contact students out onto the mat with the dude, and the guy goes into this fancy stance. He's making all sorts of noises and everything...and then *boom!*—our kid hits him with a left hook and knocks him out cold."

If the brothers seem disrespectful, they're never scoffed at. Before full-contact existed, they competed in every non-contact tournament possible.

"Sometimes we got disqualified for being overly aggressive," Benny recalls, "but it was just our style of training. None of us ever lost, and we've got closets stuffed with trophies, but you know...we were poor. We needed dough, and when full-contact came in and there were some bucks to be made, it was just natural for us to get into it. That was a while back...and now full-contact is on its way to becoming recognized as a legitimate sport. It sure has come a long way from the old days, I'll tell you that."

The days Benny is recalling were the days of the first full-contact tournaments. Those bouts were essentially elimination matches in which fighters of every size fought one another until only two remained. You might fight 20 matches in one day. There were no weight divisions, no rules and no holds barred. People would leave the ring with crushed noses, broken limbs, and teeth knocked out.

In the first public full-contact tournament, held in Hawaii in 1974, Benny kicked, spun and punched his way to the finals, in which he wound up facing a 6'3" opponent. Benny (who is 5'4" and weighs 145 pounds) knocked his 250-pound adversary out of the ring three times before putting him out for good in the third round.

"It was right then that the rest of us knew it was Ben who would go on to be a champion," says Arnold "We were all good...but Ben—he just had something special."

Arnold's analysis is right on the money. Since Benny's turned pro, he's never lost a fight. His record to date stands at 45-0, and 40 of those wins were by knockout. But as important as his ring prowess, is Benny's comprehension that fighting means more than just a barroom brawl. The fans want to be entertained. Upon discovering this, Benny promptly nicknamed himself "The Jet," and now ends every match with a victory double-back flip, to the delight of the crowd.

The Jet's image is based on a combination of flashy moves—like the jumping and spinning kicks—and scientific, almost overly-methodical fighting techniques. You seldom see Benny get mad inside the ring. Lately, the brothers have taken to kidding him about this new good-guy image, calling him "Gentleman Benny."

"I look upon fighting as a business, as opposed to a personal confrontation," Benny says. Both my opponent and myself are out there to do a job. After the fight, we're friends. In the ring, I *have* no friends."

Recently, Benny's become a national hero in Japan, after destroying two of that country's top kickboxers. The Japanese love Benny's flashy style, in comparison to the less flamboyant tactics of their own fighters. There's even a *Benny The Jet* comic book on the stands in Japan.

But success hasn't gone to Benny's head. The only visible symbol of it is his brand new Mercedes. In between fighting and filming movies, Benny spends his time with his wife, Sarah, and their daughter, Monique, in their modest two-bedroom apartment.

Still, whenever the time allows, he and the rest of the Urquidez brothers dedicate their time to teaching martial arts to youngsters in the San Fernando Valley. Their latest effort is a government-funded project in which they work with juvenile delinquents. Apparently, none of the brothers wants to forget the days when they roamed the Valley streets as members of gangs with names like The Midnight Breed, The Lynchmen, and The Group.

"We always used to fight," recalls Smiley Urquidez. "But it was Ben who got in more of them than anyone. He was little, and people just used to pick on him.

"I remember one night when we went to Bob's Big Boy down on Van Nuys Boulevard. A lot of jocks used to hang out at that place, and of course we were sort of greasers back then. Anyway, one night, Ben and I were going in the front door, and this huge football player bumps into Ben. Ben says, 'Hey man, don't you say *excuse me?*' The guy turns around, takes a look at Benny and just sort of laughs and says, 'Fuck you, punk.' And Benny just gets that look on his face."

Smiley half-closes his eyes and curls his upper lip into a semblance of a sneer, in imitation of his brother.

"So then Ben says to the guy...'*Outside*, man,' And I'll tell you...I was a little scared. I mean, that sucker was *big*. Anyway, we get out there, and there's this big crowd forming, and I'm kind of checking it out to see how many guys I'm going to have to go for, when all of a sudden Benny just jumps up in the air and kicks this fucker square in the face. And the guys goes down—*boom!*—just like that. I figured that was it, but Benny didn't stop there. He picked the guy up and just beat the holy shit out of him. I mean, *that* dude went to the hospital, man."

Smiley stops for a moment, as if to collect his thoughts. "Yeah, Benny had a pretty mean streak in those days. I felt kinda sorry for that guy. Really—I mean, he was messed up bad. But now that Ben's gone pro, he doesn't get into those kinds of hassles anymore. He's calmed down, I guess. He'll go out of his way to avoid a fight." A wistful look crosses Smiley's face...then he breaks into a grin. "Still, Benny's nobody to fuck with. I've seen him put away four, five guys... no problem. Yeah, brother Ben is one tough son of a bitch."

The Black Cat bar is located at the far end of Sunset in Hollywood, past the rows of porn theaters and massage parlors. On a Friday evening, the street—which is loaded with kids cruising the strip further down towards Vine—is deserted except for an occasional cop car. Even the hookers don't work this end of the boulevard.

Inside the bar, a couple of guys are hanging around the pool table, while a few others sit at the bar nursing beers. "Oye Como Va" is playing on the jukebox. A raven-haired Mexican girl behind the bar is dancing alone to the music.

Over in the corner, Arnold Urquidez—still wearing the red sweatshirt from earlier in the day—is yelling at someone on the phone because his shipment of Coors is late. Arnold owns the Black Cat, plus another bar, in order to bring in the money he needs to support his "martial arts habit." The only indication of the other vocation is a small-framed photo of Benny hanging on a wall behind the counter. It seems weird sitting in this place to think that Arnold will be on his way to Tokyo in the morning to sew up a fight for Benny. It won't be any vacation though. He has to be back two days later for a big fight in Las Vegas.

Between working at the bar at night and training fighters during the day, Arnold sleeps a maximum of about three hours a night. But it's nothing new. He's been doing it since he started supporting his family when their father abandoned them while Arnold was just a teenager.

"Because we were Mexican, life for us was equated with fighting. We all had plenty of fights, that's for sure," he says, sitting slumped in a corner booth. "And naturally, we got in our fair share of trouble... but it was no big thing, you know? I split for a few years, but when I came back, things had gotten really bad. All of the brothers were in gangs. There were chainings, stabbings...the whole bit. Then I caught a couple of the guys carrying pieces...and that was *it*. I had to put a stop to it. I had taken some karate during the time I was gone and I really loved the discipline of it. I was into some pretty heavy shit there myself for awhile, you know? And it might sound corny, but karate just channeled a lot of that stuff into something positive. I figured if it could work for me, it would work for them.

"In the beginning they'd hide when I came over to teach them. But I made them do it. I wanted the world to look at my brothers and respect them because I love them so much."

Hearing himself grow softhearted, Arnold is up and out of the booth, slapping the waitress on the ass and hollering at nobody in particular. "OK, it's two o'clock. Let's drink up. C'mon—*move* it!"

As I get up to leave, he's hunched over next to an old guy at the bar, the two of them laughing and talking rapidly in Spanish.

Outside, Sunset is empty, and the blackness of the cold Hollywood night closes around you like a great clammy fist.

T*okyo, Japan*—Downstairs, in the locker room of the Budokan Auditorium, Benny is looking unusually pensive. The deep-set eyes, which usually betray little or no emotion, look troubled.

Benny has made the trip to the Orient to head a card that features U.S. full-contact fighters versus Japanese kickboxers. The reason for Benny's sullen expression is that in all four matches thus far, the kickboxers have thoroughly destroyed the Americans.

Benny's opponent for the main event is Kunimitsu Okao, Japan's kickboxing champ, and a noted killer in the ring. Okao has issued a formal challenge to Benny, after having seen Urquidez—on his last trip here—knock out the number one Japanese contender in just 50 seconds of the first round. Okao has vowed that he'll put the Jet out of commission with "no problem."

As Benny sits on the dressing table, getting his final rubdown from Arnold, Tony Lopez, a young fighter from Tennessee, limps into the room. One of his eyes is completely closed, and blood gushes freely from his nose.

"Those bastards are tough," Lopez says through swollen lips. "Their fuckin' legs feel like they're made out of iron. Man, I really wanted that win..." Lopez's voice trails off. He stands, staring vacantly off into space. Then he turns to Benny. "You've got to take Okao out, Ben. You've just *got* to."

Benny manages a smile as Lopez is led off to be tended to by the doctor.

The Budokan is one of Tokyo's largest indoor arenas, and on this evening its 15,000 seats are all occupied by screaming martial arts fans. *Fanatics* is more like it.

Kickboxing is Japan's most popular spectator sport. The normally reserved Orientals become unabashedly crazed on fight night, and they make no bones about the fact that they like their fights good and bloody. No technical knockouts for these folks.

As Benny and Arnold climb through the ropes, a chant of "BEN-NEE, BEN-NEE" is taken up by a portion of the crowd. Though the Japanese are basically partisan, Benny has captured many of their hearts with his overwhelming wins over their two top fighters. Still, the real screaming erupts when Kunimitsu Okao enters the ring.

In contrast to his usual preflight antics, Benny sits soberly in his corner, while Arnold continues to rub his shoulders. Meanwhile, Okao parades around the ring—a huge grin plastered on his face. He accepts bouquet after bouquet of flowers from a kimonoed girl.

The ceremony carries on, as a long, drawn-out speech is read by a bespectacled Japanese official. Though the crowd remains fairly quiet, you can feel the tension building up with every second that passes.

When the bell for Round One finally rings, the arena becomes totally silent. Okao and Benny move out of their corners and begin to circle on another—Okao still grinning. Then, without warning, he lashes out with a hard kick that catches Benny right behind the calf. The loud *smack!* resounds through the arena. Before Benny can move, two more kicks find their mark on the same spot.

Okao is using the same tactic on Benny that has beaten the American's five stable mates—a low kick to the back of the leg...a blow that will eventually cripple a fighter if repeated often enough. It's a common kickboxing technique. The Japanese have learned to protect themselves from similar punishment by toughening their legs from childhood—kicking trees, until eventually no pain is felt.

Benny begins to circle in the opposite direction when Okao's leg shoots out again, but this time the kick is high. It whacks Benny squarely on the temple, and for the first time in his career, Urquidez is on the mat. The crowd goes berserk!

"Stay *down* there—take the *eight count!*" Arnold yells from the corner. But Benny doesn't hear him through the screams, and jumps back up at the count of two, apparently unhurt. He begins bouncing up and down, but obviously Okao thinks he's got Ben going. He wades in—but suddenly Benny's right leg arcs up and *whap!*—he stings Okao with a whipping roundhouse, catching him just over the kidney. *Whap! Whap!* Two more kicks hit Okao on the same spot. As the Japanese goes to cover up, Benny moves in and nails him with three quick, short punches, all of which smash Okao flush on the jaw.

But Okao is tough. No longer grinning, he doesn't back off either. As Benny comes in, the Japanese grabs him around the shoulders and wrestles him into the ropes. Once Ben is against them, Okao throws a knee into the pit of his stomach.

"Damnit," get off those *ropes!"* roars Arnold.

But the bell rings, ending the round.

Walking back to his corner, Benny looks distraught. In round two, Okao is the aggressor again, but Benny is dancing, Ali-fashion, providing a more elusive target. Still, Okao continues to come at him in that straight-ahead style of his. But as he moves, in, Benny suddenly whirls around and hits him in the midsection with a spinning back kick that doubles Okao up for a moment. Benny doesn't waste the opportunity. *Bap! Whap-bap-bap! Bap!* A lightning fast punch combination sends Okao's head reeling back and forth. But still, Okao gives no ground. He attempts a combination of his own, which Benny easily blocks. Then the two slow the pace, circling one another again.

Now they're in the center of the ring. Okao smashes the back of Benny's calf with another low kick. The sound causes the people sitting ringside to wince with the imagined pain. Okao stands there, as if to say, *"Come on."* Benny throws a kick of his own to the identical spot on Okao's leg. Okao returns the kick—even harder this time. He seems angered that Benny doesn't seem to be affected by his kicks.

Then Okao lets go with another. Benny smashes him back. With every kick, the crowd is grunting. The grunts grow louder as the kicks get harder. There's no finesse left in the brutal tradeoff; now it's only a matter of seeing who can withstand the most pain. When the round finally ends, the crowd seems to breathe a collective sigh of relief. During the rest period, both fighters refuse to sit down on their stools.

Between rounds, Arnold yells feverishly at Benny. In the third, Ben comes out looking more determined than before. Okao walks straight for him, a snarl on his lips. He grabs Benny and begins banging away like a madman at the back of Benny's calves again. Then he shoots another knee into Benny's gut.

Benny grimaces in pain, throwing a fleeting glance at Arnold as if to ask what to do. Benny has built a reputation as being a gentleman in the ring, but his opponent is using every dirty trick in the book.

Benny starts to wrestle his way out of Okao's grasp when another knee catches him low—directly in the groin. Benny doubles up in agony, but when he raises his head this time, there's a *different* look on his face. For a moment, his eyes seem to blaze.

As Okao comes after him again, Benny grabs the Okao's head—pulls it down, and knees him in the face—once, twice...three times. When Okao pulls his head away, he's smashed in the nose with an elbow strike. A huge spurt of blood spews from the Japanese fighter's nose. Then a whipping backfist sends Okao staggering sideways.

"That's it bro,'!" yells Arnold." Show him how to *street fight!"*

Okao attempts a high kick—but his timing is off now—and he misses sorely. For a moment, Benny appears to be backing off. Then, all of a sudden he whirls around in the air, striking Okao flush across the nose with the heel of his foot. Okao screams in pain as the bridge of his already damaged nose is snapped in half. He stumbles backward, wobbly-legged, his hands covering his face.

Benny literally runs after his opponent. When he reaches him, he shoots a hard front kick into Okao's stomach, which sends the Japanese's head forward. As the head reaches waist level, Benny unleashes a vicious uppercut to the chin. Okao begins to topple backward, blood streaming from his nose and mouth.

Benny stands stock-still for a moment, watching Okao wobble to the floor. Then, as if the descent were too slow for him, Benny lashes out with a snap kick to the side of the head, which sends Okao sprawling to the canvas.

Once on the floor, Okao doesn't move.

For a brief instant, Benny is unable to hide his emotions. A look of triumph passes across his face. Then the next second, he's high in the air as he does the back flip to wild screaming from the audience. Arnold runs up...and the two brothers hug one another.

The next second they're gone.

Okao is carried out of the ring, while his corner men work frantically to wipe the blood off the mat.

The kimonoed girl enters the ring and starts to parade round it, indicating that the fight is over.

Yes, the most beautiful and awful of sports.

The fight crowd files out quickly. Only a few hardcore fans remain, hanging around outside the dressing rooms. Finally, after almost an hour, Benny and Arnold emerge through the door and begin making their way toward the exit. Benny looks dead tired.

But the fans are insistent, and won't leave until they get his autograph. Benny, looking resigned to the task, begins signing their books and t-shirts one by one.

"You the toughest...you the toughest guy in the world!" says a kid clutching a *Benny The Jet* comic book in his hand. He thrusts his copy up at Benny. "You the *toughest*," he repeats.

Benny signs the book and hands it back to the kid, who turns and takes off running down the hallway.

Benny glances over at his brother and for a moment, he looks almost sad. "Always the same—those kids," he says.

"That's just the name of the game," Arnold replies. "They *need* that. They've got to have some sort of hero to look up to."

Benny doesn't respond.

"C'mon champ," Arnold says. "Let's go back to the hotel and get some sleep." The two brothers turn and walk toward the exit sign at the end of the hall.

Still it's possible. It could be true. Who knows? Benny might just be the toughest...the meanest....yes, the *baddest dude in the whole, wide world.*

THE SWEET SCIENCE

ONE TOUGH MOTHER

The sign outside the Los Angeles Sports Arena reads, TONIGHT—ALL-WOMEN'S BOXING CARD—SIX TITLE FIGHTS. It's 8:10 p.m., approximately 20 minutes before fight time. Inside the auditorium, the theme song from *Rocky* blares out over the P.A., as the first of the combatants climbs through the ropes.

It looks like the freak-show patrons are going to have a time of it tonight. A host of jeers and catcalls erupts as a muscular girl with a huge Afro—a gigantic pair of breasts and the face of a pit bull—boogaloos around the ring.

Her opponent is a rather pretty blonde who, though in the same weight category, looks dwarfed by her jiggling adversary.

As the two go at it, it's immediately clear that the blonde is not only smaller—she's also decidedly outclassed. She hits the canvas three times within the first minute. By the round's end, blood is pouring from her nose, and her right eye is half shut. Not a pretty sight. And as luck would have it, I've got a ringside seat, which affords me a nasty close-up of her battered face.

Fortunately, Round Two quickly ends things. The blonde is flattened by a looping left hook. She gets up, wobbly-legged, but it's all over.

Well, thank goodness for *that*.

But as the girl staggers out of the ring, a feeling that I've been suppressing all day suddenly punctures my thin resistance.

The problem is, that I have spent a good part of the two weeks before tonight's bouts with one of the participants in the next fight—Lilly Rodriguez. During that time I have watched 30-year-old Lilly train, and have learned a lot about the fight game. I've also come to know Lilly and—here's the rub—to care for her. Once you admit to that emotion, the notion of sitting back and enjoying a fight goes right out the window. The possibility of seeing someone who matters to you flat on her back—or worse—with her face cut to shreds, is not something you want to think about.

Lilly dances into the ring. Her dark hair is knotted into a ponytail, and her face shines with oil. To the delight of the crowd she does a little Ali shuffle. Meanwhile, her opponent, a toughie named Toni Lear, is fixing Lilly with the nastiest stare she can muster.

Ding! Round One.

The fighters move out toward center ring. As they approach one another, I notice that my fingers have begun to dig holes in the sides of my padded seat, and I'm sweating like a madman.

I first met Lilly in 1978, when I started studying martial arts at the Urquidez Brothers' Karate Studio, which was owned by her family. (Lilly Urquidez became Lilly Rodriguez in March 1971, when she married William "Blinky" Rodriguez.)

Out of a brood of nine (five brothers and four sisters) Lilly is the only female to have become proficient—like her brothers—at all of the traditional martial arts: karate, judo, kung-fu and boxing. But only Lilly—who was licensed in 1976—and her younger brother Benny (known in the game as "Benny The Jet") have turned pro. Both are champions in full-contact karate—a derivative of Japan's most popular sport—Muay Thai.

Benny is presently the World Lightweight Full-Contact Karate Champion.

Last year, Lilly became the Japanese Women's Kickboxing Champion by putting away her heavily favored opponent with a smashing right cross to the chin. (The blow left Lilly's Oriental opponent unconscious for nearly ten minutes.) Lilly is also the California Female Featherweight Boxing Champion. Additionally, she is a leading contender for the World Female Featherweight Full-Contact Karate Crown, as well as the Female Featherweight Boxing Crown.

When the sport of women's boxing recently began gaining popularity in the U.S., Lilly jumped right on board.

"I like full-contact, but boxing is my real love," she would tell me, "'cause my hands are where my *real* strength is." Recalling the wicked right I'd seen on a videotape of the fight in Japan, I couldn't help but agree.

These are "the facts" about Lilly—information I'd gained largely from Blinky and her older brother Arnold, who serves as her trainer and manager. After nearly two years of training in the same gym with Lilly, all I'd gotten from her was a curt nod. Not even so much as a hello. Many times, I had watched her punching away at the speed bag, or practicing a fancy new kick in front of the mirror. She always seemed aloof. Everything about her—the way she held herself, the look in her eye—said "unapproachable."

So when I arrive at the sprawling YMCA building in the San Fernando Valley for my first "official" interview, some two weeks before the Sports Arena fight, I'm feeling a mite uncomfortable.

Inside the big, empty gym Arnold is coaching Lilly as she works out on the heavy bag.

Thunk! Thunk! Lilly hammers away, feinting, bobbing and weaving, and—*thunk!*—digs a hard left into an imaginary midsection.

Thunk! Thunk!

"No, Sis!" says Arnold. "Come *back* with your right. Stick and move. Stick and move."

Thunk!... Thunk!... Thunk!

"Take your time! Jab, jab...*then* come across."

Thunk! Thunk!... Thunk!

"Good. *Now* you got it. Stick, stick, stick. Now get out of the way...keep your left in her face....attagirl!...*jab, jab, jab...*"

Arnold's voice is hypnotic, and I catch myself moving my head and shoulders to its rhythm.

Lilly goes two more rounds on the heavy bag, then three on the speed bag and three more with the jump rope. Then she dons a pair of six-ounce boxing gloves for a sparring session with Arnold. While the two trade punches, Blinky wanders in to watch.

"Whoo! *C'mon* girl," Blinky shouts, as Lilly bounces a right off Arnold's temple. Turning to me, he says, "Man, just wait'll you see her in the *ring*. That's when she *really* opens up."

I'll bet she does; but right now I wonder just how I'm going to get her to open up to *me*. I've been here nearly an hour, and she hasn't once acknowledged my presence.

Frustrated, I ask Blinky for advice.

"Just be yourself," he says, slapping me on the back. He glances at his watch. "Hey, catch you later, man. Got to make it downtown." And with that he's gone.

As I stand in the hallway, scratching my head in bewilderment, Lilly appears from the women's locker room. She's wearing jeans and an orange T-shirt; her long, jet-black hair is still wet.

I have always considered Lilly to be good-looking, but this is the first time I'm struck by the fact that she's beautiful—which makes the edginess I'm experiencing all the more acute.

"Hi," she says, walking straight up to me. "Hope I didn't keep you too long, but I needed to get in ten rounds. I'm just at the peak of my training. How'd I look anyway?"

"Uh, fine," I mutter.

"C'mon," she says, pulling me by the arm, "let's go over by the Mission. It's really old…built in 1814. And there's a park there that's real pretty. It'll be a good place to talk."

As we make our way across the lawn, Lilly says, "You know, I bet a lot of people think it's real strange for a woman to be a fighter; so I'm really glad to get a chance to talk to you. I don't know…for some reason—maybe it's 'cause I'm real serious when I train—people always think I'm cold, or stuck-up or something. I don't get it—do you?"

"No, not me," I say, plastering a dumb grin across my face.

Lilly stops to stare at a graffiti-scarred wall emblazoned with the insignias of the many youth gangs that have come and gone over the years.

"You know, it's strange training here for this fight," she says, "'cause this is my old turf. I used to hang out in this park. I got my first, real fight training right here…on the streets. Actually," she corrects herself, "I guess the real fighting started way before." There's a faraway look in her eyes. "Yeah, *way before…*"

Lilly's earliest memories are of a tiny room that her family shared in the barrios of downtown Los Angeles. "All the girls slept in one bed, all the boys in another. Mom and Pop slept where they could."

Her father was a boxer, and her mother—who now lives with Lilly and Blinky—was a professional wrestler.

"Fighting blood," Lilly says proudly.

When their father left the family in 1959, and their mother—who was unable to speak English—couldn't get welfare, it was up to Lilly and the other kids to scratch for food. Every day—with 13-year-old Arnold in the lead—the Urquidezes would make the trek from their one-room walk-up to Main Street. Once there, they'd start at the Union Rescue Mission—where the winos would line up for their afternoon feeding—and work their way up the street, hustling shoe shines and selling chewing gum. "I'd buy my gum by the pack—ten sticks to a pack—for three cents," Lilly remembers. "Then I'd sell 'em for a nickel a stick. I was a good little hustler, and on some days I'd come home with maybe ten dollars." At 30, her childhood memories are still vivid.

Besides leading the troop on their daily quest for nickels, dimes and quarters, Arnold also taught the brothers how to fight. "I was always pestering him to let me fight boxing matches with other neighborhood kids in a local alley," says Lilly. "I used to bug Arnold to let me fight, but he'd just tell me to go play with my sisters. They didn't care about fighting. But I did, and I kept bugging him.

"One day I guess he'd had enough, 'cause he said, 'Okay, girl,' and put the gloves on me. My first fight was with a little boy, 'cause there were no other girls around…and I kicked his butt pretty good. Pretty soon I was beating up all the boys in the neighborhood."

Those were "fun" fights for Lilly. But soon fighting came to mean more than just a backyard punch-out.

"I had to fight every day," she recalls. "Fight to get food...fight in school...fight to get away from the cops...fight my way through the barrios. So fighting, well—it just became a way of life."

When she was 14, Lilly's family moved from downtown L.A. to the projects, a low-income housing sector in the San Fernando Valley. Though the move may have raised their social status a notch, it presented a problem for Lilly. She'd made a name for herself in L.A. as "the baddest chick around,"—and now she had to establish her "rep" all over again.

It didn't take long. "I'd been in high school about a week," Lilly recalls, "and one day during lunch, this big black chick comes up to me.

"'Your name Lilly?' she asked. "I hear that you're supposed to be real *bad*.'

"'I guess that's right," I answered.

The ritual was standard procedure, and shortly the two arranged to meet in a tunnel under the freeway, after school.

"Now lemme tell you, this girl was *big*," says Lilly. "She must've outweighed me by 25 pounds or so. But that didn't bother me—I'd always fought bigger people. But when we met in the tunnel, she pulled a blade, and I wasn't ready for that. She cut me, too." A short, jagged scar on the inside of her right wrist attests to the knife's damage.

"Well, I'll tell you, if there hadn't been a big crowd gathered around us, I might have run—but I had my reputation at stake. All I could think to do was to stay away from her...to tire her out. I was pretty quick, and I had a lot of stamina; so I figured that that was my best shot. And sure enough, after awhile she was gasping for breath. As soon as I saw that—*ping!*—I jumped in and kicked that knife out of her hand. Then I let her have it. Beat the shit out of her too. When I walked out of that tunnel, I left her lying there."

Lilly's fighting prowess not only established her "rep," but it also earned her a position as president of a girls club called the Valley Classics.

"We weren't a gang," she stresses, "like the low riders—the *cholas*." The *cholas*, Lilly explains, were the girls "with the ratted hair and the eyebrows painted way out." And sometimes they *did* carry razor blades in their teased hairdos. "Our club wasn't like that—but we weren't pussycats either. All of the Valley Classics were good fighters. I made sure of that."

And just how did she do that? "It was easy," Lilly replies, stifling a little giggle at the recollection. "Anyone who wanted in the Classics had to fight *me*. Oh, I wouldn't beat 'em up real bad or anything. If they gave me a good battle, they were *in*."

Seeing a look of astonishment crossing my face, her tone grows more emphatic. "Hey, you *had* to be tough…it was dog eat dog. The whites hated the blacks, the blacks hated the Chicanos, and all the Chicanos fought with each other, depending on what part of the Valley they came from.

"Like, one time, these seven chicks from Pacoima jumped me. I'll never forget them, 'cause they all had this bright red hair. Mean chicks. They probably would have killed me, but luckily a cop drove by, and they split. They should have wasted me, 'cause I made up my mind I'd get them.

"Sure enough, a couple of weeks later I saw them all sitting in a car. That hair was a dead giveaway. They were stopped at a light, and before they knew what was happening, I had run up, pulled out the driver and nailed her. This other one came at me with a tire iron, but I got it away from her and just started swinging it. I was *crazy*. I hit this one girl—broke her collarbone—and when that happened, they all jumped back into the car and hauled out of there. But not before I'd smashed out a window."

Lilly's eyes are as big as saucers as she recounts the incident. "*Nobody*—I don't care how many of 'em there were—jumped *me* and got away with it!"

Shortly thereafter, came Lilly's first introduction into the martial arts—a major turning point in her life. "My brothers had begun taking judo and karate. They'd come home and say, 'Hey, Sis, let me try out this move on you,' and they'd flip me all over the place. Well, I couldn't let that happen; so I started taking lessons too. I loved it right away. The moves were so pretty—just like ballet. Plus it gave me a reason to fight. It took me off the streets, 'cause I began to fight in martial-arts tournaments instead. It was the same for my brothers, who were all into some pretty heavy stuff at the time.

"Yeah, I really think that if it hadn't been for the martial arts, some of us would have wound up in jail—or dead."

Lilly's next big change came when she met Blinky Rodriguez, who was studying boxing under Arnold's tutelage. "He was real handsome and a good little fighter, too," she recalls. "And I knew right away he liked me, but still…I wasn't sure. I had lots of guys after me at the time. I was—how do you say it?—*a main attraction*. But you see, Chicano guys are really into being macho...bossing their old ladies around—and I never went for that. I guess that's what got to me about Blink. He was so nice; I just didn't know how to take it. We went together for a long time, and sometimes I'd be really mean to him. But he just stuck right with me. He says I was like a wild, black stallion that he had to tame. In a way I guess he *did* tame me."

Her eyes grow soft. "Now that I think of it, I guess I loved him right from the start."

The sun is going down behind the San Fernando Mission, and the only sound other than the soft drone of Lilly's voice is the chirping of as some sparrows in a nearby tree. Somehow, in this serene setting, it's hard to imagine Lilly swinging tire irons and dodging switchblades.

"Oh, gosh," she says, breaking my reverie, "I didn't realize it was this late! I've got to get home and cook dinner for Blink and the kids. See you later."

Before I can reply, she's off and running across the grass.

The Main Street Gym is located in the upper section of a dingy, brown building in the heart of downtown Los Angeles. At the top of the stairs, I'm greeted by Ripley—an old black gentleman who's been there since 1938. Ripley collects the 50 cents it costs to watch a workout.

I can almost feel the history oozing out of the walls inside the 80-plus-degree gym. Every great fighter the world over has trained here—Dempsey, Tunney, Moore, Marciano, Frazier, Ali. ("Ali was the best *ever*," crows Ripley). Because of this "flavor," the place has become a favorite locale for filmmakers doing boxing movies. Both *The Main Event* and *Rocky* shot footage here.

But today there are no Alis, no filmmakers. It's just business as usual, as a dozen or so fighters go through their paces. Over in a corner, I see Blinky banging out a *rat-a-tat* pattern on one of the speed bags. When the rest bell rings, he comes over to greet me. "Lil couldn't make it," he says. "Her mom is sick. No matter how important this fight is, family comes first."

And just how important *is* this fight?

"It's a big step for her. A win here and she's the Number One contender, which means a shot at the world title. And even though full-contact karate has been good to her, she's really been working all along to make it as a boxer. It's been a long road from the streets to here."

I ask Blinky about his memories of Lilly during her street days. "Man, she was *crazy*," he blurts. "That girl was knocking out *everyone*—chicks, dudes—it didn't matter. I remember one time when we were standing in line at a hotdog joint, and this guy came up and pinched her on the ass. I was just about to step in when—*whappo!*—she turned around and flattened the sucker. Knocked him out cold. I'm telling you, man, she was *mean*. But I saw through that. Right away I knew she was special—that underneath that streak was a good, strong woman. And I was right. She's got it *here*." Blinky thumps his heart.

"Sometimes I wonder how she can do it—taking care of the kids, her mom and me—and still train like she does. You wouldn't believe how much she puts out. The other night we were running together, and I looked over at her—*pushing, pushing*—keeping up with me stride for stride. And it just made me want to put out more. She inspires me...gives me strength all the time. I'm sure I give it back. And you know, we both believe in the Lord—that He's taking care of us, guiding us—though sometimes He does it in strange ways.

"Like the last time she went to Japan to fight for the Full-Contact Championship. Right before we left, our youngest son, Gabe—he's Lil's favorite, I guess, 'cause he's the baby—got on this Elvis kick. He kept running around singing 'Hound Dog,' shaking his hips and all. Anyway, when we got over to Tokyo, the promoters told Lilly she had only five hours before her fight. *Five hours!* But there was no choice.

"I was her cornerman, and I did everything I could. But for the first four rounds she just wasn't there. She didn't *have* it, and she was losing bad. Just before the fifth round—I don't know what happened—but all of a sudden I started singing, '*You ain't nothin' but a hound dog…*' It was *weird*. It just came out of me. People were looking at me like, *What the hell is this guy doing? He's nuts!* But Lilly got the message. It was like, *Go in there and do it, girl! Do it for Gabe; do it for all the kids.* You *know why we're here!*

And sure enough, she went out there and started landing bombs—*boom! boom!*, and, well…we left Tokyo with the Japanese title.

"'Hound Dog,'" Blinky chortles. "Never really liked that song, but it's come to have a special meaning. Like I said…He moves in strange ways."

Blinky goes back to his training, and I park myself on a bench to watch. Something is bugging me...something I can't quite put my finger on. Suddenly it's obvious. All this talk about "fighting blood, fighting heart"—it's suddenly clear that these aren't just *words*. These people have really *gotten* to me. I've got a nice, fat lump in my throat to prove it.

As I walk downstairs, the gym racket fades as the street noise escalates. I hit Main Street—swallow a gulp of air to clear my head—and start walking. I walk past the rows of pawn shops, porn theaters, taco stands, bars, and the Union Rescue Mission.

The Union Rescue Mission—Lilly's old stomping ground 20 years ago. I wonder if it looks the same as it did then?

I watch the winos assemble for their free meal—it's nearly noon—when I feel a tug on my pant leg. I look down to find a skinny Mexican kid clad in a white T-shirt and jeans.

"Hey, meester!" Another tug. "Hey, meester! You wanna buy chewing gum? Only a neekel."

I'm tempted to give the kid the entire contents of my wallet, but I hand him a quarter instead. He splits around a corner.

I guess things haven't really changed much in 20 years—at least not on the streets of L.A.

It's the morning of the fight. At 8:30 a.m., I'm awakened by the ringing of the phone. It's Lilly. "Hope I didn't wake you," she says, "but there's something you asked me the other day that's been bothering me."

I'm a bit taken aback. During the preceding week, I've spent almost every day with Lilly. I've developed the view that nothing bothers her. She seems totally involved in preparing for the upcoming fight.

"Training is *the* most important thing in any fight," Lilly had said earlier that week. "Even though we fight only two-minute rounds [male fighters go for three minutes], we have to train as hard as any man does."

That statement had prompted me to ask a question: What is the difference in the fight game for a woman compared to that of a man?

"Fighting is fighting," Lilly had replied, short-circuiting the lengthy diatribe about inequality I'd expected. "Most women look bad because they fight like this." She flailed her arms around wildly. "There's a *correct* way to fight. No matter what sex you are, you tuck your chin in, get your balance, and keep your hands up. When you punch, you twist at the hip so you get your whole body into the shot. Now, I'm not saying that a woman's as strong as a man, but if she learns how to fight the proper way, she can pack a real wallop."

Lilly saw that the answer hadn't pleased me entirely, but she pressed on. "You know, people are always asking me what I think about women's lib, and I can't really give them an answer 'cause it's not an issue for me. What I mean is, I never thought about my rights as a woman when I was out on the streets. I just did what I had to do. I still do.

"The other thing I always get asked about is my sexuality. I guess people think that all women fighters are a bunch of lesbians or something. But that's *their* problem—not mine. Outside the ring, I'm a *woman*. Inside, I'm a *fighter*—and that's about all I can say."

What's puzzling me now as I speak to her on the morning of the fight, is what could possibly be bothering someone who appears to function with such gut-level, street-bred logic.

"You asked me the other day why I fight," Lilly says over the phone, "and for some reason, that question's been going through my mind. I've come up with all sorts of answers—like to make my family—Blinky, my four boys, my mom and my brothers—proud of me. That's one. Also, lots of times after I fight, young girls will come up to me—girls that remind me of myself when I was a teenager—and say, 'Wow, Lilly, you're so *bad*. We wanna be just like you.' And I get a chance to talk to them, to try and straighten them out, which makes me feel good.

But still there's something else…

"You know, when I was a little girl, I used to have this dream of being a ballet dancer, and not just any ballet dancer—but the *best*. I'd picture myself dancing in front of big crowds, and they'd be cheering for me. Of course, we didn't have the money for me to study; so it was always just a dream. Well, now I'm a fighter. And I *love* the sport;

it's been good to me, but I guess…well, I guess I still have the *dream*. What I mean is—I still want to *be* somebody."

There's silence for a moment.

"Do you know what I mean?"

I tell her that I do.

"Good," she says, sounding as if a tremendous weight has been lifted from her.

"Gotta go. Hey—you *are* coming tonight, aren't you?"

"You bet," I reply.

But more than once during the rest of the day, I still entertain the thought of missing the match. Even though Lilly's done her best to prove that she never feels any fear before going into the ring, she hasn't taken away my fear. Frankly, I'm scared shitless for her.

The bell for Round One is still ringing in my ears. I watch—frozen in my seat—as Lilly and Toni Lear circle one another. Lilly fakes a hook, then shoots a straight jab, grazing Lear's temple. Lear responds with two punches that Lilly catches on her glove, but then—*whap!*—a quick right catches Lilly.

Lilly is shorter than Lear. She's going to have to get inside and work on Lear's body. Bobbing and weaving, Lilly attempts to bull her way in, but Lear—who's throwing more punches than Lilly—tags her again. From ringside, the sound of the blows is horribly loud.

Whap! Lear's long, looping right smashes against Lilly's temple.

"Attagirl, Toni! Show her who's boss!" yells a fat guy two seats down from me.

Lear comes after Lilly now, but her punches are wild. They all miss their mark. Lilly gets in a good, hard right as the bell sounds. As she walks back to her corner, she looks confused.

In Round Two, she comes out looking more determined. Immediately, she gets inside, and digs a hard left to Lear's midsection... then another, which—just for an instant—buckles the larger girl's knees. There's no question who hits harder. But Lear is game, and she comes back with a wild barrage of punches, the last of which connects with Lilly's jaw.

"Awwwright, Toni! You got her now, babe!" hollers the fat guy.

Stupid schmuck, I think. Who the hell *is* he anyway?

"Let's *go*, Lilly. She doesn't have a punch!" I yell.

The fat guy shoots me a menacing glance. But as if on cue, Lilly ducks underneath a whistling left hook from Lear and bangs a hard right to her liver. Lear grunts, and the next second her head is snapped back by a vicious uppercut.

"C'mon, Lilly!" I holler. But the round is over.

In Round Three, the two hunt and peck for the first 30 seconds. Then Lear decides to get cute. She makes a motion with her hand as if to say "C'mon." She follows by sticking her mouthpiece out at Lilly.

"Yaaaaaaahhhhhhh!" screams the fat guy.

Lear—feeling her oats again—steps inside, wanting to trade punches. It's a mistake. She hits Lilly first—a glancing hook that has nothing behind it. Lilly answers with a wicked right that thunks against Lear's temple.

Bap! Bap-bap-bap! Four more punches—quick as lightning—send Lear's head reeling back and forth. Lear is still swinging, but her timing is way off.

Whap!—she catches one again just over the eye.

Lilly treats Lear like a heavy punching bag now. She pounds Lear all over the ring....and, before I know it...I'm up and out of my seat, screaming at the top of my lungs. *"Kill her, Lilly! Kick her ass!"*

At the bell I'm still shouting.

The next few rounds are all Lilly, as Lear is rocked again and again. Though she's still on her feet at the end of the eight-round fight, when she wobbles back to her corner, there's no doubt as to the winner is.

The crowd roars, and I roar along with them, as Lilly's hand is raised.

Just for an instant. I see a trace of a smile pass across her face.

I look over towards the fat guy. He's gone.

There are more fights on the card, but as far as I'm concerned, the night is over. As I head out to my car, I have the most peculiar sensation that I'm floating on air. Somewhere in the back of my head, I'm aware that sooner or later I'm going to have to deal with the reality of a grown, supposedly civilized man—screaming for the blood of some poor, innocent girl who's never done him any harm. But that'll have to wait—because right now everything feels *just right.*

I get into my car and automatically flip on the radio. The second I hear the music, I'm hit by a rush. The rush of knowing that—how to put it?—*things are as they should be.*

I sit for a moment, letting the music reverberate inside me.

As I edge out toward the street, I stop to crank up the volume. There's a twinge of self-consciousness, as I hear Blinky's voice in my head...

"He moves in strange ways..."

I put my foot to the floor, laying about 15 yards of rubber out onto Vermont Avenue, as I slide giddily into the nighttime traffic.

There's no reason for the self-consciousness really. No mind readers around here, right? Besides, should anyone be...er, observing me, he'd never suspect me of thinking such high and mighty thoughts.

I'm safe. Just a typical Joe, on a typical Saturday night—cruising the streets of L.A.—with "Hound Dog" blasting from my car speakers, which are cranked up as loud as friggin' possible.

Lilly Urquidez Rodriguez passed away on Jan 13, 2007. She was 59.

NIGHTMARES

NIGHTMARES

TWO GUYS NAMED OTIS

It was 5:30 in the morning in downtown L.A. and the sun was coming up reddish-yellow over Bunker Hill. It was still quiet at this time of the morning, though soon enough the street people would be stirring.

In front of the Lucky Market, two guys named Otis were sleeping. While it was true that both their names were Otis, neither of the two men ever stopped to discuss the fact. In fact, they didn't find it in the least bit remarkable.

The first Otis was curled up on a little piece of cardboard near the doorway of the market. He'd been sleeping here every night for the past month or so, and he was quite happy with the spot. Meanwhile, Otis Number Two was rolled up in a sleeping bag, which he'd bought for $19.95 from the Salvation Army Store.

Soon, an old white Chevy pulled up in front of the market. A short Chinese man emerged from the car. This was Mr. Wong, who owned the market. He usually arrived at this time. He enjoyed the early morning hours at the market when he could read his paper and sip his coffee without his wife nagging at him.

Otis Number Two began to stir inside his bag. He popped his wooly head up from inside the bag and looked around—just like an old groundhog—and surveyed the territory around him. He looked over at the sleeping figure of his friend curled up on his little piece of cardboard. In between Otis Number One's legs, the top of a bottle emerged. Otis Number Two moved a bit closer. Then, *very carefully*, he put his hand on the bottle and, ever-so-slowly, he began to inch it out from its resting place between Otis Number One's legs.

"Hey! Whassahappenin? Say man, *whatthefuckyoudoin?"* Otis Number One exclaimed. He was wide-awake now, his old eyes popping. Both men looked at the bottle. The label said Ripple. There was only a teeny bit of the red liquid remaining in the bottom of the bottle. Otis Number One unscrewed the cap and held it to his lips. He let the liquid go down slowly, holding it in his mouth and swishing it around before swallowing it with a noisy gulp.

"Say man…save sum a dat fo' *me!"* Otis Number Two said, grabbing at the bottle. But by the time he'd gotten hold of it, Otis Number One had emptied its contents. "Shee-it, man…how cum you wanna do me like that?" said Otis Number Two. "*Shee-it…*" He looked very hurt, but even Otis Number One—who wasn't particularly bright—could see that his pal was hamming it up.

Otis Number Two was rattling around in his pockets now. Soon he emerged with some change, which he began to count. Otis Number One watched him with great curiosity.

"Say, watchoo doin' man?" he said. Otis Number Two didn't look up. He just kept right on counting. "Gonna git me sum wine…" he finally said, as he got up to go inside the market.

Inside the store, Mr. Wong sat behind the counter, reading his racing form. He looked up as Otis Number Two came in, but didn't say anything. He knew that Otis Number Two would be heading for the liquor section at the back of the store, as he did each morning. But on this particular morning, Otis Number Two felt like wandering around, looking at the various items on the shelves.

First, he went to the rack that held the magazines. He picked up a copy of *Big Black Boobs* Magazine and opened it. He leafed through it until he found a two-page spread that had a picture of a beautiful, dark-haired girl. She was very naked. The photo was taken in a jungle setting, in which the girl was being carried off by a monstrous ape.

Otis Number Two noticed that the girl had huge tufts of hair sprouting from underneath her armpits. As he looked at the picture, his cock got hard. But suddenly, he felt something peculiar…as if someone were staring at him.

There, at the other end of the rack was a youngish Mexican man wearing a green army jacket. He also had a magazine in his hand, but he wasn't looking at it. Instead, he was looking at Otis Number Two.

The man was quite tall, had wild, disheveled hair, and coal-black eyes. There seemed to be a tiny point of light directly at the center of the man's eyes. But when he saw Otis Number Two looking at him, the man quickly looked down. Then he put his magazine back on the rack, and disappeared around the corner.

Otis Number Two headed for the liquor section. Something in the man's gaze had made him feel queasy. He needed a drink.

In the back of the store, Otis Number Two selected a bottle of Thunderbird. It cost $1.34. It tasted bad, Otis Number Two knew, but it would do the trick. He took the bottle and headed for the cash register...but as he turned the corner he bumped into the man in the green army jacket.

"Unhhh, sorry, man," Otis Number Two said. Again, he noticed the man's eyes. They seemed to bulge when he saw Otis Number Two—then they rapidly clouded over. The next second, the man brushed past Otis Number Two and left the store, walking very quickly—as if he had somewhere terribly important to be.

Mr. Wong was waiting for Otis Number Two at the counter. He had his little black-and-white TV turned to a rerun of "I Love Lucy." Otis Number Two put the bottle down on the counter and plunked down some change.

Mr. Wong counted the money. It came to $1.16. It wasn't enough, but Mister Wong just clucked his tongue and took Otis Number Two's money. Otis Number Two took the bottle, now wrapped in a brown paper sack, and exited the store.

Outside, the sun was high and yellow. Otis Number Two knew that it was going to be a scorcher. That was the way it was down here—freezing nights, unbearably hot days. You couldn't win.

Otis Number Two plunked himself down next to Otis Number One, who was still sitting in the same position he'd been in when Otis Number Two had left. Otis Number Two wanted to tell his friend about the man in the green army jacket with the strange eyes, but then he changed his mind. He'd just drink his wine and forget it.

Everyday it was the same. The two men would wake up, drink some wine, maybe have a smoke or two. Sometimes they'd talk about things, better times maybe... Sometimes they'd just sit and watch the morning pass by.

For the next hour or so, they passed the bottle back and forth, saying very little to one another. It was as pleasant a way as any to pass the time. Soon—as they would do each day—they'd stash their gear in the field next to the market and take a nice, slow walk over to the Union Rescue Mission for the noon feeding. After lunch, they'd probably sit and jaw with Father O'Reilly awhile, for he always had a good story to tell. Later, they'd head down Main Street...maybe do a little panhandling or catch a catnap on the bench in the Greyhound bus depot. Finally, around 4:00 p.m. or so, they'd head back to their spot next to the market and get ready for the long night ahead.

The sun glowed reddish-orange as it set over Bunker Hill. It was a quiet time—perhaps even serene. By 6:00 p.m., the two Otises prepared to settle down for the night. Otis Number One found his little piece of cardboard, and set it down close to the doorway. Otis Number Two got out his sleeping bag, unzipped it, and crawled inside.

"G'night Otis," Otis Number One said to his friend.

"'Night Otis," Otis Number Two replied.

Soon the two men were fast asleep. Otis Number One slept peacefully, snoring those big, long snores of his. But Otis Number Two's sleep was fitful. He tossed and turned. Strange images flitted through his head. After a while, he fell into a terrible dream.

In the dream, the landscape was black—pitch black—yet somehow everything glowed with an eerie silver hue. There was a hum in the air—a strange, electric hum that began to grow louder and louder.

In the dream, Otis Number Two was hovering in the air so that he could look down and see everything around him. He floated over the sleeping figures of himself and Otis Number One, lying on his little piece of cardboard near the doorway.

Then from out of a doorway, a figure emerged. At first it was just a dark shadow. But as the figure moved under the streetlamp, Otis Number Two recognized the tall man in the green army jacket, with the wild hair and the coal-black eyes.

A knot arose in the pit of Otis Number Two's stomach. The electric hum in the air grew louder. The man was looking around, back and forth, and over his shoulder, as if he were afraid. In his hand he clutched a brown paper sack. Otis Number Two was feeling sick inside now—sick to his stomach—as if something wanted to erupt from his guts.

As Otis Number Two watched, the man approached him. He stood over Otis Number Two, looking down at him, and slowly moving his head back and forth. He was mumbling something—an incantation of some sort—but Otis Number Two couldn't tell what it was. The hum in the air grew louder—

Now, the man turned from Otis Number Two, and walked over to the sleeping figure of his companion. He regarded him for a moment, then reached inside his paper bag and extracted something. Under the glow of the streetlamp, Otis Number Two saw the glint of a long, shiny blade.

Now the incantation grew louder.

"*Nimroth, lagog, malakai, sheboth…bala sham narog. Balac ma aree…*BALOC, NAROG, MALAC, GEDULA."

The words grew louder, more rhythmic.

Now the man raised the long blade high over his head…

"BALAC! NAROG! RAM! NAROG!"

And with that, the man plunged the knife deep into the chest of Otis Number One. As it punctured the skin, there was a distinct popping sound.

When the knife entered his body, Otis Number One sat straight up on his little piece of cardboard.

"Ahhhh!" he yelled, "Jesus, *God!"* But before he could yell again, the tall man grabbed Otis Number One by the hair, pulled his head back, and slit his throat—*zut!*—just like that.

For a moment, Otis Number One's eyes seemed to bulge out of their sockets, and the scream became a gurgle. Otis Number One's mouth remained open, but now, no sound came out.

Then the man took the blade and slowly—ever so slowly—put it to his lips. He tasted the blood. Then he took the long, thin knife and held it high in the air. For a moment it glinted under the gold glow of the streetlamp.

"This is for you, my Dark Father," he said.

Then he plunged the knife into Otis Number One's left eye. In one swift motion he scooped the eyeball out of its socket. Then he swiftly cut out the other eyeball. Both eyeballs were plopped into the paper sack. Quickly, the man turned on his heel and walked down the alleyway, disappearing a moment later into the shadows.

For what seemed to be a very long time, Otis Number Two continued to hover over the scene. It was as if he didn't want to disturb anything, for it seemed to him that something sacred had taken place.

The next moment he tried to wake himself, but found he could not. He tried and tried, but he just hung there in the air, looking over the figures of himself and his friend.

Soon he stopped trying—then, quite suddenly, he felt himself falling. Falling and falling—through one door, then another.

With his stomach reeling, he continued to fall into the blackness.

Today, the sun rose bright and yellow over Bunker Hill. Otis Number Two awoke, as he did on many days, to the sound of the streets sweepers, the clang of the little bell and the splash of the water as it whooshed into the street, clearing away the stench and stink of the night.

It was freezing outside, so Otis Number Two hunkered down in his sleeping bag. He'd stay in there as long as he could—that was for sure. He looked over at his friend, who was still sleeping soundly. Then the thought struck him that perhaps Otis Number One had another bottle stashed somewhere.

Quietly, ever-so-quietly, Otis Number Two crawled out of his bag, and snuck over to where his friend lay. Sure enough, he was sleeping peacefully.

"C'mon shit fo' brains," Otis Number Two said, shaking his friend. "Get yo' lazy ass up." He thought he heard Otis Number One grunt now, so he pulled him by the shoulder.

It was then he saw the face—the mouth open in a frozen scream, the red gash across the throat, and the dark empty eye sockets. Otis Number Two stood looking down like that for what seemed like a very long time.

"*Shee-it*, man," he whispered. "*Shee-ittt*."

Then Otis Number Two turned and began walking very fast down Flower Street. He didn't want to run, because it might attract attention...yet soon he was running anyway. He ran and ran and ran until he was out of breath...and still he ran. He ran until his legs wouldn't carry him any more. And all the while he ran, he heard the strange incantation of the tall, dark man in the dream and he could see the man's terrible eyes staring coldly at him from under the streetlamp.

Otis Number Two was still running when he hit Main Street, nearly a mile away.

Back in front of the Lucky Market, the body of Otis Number One lay, curled up like a sleeping fetus on the sidewalk. When the morning street people came out, most of them walked right by it. Some went around the body; others simply stepped right over it.

At 4:00 p.m., the body was still there. Flies were hovering over the face now, and ants had begun to feed on the empty holes where Otis Number One's eyes had once been.

Finally, at 5:00 p.m. a police car arrived.

Two officers got out. One was a handsome young rookie. The rookie had dark brown hair with little flecks of grey in it. His partner was a young female officer with blonde hair pulled back into a ponytail.

The two officers went over to look at the body. Then the girl walked back to the car to talk on the radio; meanwhile the young rookie wrote something in his notebook. After he'd finished, they both got in the car and left.

It was approaching dusk now. Finally, a little past 6:00 p.m., a white police van arrived. Two men got out of the van. They went over to the body, and slipped a stretcher underneath it. One man took a brown plastic bag and stuffed the body into it.

The bag was zipped up. *Zip!* it went. Then the men hoisted the stretcher into the back of the van and drove away.

It was nearly dark now, and the streets were almost empty.

A pretty little black girl—maybe eight or so—skipped along the sidewalk. She was bouncing a large blue ball and humming a tune that almost sounded familiar.

A drunk stumbled out of a bar across the street from the Lucky Market. He stood there a moment, just weaving around, then sat down on the curb. After a moment, he threw up between his knees.

Soon, Mr. Wong came out of the market. He put the padlock through the door, lit a fat, black cigar, then climbed into his Chevy and drove off.

Now the streets were barren. Save for the wail of a siren a few blocks away, the streets were strangely quiet.

Night had fallen in downtown Los Angeles.

Another day had passed.

PIN MAN

Donna Brown was sleeping over. She'd been staying at my place for the last couple of weeks pretty steadily, sharing the little twin bed I had—the one with the bumpy springs and the orange bedspread. It was really much too small a bed for two people to sleep comfortably on (I liked a lot of space so that I could roll around). But I liked Donna Brown a lot and I liked the fact that she'd left her apartment and her roommates Lucy and Joyce. I liked the fact that she wasn't in that place with the crummy stereo and the guitar leaning up against the wall and the poster of the bullfighter and the cans of corn and peas with the prices still marked on them in the cupboard.

I didn't really like my apartment much. Somehow it didn't feel *safe*. What I mean is, you could actually feel the people in the next apartment over—the guy with the Joe Palooka chin and his stupid girlfriend that played records by really terrible rock bands early in the morning and they'd walk to school holding hands and you knew that they'd probably get married someday and live in Orange County or somewhere equally depressing.

Actually, I didn't mind the noise so much—I mean, you could hear it when they fucked—the bed banging against the wall and the awful sounds they made. It was horrible. But worse still, you could actually feel their vibes—whatever the hell you want to call those things—coming right through the wall.

Sometimes it made me dizzy and feel like vomiting.

My friend Otis slept in the bedroom. I slept on a lumpy twin bed in the living room. I'd known Otis for a long time—ever since the sixth grade, to be exact. Back then he'd weighed almost 200 lbs. We used to call him "The Crusher." This was because he'd sneak up behind girls, wrap his huge arms around them, and *crush* them until they screamed at the top of their lungs! Actually, this was Otis' way of telling girls that he *liked* them—though they didn't seem to understand this too well.

Anyhow, like I said, Donna Brown was sleeping over. She would come over to our place just every night about 6:30 and cook Otis and I dinner. She wasn't a very good cook—but that didn't matter. It was just the idea that she'd do it that I liked.

After we'd eat, Otis would go off to his room and maybe read or watch TV. Donna and I would just sit around and talk, and then we'd get in bed and talk some more...and finally we'd make love.

I really liked her a *lot*. In fact, sometimes I sort of thought maybe I was actually in love with her!

Donna had blond hair, gray-brown eyes, and one of those plain, pretty faces—the kind like you see on the women in those old Western movies. And she was very nervous. She had this high, nervous little laugh—sort of a twitter almost—that always bugged me. Sometimes I thought to myself that she'd probably commit suicide one day.

But we had a lot of fun in that apartment. We really did. We'd tell stories and laugh and joke...or sometimes Donna would read to us—she had a very nice voice—and it was sort of like she was our mother or our sister, and the three of us were really good pals, but she was *mine* and she slept with *me*.

One time I got pretty drunk and I was in the bathtub. I was splashing water all over the place and I let the water run out of the tub until it overflowed onto the tile floors and then out into the living room where it soaked into the crummy brown carpet.

"Oh, Martin is drunk! He's making a mess!" Donna said.

She was laughing. "He's so crazy. Oh God!"

"He's just trying to get attention, you know," Otis said.

He was right, of course. But it *was* nice splashing around in that tub and singing and yelling and making a big mess of everything. To tell you the truth, I was enjoying myself for the first time in months.

Anyhow, it was later that night and Donna and I were in bed. She slept in one of those thin satin nighties that I thought was quite sexy—and she smelled *really* good. I can still smell her even now.

Pretty soon she fell asleep. But I couldn't sleep. I was wide awake. So I lay there in the dark, just sort of looking at her. She was sleeping on her side; her mouth was twisted up kind of funny, and she didn't look so pretty.

I just lay there watching her.

I really couldn't seem to sleep very well.

A few minutes later I heard this *whooshing* sound.

Then, a second later I smelled something *really* awful.

Donna had farted in her sleep.

It was *terrible*. I thought that she must have had maggots crawling around inside her stomach for her to let one that smelled that bad.

So there I was, wide awake—just lying there—and for some reason I started thinking about Pin Man.

It was a little scary. But not nearly so scary as when I'd first seen him.

I must've been around six or so, and I was watching one of those Saturday morning cartoon shows. It was one of those old black and white cartoons about this little place called Thimbletown. It was this tiny village that was inhabited by these little bug people—*you* know the kind.

The little bug people just ran around doing their chores and stuff. They seemed like they were very hard workers.

And then Pin Man came.

He was this, well—this big pincushion with pins sticking in him...and he had lots of long spindly legs. Sort of like a gigantic spider. He had horrible eyes and big, sharp yellow teeth. And what he'd do was, he'd run after the little bug people—and though you never knew exactly what he did when he caught them, you knew that probably he gobbled them up, or maybe even something even more horrible.

I just kept lying there and thinking about Pin Man and watching Donna Brown and her twisty little mouth and listening to her breathe.

Then I started to do something really terrible.

"Pin Man." I whispered it—very softly—into her ear.

She didn't move.

"Pin Man!" A little louder this time.

I was feeling pretty peculiar, if you want to know the truth. Something was building inside. I could feel it.

"Pin Man!" I did it again.

This time she moved a little.

"Pin Man!" I could feel him now, taking over my body. My body turning into that big fat pincushion with needles—long sharp needles sticking out of me and my eyes were red and my teeth were sharp and smeared with blood.

"PIN MAN! PIN MAN! PIN MAN!"

Donna awoke with a start. Her eyes were wide open and she was staring into my eyes.

My terrible yellow eyes.

I looked at her and smiled.

"Pin Man," I whispered again.

"What's wrong? What are you doing?"

"Pin Man!" I could feel the bile rising in my throat.

"Stop it! What's wrong? Jesus—what are you *doing?"*

I could feel him coming now. He was almost entirely there, and my face was shrinking, shrinking...changing into a horrible, distorted, twisted mass.

"*Pin Man!*" I hissed.

Then Donna Brown screamed and took one long claw at my face, drawing blood with her long fingernails. The next second she jumped straight up out of bed and ran out the door. Out into the cold 2:00 a.m. night in her white silk nightie. Out across the wet lawns scattered with glistening dogshit. Out and through the driveways and backyards and alleyways, down the streets in her bare feet, cold and running, running. Running back to her apartment with the guitar in the corner and the bullfighter poster on the wall and the cans of corn and peas in the cupboard with the prices still marked on them. Back to her two sleeping roommates, Joyce, who sort of played guitar OK but not really, and Lucy, who always had bad breath.

I lay in bed and stared at the ceiling. It was one of those stucco ceilings like all crummy apartments had. I'd always hated them, but for some reason now, I could actually imagine that I was looking up at the stars.

I felt very peaceful.

I lay in bed like that and I could feel the blood still wet on my face, but I didn't want to wipe it off. Finally I swiped my finger in it.

Then I stuck the finger in my mouth.

It tasted sweet.

I was sort of hungry. I thought about eating the leftover salad in the refrigerator that Donna had made for dinner. I'd always liked cold salad, but for some reason I didn't feel much like eating it.

So I just lay there like that.

After a while I fell asleep.

I don't think I had any dreams, but I can't really say for sure.

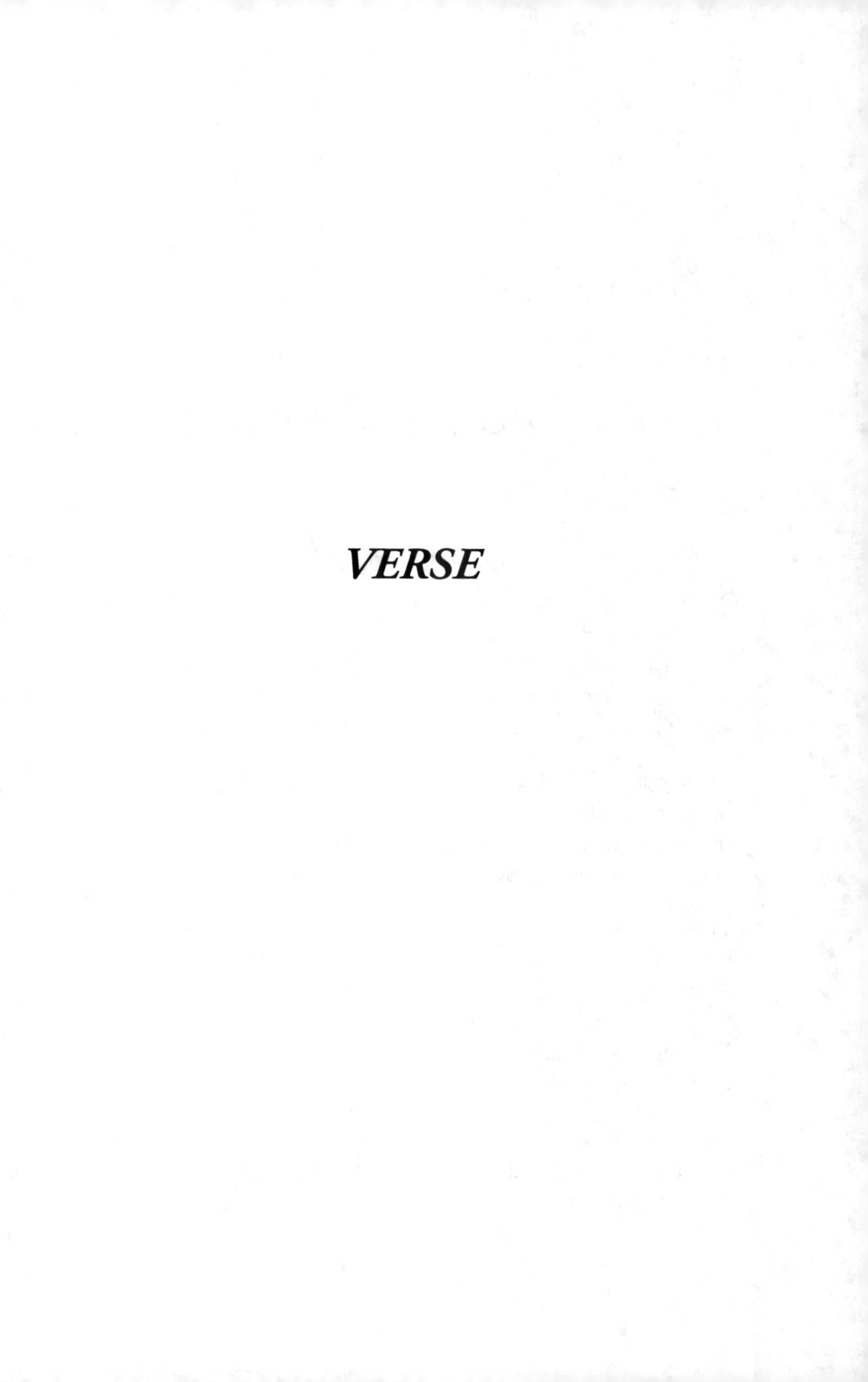

VERSE

VERSE

THE HOUSE ON RYE ST.

It's still there
On the corner. The lawn freshly cut
Mailbox out front
12403 Rye St.
I squint my eyes (glasses now). On the box it says—
THE JONES.'

Are they actually inside there—30 years later?
Could it actually be?
I get out of my car and—queasy stomach—
go up to the door and knock.

An eternity—
Then, a figure at the door
Maryanne—
Maryanne Maryanne Maryanne. You're still *here!*
And you know what?
She looks the *exactly* the same!

Hi, it's me—
For a moment, nothing. Then she remembers
"Oh my gosh! Come in, come in—"

Maryanne Jones sitting in a chair with a glass of wine
Maryanne Jones in a yellow summer dress
Maryanne Jones—still beautiful
Grace Kelly ain't got nothin' on you—
Ingrid Bergman—forget it
And my 30-year old crush—yep—it's still there.

Maryanne—
Always the perfect hostess
Ice tinkles in the glass
The house is cool inside
We sit and talk...as easy as pie
And as we do…it all comes back—

The first thing is the pool
Yeah, of course! The magical Jones pool!
And it *was* magic…it really was.

I remember swimming, wanting to always be underwater (I thought
I was Flash Gordon swimming upside down in underground caves,
my goggles some kind of weird space helmet)
The drain at the bottom—*that* was the goal
I can touch the drain!
No you can't!
Yes I can!
No you can't!
Yes I can—

Kids galore
Jerry and Jill Feldberg, me, my sis—moms, dads, cousins, friends
(the whole bloody neighborhood)!
Sandwiches and Cokes all around
"You can't go in the water for an hour after you've eaten!"
all the moms say
Nobody listens.

Lori Jones, a tiny round thing—brown as a berry
Swims like a fish
Swims better than all the guys, in fact
Something *about* her—

On the deck something wonderful and awful happens
As she lies sleeping in the sun, the bottom of
Cindy Feldberg's breast emerges from her bathing suit top—
I am astonished, amazed, frightened, shocked and delighted
I want to look, but I don't want to get caught
Cindy's eyes are closed
I hear what sounds like a snore
Screw it—
I feast my eyes
Ahhhhh.

Aunt Flo and Uncle Norm's house around the corner
Cut across the lawn, barefoot—
Feet feel good against hot pavement
Cokes and pretzels and TV waiting for me
Even then I remember thinking to myself—*this is the life!*

Nighttime
Magic, eternal summer
A garage full of Cokes, RC's, Dr. Pepper, 7-Up
(12 oz. bottles only, please!), ice cream—Chocolate, Rocky Road,
Neapolitan, Coffee (my favorite) pretzels, peanuts (salted only)
Boxes and boxes of Almond Roca, Mike Lyman's chocolate bars—
Comic books!
Model airplanes!
What *else* does a kid need?
Nothing—*that's* what.

Aunt Flo's studio out back
Paintings on easels
Lots of weird looking people
Fat people, bums, wino looking guys, gypsies—
Whoops—*naked ladies!*
I feast my nine-year old eyes

Thank you Auntie Flo!

Red ants in the dirt out back
Millions of them
Mean sons of bitches
Jerry and I make a secret potion out of all kinds of stuff to kill them
Pour it down the hole
Pee in it for good measure
Hee hee
Take *that*, you fuckers.

Barefoot boy, running down the streets...running, running
Feet leather tough
Warm summer nights
Sleep out in the backyard on the chaise lounge
Crickets loud
Telescope
Look up at the moon
Hello moon
Hello stars
Hello Heaven—

Funnies and coffee in the morning
Jerry comes over to play
Later we do this thing where we pretend to be Flash Gordon
and Ming and the bad guys are after us and we climb up on
the fence and jump off into space
(landing safely on the grass on the other side)
Up up and *awayyyyyy!*

Later, a magic show in Jerry's back yard
Make the kids pay a quarter to get in
Suckers—
Already a hustler at age nine.

Jerry playing bad clarinet in his room
Honk honk honk
SHUT UP! somebody hollers
Ooops, it's *me*.

Jill probably off somewhere eating her boogers
Cindy in the kitchen cutting up vegetables
Mort, walking around the house with hair popping out of his chest
all over the place
Why don't I like him?
He smells sour
He has bad breath
He has no sense of humor
Reasons aplenty.

Bob Jones
Maryanne's husband
My trumpet teacher
One cool cat
Be bop man
Hang out with him in his studio
Sheet music piled high in the wood paneled room.

Records galore. Stacks and stacks of them
Doris Day. *Que Sera Sera*. Harry Belafonte, *Day-O*,
Sinatra, Rosemary Clooney, movie theme music—
Strange looking jazz guys
wearing lime green Hawaiian shirts and beards
I don't quite get it yet, but I know it's cool
Yeah—
Screw the William Tell Overture.

Ice cream truck! Ice cream truck!
Auntie Flo, Auntie Flo—can I have a quarter?
Money in hand, I run outside
Kids line up
Squeeze in
Drumstick or cherry popsicle?
What a decision
Both—of course!

Jerry and I throw a bunch of plums over the fence where they land in
Maryanne's pool

Splash, sploosh, splash
Heee Heeeee

Later, Maryanne invites us over swimming
I am mortified by guilt as I watch her scooping plums
out of the pool
Some kid over there…I don't know him and I already don't like him
Buddy Sheibal
Another clarinet asshole. (Only trumpet players are cool—
everybody knows that!)
But his sister Sara is kind of pretty and I can tell she likes me.
And why not?
I am the coolest.

I don't like Buddy Sheibal
Maybe jealous of him
He has straight hair, cut in butch
My hair curly—Jewish
Eechhh
Sara already growing breasts
Hmmmm—
Maybe if I'm nice to her she'll let me look at them!

I pull Jerry's pants down in front of everyone
He starts to cry and runs home
Wah wah wah
What a sissy
Later, Cindy says come over for an avocado sandwich
I don't like avocado
It reminds me of Jill's boogers.

Feldberg house lunch
Dry
Dry white bread
Dry boloney
Dry people, dry house, dry everything
I like Aunt Flo's house better
I'm outta here—

I beat the crap out of Jerry Feldberg
He tries to claw my face like a girl
I get him on the ground. Headlock followed by a leg trip.
My favorite move.
Unbeatable
He's crying now—
There he goes, running home to his mommy
Nyah nyah na na nah!
Uncle Norm says, "You did good, Hoppy."

Fourth of July
Jerry and I hide firecrackers under a fat lady's chair
in Aunt Flo's backyard
BANG! BANG! BANG!
Fatso screams and jumps up and everybody starts laughing
Yeah!!!

More fireworks—
A gigantic box full of strange, wonderful looking things
Thirty bucks worth
The girls like the sparklers
Stupid girls
Everybody knows that the rockets are the best!

Jill's dress catches on fire
My mom beats it out with her hands
She's declared a National Hero.
And I—her wonderful, stupendous and most admirable
young son—am a hero by virtue of genetics, am I not?
I yam I yam I yam.

Radio playing at night
Jailhouse Rock, Peggy Sue, That'll Be The Day, Be Bop A Lula
I lie in my underwear on Barb's bed
Let the music go inside my stomach
Magical sounds.
Thick, fat sounds
I picture me and Elvis and Buddy and Gene—all of us onstage

This must be it—when I was first infected
Oooh weee, mamma
I gots da rock 'n' roll demon.

"Hey Hoppy," Uncle Norm says to me when he gets home from work
Lights a cigar
Ahhhh—
I love the smell
Aunt Flo drinking iced coffee in the kitchen
Yellow formica table top
"Hey Studie—how 'bout a soda?"
A soda?
Sure. Of course!
Vanilla, coffee or Rocky Road?
All three, please—
Here you go, Studie—

Uncle Norm lounging on his favorite green chair in the den
Jazz playing in the background
Cool sax wafts thru the house
It's five o'clock in the afternoon and the sun is going down and everything is right—
I love it here.

Another summer
The best—
Lots of TV. Black and white only (screw color!) *The Cisco Kid, Crusader Rabbit, Kukla, Fran And Ollie, The Lone Ranger, Spin And Marty, Sherriff John*, and my favorite—*The Mickey Mouse Club.*

Annette Funicello
I'm so crazy over her
Darleen and Cheryl are both cute—but it's Annette for me!
And guess what?
She lives around the corner!
From ME!

I could walk over there right now if I wanted
In fact, I think I will...
I don't know who God is, but I thank Him anyway.

The drawers in the living room cabinet stuffed with...
EVERYTHING
Extras
Extra candy, extra comic books, extra chewing gum—
Wrigley's Spearmint, Juicyfruit, Beeman's Pepsin,
Blackjack, Doublemint, Dentyne
I chew a whole pack at a time. And why not?
There's always MORE—

Mike Lyman's chocolate bars. Giant ones
You want almonds? No problem
Licorice—red and black
Those weird sour red balls that make your tongue burn
Lighters
Tons and tons of Zippo lighters—
Click click click they go
Wonderful sound
I love the smell of the metal—

The bookcase in Aunt Flo's den
I know each book by heart
I like the cartoons the best
Droodles by Roger Price. *The Adams Family, Dick Tracy, Li'l Abner*
Pocket books—dozens of them: Mickey Spillane, cowboy stuff,
science-fiction, scary stuff, sexy stuff (I know where all the
dirty words are in each and every book).

And of course, Aunt Flo's art books,
Chock full of wonderful pictures of—yep—
Naked ladies (colloquially called *nudes*).
Musn't forget those now, must we?

I play the piano in the hallway
Boogie woogie

C, G and maybe B flat
Eleven years old and I can play the blues.

Me, drunk as a skunk at a Passover Seder
Manishevitz wine does the trick
All the relatives there
Pinching my cheeks like crazy
Too much Jewishness—
Aghhh. Suffocating
Lemme outta here—
Sneak out back door when nobody is looking
Dark outside
Cut across Feldberg lawn over to Maryanne's house—

The light is on in the window
Maryanne at the door now, wearing black pedal pushers
and a yellow blouse
My heart goes *zing!* at the sight of her
Come in, come in! she says (I wonder if she can tell I'm plastered?)
She offers me a coke (as always). With ice—
The ice goes *clunk clunk clunk* in the glass.

We talk about I don't know what
Doesn't matter
I just want to listen to her talk
The sound of her voice—like music
I could listen to it forever
That's the problem. I want it to last forever
I want *everything* to last
Even drunk, I know it won't—

Marayanne's house
So...*American*
So *not*-Jewish
I want to live here. I am jealous
I want to be one of *these* people
I want to be a Christian with perfect teeth and straight hair

And a name like Jones
Hey, maybe they'll adopt me—
Shut up stupid—you're drunk!

TV, TV and more TV—
Beany and Cecil. Howdy Doody.
That word—*doody.*
I say it over and over. It tickles my tongue
Princess Summer-Fall-Winter-Spring, Clarabell, D.J.
(Dishonest John), Buffalo Bob
Hey! Where's Crusader Rabbit and Rags?

Comic books stacked high in my room
Piles and piles of them
Little Lulu, Uncle Scrooge, Donald, Mickey and Goofy
Tales From The Crypt, Mad (the 10 cent kind!)—
I go in the den (my favorite room), pop open a Coke
I can drink twelve of them in an hour and not even feel sick!

Flip on the TV
Medic with Richard Boone (he's not Paladin yet)
He has acne, but that's OK. He's cool. Major badass...
My kinda guy
77 Sunset Strip. Cheyenne. Sugarfoot, Hawaiian Eye—
Efrem Zimbalist Jr., Connie Stevens (another teenage crush)
Kookie, Kookie, lend me your comb—

Some movie producer guy lives across the street
Directs *Gunsmoke* and *Have Gun Will Travel.*
I get to go on the set! Meet Matt and Doc and Kitty
Autographs all around...
Oh man—wait'll I tell my friends back in Cleveland!

More magical summers—'55, '56, '57.
(Was I really alive then? Where did it *go?)*

Cousin Barb away at college now
I have taken over her old room
We used to share that room

One time I watched her undress in the dark
Couldn't really see much
Outline of a nipple
The clock next to the bed with the too-loud *tick-tick-ticking*
I still crave that sound 'cause it can almost get me back there
Almost...but not quite.

Lori Jones comes over to Aunt Flo's
White summer dress
Older now
Long hair
Brown from the sun
I think to myself—hmmmm, she's kind of pretty
Too young, Stu—too young
Nah, forget it
Still, I think maybe I'll look her up in a coupla more years.

Another summer
More magic
That's all—just plain magic
The nights, especially
Coke and pretzels in the den
Crickets outside
Fireflies.

Night Of The Hunter on TV with Robert Mitchum
(one scary sonofabitch of a movie).
Two kids floating down the river at night in a raft
Gorgeous black and white—
Moon reflects in the water
Mitchum up on the hill, stalking
Coming for them now—

Then out of nowhere Aunt Flo says "You know, he's a drug addict!"
I don't know what a drug addict is and I don't care
She goes on (and on and on and on)
Shut up, Aunt Flo. Please just SHUT UP will you?
Don't you get it? Mitchum is *cool!*
Just look at those eyes. Just like Elvis.

I saw him once over at the park by the merry-go-round.
Had a couple of kids with him.
I dunno...looked like a regular guy to me.
But I know he probably does secret stuff—bad stuff
I want to follow him home...spy on him
No that's not it—I want to *be* him.
I want to be *everybody* (everybody but me it seems).
How come we only get to be one person in this stupid life?

More years—
Junior high school now
I walk to school, books banging against my leg
Girls with brand new breasts, guys with brand new muscles
A whole different deal
Shitty spaghetti at lunch
Fifteen cents
I feel...*different*. At first I don't know what it is
Then I do
I'm scared—

Some kid slugs me in the stomach after school
He's bigger than me
I have an attack of cowardice
I don't fight back.
My mom picks me up after school and I am ashamed
She buys me a drumstick at the liquor store to help me feel better
Drumstick, peanuts and a Coke. *Mmmm, mmmm*—

At night I dream of how I'm going to fight the kid
Punch his stupid face into the ground in front of everyone
right in the middle of the lunch yard
Gonna have to grow some new muscles first I think—

Mickey Dolenz (pre-Monkees) walks home from school
I follow him down Moorpark, tagging along behind—
Wonder what his life is like
He's on some show called *Circus Boy*
Corky—that's his name

He has this weird underslung jaw that makes him look sort of like
a piranha fish
But *he's* on TV
I am *not* on TV
This is decidedly NOT FAIR!
I am awfully handsome I think
Handsomer than *him* anyhow
So how come *I'm* not a TV star?
Too Jewish, I guess—

More years go by—
Another summer
I drive by the Jones house
The sign out front on the mailbox. It's still there!
Eternal, oblivious to the rot and death and stink
that's gone on out there in the world.
I knock—
Hi, Maryanne Jones...

Maryanne tells me she still goes to the little church on the corner
The same merry-go-round out back
I thank the Lord for things that last
I don't want to leave—

Uncle Norm has cancer now.
He stumbles through the house naked, dazed.
"I hope I'm gonna be allright," he says
I know he will not
He will die
The house smells like death
I don't want to be near it. Don't want to smell the death.

I'm sorry, Uncle Norm. Please don't go—
Two months later he's down to under a hundred pounds
Shits in his bed
Aunt Flo waiting on him night and day
I sit by the bed...say meaningless things
He's suffering...unbearable fucking pain

Why why why why why?
I keep trying to talk to God but He won't answer me back.

A week later some doctor guy administers an OD of morphine
Norm dies in his sleep an hour later.

Another ten years
Gotta go back—
On the way over I wonder—will the Jones mailbox still be there?
I say a small prayer
They don't know it, but it's my signpost
My connection—

It's there!
The magical house on Rye St.
I knock—Maryanne comes to door
She doesn't recognize me at first
But then, she smiles that smile
She invites me inside
I sit at the counter
Cokes in the kitchen
Clunk clunk clunk in the glass
Just like old times
But not quite...
The Jones pool—the magic pool—now empty
God, it's so *small*
Could it really have been that small?

Bob Jones is gone now
Heart attack
Lori's room is empty...
Moved out—
Married to a singer or something
Her picture on the mantel
Same moon face
Still pretty
I wonder if she ever knew I phoned her once in junior high
Drove over there in my '57 Chevy to show off, but too chickenshit
to knock on the door.

We sit in silence
Then Maryanne says something terrible—
"It's not the same anymore…"
I feel like somebody just slugged me in the stomach
I don't know what to say
There's nothing *to* say
I wait until I get in my car and then bawl like a baby
all the way home.

Aunt Flo is dying now
They stick her in some goddamn little apartment with a nurse
that feeds her cereal
Her hair is white. She drools
I'm sorry Auntie Flo
I was a stinking coward
I left. I couldn't look at you like that. Feeding you with
a fucking spoon
"Bye Auntie Flo," I said as I drove down the street in my red VW
Playing the radio full blast to try to drown everything out
I knew I'd never see you again—
You died while I was in Europe that summer
I missed your funeral
The truth is, I wanted to miss it.

Please God, no more death
Please—no more—

But the cancer came. The cancer came and the brain rot came and came and came and took them all: Uncle Norm, Aunt Flo, Aunt Adeline, Aunt Charlotte, Grandma, Grandpa Jake, my Mom and Dad, cousin Barb. They all went. Just like that—
I punched holes in the wall and cursed and screamed and howled at the moon and it didn't help and I knew I was powerless.

Death death death. Hospital death, car accident death, diabetes death. Operating tables and legs hacked off and wrong diagnoses and mean-assed nurses and arrogant doctors playing God…

And nobody could do anything—it was a stupid charade
And they all just fucking died.

And then there were no more seders, no more summers, no more lawns, no more bare feet, no more firecrackers, no more Cokes, no more TV, no more, no more...and it was gone and the music and the nights and the crickets and sneaking out Barb's window and Uncle Norm and his wonderful Vitalis hair and cigars and clean starched shirt and Auntie Flo drinking coffee at the kitchen table and her saxophone over by the piano...and it was all gone—
And I didn't know why.

But you know what?
The Jones house was still there!
And I left and ten more years went by and I got married
and I moved back around the corner, and it was STILL there.
The Jones house
On the corner
The lawn freshly cut
The mailbox out front
And I thought, I'm back…I'm back!

Only I wasn't back—

And then Kathy left me and I was in the house alone by myself and I turned into Frozen Man and lay there on the couch thinking about killing myself but I was a fucking coward and I didn't have the guts and I ran out into the street and I threw the wedding ring out there and it went *cling clang cling* and cars ran over it and I watched until it was crushed and it was night and it got darker and darker and finally I went back home.

Still...something was left. I don't know what to call it but it was there. The Jones house, the mailbox, the Maryanne, the lawn, the summer, the grass, the Feldbergs, the boat, the red ants, the ice-cream truck, the streets with no curbs that you could walk barefoot on in the summer and your feet would get tough and the grass underneath your feet would feel so good, and the little church and the merry-go-round, and Annette's old house and the sidewalk where

Mickey Dolenz walked and the Ringside Liquor Store and the Shell gas station on the corner and my old house on Sarah St. and the smell of it all—yeah—it was still there and that was...well, that was a goddamn miracle! I mean, what the hell else can you call it? And then I realized something
And what I realized was this:

Something always remains.

Five more years
Grey hair now
I go by the Jones house
It's still there
No, I won't knock
Someone's in there...I see the light on inside
The light on is enough.

OK, I'm going now
So, bye Maryanne, bye Bob, bye Lori, bye Jones house,
Bye Auntie Flo, bye Uncle Norm, bye barefoot Stu, bye grass,
Bye sidewalks, bye Jerry and Jill boogerwoman.
Bye everybody, bye now—
I'm sorry you all died and I'm still here, but I can't help it.
That's just the way it worked out.

OK, gang—see you guys in heaven, OK?
Maybe I'll bring my guitar
We'll play some blues. Yeah, sure we will—nice and slow.
In B flat (the best key!) And you know what?—it'll be great.
It'll be *cool!* Really it will—I promise.

Gotta go now.
Stuff to do
You know the deal
Gotta keep busy. That's what they say—
Anyhow, I'll be seein' you all real soon
And then, well...it'll be just like old times
It'll be *summer* again—
Summer's were the best, weren't they?

Ah, shit…I'm no good at this
Never could stand goodbyes—
So...I'm outta here
Later, alligator.

Get in my car and pull away from the curb.
A block away...and I can't help it
I hang a U and drive by one more time—just for good measure.

The sign
The name on the mailbox
THE JONES'—
I sit there and stare at it. Drink it in one more time—
Trying to suck it inside myself—

Then I'm gone.

VERSE

I'M BLEEDING

I'm bleeding, I'm bleeding, from every pore and hole
In my entire body, Oy vey it's getting old
I'm bleeding from my anus, I'm bleeding from my gums
I'm bleeding from my tuchus, I'm bleeding from my thumbs

I'm bleeding from my kishkas, I'm bleeding from my face
I'm bleeding bleeding bleeding, gosh it's getting all over
the place
I'm bleeding from my eyeballs, I'm bleeding from my pores
I'm bleeding from my big black nostrils, gee everything is sore

Oh doctor dear please help me, this wound it needs a dress
It's getting on my brand new pants, it's certainly a mess
Look here I'm bleeding on the couch, goddamn it just won't stop
Will someone please call a nasty nurse, tell her to bring a mop

I want to call my mummy dear, she'll fix me right away
C'mon now doctor dearest, won't you let me have my way
Here I sit in the Kaiser waiting room, bleeding all over the place
But nobody's paying any attention, it's truly a disgrace

And now I'm getting oh so tired, the room it's getting dim
As I lie here in a pool of blood, my head's beginning to swim

I think I see an angel now, oh doesn't she look sweet
Oh gosh oh golly I'm bleeding to death, but y'know it's kinda neat!

Well here I come Lord, so if you're there, I hope you'll let
me through
Those pearly gates of heaven, though I'm just a filthy little Jew
I've tried my best to be a good boy, to live by the golden rule
To do unto others as they'd do unto me, now don't you think
that's cool?

So as the last drops drain out of me, I look to a life beyond
I just hope there'll be an angel there, and please—make her a blond
They tell me that the next life, it's got to be better than this
And that I'm sure is very true, cause bein' here ain't exactly been bliss

My mind is going blank now, I've bled and bled and bled
So here I go, now one...two...three
That's it
I'm finished
I'm
Dead.

At 2:20 a.m. on the morning of July 23, 1987, while filming a scene for Twilight Zone: The Movie, veteran character actor Vic Morrow was killed when a helicopter went out of control and crashed, decapitating Morrow in the process. This poem is dedicated to him.

VIC MORROW'S HEAD

It's four o'clock as I sit here
Sadly watching reruns of *Combat*
And I think about old Vic Morrow
And know he'll nevermore wear a hat

Not a bowler, a 10-gallon, not even a yarmulke
Be they green or blue or red
For you see our dear friend poor old Vic
No longer has a head.

I'm sure you recall that fateful day
They were filming *Twilight Zone*
Someone shouted "A helicopter's gonna crash,
Look out! It'll cut you to the bone!"

But alas Vic heard the warning
Just a little bit too late
The copter came down and loped off his cranium
And now Vic no longer has a pate!

Oh dear, oh shit, the people yelled
Leaping hither and thither and yon
They looked about for dear Vic's head
But alas it seemed to be gone!

They searched high and low and far and wide
Under every tree and rock
But old Vic's head was not to be found
It certainly was a shock!

To all of us who loved him
To all of us who cared
Vic Morrow was the baddest of the bad
Never ever was he a square.

Remember how in *Blackboard Jungle*
He called Glenn Ford "daddy-o?"
He sneered and snarled and acted real tough
Yeah old Vic knew the way to go.

In *King Creole* he bonked Elvis' dad
On the head with a big fat brick
Now even as a little kid
I thought that was pretty slick!

And when he'd flick his switchblade
You knew he was truly bad
That's why picturing him without his head
Well it really makes me sad.

After all what's a tough guy without his cranium
He's not so tough then, you'll have to admit
Why without that mean old puss of his
Vic would be just another stupid twit.

So mourn we must for poor old Vic
A true villain he really was
Not like Stallone or Bronson or Norris
Those jerks just give me the blahs.

Y'see Vic was lean and Vic was mean
It came naturally to him
From the glare in his eye to the sneer on his lip
To the stubble on his chin.

Yeah Vic was macho before it was cool to be macho
He was ugly, nasty and rough
That's why imagining a headless Vic
Don't you see it's really tough?

Now as for Mr. John Landis
For him I couldn't care less
All he's got to deal with is a lawsuit
Heck, he didn't even stop to clean up the mess!

For losing a head, well it gets pretty bloody
If you want to know the truth
I mean it's not like Vic suffered a broken bone
Or the removal of his tooth.

See, Vic lost that thing that made him Vic
That impenetrable, inscrutable face
And goodness knows, that ain't no way to die
I mean heck, it's a real disgrace.

To be a headless villain
Why that's a plain silly thought
And once you lose a head, it's gone
A new one can't simply be bought!

I'll bet he didn't grumble though
I'll bet he took it like a man
Even though in his heart of hearts
Vic knew it'd be his last suntan.

Yes, Vic Morrow was a man among men
I'm telling you he was mean
And even when he went through this terrible time
I'll bet he didn't make a scene.

Now I know what you are thinking
How could he, after all
For he'd passed on from this life
But hell that's not so bad at all!

When you stop and think about the daily grind
The boredom, the struggle, the strife
You'll see that dying, it ain't so bad
I mean, hell, what's one silly little life?

That's what Vic would've said
I know I'm right
I'll prove it if I can
Vic wouldn't have whined about losing his head
He'd have taken it like a man.

So if you want to remember Vic
The man we all loved and knew
Just wipe away that tear in your eye
And I know he'd be proud of you.

Yes dry your eyes and steel your heart
For though Vic may be gone
Inside our hearts and inside our minds
He'll live on and on and on.

So sing the song and walk on young man
And think not of the dead
And when you start feeling sorry for yourself
Just think about Vic Morrow's head.

VERSE

HOW TO LIVE A STUPID LIFE

Get born
Develop an Oedipus complex
Go to school
Quit school
Wonder why you're here
Get no answers
Fall in love
Get rejected
Fall in love again
You reject her this time
You realize this is better
Work at a bunch of jobs you don't care about
Quit those jobs and go to Europe
Go into therapy
After five years realize that therapy is stupid
Get freaked out at around 30 that life is passing you by
Get married
Realize that you hate your wife
Get divorced
Get really freaked out that life is passing you by
Talk to people about this
Realize that nobody knows what they're doing

Get religious
Join a cult
Get out of the cult
Get totally freaked out that there are no answers
Pray to God for answers
Get none
Read the obituary columns to see how many of your friends are dying
Pray to God some more for answers
Get none
Become a Christian as a last resort
Turn into a boring person
Quit Christianity after getting completely disgusted with it
Get totally depressed
Watch a lot of TV
Remember your life
Make times that were really shitty good when you're remembering
Watch more TV
Think about asking God again for answers
Say fuck it, there are no answers and this is all really stupid
Get totally freaked out and despondent
Sit around and do nothing of value
Sit around some more
Get to like sitting around
Get old
Get older
Get older still
Get cancer or one of those diseases
Die.

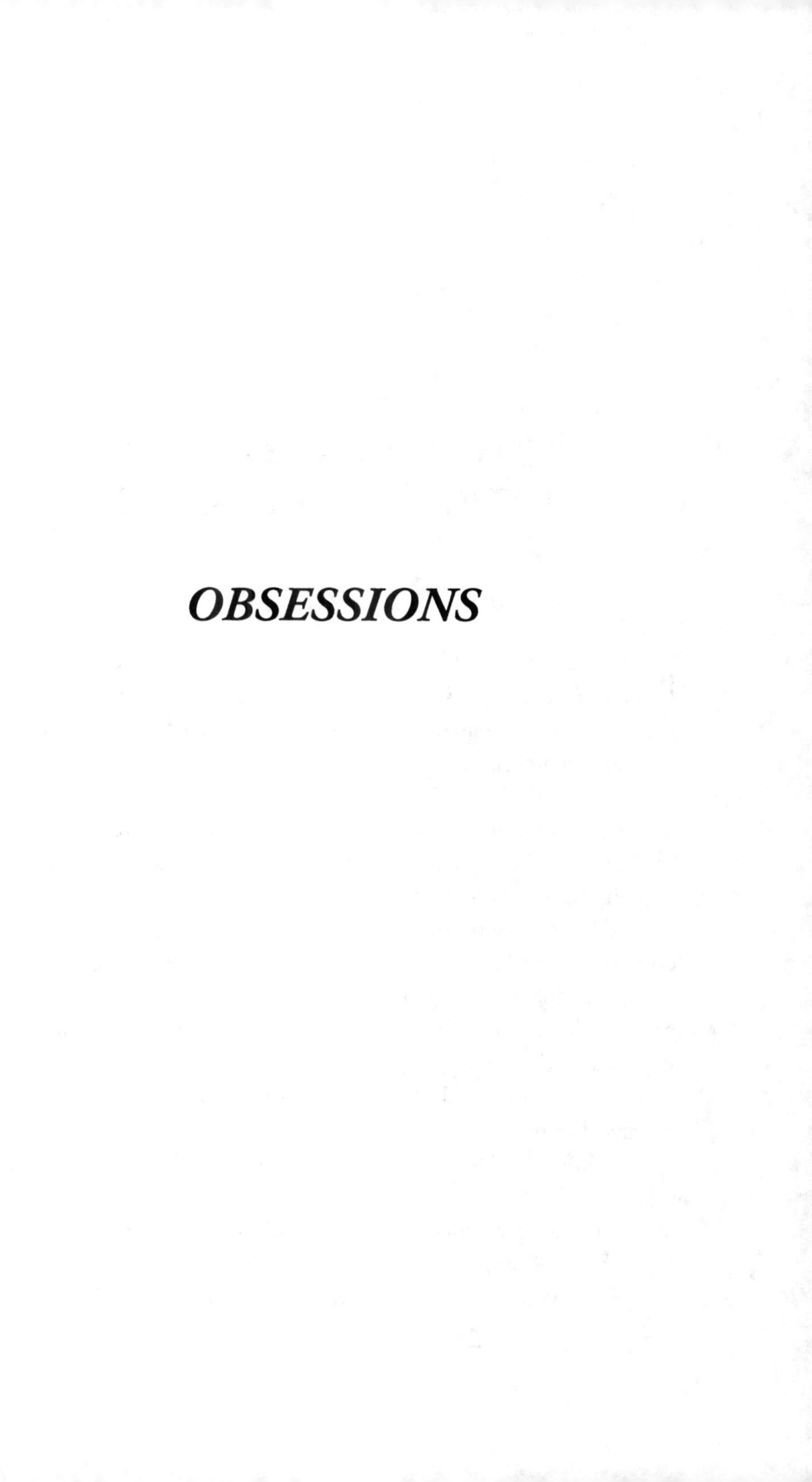

OBSESSIONS

OBSESSIONS

UNTER DER EGG UND UNTER DER ARKARDEN

It was just past midnight when they met on the staircase. Everyone else in the old Swiss schoolhouse was fast asleep, and it was dead quiet. They sat silently in the darkness for a while, just listening.

She lit a cigarette.

As the match flared, he saw the outline of her face. How beautiful she was, he thought. He wanted badly to touch her, but he felt afraid. Actually, what he wanted to do most was just to reach over and touch her hair, but he couldn't. Not yet.

They sat like that for a while, tearing off huge hunks from the long loaf of bread and chewing noisily. Soon, he took a fingerful of the jam they'd stolen from the kitchen and smooshed it on her face. For a moment she seemed shocked, but then she started laughing, and soon they were both laughing.

She got a handful of jam and put it in his hair, until they were convulsed in fits.

"Shhhhh, shhhhh," she giggled through cupped palms. "We'll wake everyone!"

They both decided at the same instant. Of *course!* They'd run away! It was *perfect.*

Silently, they went to their rooms to pack their clothes.

By 3:00 a.m. they'd gotten their stuff, crept silently through the halls, and out the front door.

There, the night. Cold, black, silent.

They padded through the empty streets, across the fields and down the hill to the little train depot. A cowbell clanged in the distance. The train wouldn't be coming for another couple of hours and it was cold—freezing cold.

She was wearing that green parka thing—the one given to her by her brother who'd drowned in the swimming pool accident. It was awfully thin, so he let her get inside the thick wool sweater with him to keep warm.

Ah, there.

Soon she was asleep, snoring just a little.

He looked down at her, at her straight brown hair, so unlike his own mop of black kink. At her soft features.

He especially loved her mouth. On one side, the lip had a tiny flaw. It sort of went down over her teeth, just a little bit. He traced his finger along the outline of the lip and felt the warm breath coming from her nostrils. How heavily she breathed!

Just before dawn the train arrived, shocking them both out of sleep. They decided on Nice. Sure, why *not?* The French Riviera! *Real* food—after all that vegetarian crap. Swimming…suntans… warm water!

Later that day, they changed trains at Montreux. There, they walked the streets and gazed at all the stuff in the store window—jewelry, trinkets, and a million watches. Oh, it was junk all right—but somehow it was better than the junk in America.

And then they found these wonderful postcards—cows, just after the slaughter. Blood poured from the open wounds where they'd been freshly beheaded. They bought a whole handful. The first one was sent back to the people at the school. It was a particularly bloody one.

"Hi there! Wish you were here!"

Hah! Take that, you vegetarian sissies! You macrobiotic assholes!

As soon as they arrived in Nice, they went shopping. She bought a black bikini that would show off her skinny, muscular body. And she bought him a pair of silly orange corduroy pants—very French and all.

For the next few days, all they did was eat and swim and sit on the beach, watching all of the curious French people (how *French* they all looked!) and get black black black from the sun.

Oh man, that sun felt so good!

At night, they'd go to this one little cafe and sit and drink wine or beer, and play the jukebox, which was full of good American songs—not the stupid French stuff. She played "The Sounds Of Silence," over and over, and once, she actually started crying. He thought it was kind of dumb; but years later, after she'd died, whenever he'd hear that song, he would always remember the scene.

Late at night they'd lie on the bed in their upstairs flat and watch the whores on the street. They especially liked this one old whore.

"Look how *serious* she is," she said. "She's not like the rest."

Sometimes they tried to wave at her or to get her to notice them, but she'd never look up. Strictly business.

But it's funny how quickly good things can turn bad. It happened one night just after they'd made love. He noticed that she was crying.

"What's wrong?" he asked, but she wouldn't answer him.

Finally she said, "We can't do that anymore."

He didn't understand. "But...*why?"* he asked, stung.

"We just *can't*—that's all."

And then she turned her back to him and went to sleep.

He lay awake, looking out the window at the blinking neon from the bar across the street. He looked for the old whore, but she was gone.

He didn't know what time it was, but he could tell that soon it would be morning. He tried and tried in his head to keep it from being morning. He didn't want to see the light, but he knew he couldn't stop it. He kept thinking maybe she'd wake up and say, "Oh, it was just one of my moods" (she was quite moody), but she didn't.

In the morning they waked to the little cafe for coffee and croissants. They didn't look at each other as they walked. They both knew it was bad.

"Shall we get the train back?" she finally said.

"I guess so," he answered glumly. He just felt dead inside.

On the train they were both silent. She smoked a bit, then she fell asleep on his shoulder. He noticed that she had a tiny nosebleed, and he took his finger and swiped at the trickle of blood which was coming from her nostril. He put the finger to his lips. It tasted sweet.

The train changed at Lucerne. It was just past midnight when they arrived. The conductor told them another train wouldn't come 'till morning. The train station was gray and rather depressing, so they decided to walk the streets.

The town was silent—so silent. There were little lights shining from all the windows, yet nobody seemed to be behind them. Their heels went *clippity-clop, clippity-clop* on the cobblestone street, as they walked.

Soon they came to a very old bridge. In the full moonlit night, a thousand spider webs were silhouetted. It was very beautiful—yet somehow it didn't look quite real.

The bridge had a mural painted on it. In the mural scene, many skull people on horseback were slaughtering the people of the town. The skull people were terrible, but their horses—all muscle and power and steam coming from their nostrils—were even more frightening.

The skull people seemed to be smiling as they thrust their spears and their swords of steel through the bodies of the townspeople, as they tried to run away. Some of the people writhed on the ground, as the skull people laughed and drove their long spears through their hearts.

For some time they stood and looked at the mural.

"This isn't good," she said after awhile. "I want to go from here." Her voice sounded funny.

They walked some more. After some time they came to a gray and very silent part of the town. There seemed to be no life there at all. At the very end of the street, a single lamp shone down upon a sign affixed to a wall. They came closer in order to read it. The sign read:

UNTER DER EGG, UND UNTER DER ARKARDEN.

There was at once something terribly silly and yet awful about the sign. It seemed important to know what it meant—but neither of them could read German.

They both read the sign aloud, laughing—but kind of a forced laugh. "God," he said. "That's *terrible!*" He looked at it again.

"I wonder what it means?"

"I don't think we're supposed to know," she said. "It's just... *Unter der egg und unter der arkarden.*"

He knew that she was right. She was, he thought, very wise for someone so young.

After awhile they made their way back to the train station, where they sat on a wooden bench by a fountain.

A cloud passed in front of the moon.

She was having her period, and her underwear was soaked with blood.

She had no tampons, so she took off her pants and underwear and threw the soaking panties behind some bushes.

He watched her naked bottom in the moonlight, but he had no desire to touch her.

Something was in the air. Something peculiar, something strong…maybe even a bit foreboding. It had a story to tell.

She sat on a wall and lit a cigarette, and suddenly he was overcome with despair. It just welled up inside him like black vomit. It was very bad.

Soon he came over, got on his knees, and buried his face in her stomach.

What he really wanted was to put his face into her crotch, into her cunt…to have his face wet with blood.

More, he wanted to *be* in her stomach, to crawl up inside there—inside the warmth and the wetness and just to be in there, surrounded by blackness.

She seemed to know, but she said nothing. He was crying and sort of praying to himself now, and she told him it was OK and pressed his face harder into her stomach.

Near dawn the train came. They were both so goddamn cold and tired by then that the warm car seemed like a blessing from heaven.

They shared the car with an old man, a soldier, and a stoic German girl with a fat, black mole on her cheek. They all nodded greetings to one another but said nothing. The soldier offered him a cigarette, but he said no. The German girl stared coldly and snuffled.

After awhile, she put her head on his lap and promptly fell asleep. In the dim morning light of the car he looked down at her. *God, what a wonderful face*, he thought. He couldn't believe how beautiful she was...how wonderful she smelled. Always that smell...

He looked at her—at the faint trace of a moustache, at the little flaw in her lip, at her lovely swan-like neck, at the many different colors in her hair. He put his hand inside her shirt, on her naked breast, and felt her heart.

Still she slept.

He felt the heart pounding—oh so fast it seemed.

Someday, he thought to himself, this heart will stop. It seemed impossible, yet he knew it was so.

Soon the sound of the train and the warmth of the car made him drowsy.

He fought sleep. There seemed to be something terrible in it—something to do with the strange sign and the skull people and their awful smiles and great, gleaming swords.

But soon the sleep began to overtake him, and suddenly he was whooshed into a gray place—a long, gray place full of speed and sound and dizzying nothingness.

OBSESSIONS

A DIMESTORE TALE

Once upon a time there was a young boy. He lived in a room. The room was on the second floor of a house, but the boy didn't know who lived in the other part of the house because he did not ever come out of the room. There may have been other people in the house. There may not have. That is not important.

Sometimes in the deep of the night, the boy would arise from his bed and go stand at the window. Down below, on the front lawn—under a lone tree—stood a wolf.

The wolf had yellow eyes and sharp teeth and a long red tongue. It was looking up at the boy standing in the window. The boy looked down at the wolf, and as he did, the wolf smiled up at him.

Then the wolf called to the boy in his soft language.

"Come down little boy. Come down," said the wolf.

But the boy would not come down. Of course not—for if he did, he knew that the wolf would eat him!

Yet something inside the boy called to go down—that is, something of himself actually *wanted* to go down. Something in him wanted to feel the bright, sharp horror as the wolf took him into his grasp. Into his mouth.

But the boy did not go down. No. He stayed in his room and did things. Many things.

He read many books—books of lands far away. Books about pirates and spaceships and dashing men with glittering swords. Stories of men who had fists of steel—stories of the good men and the bad men and the Supermen and the Robin Hoods and how they came charging in and beat the bad guys down, down—into the bush. The bad guys were crying—yes they were. Oh, it was sweet!

And so the boy stayed in his Story Room, for that is what it was. It was a room in which to have adventures. To explore. To find magical things.

Oh, yes—one more thing.

Our boy knew a secret. And the secret was this: as long as he stayed in the room, *nothing* could ever hurt him.

Outside was the wolf, and many other terrible things as well. But as long as the boy stayed in the room, none of these bad things could touch him. He could not be harmed in any way.

All right.

Now you understand.

One night the boy did something strange. There was no explanation for it, really.

What he did was this: he reached into a cabinet in the room and pulled out a can of shaving cream (the boy kept all of his things in the room!) It was the old fashioned kind—the really thick, puffy kind of shaving cream. *You* remember—the kind that came in bright red and blue striped aerosol cans.

Now the boy went to the window, carrying the can of shaving cream with him. He opened the window—then he took some of the shaving cream and squirted it into the palm of his hand. Then, the boy began to send the little puffs of shaving cream floating out the window.

Down and down and down went the puffs. To where, it was impossible to say. They just floated off into the sky.

Somehow it was all a part of something much bigger. Something the boy could feel, but that he had no name for. The shaving cream puffs floating off into the sky…out the window...out into the cool summer night air—into the darkness.

And so the boy sent the shaving cream puffs floating off into the night.

Whoooosh. Off they went!

Bye, bye.

Down below, in the yard, under the tree, something moved.

The boy squinted his eyes. He thought perhaps it was the wolf, watching him. But no matter how hard he looked, he saw nothing.

After all the shaving cream puffs had been sent off on their journey, the boy climbed into his bed. The sheets were clean and white and cool.

Then the boy pulled the blankets right up to his neck. Then he settled back into the pillows.

Ahhhhh—

After a while, the boy began to do something. It is a bit difficult to describe, but if you listen carefully, you'll understand.

What the boy would do is this: he would let his mind float outside of his head. It was not a magical feat or anything like that. In fact, it was a very simple thing to do.

And so the boy's mind would float out of his head, like the puffs of shaving cream floating out the window.

First, it would float up to the ceiling, where it would bounce around—*ping! ping!*—Like that. Soon—when it got comfortable in its new surroundings—the mind would float off to other places. While it was out there, the mind would grow to various sizes—kind of like a balloon that gets bigger or smaller as it needs to.

Now came the really nice part. Once he knew that his mind was happily (and safely) on its own little adventure outside of his head, the boy would do the second part of his special trick.

He had a name for it.

He called it simply, "melting."

What he would do is—the boy would kind of go all soft inside. He would melt himself away until everything outside of him began to come inside him.

Oh, it was *magic* all right! No doubt about that.

What would happen is—the empty space inside the boy was so big—think of the Grand Canyon, if you wish—that it could fit all kinds of things into itself.

Do you see?

Of course you do!

And so, with all that space, the boy could let all kinds of things come inside him so that he could taste them and smell them and sample all the different treats—because that's exactly what they were.

Special treats.

Sometimes the things would be like food or music. Or perhaps they were like two children floating down a river at night. The moon is hanging over them in the sky and they're floating down there on a raft—fast asleep. The moon is bright yellow and hangs low in the sky. And down below, in the water—deep down at the bottom of the river—is a woman. She is dead, and she is very beautiful. Her hair floats out from her head and her eyes are open and they are blue and they are nice. She is down there in the water and she is dead and it is good because the water is a very peaceful place to be and it wraps around you and keeps you safe.

And up above, the two sleeping children would be floating down the river, fast asleep on their magical wooden raft. And the best part of all, you see, was that was only the tippy-top of the thing—the thing that floated around inside the boy's head.

Much of the inside of the thing was water.

Or things in water.

Fish floated by saying, *hullo, hullo...*

They made those curious little O things with their mouths and looked about with their big goggle-eyes, all happy and amazed.

Many things would float by in the water. People waving. Ships in bottles. Children flying kites. Even a girl in a black sweater, I think.

Her name is Julie.

She is beautiful and has blonde hair that floats out from her head in long tendrils.

And so the boy would swim around in the water that was in the space inside his head where his mind used to be. He was inside himself, you see, and he could just float around in there.

It was a very sweet feeling, this swimming around inside your own head, because you could go upside down or right side up or *waaaaay* down to the bottom—deep, deep—down by the funnel (some people preferred to call it a drain).

And down there you could look up through the crystal blue of the water, and you weren't really upside down or right side up, because of course we all know that inside a mind there *is* no up or down or right or left or anything like that.

So our boy could play like that for hours, or even for days at a time, if he wished. And finally, when he was done melting, he would sleep. And when he slept, his mind (which had been bouncing around on the ceiling, having a fine old time) would come back inside his head. *Bloop!* And then it, too, would fall asleep, because it was very tired from having its own set of adventures...exploring all the nooks and crannies of the boy's room.

So you see, all these things worked together, and that is what made it so nice. And it could happen again and again. The boy had learned the trick of doing it, even though he didn't think of it as a trick.

All right, now we'll tell you another story. Our boy is sleeping now—so let's just let him sleep for a bit. Don't worry, we'll come back to him after he's had his rest.

This story is about a parakeet. A parakeet named Samson. Somebody had named Samson *Samson*, but we do not know who. Maybe it was our boy, or maybe it was somebody else. It doesn't matter, really.

Samson was your typical parakeet. An ordinary, green parakeet—that's what he was.

Samson lived in a cage with several other parakeets in a Kresge's five-and-dime store in a nice neighborhood in Shaker Heights, Ohio. The dimestore was full of all the things that are always in dimestores—needles and thread, clothes (cheap but clean), red-checked tablecloths, a section of candies, books, magazines, balls of yarn, bottles, picture frames... Oh, *you* know—all these kinds of things!

Samson lived in the part of the store where the animals were kept. There were, beside himself, lots of other birds. They were a very noisy bunch indeed!

Also, the store contained many aquariums filled with fish and snails and things. Little bubbles went *bloop, bloop, bloop*—and the store owners played *"How Much Is That Doggie In the Window"* on a small radio that they kept behind the counter.

All of the ladies who worked in the dimestore were old and very nice. One lady—old Mrs. Curry—would feed Samson every day.

She'd give him clean water and fresh birdseed, and every so often—for a special treat—she'd stick in a piece of fresh green celery, which she knew was Samson's favorite.

"There you go, birdie," Mrs. Curry would say. She kind of chirped when she said it. She was really very old, and Samson knew she probably wouldn't be around very much longer.

One day, a young woman and her son came into the dimestore. The woman was very pretty, with dark shiny hair and a very nice smile.

Her boy was named Norman.

Norman was not quite so nice as his mother. He would sometimes do mean things—mostly to his little sister, Sippie. But fortunately, Norman was not the kind of mean child that would later grow up into a terrible person or anything like that. No—he just liked to play tricks on people, which many children do, you must admit.

So Norman and his mother brought Samson home and put him in his cage on a wooden table in the dining room and they fed him every day. On special occasions, they would let Samson out of his cage so that he could fly around and explore the house.

But the problem was, Samson would always get lost or try and hide in the curtains or behind the couch.

Finally, Norman's mother told him that Samson had to stay in his cage.

One day, Norman was home alone. His mother was at work at the dance studio—which was located above a delicatessen in a not-so-nice part of Cleveland.

She had to work long hours, especially after her husband (a rather rotund man, jovially referred to by his friends simply as "Fat Pete") had died of a liver ailment.

On this particular day, Norman decided that he'd let Samson out of his cage.

Poor old Samson needed to fly around—stretch his wings and all that stuff.

Norman's mother would only be gone for a little while, she had told him.

Now, while Samson was flying around, batting into the curtains and windows (Samson was a bit retarded, if you must know the truth),

Norman went down into the basement, where he had a secret room that was all his own.

He kept all his special things in there—his chemistry set, his inventions (stink bombs and such), his comic book collection (*Uncle Scrooge* and *Little Lulu* were his favorites!), his electric trains—all of his favorite things. Norman even had a lock on the door of his secret room and a big sign posted on the door saying KEEP OUT!

Well, what happened was this. You've probably already guessed it. While Norman was down in his secret room, working on one of his inventions, Samson accidentally flew right into the gas burner on the kitchen stove. Norman's mother had left last night's beef stew warming up on the stove, and Samson flew right, smack into the fire and burned up—just like that!

When poor Norman came upstairs from his secret basement room, he found Samson lying on the kitchen floor, right near the stove. He was all brown and crispy. He didn't really even look much like a parakeet anymore.

Norman was very scared of what his mother would do to him when she got back home. He thought of going out and buying another parakeet, but he knew *that* probably wouldn't work. His mother was too smart for that—and besides, Norman had a way of looking guilty when he did bad things (which was fairly often).

Instead, what Norman did, is—he carried Samson out into the back yard and buried him. He decided that whatever punishment his mother gave him, he deserved it, and he'd take it like a man.

But then another thing happened. It was kind of bad.

As Norman's mother was leaving the dance studio, she was hit by a car—a green, 1953 Plymouth sedan, to be exact. She was killed instantly, they said. The driver of the car that killed her was never found.

By now you have probably already guessed that Norman is the boy who lived alone in the room that he never came out of. So really, this isn't two stories at all—it's just *one* story. A story with many parts. But in order to understand this story, you'll have to go along with the fact that it must be told in a very precise order. Otherwise, it will simply not make any sense at all.

All right, then. Now that you understand that, let us go back to the boy sleeping upstairs in his room. You now know that his name is Norman. He is nine years old and he doesn't go to school. He doesn't do any of the things that most nine-year-old boys do. He is indeed, a very special (if somewhat neurotic) boy.

Unfortunately, as Norman is sleeping, a terrible thing happens.

A wicked old witch (who had been hiding in Norman's closet) decides to put a spell on Norman. Since Norman likes to sleep, the old hag decides that a Sleeping Curse would be very appropriate.

So the witch waves her magic wand and—presto!—Norman is put into a deep, deep sleep. The witch decides that Norman will stay asleep for 30 years.

And that, my friends, is where our story ends—at least for the time being.

Don't worry, though—Norman's adventures will resume—we *promise* you. And with that, we leave you with the traditional—(to be continued).

And it really will—we promise you!

OBSESSIONS

PERFECTMAN

When I was growing up, I didn't want to be Superman, Batman, or The Green Hornet—none of those guys. Nope, I wanted to be (am I *really* gonna admit this?)

Perfectman.

Yep, it's true. I'm not exactly sure when it started, but I can remember as far back as the third grade sitting in class and drawing these faces on my notebook. It was always the same face—the profile of a man with a straight, aquiline nose, well-set mouth, good square jaw, steely eyes, and blonde hair...with just a little bit hanging over the forehead. I didn't know who he was at the time.

It was only later I'd give him a name—Perfectman. (Jesus, this is embarrassing.)

I didn't know much about Perfectman. I doubt if he was even particularly intelligent. But that didn't matter. He was *perfect*. And I wanted to be him. (There, it's out.)

Alas, even at that early stage in life, it was painfully obvious that I was not. All I saw when I looked in the mirror was my roundish face, my (even then) Jewish nose, and curly (make that kinky) hair.

God, how I *hated* that hair! I tried everything under the sun to make it normal, finally settling on a suspicious (and very smelly) product called Perma-Strate, which my poor mother had to travel to the black section of Cleveland in order to purchase.

Still, straight hair was an absolute prerequisite for being perfect.

Then there were the clothes.

Back in junior high, I strong-armed my parents into buying me hundreds of dollars worth of these extremely "in-crowd" shirts. Sir Guys, they were called. My closet was filled with the god-damned things.

Of course, I worked on my hair constantly, gunking it down with Fitch Brilliantine or even sometimes plain old Vaseline. I'd pat it, push it, pull it, and I'd bring down that little piece *just right* over my forehead—just like Elvis.

Actually, one time this girl told me I looked just like Frankie Avalon.

Hell, who was I to argue? The problem was that the girl—Carol Black—was far from perfect herself.

Come to think of it, she looked sort of like Karl Malden.

Oh, how poor Carol pined for me, but I was having none of it. I, you see, was in love with Laurel Whittaker, a lovely young thing made up of equal parts Annette Funicello, Cheryl Holdridge, and Sandra Dee (that's two Mousketeers and one Gidget, so you can see where *I* was at).

Laurel and I went out a few times...even did a bit of smooching, but one terrible night she told me she thought it'd be better if we'd just be friends (remember *that* line?).

Needless to say, I was heartbroken.

Still, all through high school I kept up my quest. Studies be damned! My priorities were firmly established. Being Perfectman was what I craved!

Oh, he was no longer the guy on my third grade notebook. In fact his face changed many times over the years—though it was always an approximation of the same guy. Elvis, Fabian, James Darren, Robert Culp (*Robert Culp?*), Steve McQueen, Tony Dow (notice all the blonds?), Clint Eastwood—all made their way onto the list. But no matter who the model, I was never *quite* there.

But one of the (few) nice things about growing older is that I've become more and more comfortable ignoring styles, trends, looks, and fads (all the guises of Perfectman).

Somewhere in my 20s, I realized that his hold on me was lessening.

Nevertheless, a couple of years back, noticing my ever-growing pot belly, I plunked down my money and joined the Holiday Health Spa.

The only problem is that I hate exercising, though I *do* find that I enjoy the ritual—the basic sweat and stink of it all. And occasionally, just like the other guys (who ever said men aren't vain?), I catch myself flexing the old biceps in front of the mirror.

Yep, old Perfectman, still at work.

I rather enjoy watching the people at the spa. It's always a good show.

One of the more curious things about the men there is that they all seem to be either grimacing or smiling—I really can't tell which. I guess perhaps they're sort of smiling *painfully*.

My problem is, I can't figure out what they're smiling *about*, unless they're secretly delighted just to be at the gym, getting in shape.

The worst thing, though is, if you don't watch it, *you* start doing it too. And I don't know about you—but I don't want to be walking around with some crazy grin on my face.

By contrast, the women at the spa all look fairly grim.

It's no wonder though—the old Perfect Monster is *really* on their backs.

For the women, the whole thing is also kind of a style show.

Boy, do they ever get decked out!

Still, if they don't meet the criteria for perfection, which is pretty much the same as it's always been (blonde hair, big tits, tiny waist), all the Danskins and legwarmers in the world ain't gonna make a bit of difference.

I have this one friend—a very pretty girl—who happens to be short, very dark-haired, and has a slight tendency to gain weight. Now when she goes to the spa, she gets out there in her leotards and twitches her little butt all over the place. But alas, she just can't seem to meet any "real" men. "The only guys who try to hit on me," she complained, "are Iranians and Mexicans!"

Now, personally, I wouldn't give one of those Danskin/legwarmer bimbos the time of day.

No way, José.

Those chicks *scare* me!

No, give me a girl who looks like Mariel Hemingway (before the silicone implants)—a girl with voodoo eyes and a pawn-shop heart. Somebody who's strong (hearty is a better word), maybe a little bit sad (but not *too*); somebody who knows how to be *quiet*.

And for God's sake, give her a couple of flaws.

Maybe a slight overbite (I'm a sucker for those)—even a tiny little limp.

Make her somebody who likes to wear dresses...maybe even green knee socks and scuffed up loafers.

Yeah, *that's* my kind of gal.

Hey, now don't get me wrong. I like them ol' big-titted blondes as much as the next guy and sure—I'd love to grudge-fuck Charlize Theron up against a brick wall—but for anything more than a quickie—*forget* it, Charlie.

Nah, I'll take a chick that looks like a French newsboy *any* day over some goddamn Drew Barrymore zombie.

Those poor goddamn women!

Do you even *begin* to realize what they go through just so they can look like an approximation of Wynona Ryder?

Face lifts, breast implants, thigh suctions, tummy tucks—

The cutting of the flesh, baby.

Know what I saw the other day in one of those fitness magazines? An ad by some doctor who'll surgically implant something in a woman's nipples to keep them permanently erect!

Jesus God...let them have *nipples erecti*, so that they can put on a T-shirt and go parading around the mall and watch the junkies drool all over themselves.

Dear Lord—save me from the dreaded Perfect Monster!

See, the deal is, you've got to give it up.

Kick the habit.

Drop it like a goddamn hot potato.

And it ain't easy, my friend, because *everything* out there makes us want it all the more.

But I've got a little tip for you.

You say you wanna kick the Perfect Jones for good?

Okay, it's simple.

Just go down to the hospital—any one will do—and walk around one of the wards for a while.

Don't pick any lightweight stuff.

Hit the post-op or the cancer ward if possible.

Walk past the rooms.

Stop, and look inside.

Take your time; nobody'll bother you.

Listen to the moans and groans.

Check out the hollow-eyed people staring up at the ceilings.

God, look at all those tubes going into all the orifices.

Listen to the rattles in the chests.

Jesus, *look out!* You almost knocked over that old guy—the one shuffling down the hallway, lugging that catheter bag.

God will you look how *slo-o-ow-ly* he walks.

How every step is *painful.*

And yet you'd swear he's…yeah he *is*—he's *smiling.*

Almost as if he's *thankful* for every step he takes.

Wait a sec. Don't leave yet.

Stick around, relax.

You need to breathe in the smell of people dying.

Feel the death—you *can*, you know.

Feel it flitting through the hallway, in and out of the rooms.

Breathe it in. Smell it, inhale it. Let it soak into your bones.

Had enough?

Okay, let's get the hell out of here.

Listen, I'm telling you—it works!

You're gonna walk out of that hospital, out into the sunshine, and you're gonna look up, and you're gonna thank the Lord that you've got all four limbs—and if you've only got three you're gonna thank him for *those.*

And the best part is, that old Perfect Monster isn't gonna be anywhere around.

But listen, there's one thing I forgot to tell you.

I was at the gym the other day and I finally saw him.

Perfectman—that's who!

Yep, he was in the shower stall right next to mine.

I'll admit it, the guy was fucking *beautiful.*

That face—the perfectly proportioned bone structure.

The body of a Greek god.

No doubt about it—he was the guy in my third grade drawing come to life.

And then, God forgive me, I glanced down at his crotch.

I just *had* to see—you understand, don't you?

And when I finally did, I was hit by a wave of shock.

For there—where there should have been a mighty salami-of-a-John-Holmes-schlong—was the *tiniest* little weenie I've ever seen in my entire life.

I'm not kidding...we're talking *microscopic.*

Oh, God—that poor man....

What he must go through every time some hot 'n' horny chick comes onto him—raking her nails across his perfectly hairless chest, kissing his nipples, traveling down his stomach, down down down... slowly slipping off his shorts and then—*surprise*—

Heeeeeeeere's Johnny!

Now that, my friends, isn't poetic justice—that's just one motherfucking cruel twist of fate.

But that's how the old Perfect Monster works, y'see?

I got dressed and split.

Outside the gym I passed a group of semi-perfect Spa People hanging out in the sun, showing off the old bods.

I got in my car and sat for a minute, just watching.

The parking lot was full of people carting bags full of groceries to their nondescript little cars.

Somehow, all of the Parking Lot People looked bent or slightly deformed in one way or another. Not badly or anything—but they were all just a little bit *off.*

Then I noticed that occasionally one or two of the Parking Lot People would glance sort of longingly over at the Spa People.

But the Spa People refused to acknowledge them.

They just kept on flexing and jabbering away.

They were sort of Spa Snobs, I suppose.

The Parking Lot People continued their sad little treks to their cars with their bags full of Spaghetti-O's and Spam and stuff.

I wanted to tell them that it was really okay…that the Spa People were really no better off—in fact they were *worse* off—because they didn't know that you couldn't *be* perfect.

I wanted to tell them that some of the Spa People would probably even *be* Parking Lot People someday—but I finally decided against it.

You can't tell people stuff like that. You really can't.

I sat for a while and watched some more, but I knew if I stayed much longer I'd start to get depressed.

And there's nothing worse than being depressed, sitting in your car in some crazy parking lot when it's about 100 degrees outside.

Finally, I gunned my engine—flipped on the radio to my favorite evangelist—and headed over to the 7-Eleven to get a sandwich and a copy of the *National Enquirer.*

OBSESSIONS

THE KID FROM CLEVELAND

C*leveland, Ohio*—I know. You don't have to tell me. You can't go home again. But just for the hell of it, I'm gonna give it a try.

I'm on a mission here, you see. A sort of Proustian pilgrimage back to the place where I grew up. I haven't been here for almost 30 years. Now I'm a man. And yet, over those years, this place has—in some strange and very powerful way—inhabited my being. For no matter what guises I've assumed, underneath it all I've always felt like I was really, well—just a kid from Cleveland.

It's funny. Everybody I meet here says the same thing. "Oh yes, you really must see…*blah blah blah*," they say. How do I explain to them that I don't *care* about how Cleveland has progressed—that I don't *want* to see anything new. That the new is my *enemy*.

What's important to me aren't even specific places. It's more… well…smells, corners, certain angles—perhaps the way the shadows are cast at a particular time of day.

First, I drive to the corner of Kinsman and Lee—a personal landmark.

I am in shock. What was once the place where I used to spend countless lazy Saturday afternoons is now nothing but a burnt-out array of second-hand stores, grubby burger joints, and empty shop fronts.

I am mortified. But *there*—across the street—my first school: Moreland Elementary.

Aside from a slight sense of smallness, it looks uncannily the same.

I cross the street and walk onto the playground.

Something about the way the grass is shaped into little hillocks—the roundness of everything—causes a wave of nausea to pass over me.

A large rock embedded in the grass gets my attention.

Of course!

Hey you…*rock!* Remember *me?* The kid who used to go to school here in the first grade.

Yeah, that's right…I'm *back!*

Though it looks positively forbidding, I go inside the building. The polished emptiness of the corridor hits me. There is a knot in the pit of my stomach.

What is it?

Then I recognize it. That old, sickening sensation of being in school on the first day.

For a few seconds I am, deliciously, seven years old again. I look around the halls, terrified, afraid that a teacher will come out and scold me.

Giddy with the sensation, I split.

I drive down Van Aken Boulevard to Shaker Square.

My God, there it is! Pristine. Untouched. That wonderful circle of neat brown-and-white shops where I spent so many wonderful boyhood hours.

I park my car and begin walking.

Immediately, the memories come flooding back.

Drinking cherry Cokes in the colony drugstore. Reading movie star magazines and comics. Buying my very first record ("Black Denim Trousers and Motorcycle Boots"). Getting caught for throwing tomatoes in Stanyon's department store. Sitting in the Rapid Transit coffee shop, listening to "Short Fat Fannie" and "Don't Be Cruel" on the jukebox.

As I walk around the square, every archway, every brick, seems pregnant with meaning. They seem to tease...not quite willing to reveal themselves to me.

How odd. How strange that the world has gone on—that people have walked in space, wars have been fought, people been born, people have died—and through it all, these buildings have been right here.

At the moment, it seems nothing short of miraculous.

Sitting on a bench, I spy a wizened old bum, who, over the next three days, I will constantly see here.

As is my custom, I give him a name. He is christened (what else?) the Shaker Square Bum.

This guy bothers me. Some bums are happy being bums—but this guy looks like somebody who *wasn't* a bum once, and doesn't like being one now. Worse, his eyes are yellow. He looks like death warmed over.

I want him to go away. Somehow, he's a bad omen.

Back in my hotel room, I leaf frantically through the phone book, trying to look up names of old friends.

Wait a second! What are you…crazy? You're talking thirty years, man! Naturally, nobody I remember is listed.

Still, somehow I keep expecting the phone to ring:

"Hey, kid…is it really you? Are you really back?"

But the phone doesn't ring.

This depresses me.

I comfort myself with massive doses of junk food from the machine in the hall.

The next day, I've arranged to go back to Ludlow, my second elementary school.

Here, I make the rounds of the classes, being greeted by kids in each who are anxious to meet the "famous writer" from L.A.

A gap-toothed kid sitting in what used to be my old fifth grade classroom looks up at me.

"You Matt Houston?" he asks.

"No. I'm *Goldman*."

The kid eyes me warily. "If I come t'Hollywood, kin you get me in the movies?" he asks.

"Call me when you get to town, pal," I say, handing him my card.

From the school, I trace the route I used to take home.

As I walk, I seem to remember every crack in the sidewalk.

God, look at those cracks!

What *fantastic* cracks!

Hey, you—*crack!* It's me…your old pal. The kid who used to walk home this way. Yeah, yeah, I know. How time flies...

Passing the houses. Remembering.

There—the house of the evil Timmy Cain, my crazy friend who threw up on the rug while watching *Howdy Doody* and who later tried to set my house on fire when my mom banned him from the premises.

The house of my best friend, Jeff. I always loved his house because his mom made better hamburgers than mine, and because we got to stay up late and watch Sid Caesar on TV.

In the driveway a kid is playing basketball.

He eyes me warily as I pass.

Hey, kid! It's me! Me, who used to play in that very driveway where you now stand. So know this, my young friend: someday, someone shall play in *your* driveway! Yes, know this, and tremble with the knowledge, my dear young chublet, for I—the Kid From Cleveland—have spoken!

Finally, the end of the street. And there it is. My old house: 14112 Becket Road. Oddly, as soon as I see it, I recall my phone number: Wyoming 1-4021.

Weird that all that stuff stays locked in the brain.

The owners have painted the place a hideous shade of blue.

Nonetheless, it's still a magnificent house.

I let my eye trace every shingle, every window, every doorway. And as I do, it all comes back—all the many wonderful and terrible things that took place during the three years we lived there.

How odd that the people living there now know nothing of these stories.

How could this *be?!*

And then I realize that *every* house contains a multitude of strange and wondrous tales.

How they must *ache to* tell them!

I walk around the corner, onto the next street.

Suddenly the neighborhood grows shabby.

Sullen-looking blacks sit on stoops, staring out at nothing.

I walk down the street.

It's getting dark now.

Suddenly it strikes me that this neighborhood might not be so safe at night.

But safety be damned!

Don't these fools know whom they're dealing with?

Don't they realize that I—The Kid From Cleveland—have risen from the dead, and can smite them with but a mere flick of my wrist! That I carry doom and destruction within the very fiber of my being?!

From the other end of the street, a lone man approaches.

I knot my fists up, readying myself.

C'mon sucker. Try something. I'll bite a hole in your throat! I'll rip your eyeballs out and eat them if you so much as look at me cockeyed! Come on! Make a wrong move and meet your death!

The guy is nearer now.

As we get close to one another, I see that it's an old Jewish man of perhaps eighty or so.

Still, I emit a tiny growl as he passes.

Night has fallen.

The lights inside the houses are now on.

Everything looks magical.

I stop in front of one house—a handsome, white, two-story affair.

God, how many times did I stand here just like this, looking up at the second-story window. Hoping upon hope to catch a glimpse of my true love (though she never knew it), the wonderful Polly Schuster.

I'd been completely crazy for her—that is, until the day after Elvis appeared on *The Ed Sullivan Show.*

The following day in school, when I spoke excitedly of Elvis's appearance, Polly's pretty face suddenly turned terrible.

"Eeeewww. He's *ugly!"* she scoffed. "He looks like a drug addict."

Ugly? Drug addict? Why, you pathetic little greaser! You whore of Babylon! You preposterous pile of putrefied pig feces!

A curse on you, I say.

Yes, you evil fuckstress, I pray that your moustache grows, and that all of your children are cursed with large nostrils like yours!

Needless to say, it was the end of a beautiful romance.

For the next day, I've saved a ritual that was most prized to me: taking the rapid transit to downtown Cleveland.

From Shaker Square, the ride used to cost a quarter.

Now it's a buck.

But once I reach my destination, there's more heartache in store.

What used to be a magical place is now just another depressing downtown, populated by assorted bums, winos, and guys with no legs.

As I cross the street, I spot an incredible old guy wearing a straw hat, a blue alpaca sweater, a red and blue striped tie, and sandals with socks.

He's bearing a hand-lettered sign proclaiming Jesus as the savior.

Somehow, I like this guy.

I dunno, he's just different from the rest of the street people.

I ask him if he minds me taking his picture. He says no, and preens properly as I snap away.

Then something really strange happens.

As I am about to round the corner, I'm struck by a sensation so powerful it almost knocks me over.

I'm so dizzy that I have to sit down on a bench.

It takes me a while to realize what's happened.

How to describe it? It's like the opposite of *déjà vu*.

I've seen this place before. But not really.

That's it—I *dreamed* it! And by dreaming it, I've somehow created it in reality! In my dream, I've come close to this corner many times. Yet I've never rounded the bend, because I knew instinctively that if I did, something terrible would happen. You'd enter this long, gray corridor and then—before you knew it—you'd take one step too many and you'd fall off an edge, and you'd just keep falling—down and down and down.

And now I am at this very spot.

Incredible!

I am tempted to walk around the corner, yet somehow I know that I must not.

No—in fact I must leave the Dream Corner immediately, for it is a border never to be crossed.

Back in Shaker Square, dusk is setting, and the place has an odd, surreal quality about it.

Timeless couples saunter around the square, gazing into shop windows.

Nobody seems to be going anywhere special.

Nobody is in a hurry. It's as if they have all the time in the world. As if they have always been here and always will be.

As I'm basking in this nether reality, suddenly I hear a terrible sound behind me—sort of like "HAWWWWWWCH!"

I turn around to see the Shaker Square Bum. He's adjusting a piece of newspaper on a chair, to keep his skinny old butt from getting cold.

Something about the guy makes me extremely nervous. I don't want to look at him because I know he's dying and I don't want him to know that I know.

The signs are clear.

It's time to leave.

I walk one more circle around the square.

The sun has almost set now.

Some pigeons dart crazily across the sky.

The red glow from the Colony Theatre comes on. It seems to me I can smell the popcorn.

God, it's so pretty here.

So, goodbye Shaker Square. Goodbye kids. Goodbye house. Goodbye Rapid Transit. Goodbye lawns. Goodbye sidewalks. Goodbye rock. Goodbye lights. Goodbye trees. Goodbye schools. Goodbye drugstore. Goodbye Colony theater. Goodbye comic books. Goodbye Elvis. Goodbye Polly Schuster. Goodbye Jesus Man. Goodbye Dream Corner. Goodbye, goodbye, goodbye.

And may God bless you, each and every one.

OBSESSIONS

I'M SCARED

I'm scared.
I can't see. I'm going blind—
I'm scared of those guys unloading the truck across the street.
Noises scare me (the only thing that makes me feel good is a rag on my forehead).
I'm scared that they're going to come and get me.
I'm scared I'm going to be arrested and thrown in jail. (I feel like I did something wrong.) I'm guilty!
I'm scared that poisonous molecules are getting into my system.
I'm scared to take a blood test.
I'm scared of mean nurses (and mean librarians and postal clerks, too!)
I'm scared of noises. Everything is too loud. It hurts me.
I'm scared that people will really find out that I'm a liar. That I really am—am what?
I'm scared that everybody around me is going to die. (Wait a minute—they already have.)
I'm scared of people getting too close and touching me and rubbing all their stinking stupid "vibes" off on me.
I'm scared that my computer is going to crash.

I'm scared that someone behind me in the movies will start eating popcorn real loud and I'll be too chickenshit to tell them to shut the fuck up.
I'm scared that everything is going to disappear.
I'm scared that people are going to yell at me.
I don't feel very good. I must be getting sick. Do I look sick?
Karyn's check in my wallet makes me scared.
I'm scared shitless of trucks
—of things bigger than me
—of movie theatres
—of long, empty fields
—of too crowded restaurants
—of people talking too loud for no reason
—of hangup phone calls
—of stupid people with blue eyes in positions of power
—of not finding any place quiet
—of everybody having an IPod and I don't know how to use one
—of people with no imagination
—of what happened to black and white
—of Peter And The Wolf
—of getting caught jerking off to pictures of Dolly Parton
—of Zeppelins
—of being in an elevator with a midget
—of feeling like I'm upside down sometimes
—of why people wear backwards baseball caps
—of people breaking into my house
—of a wart on my elbow
—of my face disappearing
—of knowing that I don't give a fuck about anybody but myself
—of "have a great day!"
—of Hillside Memorial Cemetery
—of kids who aren't kids
—of gardeners who leave their cards on my front porch
—of an eyeball being slit open (fuck you, Dali!)
—of why Bob Dylan got old
—of...no—I can't say that word!
—of why Elvis had to die
—of tough guys with tattoos beating me up

—of being ashamed
—of everyone being mad at me and rejecting me
—of not being able to wake up from that dream
—of Karyn's ghost
—of all the ghosts
—of why I want to look at porn
—of people who talk too loud
—of elevators that don't say Otis
—of people who pronounce words wrong
—of falling off the high diving board at the Riviera Hotel in Las Vegas
—of people whose heads are too big for their bodies
—of no more black and white TV
—of New Orleans just disappearing like that
—of people with stretched-out faces
—of beautiful people
—of cripples
—of spiders (don't even SAY that word!)
—of the wolf under my bedroom window
—that he'll gobble me up and then smile...
—of the Troll under the bridge *(trip, trap, trip, trap!)*
—of when my dad called me a sap
—of empty hospital hallways
—of demon-possessed nurses
—of the teeth being embedded in the steering wheel
—of tiny dogs that I want to kick in the face
—of the brown spot in my underwear
—of people smiling for no reason
—of not having enough...
—of the word "oncologist"
—of why Timmy Cain threw up on my parent's rug
—of doctors who wear turbans
—of why some girls won't like me
—of hair in the sink
—of hair growing in my ears
—of people who insist that you love their dogs
—of people who insist that you love their babies
—of people who insist *anything*...

—of Spam (both the food kind, and the computer kind)
—of 7-11's
—of getting diarrhea on an airplane
—of cash registers
—of typos
—of Xerox machines (no that's a lie—I love Xerox machines).
—of why I can't stop lying
—of four girls stretching a guy at recess until he cries for his mommy
—of Iranians who own computer stores
—of not being able to run
—of a jellyfish in my mouth
—of drinking buttermilk
—of wanting to bite that lady in the eye
—of a big hair growing out of a wart
—of liver
—of the fact that my ex-wife used to refer to her pussy as "my little liver"
—of someone seeing me picking my nose in public
—of what ever happened to Kukla, Fran and Ollie
—of the time I saw my mother naked
—of being the last guy chosen
—of crying in front of everyone
—of why I start crying every time I see a crippled person
—of killing Willie's duck with a water balloon
—that I'm being followed
—that something bad is inside my head
—that my legs won't work
—that I have a double chin
—that they'll all laugh at me
—of pulling my teeth and gums out but I can't get the last one
—that my colon is rotting
—that the two squirrels that live in my backyard are gonna die
—that I can't find my way home
—that someone is trying to poison me
—that something is sucking my brains out of my head

I'm scared that there is no God.
I'm scared that Jesus is not real.

Well—*is* He or *isn't* He?
I'm scared that everything really is chaos and that it's not just my stupid goddamn brain chemicals…

I'm fucking scared.

PULP

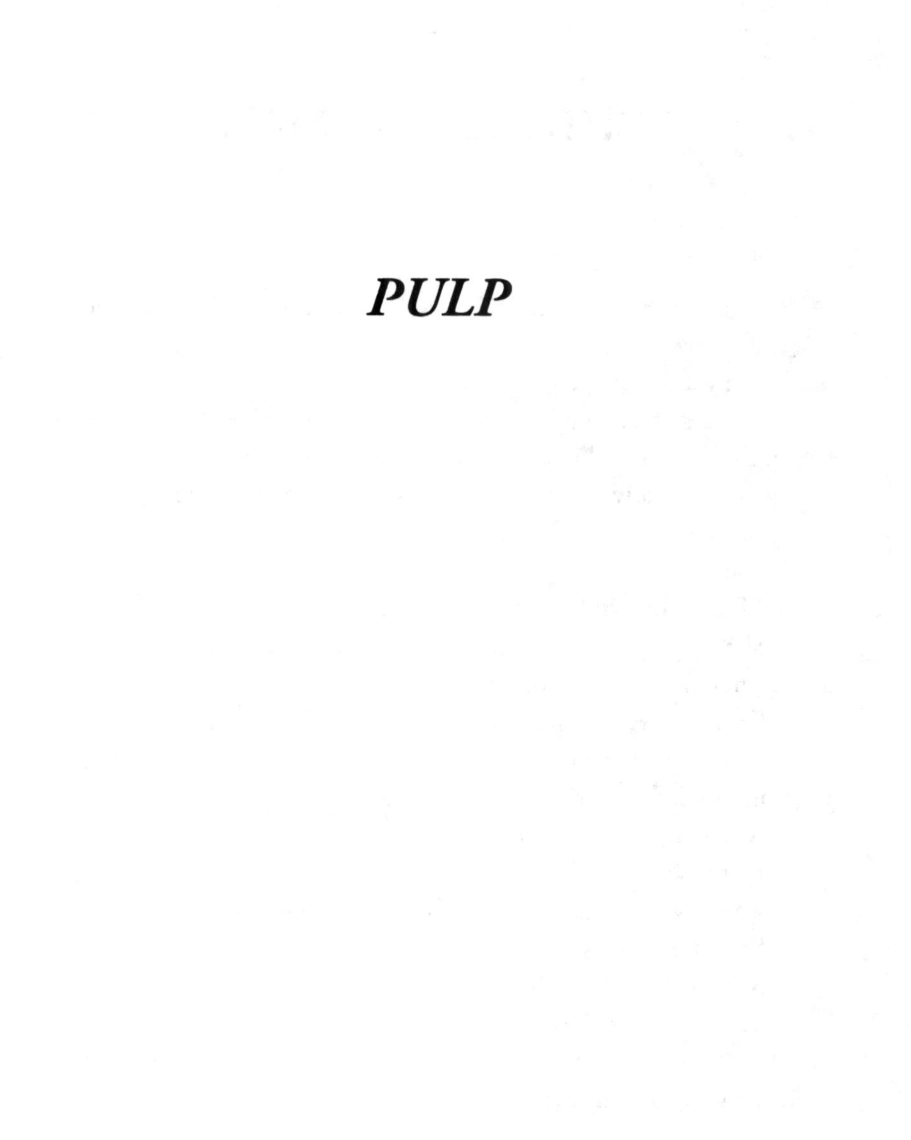

PULP

CHICKEN WOMAN

Sitting in a Chicken Delight joint. Somewhere in America—dunno where.

Only a couple people in the joint.

Some sad old guy wearing one of those cheap suits like he's trying to dress up to look for a job...only he looks like he's been in the deep sweats for a week and he's been sleeping in the fucking thing.

Another chick sitting in a booth.

Plain Jane.

Mousey brown hair, balding a little.

She's eating her food real slow, savoring every bite, like she was at the goddamn Ritz or something.

Coupla greasy Iranian bastards behind the counter.

One guy takes a good pick at his nose, then goes back to making the potato salad.

Real class A-1 joint. Yeah, yeah.

Pretty soon the front door squeaks open.

These two old broads—maybe 65 or so—come in.

Sad cases.

Salvation Army clothes.

Those kinda hairdos where it looks like they just came outta the beauty salon and the hair is rolled a little too tight, wrapped around their shrunken old heads like a little hair hat.

How come old broads always wanna get their hair done, anyhow? Like as if anybody cares.

Ah, fuck it. Anything to kill time. Stave off the hours 'til death comes and whisks you down that long, dark alleyway.

They go to the counter and the one old bag is squinting—trying to read the menu. She reads the whole goddamn thing aloud to her friend, who doesn't seem to hear a word of it. Deaf, probably. Finally, after a million hours, they both order the chicken—natch.

One gets "spicy," the other, "regular."

They go over an' sit down at a booth by the window. The sunlight is shining right smack in the one old broad's face. She keeps squinting into it, covering her eyes, but doesn't think to move.

Queer, man, *real* queer.

They start eating their chicken.

Both of 'em have real different eating styles.

The deaf one—ever-so-delicately—picks at her food, taking eensy-weensy little bits, eating only with the tips of her teeth, then sucking off a tiny morsel at the end. *Zup!*

Meanwhile, the other one, she's just yarfing it down, shoveling it right into the old wazoo as fast as she can. Grease all over her puss. Oh, my my my!

All the while they eat, the two of 'em are yapping about something or other.

Dunno—can't hear. Something about a gall bladder operation.

Jesus, how come all old people ever talk about is their goddamn innards and stuff?

Both of 'em are blabbing away in these monotone voices, but you can see that neither of 'em is listening to what the other one is saying.

Blab blab blab.

Anyway, the one old bag—the one shoveling it in like there's no tomorrow—she's working on a breast now.

Big ol' flap of skin hanging outta her mouth, but she just shoves it right back in.

Her lips are all red and pointed.

Then something kinda weird starts happening.

When she removes her fingers from her mouth, you can see that a little piece of her lip is bloody.

Funny, the chicken looks pretty well-cooked and all.

She grabs another piece of chicken, stuffs it in her mouth.

Gnaws at it voraciously…but when she takes her hand away it appears like a piece of her lip is gone.

Then it's clear. The next time she puts the chicken to her mouth, the chicken takes a bite right out of her face.

Snipper-snap! Just like that. Real quick and sneaky like.

But the old bag is so engrossed in stuffing her puss, she don't even see what's happening.

Still, every time she bites into a piece, the chicken rips another hunk of her face off.

Oddly, her friend doesn't seem to notice any of this.

Shit, maybe she's blind *and* deaf!

Pretty soon, the woman's face is a mess. It's being flayed to ribbons. Huge open wounds are everywhere.

With her next bite, the chicken chomps off a huge chunk of her cheek.

Snap! Snap! Snippety-snap!

It appears to be a contest as to who will consume who first. The chicken is now ripping off bigger and bigger hunks of the old bat's face. Meanwhile, she's gobbling away—faster and faster. She's making these sounds while she chews. Kinda like *gnnunnk, gnnnucckk, gnuckkk*.

The old lady bites into a thigh.

The chicken removes half her nose!

She devours a wing!

The chicken chews off her lips!

Her face is a mass of open sores now.

Big hunks of bloody skin are hanging down all over the place.

Still, she chews away—faster and faster now.

She's nearly sucked the chicken to the bone, but the chicken isn't quitting!

It tears off a big hunk of meat from the fleshy area under the lady's neck.

Zurrrrrp!

By the time she finishes the last piece of chicken, the old broad's face looks like raw hamburger. None of the features are distinguishable from one another. But she doesn't seem to notice.

She tamps up a cigarette and tries to put it in her mouth.

Unfortunately, she doesn't have a mouth any longer.

Her friend, the dainty one, finally finishes her meal.

Old Hamburger Face tries to say something, but the only thing that comes out of her is this weird kind of gurgle.

Now the delicate one wipes the crumbs from her lap, then stands up. As she does, she lets out a huge fart.

Old Hamburger Head looks kind of weird, with her blue hair and not much of a face to speak of—but it certainly don't seem to bother her.

Just another grand old day!

Finally—without ever bothering to clean up their trays!—the two leave the restaurant and climb into this beat up, blue Mustang.

Old Quasimodo is still trying to light a cig, but she can't find anyplace to put it.

Ha, ha, what a card!

The car won't start, natch. It whines and wheezes and coughs. Lots of black smoke erupts from the tailpipe.

Finally it kicks over, and the two old birds putt out onto the road.

The car gets smaller and smaller.

Soon it disappears down the highway.

The place is empty now, save for the two Iranian guys behind the counter.

Finally, one of them stops wiping down the stove and turns to his buddy.

"Didjew see that, Amir?" he says.

The other guy looks up.

He has a moustache that's so thin it looks like somebody drew it on his face.

"Yeah," he says.

The first guy thoughtfully scratches his balls.

"I guess we better not make any more of that spicy for a while," he says.

"Yeah," says his buddy. "Guess not."

The first guy walks over to the window and looks out—almost longingly—at the empty highway.

"Hey, Amir," he says, "You ever miss your mother?"
The second guy stops and thinks for a moment.
"No," he says. "I've always hated my mother. Why do you ask?"
"Aw, I dunno," says the first guy, picking his rear.
"Sometimes I'm sorry we came to America, that's all."
The second guy dumps a batch of potatoes into the fryer.
Lights up a Kool unfiltered.
"Yeah," he says. "I know what you mean."

PULP

HOMEWARD BOUND

The car sped along the desert highway. Inside, Sheri and Lou both looked slightly worn. Well, it was no wonder. They'd both just gotten out of the hospital less than an hour ago where they'd each undergone the identical operation. In non-medical lingo, it was called "stomach stapling."

In fact, that was a pretty accurate description for the procedure. The lining of the stomach walls had been sewn shut, so that food would bypass the organ, being routed directly to the colon. The result, Doc Schaffer had promised, would be a weight loss of up to 150 pounds.

But now the two women were getting tired of driving. It would take six hours to get back to their homes in Bakersfield. Sheri figured that if she averaged 75 or so, they'd make it back by eight that evening.

"Say, hon, ya wanna stop soon?" said Sheri. "I think there's a Howard Johnson's coming up."

"Why not?" Lou answered. She was hoping there might be another piece of that lemon meringue pie she'd eaten at the last rest stop.

Both of the women were extremely fat and sweaty. Unfortunately for them, the air conditioner in the old Merc was broken, causing their backs to stick to the plastic seat covers.

"Is there another Dr. Pepper in the cooler?" Lou said. "I'm sweatin' like a damn pig."

"Just Orange Crush," said Sheri. "Probably warm b'now."

She reached over and handed Lou a rumpled brown paper sack.

Lou took the can of soda, popped it open, and downed half of it in one long gulp. Then she took out a pack of Camels—pulled out a cig, tamped it down on the dash—then lit up.

Sheri was having trouble staying awake now. The flat brown landscape seemed to have some sort of hypnotic effect on her. Occasionally, the bleakness was broken up by a gas station... maybe a 7-Eleven, but other than that, there wasn't really much to look at.

Sheri began humming a little song in her head. She didn't really remember all of the words, so she just sang, "*Pepsi Cola hits the spot... Pepsi Cola hits the spot...*" over and over and over. Somehow, singing this made her feel better.

"Hey, girl," Lou said, stifling a belch, "how're ya feelin', anyhow?"

Sheri wiped a bead of sweat from her upper lip.

"Oh, not too bad, I guess...little tired's all." She didn't want to tell Lou about the blood in her stool that she'd discovered at the last rest stop. No use worrying Lou. Heck, Lou worried about everything under the damn sun, anyhow.

The heat bore down on the old Merc.

Vapors of steam rose from the hood everytime they hit in the road.

Lou swiped at her neck.

Sheri opened the window, causing her dull, brown hair to poof up into little tufts along the side of her head.

Lou flipped on the radio, turning the dial until she settled on a country station. She cranked the volume up a notch.

"Oooh, I jus' *luvvv* my Barbara Mandrell—don't you, babe?"

But Sheri didn't answer. She was off now...lost in the song she was humming inside her head.

"Y'know, hon," Lou said..."I was thinkin' that mebbe you an' me an' Tom 'n' Wes could take one a them Greyhound bus tours...y'know—mebbe t'Las Vegas or sumthin'. Heck, I could leave the kids with my sister Jesse. Whaddaya think, babe?"

"What?" Sheri said absently.

"I said, I was thinkin' mebbe when we got all healed up an everythin', we could all take off fer Vegas. We don't have t'stay in one a them expensive places. Heck, they got some real cute little motels off the strip. Got gamblin' an' everything in 'em too!"

Sheri looked over at her friend.

"Lord," she said after a moment, "I dunno. I mean, I don't think Tom could get off work. 'Sides, Vegas kin be real expensive, y'know? I guess I'd like it—I mean, I hear Wayne Newton's there all the time. Mebbe I could get him to sign that album of his—you 'member...the one I bought at Kmart last week?"

Lou looked over at Sheri now. Something was off...something in the tone of her voice.

"Hey, girl," Lou said. "You okay?"

"Sure, babe...I'm fine," Sheri replied. She wiped a wet strand of hair from her face and turned down the radio a bit. "I was just thinkin' that—well, life's funny, is all," she said.

Lou downed the last of her soda, then tossed the empty can out the window. It bounced along the highway before another car ran over it.

"Whaddaya mean—*funny?"* she said, shaking another cigarette out of the pack, then tamping it down on her wrist.

But Sheri wasn't listening again. What she was doing was—she was remembering the time when she was a little girl—maybe eight or so. The boy next door, Buddy McQueen—that was his name—had asked her to take off all her clothes. Right there in the living room and all. When she'd finally done it, Buddy just stood and looked at her for a long, long while. Then he had touched her—down *there.*

Sheri recalled how she had put her hand on the back of Buddy'a head. She'd just stood there petting his head, kind of the same way she petted her dog, Whizzer.

Buddy's hair felt so soft. So nice. It smelled good too. Sort of like—what was that stuff that all the boys used to use? *Brylcreem*—that was it.

That smell, that feeling—somehow it had been very important to Sheri over the years. It led, like some long, invisible string, to other things—other rooms in her mind. And somehow, though Sheri didn't really understand it, it had been connected to the years she'd spent as a stripper, and even later to those porn films.

Still, that was long ago, when she'd been young. She'd had a great body back them.

Oh yeah, the guys used to *love* her body. Especially her breasts. But after she'd married Tom and had the boys, Sheri could actually feel herself getting soft. Yeah—kind of soft and mushy. She didn't mind though—she was too damn tired to mind. In fact, in a funny sort of way, getting soft felt kind of *nice*. It really did.

But now something seemed wrong. Somehow the other end of the string had disappeared, and now Sheri couldn't seem to find her way back.

Lou was quiet now, too. She was thinking about that lemon meringue pie again.

Oh, man, she could *taste* that pie!

As she thought of it, Lou ran a finger over one of her dry, old nipples. To her surprise, it was erect.

"Hey, girl—we gonna stop soon?" she said. "I gotta go winky tinky."

But Sheri still wasn't listening.

She was trying to climb back up that long string. Back up to... to *what?*

Suddenly Sheri felt scared. She had been trying to remember what her husband Tom and her two boys looked like, but no matter how hard she tried, she couldn't see their faces.

She began to feel panicky, so, inside her head she started singing the song again.

Pepsi Cola hits the spot...Pepsi Cola hits the spot...

But it didn't seem to work—

Sheri looked imploringly at her friend.

"Lou?" she said. "Remember when you an' me was in high school...that time those guys came t'that slumber party we had at Laurie Nicholas' house? Remember that boy, Rodney Dillingham? How he kept tryin' t'get me to go in the bedroom with him so we could, y'know...make out an' stuff? 'Member that?"

Sheri knew she'd better keep talking. She was really beginning to feel quite peculiar. Alone, *that's* what she felt. So alone—as if she just wasn't attached to anything in the world. It was a very bad feeling. It made her feel like she might vomit at any second.

"I never went back there with him, Lou—you *know* that, don't you, girl?"

Sheri's voice etched up a notch. It was almost a whine now.

"Lou...I was a *nice* girl back then, wasn't I? Please, Lou—just tell me I was a nice girl...will ya, hon'?"

PULP

THE BOXERS

Both fighters are in their corners now. In the blue, a lanky black kid with a little goatee and a huge Afro is doing an Ali shuffle, showing off for the crowd. In the opposite corner, a Mexican guy with a three-day stubble of beard is taking last-minute instructions from his cornerman.

The ref calls the fighters to ring center. The black dude gets right up in the Mexican guy's face, trying to do the old psych-out job on him. The Mex looks down at the ground, refusing the stare down. As the ref finishes reading the rules, both fighters return to their corners. The Mex gets down on one knee and does a Hail Mary.

The bell rings.

Both fighters come out fast.

The black dude is quick, but his punches are wild. The Mex is catching most of them on his gloves. But the black keeps lunging in.

Out in the audience a huge, fat colored woman—obviously the kid's mother—is bouncing up and down in her chair and screaming at the top of her lungs.

"Hit him, sonny! Knock his block off!"

Just before the bell, the Mex wades in and digs a pretty good hook to the black guy's liver, which buckles his knees for a second.

"Shake it off, baby!" Shake it off!" his mama hollers.

In Round Two, you can see that the black guy is already tired. The Mex is starting to connect with some pretty good jabs now. "C'mon sonny—you can do it!" the black guy's mama yells. She's eating a hot dog and pieces of it are flying out of her mouth all over the woman in front of her.

The black guy is backpedaling now, trying to cover up...but suddenly the Mex connects with a whistling right to the temple and the black goes down on one knee. He bounces right back up, but you can see his legs aren't there anymore.

The Mex smells blood.

He wades in, face squared to his chest. Little slit eyes looking upward like a crab, searching out his quarry.

The black steps in and lets go with a wild right.

The Mex ducks, takes a little step inside and comes in with a choppy right to the black's left jaw.

A crunching uppercut follows. It's not quite on the mark. It catches the black in the throat instead of on the chin.

He goes down on one knee now, clutching his throat and gasping for air.

He's not getting up—that's clear.

He's on his back now, clutching his throat and making these awful hacking noises.

The ref kneels down to see if the guy is OK, while a fat white-haired doctor with a yellow and black checkered sport coat jumps into the ring.

They drag the black guy to his corner. All the while he's still gasping and retching.

Out in the crowd, his mother buries her face in her hands.

The audience is silent now. Everybody's watching the kid. A strange transformation has come over him now. He's no longer the tough, cocky fighter who strutted around the ring. Now he's just a young kid, scared and hurt.

And then a terrible thing happens. The kid starts to cry—the humiliation and the pain of it all have gotten to him.

The audience is silent, uncomfortable.

This is definitely *not* cool. Puts a damper on the bloodlust.

The announcer sees this, and begins babbling into the mike.

Now the ring girl—a sumptuous blonde with monstrous silicone tits, which are barely covered by a tiny bikini—parades around the ring.

The audience, eager to escape the ugly drama taking place in the corner, begins to hoot and holler.

The black kid's mother gets up and goes over to his corner. He's stopped crying now, and he's escorted out of the ring and back to his dressing room.

The lights dim.

The big tits girl finishes her walk around the ring to a host of catcalls from the crowd.

The next two fighters climb into the ring.

The crowd screams, relieved that things have returned to normal.

Somebody throws a cupful of Pepsi into the ring, which barely misses the announcer.

Out in the crowd, the chair where the black kid's mother sat is empty, save for a half eaten hot dog and a worn looking instamatic camera.

Pretty soon, two little kids trot by—their arms full of popcorn, cokes and candy.

One of the kids spies the camera. They eyeball each other for a sec—

Then the first kid grabs the camera and then they both scoot off—lickety split—into the crowd.

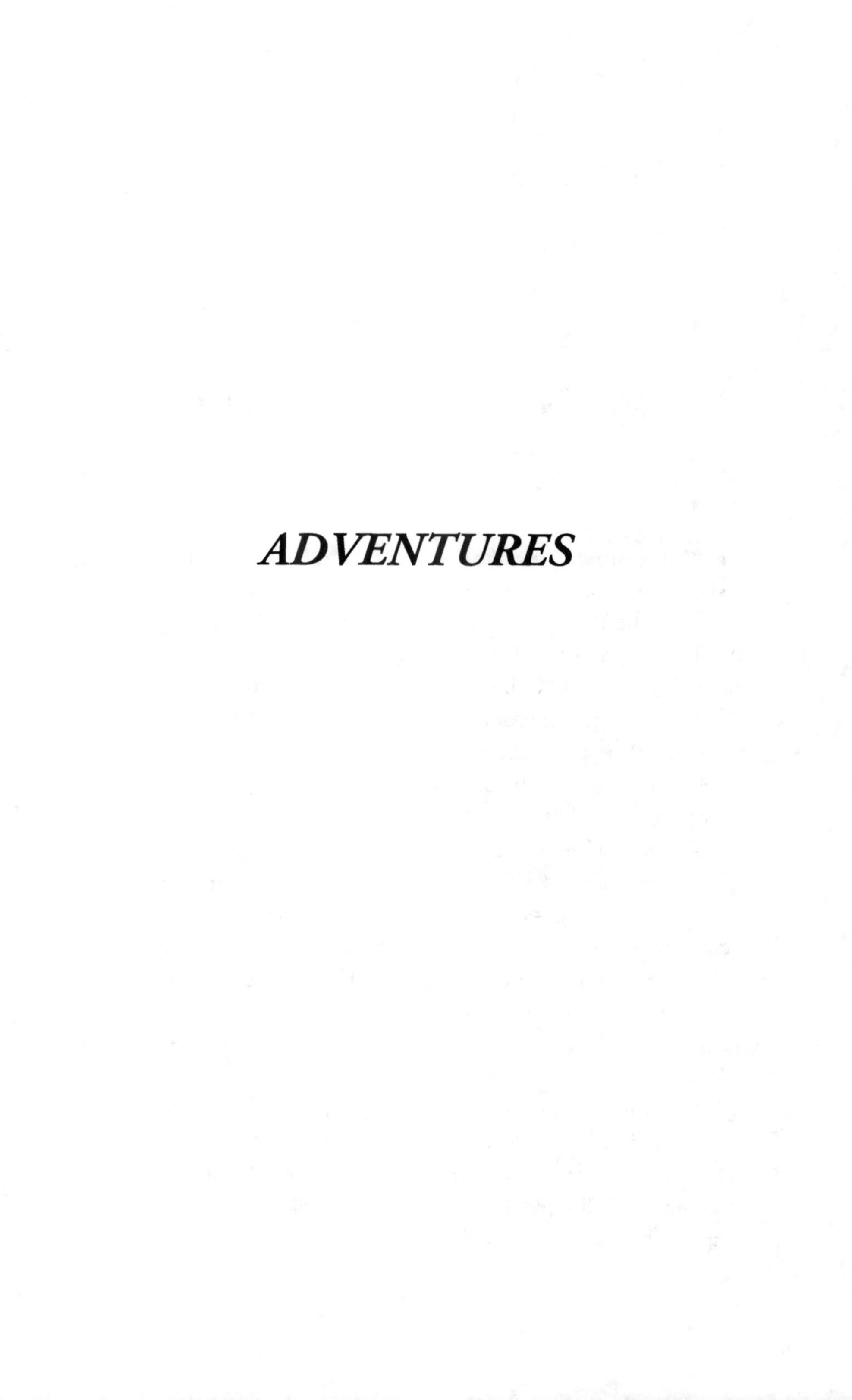

ADVENTURES

FRANNY'S ADVENTURE

The central figure of our tale is Franny Westinghouse—a lovely young actress who began her film career at age 14 as the star of the 1961 low-budget film entitled *The Cheeseburger Twins*. The film was an instant hit, and made tons of money for its producer, Charles "Cubby" Lundquist, head of England's Acme Studios.

Prior to her appearance in *The Cheeseburger Twins*, Franny had worked in several English-made horror flicks and had already distinguished herself before becoming a bona fide low-budget film starlet.

Franny had a curious combination of the child and the adult in her, which always kept her performances interesting. But there was another quality—something lurking underneath—a softness, a roundness, a freshness—that simply made you *have* to watch her. It was almost as if she were bursting forth from underneath her skin. No matter who else was onscreen, your eyes would fix on Franny, and the other people in the scene would immediately fade into the background.

Not that Franny was a scene stealer, nor that she employed any of the disgusting mechanisms—the overly cute demeanor or the tiresome show-offy manner employed by other child starlets like the hideous Shirley Temple. No, it was nothing like that. Franny simply occupied her space with such a strong presence that she took over whatever scene she was in. She did this quite effortlessly, which is, of course what made her so effective. It was magic—pure and simple. Nothing more, nothing less.

The making of *The Cheeseburger Twins* was really quite an effort for young Franny, who turned 15 while the film was in its second month of production. (Though it was allegedly set in England, the film was shot primarily in the town of Yucaipa, California.) In the film—which was about a pair of twins lured into a life of prostitution by the owner of a string of whorehouses disguised as hamburger stands—Franny played both roles. That is, she played both twins—Nelda and Nancy.

In some instances, this involved the use of a double—a young actress named Sara Domergue—who would, at the young age of 19, commit suicide by swallowing battery acid.

Domergue, in fact, looked nothing like Franny, who was blue-eyed, smooth-skinned and naturally cheery. Domergue, by contrast, had one brown eye and one green eye, and even at 13, she was already sporting a nasty case of acne, which was to leave her skin badly pitted for the rest of her short life.

However, the body structure—lithe, long-legged, just the hint of new, young breasts—of the two young girls was almost exactly alike. And when Domergue donned her blonde wig—when filmed from the proper angle—she was a dead ringer for Franny.

Domergue was used only in limited scenes. For the bulk of the film, Westinghouse had to separately shoot the part of both twins. Later, when the film was edited, the two parts would be put together via split screen—a technique which has since faded from popularity. For these scenes, Franny would—in order to get the timing right—read her lines to a person off camera, who would then read back the line of whichever twin was not in the actual shot. Because the producers (a decidedly cheap bunch) had never assigned a particular person to this task, every day the job was performed by a different person.

On some days it was the associate director—a snippy young pretty boy named Dirk Smedley (whose friends called him "Duffy"). Smedley read his lines without enthusiasm or flavor, which infuriated young Franny. At other times the task was given to Otis Pettigrew—the go-fer on the set. Though he was in his mid-30s, Pettigrew looked closer to 50. He always sported a heavy three-day growth of beard. He also stunk.

Franny—always the trooper—never once complained. She simply did take after take after take, until she was satisfied that she'd got her shots exactly right. Even at her young age, Franny was a perfectionist.

After completing *The Cheeseburger Twins*, Franny starred in 12 other low-budget films—everything from sci-fi to horror—to a host of teen hot-rod flicks. She also made a very bad record album featuring terrible remakes of rock 'n' roll hits of the day, like "Ballad Of A Teenage Queen" and "The Peppermint Twist."

By the time she was 16, Franny's parents had divorced. She divided her time between a small flat in the town of Derbyshire and her mother's home, located in Reseda, California.

As was the case with many child stars, gradually there was less and less demand for Franny—as younger, cuter girls took her place. Soon she resorted to taking jobs in soft-core porn films. But Franny didn't do that for long. She'd decided to pursue a career in animal husbandry. In the fall quarter, she enrolled at Pierce Junior College in Woodland Hills, California.

Franny seemed perfectly happy in her post-teenage life. She didn't go the way of many child stars, falling into major depressions or contemplating suicide. She simply got on with her life.

Franny looked into the mirror. She blinked her eyes. She blinked them again.

Damn, this mirror was dirty! There were no tissues, so Franny rubbed the dirty film off the mirror with the sleeve of her blouse.

There. Now she could see.

She looked at her face. It was odd—every time she looked at herself, she looked different.

Who was *this?*

Is this *me?*

Hullo, hullo?

The only thing that looked somewhat the same each time she observed herself was her lips. Yes, they were the same full lips that she'd always had.

Franny ran her tongue across them, pursed them at herself. She tried to focus on her lips, but other parts of her face kept getting in the way. All she wanted the face in the mirror to do was to hold still for one or two seconds, so she could get a fix on it. Make some *sense* of it.

But it wouldn't work.

First she'd look at her eyes—the wrinkles around them. Then her nose, cheeks, chin, etc.

Franny regarded the thick mat of caked, brown hair on her head, splaying out in little bits at the sideburns.

So much *hair* on the face! She'd had it when she'd been younger—this fine covering of ultra-light blonde hairs. But over the years they'd grown longer and darker.

My God, I actually have a beard! Franny thought.

Franny Westinghouse with a beard!

Franny moved in for a closer look.

"*Dekudisha*," she said.

She said it again.

Franny didn't know why she said *dekudisha*. But she knew she had to say it. It didn't mean anything—nonetheless she said it often.

Franny often did this with words that may have sounded like nonsense to the average person. But saying the words—which would change whenever she felt the need—would put something into a certain shape inside her stomach. And as that thing went into shape—somehow the events of the world would become—at least for a time—solid.

It was only at these times that Franny felt completely "normal."

Most of the time, it seemed to her, everything was about to fly apart.

Franny stepped back in order to get a longer view.

She was wearing only a thin brown shirt—one that she'd had on for days, and a pair of cheap cotton underwear that she'd purchased at Kress' dime store.

The top three buttons of the shirt were undone.

Franny reached up and undid the bottom one, then opened the shirt to reveal her breasts.

Franny had never had large breasts, and thankfully so. Even now, they stood upright and firm. Her nipples were larger, or rather, they protruded more than they had during her girlhood. Back then,

Daddy had made her put tape across them. (Franny had insisted on not wearing a bra when that became the fashion during the late '60s, so her rather large nipples would show through her clothing.) Daddy had always been somewhat of a prude, but this tape-over-the-nipple business was the final indignity.

Franny's body was still long, lean, and fairly fat-free. Only a few sections around the thighs and above the navel were mottled. Other than that, her body could have belonged to a 25-year-old.

Only her face seemed to have aged. And, unfortunately, it had aged poorly. Though she was thin, poor Franny—unless she kept her head perfectly straight—had at least three chins. And the skin around her neck was totally wrinkled. Hell, she looked like damn turtle!

Franny turned her head this way and that—struck one pose after another—but she couldn't change the fact that she had the face of an old woman—a terrible, wrinkled old woman!

It was 1991, and Franny Westinghouse was 43—going on 44. She hadn't gone the way of many so-called child stars and faded into total oblivion. In fact, she still found guest roles on the occasional TV shows. Her last had been an episode of *Murder, She Wrote*, in which she'd played a woman suspected of chopping up her cheating, lawyer husband with a rusty meat cleaver. At the conclusion, she's found innocent (with the help of Angela Lansbury, naturally).

Of course, in the '90s, most people didn't know who Franny Westinghouse was, nor that she'd once been a low-budget teen film star. To them, she was just some older actress. And a not very interesting one at that. Whatever charm Franny had exuded as a teenager had faded over the years. She wasn't a terrible actress—she was just, well... mediocre. Nonetheless, with the help of her agent, she managed to keep enough jobs to give her enough money to get by on.

Given all this, the fact that Franny had chosen to move into the Hotel Eddy—a rundown flophouse in the Tenderloin section of San Francisco—might have seemed strange...but in reality, it wasn't.

You see, Franny needed an *adventure*.

That was all there was to it. She needed something that would totally disconnect her from the life that had led up to the present moment.

Though when she looked at it, her life *did* seem all disconnected, yet there was a string that somehow kept all the pieces together. Franny didn't know what the string consisted of—but it was there, nonetheless.

Now it was time to break the string.

Franny had been through three marriages...each time to a man who'd abused her. She'd been a housewife, a schoolteacher, and a businesswoman. She'd done her share of drugs and had become an alcoholic—though she'd cleaned up after joining a 12-step program. She'd been through therapy—Freudian, Reichian, Gestalt—you name it. All typical stuff for a woman, her age, *right?*

The way Franny came to be a resident of the Eddy Hotel was like this:

Franny had been up in San Francisco one day to shoot a talk show about—you guessed it—child stars who were "still in the business."

After the taping, rather than take the limousine back to her hotel, Franny decided to walk.

A half hour later, she found herself in the Tenderloin—an area of the city that catered primarily to prostitutes, drug addicts, bums and other undesirables. For some reason, Franny often liked to walk through such sections of town. She liked to imagine each of the people as children, and then try to figure out by what path they had come to where they were at this moment of their lives.

Franny stopped in front of the Hotel Eddy—a weather-beaten old tenement that sat next to a liquor store—and looked inside. In the lobby, there were a dozen or so old people gathered around an ancient black-and-white television set.

Somehow the scene was comforting.

Suddenly it hit her.

This is the beginning of my new adventure! Franny thought.

Franny went inside the hotel.

The desk clerk was a small, mousy girl with a harelip. Her name (Franny was later to learn) was Mary Spudlinger. She had been born in Bakersfield to low-class parents. Her father, William "Benny" Spudlinger, was presently serving a life sentence in Folsom for murder. Her mother had recently suicided. Mary Spudlinger was—despite the harelip—somehow oddly pretty. In fact, Franny noticed a slight stirring in her loins as she observed the girl. Whether this was actually due to a physical attraction to the girl, or was simply the excitement from beginning her new adventure, Franny didn't know.

"How much for a room?" Franny asked.

The girl looked up from her movie magazine. "Eight bucks a night," she answered in a dull monotone. Twelve 'fyou wanna bath. Fifteen for your own TV."

"How much for a week?" Franny queried.

"Don't rent 'em buy the week," the girl said. "S'cheaper by the month."

Franny reached in her purse and pulled out a wad of cash. "I'd like to pay you for the month," Franny said. "I want a bath. No TV."

The girl took the money and pulled a key off the rack.

"We don't got no extra," the girl said. "If you want one, you'll haveta pay for it.

"Thank you," Franny said, taking the key.

Thus, Franny became a resident of the Hotel Eddy. Her plan during her stay was to...well—to do *nothing*, actually.

What she wanted to do was to *stop the flow*. Let everything fall apart. Whatever was left—after the falling apart—would be the actual facts—the *stuff* of everything. Only after this took place could Franny consider carrying on with her life.

Much of the time, Franny simply lay in her room and thought. Not *thought* actually—she just let things take shape in her mind.

Sometimes a particular thought would completely take her over...and she would simply go with it. Other times, the thoughts had no force or energy, and she would let them go out of her head, where they would bounce around on the ceiling.

After a time, Franny got to know some of the other inhabitants of the Eddy. They were a fairly interesting lot.

In room 203—just down the hall—was Trixie Bixel, an old crippled woman who went lickety-split around the place in her wheelchair. Trixie had once been a stripper. She'd also been a taxi dancer (in those days they called them "dime-a-dance girls") at the Roseland Ballroom in New York. After her accident, Trixie decided that she would try to set a record by going across the U.S.—from New York to California—in her wheelchair.

Unfortunately, she only made it as far as New Orleans, where she was run over by a drunk in a pickup truck. After she recuperated, they shipped her out to California, where she'd lived with her sister-in-law, Flo...who'd recently died of a strange brain ailment.

After this, Trixie became a resident of the Hotel Eddy.

In room 304 was a squat, little man named Douglas Bendix. He was hideously ugly, with a sour red face that had gigantic welts all over it. He also seemed to have a hunchback. Bendix's teeth were all black and rotted, and his breath was constantly putrid. Given that, Franny was amazed to find out that he was a male prostitute!

"Women *like* me!" he said, taking a pull on a bottle of Ripple. "I don't know why...they just *do!* On a good night I can make me a hunnert bucks...mebbe two!"

He pushed the bottle at Franny. "Here, ya want a pop, hon'?"

"No, thanks," Franny said, lighting up a Camel unfiltered.

Franny liked listening to Bendix—even though she didn't much care for him. The thought of actually having sex with him made her want to puke.

The man was the ugliest thing she'd ever seen in her life! Plus... he *stunk!*

Franny's favorite resident of the Eddy was Bedford Delmont—a graceful black gentleman of about 60. Belmont was a preacher. Every Sunday morning, he held a service—right there in the lobby of the Eddy! Most everybody came.

Delmont was not a bible thumper, per se, but his sermons could get pretty fiery.

"WE BATTLE NOT AGAINST FLESH AND BLOOD, BUT AGAINST PRINCIPALITIES AND POWERS IN HIGH PLACES!" Delmont shouted at the top of his lungs.

Something about this got to Franny.

She did, indeed, feel that she was always battling against *something*—an actual, tangible force—not just her stupid subconscious, or her "past" (that's what the shrinks always said).

Franny became fascinated by the sermons, and even began reading the Bible that she'd found in the desk in her room.

She thought to herself: *If this Jesus stuff is really true, and God actually made us...then people today are no different from what they were in the Bible days. Everything is the same as it's always been!*

But it was hard to imagine the residents of the Hotel Eddy—or anybody in her life for that matter—to be figures with the force and power of the characters in the Bible.

Most people seemed so flimsy.

Somehow they were all just cheap versions of one another. They lived and died and it hardly mattered. Nothing would be changed by them.

Franny especially liked reading the Old Testament. It made sense to her. God was so *angry!*

But of course! After all, He *made* people, and they'd simply gone ahead and made a hideous mess of things.

And when it came time to pour out his wrath, God didn't fool around. Why people always made all this noise about God being kind and good and loving, she simply didn't understand.

God was *pissed!* And He bloody well had a *right* to be!

"YOU MUST REPENT!" Delmont had shouted on a recent Sunday. "YOU MUST GET DOWN ON YOUR KNEES RIGHT NOW—NOT TOMORROW—AND ASK GOD TO FORGIVE YOUR SINS! AND YOU'D BETTER MEAN IT! BECAUSE GOD CAN SEE INTO YOUR HEART, AND IF YOU'RE NOT SINCERE, HE'LL KNOW IT!!"

This scared Franny.

She thought back over her life; she thought of all the things she'd done to make God angry. But no matter how much she tried, whenever she tried to repent—she didn't really *mean* it.

She didn't feel sorry for anything. *That* was the problem.

"How can I make it up to God?" she thought. "How, how, how?"

But even as she said this, Franny didn't really mean it.

Hell—all this stuff about God could be just a lot of *bullshit!*

Franny had been in San Francisco for six months now. Nothing particular had happened. She'd just wandered around the city. One of her favorite places was the old Kress's five-and-dime down on Market Street. It reminded Franny of her childhood.

Everything seemed old. Even the items on the shelves looked like they'd been sitting there since the '40s.

Kress's was wonderful. There was a counter where you could get coffee…and it was still ten cents a cup!

Franny would order coffee and sit for hours in the dime store, letting the thought bubbles in her head go *pop, pop, pop!*

She'd wander up and down the aisles, looking at all the wonderful items—the soaps, bubbly shampoos, bathwaters, etc.

She especially liked the "colored" section of the store which sold items like Hair Sheen, Razor Bump, and assorted skin lightening creams.

Black people are lucky! Franny thought to herself. *Look at all the terrific items they can buy!*

To be completely honest, Franny often thought of herself *as* a black person. Not that she thought she actually *was* one, but simply that she felt more black than she did white.

One night, in her wanderings around the city, Franny went to the Mitchell Brothers Theatre—a porno film house on O'Farrell Street, which was a couple of blocks from the Eddy. Besides films—which tended to be ultra-kinky—the Mitchell Brothers Theatre also offered live sex shows.

Franny paid the $10 to see a film called *Big Baby Man*. Like most movies of this sort, the film—which was about a fat guy who sat around in diapers and liked to have women urinate on him—didn't have much of a plot. After about ten minutes, Franny grew bored. She got up and went into the room where the live shows were held.

This, too, was a pretty disappointing affair. On a stage lit by only a dim red bulb, a silicone-titted blond was shoving a dildo up the crotch of a red-haired gal with snake tattoos all over her body. For some reason the tattoo lady kept going *Moo, moo, moo*, as the other girl worked away with the dildo.

Franny stifled a yawn. Pretty soon she got up and exited the theatre.

It was dark when Franny got outside.

There were a few hoots and howls from street-corner people as she walked.

Then, as she turned down the corner of Larkin Street, a black man materialized from the darkness of a corner stoop. A cigarette dangled from his lips.

"Got a light?" the man said.

Franny knew she should have felt afraid, but she didn't.

She pulled a Bic lighter from her purse and snapped it open. In the light from the flame, she could see the man's face. He was older—mid-50s probably—but strangely good-looking. Little sprouts of beard popped from his face. Franny noticed that the man's beard hairs were spaced wide apart.

After his cigarette was lit, the man's eyes held hers. There was something in them, but Franny couldn't say what it was.

Franny looked away from the man's gaze.

"Not safe for a lady walking in this part of town at night," the man said in a soft voice.

"I suppose not." Franny said. "My hotel's not very far from here."

She turned to walk.

The man fell into step beside her. Franny offered no protest.

"Name's Homer—Homer McGriff," the man said. "I'm from Seattle."

"Franny—Franny Westinghouse."

The man didn't react.

"You don't mind if I walk with you, do you?" he asked.

"No, it's okay," Franny said.

Oddly, something about the big black man was comforting. Franny felt safe and secure in his presence.

When they got to the Eddy, Franny stopped.

"Well, this is it," she said.

The man just stood there looking at her.

"Uh...haven't I seen you somewhere before?"

"No," Franny said. "I don't think so."

There was a moment of silence.

"Well, good night," Franny said.

"G'night." McGriff said. Then he turned on his heel and faded into the darkness.

That night Franny had a dream. She was in a city somewhere—she didn't know where. It could have been any city really—the buildings were tall and the sky was overcast and brown.

Something about the daylight was foreboding—it brought everything too close together.

Things seemed out of proportion.

Franny walked down into a subway to wait for the train.

People weren't speaking to one another.

They all looked ill—their faces gaunt and white.

In the dream, there was no language; nobody spoke—there was no need to.

In the subway, people sat on seats. A lot of the people looked familiar to her—as if she'd once known them—but Franny didn't know from where. Some of them seemed to be people she'd once gone to school with, but now they were old—perhaps near death, even.

An old woman sat in the seat across from her.

The woman pulled up her skirt. She was wearing nothing underneath; she had a huge, swollen vagina. It had red sores on it.

The woman spread her legs, and began stroking herself.

Nobody paid attention.

People came on and off the train—on and off.

Finally, Franny got out at a stop and went up the stairs.

It was just turning to dusk outside.

She wasn't in the city anymore. It was somewhere else, something like a beach—the ground was covered with something strange.

Franny's feet made *crack-cracking* sounds as she walked.

After a time, Franny realized that the ground was covered with the bodies of dead fish. They stretched for miles and miles—and far out beyond them lay the ocean.

The stinking dead ocean.

Franny began to walk faster. Soon she was running.

Crack! Crack! Crack! went the sounds of Franny's shoes as they scuttled over the bodies of the dead fish.

"Shutup, shutup shutup!" she cried as she ran.

Something was rumbling under the cruel dark sea.

Franny tripped and fell face down in a pile of stinking, dead fish.

Crack! went her skull.

"SHUTUP, GODDAMNIT, OR I'LL BITE YOU!" she yelled.

She opened her mouth and took a big dead fish inside it. She bit as hard as she could. Black blood spilled from the corners of her mouth…

When Franny awoke from the dream, she was covered with sweat. She went to the bathroom sink and gulped water until her stomach was bloated.

Franny would continue to see Homer McGriff. He'd pop up at odd times and what seemed like strange places. The two would have coffee, or sit in the five-and-dime on Market Street.

Once, McGriff took her to this old place in Chinatown where the waiter—a crazy old Chinese guy named Fo Wing Yung—ran around and yelled at people and served them the wrong food.

McGriff never talked about himself. He wasn't at all like the other people on the street. He was bright, obviously well-read...and he had a quality about him—a gentleness—that caused Franny's heart to go all soft inside. McGriff always walked Franny back to her hotel—and he never once made an advance, or asked her if he could come up to her room.

Franny felt like she'd been gone forever. Her old life didn't feel like it belonged to her anymore. Occasionally, her agent would send her offers for this audition or that—but Franny didn't want to do anything yet. She hadn't figured things out—though underneath, she could feel things falling into place.

Sometimes she'd have a strange memory that would come back clear as day. One day, she recalled that Sir John had attempted to have sex with her. She'd been about six. Franny could see the whole thing—Sir John's big red monkey-penis popping up from his trousers as he leaned towards her on the bed.

"It's okay, sweetie," he said. "It's just another way for Daddy to show how much he loves you." Although he never had actually penetrated her, he'd tried to on several occasions.

Somehow, the memory didn't upset Franny. It simply filled up another space inside her.

Franny also remembered getting into a fight with a little boy with red hair who lived down the row at Chancery Lane. Franny was a tomboy, and much stronger than her opponent. She had smashed his head into the pavement several times before the boy's mother whisked him away, shouting insults.

The memory pleased Franny. She could actually feel the boy's head smacking into the ground.

Whack! Whack! Whack!

Oh, it was such a lovely sound!

Other strange people and incidents would pop up in her mind—people she hadn't thought of in years...and yet there they *were*. Just like that! She could see them perfectly. It was all really quite marvelous!

One night, McGriff had walked her to her front door. They stood on the door stoop, not saying anything.

"Would you like to come up?" Franny asked.

McGriff said nothing. He held her eyes for a moment...and then followed her up.

When they got in the room, Franny took off her clothes. McGriff sat in a chair opposite her. He said nothing. He looked like he was going to cry.

Franny came to him then and held his head in her hands.

Then she led him to the bed.

They made love wordlessly. He was very gentle, just as she had expected.

Soon McGriff was snoring beside her.

Franny couldn't sleep. She lay in bed and stared out into the darkness. She couldn't stop thinking about everything. Everything came at random and scattered around in her mind—but it was different this time.

It was not good at all.

Soon a terrible fear came over her.

How can I get God to forgive me? she kept thinking. Franny felt so dirty—so vile—that it seemed nothing could ever wash it off.

Franny got up and sat in the chair by the window.

Outside there was a clatter of garbage cans.

Franny looked out.

Two old bums were fighting in the alley below.

After a bit of scuffling, one old guy knocked the other one to the ground. He laid a boot heel to the side of the head, then scuttled into the darkness.

Franny felt dizzy. She picked up her Bible and clutched it to her chest.

She looked over at McGriff, who was snoring heavily.

Then all of a sudden it came to her. She realized the purpose that Homer McGriff had in her life.

Yes—it was clear as a bell.

I must make a sacrifice! A sacrifice to God! Just like the people in the Old Testament! That's what I'll do!

Franny was, of course, insane. She had halfway known it for years.

Now she went to her purse, where she kept a long folding Swiss Army knife.

She took the knife out, pulled the blade open—then went and sat on the bed next to McGriff.

"Dear God," Franny said, "please forgive me for everything I've done. I offer this man up to you—this good, kind man—and I hope that you will be pleased with my offering."

McGriff stirred in his sleep.

Franny raised the knife over McGriff's chest and closed her eyes—

The next morning when she awoke, the clock on the dresser said 10:30. McGriff lay soundlessly next to her. He didn't move. Franny got up and went and sat in the chair by the window, looking at him.

About ten minutes later, McGriff stirred. He rubbed his eyes, then sat up, propping himself on one elbow. "Monin'," he said.

Franny just sat on the chair and looked at him, saying nothing.

"What's the matter," McGriff said. "Are you okay?"

Franny continued to stare.

"Get out of here," she said flatly.

McGriff looked puzzled.

"What?" he asked.

"I said, get out of here—you fucking, stinking, nigger ape!"

McGriff didn't say anything. He just got up and put on his clothes. There were tears in his eyes.

When he was dressed, he looked over at Franny. She stared right through him.

He opened the door and stepped into the hall without looking behind him again.

After he was gone, Franny continued to sit in her chair by the open window. She felt dead inside.

Dekudisha, she whispered to herself.

Outside there was a din of noise—a terrible pounding. It was coming from the streets. After awhile, Franny recognized the noise as the strains of a Jimi Hendrix song—"Manic Depression."

Franny got up and put on a shirt and jeans. She opened the door and went downstairs. When she passed the front desk, Mary Spudlinger was not there. An open copy of *True Detective* lay on the desk.

A few of the old people were sitting around the TV in the lobby watching reruns of *Dragnet*. Trixie was snoring in her wheelchair. Her head had fallen back, and her mouth was agape. As Franny passed her, Trixie emitted a long, creaky fart.

Franny went outside. It was unusually hot and sticky. The sky was overcast and brown. She walked down Eddy to Powell Street—next to the cable car tracks—following the sound of the music.

When she got to the corner of Powell and Market, Franny saw that a crowd had gathered. The crowd consisted primarily of assorted derelicts and street people. In the center of the throng, a very bad three-piece rock band was playing instrumental versions of '60s songs. The guitar player—a dreadlocked black man—appeared to have only one nostril. He was playing very fast—but his playing didn't mean anything.

People gathered around the band.

Hell—it was a *party!*

A drunk man stripped off his shirt. He had a perfectly white, probably once-muscular body—now gone soft, with tattoos all over. The white tattoo man began to dance around, waving a bottle of beer. The beer was splattering people, but he didn't notice. The man would dance up to people and poke them in the chest, saying things like "Awwright!" or "Let's party *down*, dude!" Then he'd dance away like a fat, white fairy.

Then, what appeared to be a very old woman got in the center of the circle and began to dance wildly. Franny recognized her as the woman on the train from her dream.

The old woman danced a terrible, evil dance. It was so hideous that Franny could barely look at her. The old woman waved her hands over her head and laughed and spit on the ground.

It was obscene.

People were terrified of her.

Soon other people began dancing.

The music grew more furious.

Franny stood off to the side and watched the scene.

Something was wrong. *Something was terribly wrong!*

Suddenly she saw it. These really *were* the Bible people! That is—they were the *same* people that had always existed on the earth. They were creatures of God. Creatures gone astray. Creatures who—by their own choice—had been polluted and corrupted by all things vile and evil and rank. And now they danced—they danced the terrible Death Dance—as things fell apart around them.

Franny went weak in the knees. She wanted to yell. She wanted to cry. She wanted to shout. "Stop! For God's sake—don't you *see?!* You've got to *stop* before it's too late!"

But Franny couldn't say anything. Nothing would come out of her mouth. "Please God," she said inside her own head. "Please—don't let it be like this!"

Franny looked up at the sky. Things looked wrong. Something about the angles. Everything seemed crooked—off kilter. Not just that—things were too *close.*

The sky—brown and hideous now—seemed to actually touch the buildings, which looked tilted to the sides. Something was going on behind the sky—a huge commotion. The sky looked like it was about to crack open. Franny could almost see a war in the skies—with the Archangel Michael and his troops fighting a terrible battle with hordes of ferocious demons.

Then, Franny was overcome by a nameless fear. It was the worst thing she'd ever felt her life—a horrible, black fear that completely paralyzed her. She didn't know what it was—it wasn't the fear of death, or of torture, or of suffering or of anything she could name. No, it was much more than that—

With all the strength she could muster, Franny tried to latch onto something—an idea, a thought, *anything*—but she could not.

Nothing was solid. Nothing would hold.

Then all of a sudden, a terrible thundering began to well up from underneath the ground.

It was horrible.

People knew instantly and started running—but they didn't know where to run.

Almost immediately, a wail of sirens began to howl.

The ground rocked and swayed.

Franny looked up.

Buildings were swaying to and fro—almost in slow motion.

Across the street she saw a department store shaking back and forth. Then suddenly—it simply fell apart.

A gigantic crack opened wide across Market Street, splitting and twisting the old trolley car tracks.

In the distance, another building crumpled, crashing to the ground.

Franny stood still, not moving.

Around her, people were running and screaming and clawing each other.

Franny no longer heard the din of things falling apart around her.

Something was enveloping her—something that pulled her with a terrible force into its cold, black center.

As she fell into the thing, Franny cried out.

"DEKUDISHA! DEKUDISHA! DEKUDISHA!" she wailed.

Only this time, it didn't work.

ADVENTURES

JEWS LIKE US

I was talking on the phone with my friend Mitzi the other night when she said something that stopped me in my tracks. Frankly, I don't even recall the exact statement. All I remember are those three deadly words: "*Jews like us*" (Mitzi and I are obviously both Jewish.)

My God—there it was again! After all these years! That horrible onus!

Oh Mitzi, how could you *say* such a thing? I *trusted* you! I thought you were my *friend!*

You see, I've always had this...*thing* about being Jewish. Of course now that I've "matured," I've gotten over it. But while I was growing up, being a Jew was nothing short of a curse. In the beginning, I didn't even know that it was my Jewishness that was causing my problems. I just knew that something was *terribly wrong.*

For example, back in elementary school, when I liked certain girls, they didn't like me back. No, they liked self-assured, blond-haired guys with straight noses—guys that played baseball and football after school (while I was studying).

But it was when we moved from Cleveland to Los Angeles that things really got bad. It was in that golden state that I got my first taste of terms like *kike* and *Jewboy*. Oh, how they hurt—right down to the quick. Once, some guy in junior high actually called me a *matzoh head.*

Needless to say, I was devastated.

Another bad thing about my new domicile was that in Cleveland, the Jew/goy ratio had been fairly even. But in California—it seemed like there were no Jews at all! If they *were* around, they must have been in disguise.

But by that point, I didn't want Jews for friends anyhow! No sir, I wanted athletic guys—guys who swore and spit and could act tough! Guys named Chipper and Terry and Buzz. Surely, those were *my* kind of people. I didn't want any more friends named Hymie and Pinkus—those soft, little boy/men who already had mustaches at age ten and wanted to grow up to be scientists.

I quickly adjusted to my new situation by becoming rabidly anti-Semitic. I cultivated exclusively non-Jewish friends. I loved going over to their houses. I loved my *own* house because it was big and spacious and *very* non-Jewish. A long, sleek, California-modern house, with a pool and everything! This was definitely *not* the house of a Jew—no siree!

Still, whenever we'd go to visit my relatives, the magic would instantly vanish, and I'd be back in those houses with the dim, gray hallways and the depressing floral wallpaper. Back with the aunts and the grandmas oozing onions and melancholy. *You* know—the ones who constantly pinched your cheeks and kept telling you that you were a genius.

I tried with all my might to create a new persona. I straightened my hair with an extremely smelly substance called "Perma Strate," which my poor mother had to travel to the black section of town to purchase. I practiced sucking in my cheeks to overcome the roundness of my face. On a good day, if I tried *really* hard—striking the proper pose in front of the mirror—I could manage to look *almost* like Tony Curtis, (born Bernard Schwartz), who I hadn't realized was Jewish!

Still, no matter how many preventative measures I'd take, suddenly, out of the blue—horribly, unexpectedly—it would come: "Hey, Jew! Hey, you—*Gee-yew boy!*"

God, the *sound* of it!

GEE-YEWWWWWWW!

Paranoia rapidly set in. Like if somebody would say, "You want a glass of orange juice?"—what I heard was *orange Jews*. Or if somebody asked, "What'd you eat for lunch?" I heard *Jew eat?*

It was horrible.

Oh, Lord, there were a million reasons to hate being Jewish: Moles with little hairs growing out of them...fish breath...soft arms... smacking lips...your grandmother picking food off your plate... songs in a minor key (I've always hated minor keys. Give me major anytime!)...people *zuuppping* their soup, and—worst of all—the dreaded *chach-ing* sound (for those not in the know, the sound I am speaking of resembles someone trying to eject an olive pit stuck in the back of his throat).

And then, there were always the "six million."

You didn't really think I was going to forget the *six million*, did you? My God, how *could* I? That's all I ever heard about! Would we ever be allowed to *forget?* Absolutely not! We were constantly reminded of how our people had suffered. What's more, we were told that we would continue to suffer for *their* suffering...and on and on and on—ad infinitum. Moreover, we were subtly encouraged to feel guilty if we didn't *keep on* suffering.

For a true Jew, life *equaled* suffering.

Damn those six million, anyhow! Because the truth is that there were *twelve million* people killed in the Holocaust. Do you hear me? *Twelve million* is the correct figure!

Besides—you didn't hear Catholics or Christians carrying on about *their* six million. No, they went *on* with their lives. Only the Jews seemed determined to suffer and *keep on* suffering.

Still don't think I have a case, eh? You want more reasons?

Okay, fine.

How about the fact that goys got to *celebrate* Christmas, while Jews had to *observe* Chanukah.

Goy guys had *dicks*. Jewish guys had *dongs*.

Goy girls had *vaginas*. Jewish girls had *pupiks*.

Goys said *"Shutup!"* Jews said *"Shah!"*

Goys said *"Sonofabitch!"* Jews said *"Oy vey!"*

Goys *pissed* and *shit*. Jews made *sissy* and *doody*.

When goys farted it went *braaap!* When Jews farted it went *phuudd*.

When goys spit, it went *pttttt-ding!* When Jews spit, it went *chachhhhh-ptooey!*

See what I mean? *There's* that horrible *chaching* sound again.

Truly, that bloody sound is the blight of the Jewish life!

At least, *my* Jewish life.

In fact, right this very minute, I feel the overwhelming urge to make some Jewish sounds. I'm sorry, but I simply *must*. Ready? Okay, here we go—

Chacchh! Chaachhhhh!

Challah! Chatzah! Chooey!!!

Matzey! Schotzy! Yahtzy! Plotzy!

Zuck, Zuck—ZUCKERMAN! (oh God, please help me—I can't stop).

—OY! OY! OY YOY-YOY!

—NNN...NNNNNN—NACH!!!!

—NACH, NACH, NACHAS!!!

—CHHAAAACCCCCHHHHHHHHH-PTOOEY!!

Ah, *there*. Now I feel better.

By the time I'd reached my late twenties, I'd moved out of my anti-Semitic phase and into my I-don't-care phase. By then, it'd turned out that a lot of very cool people were actually Jewish. People you didn't expect—like Cary Grant, Lauren Bacall, Kirk Douglas, Robert Redford and Bob Dylan. In fact, it even began to be sort of *cool* to be Jewish. Apparently, lots of goy girls actually wanted to marry Jewish guys!

But a lot of good this did me.

Where were all these Jew-lovers when everyone was yelling *Jewboy* and *matzoh head?*

Because of my negative feelings about being Jewish, I'd managed to stay out of a synagogue since my bar mitzvah. However, I recently had an occasion to attend a Friday night service. I wish I could tell you that it turned out to be a wonderful experience, but unfortunately that wasn't the case. Basically, it was just as depressing as when I was a kid.

Still, the evening wasn't a total bust, because of a very interesting character I encountered. He was this little old man who had been stationed at the front entrance of the synagogue. He'd obviously been posted there to direct people—to give them information.

As I watched, people would come up and ask him a question—things like, "What time does the service start?" or "Where's the bathroom?" Easy stuff.

Yet to each and every question, the man's reply was identical. He'd scratch his chin, look skyward for a long moment—then he'd turn back to the questioner and reply, "I really don't know."

I found this quite perplexing. Here was a man who was purportedly in a position of knowledge—minor knowledge, to be sure—but knowledge nonetheless. And yet each questioner was given the exact same answer:

"I don't know."

I found this to be absolutely incredible!

There he stood—*not knowing*.

But was he ashamed?

Was he embarrassed?

No!

Worse, the temple-goers accepted the man's flagrant *not-knowing* without so much as batting an eyelash—as if *not knowing* was the proper response to the questions of life!

Soon, I came to see The I-Don't-Know Man as a symbol for the entire Jewish predicament. For really and truly—they did *not* know.

However, upon reflection, I decided that I admired The I-Don't-Know Man. For to stand there—*not knowing*—and yet to *persist*... surely this was an act of the utmost bravery!

For this act alone, you had to admire the Jews. In spite of all odds—they *always* persisted.

Despite such humanitarian sentiments, I still couldn't get that hideous phrase out of my head.

—Jews like us—

It haunted me.

It invaded my dreams.

So last Saturday, I decided to wander down to the Fairfax area of Los Angeles (known to locals as "The Borscht Belt"). I guess I wanted to try to cure myself of my ailment, once and for all, by experiencing as big a dose of Jewishness as possible.

When I got there, the first thing that hit me were the smells.

All those incredible smells!

And the *faces*. They all looked so wonderfully—*ethnic*.

I don't know, maybe I was in a weird mood—but I felt a strange new sense of camaraderie with everyone. Somehow, I wasn't bugged by how the old women jaywalked—ever so slowly—across the boulevard while shaking their fists at the honking motorists. I didn't even mind the all-black-clad, dreadlocked men with the horrible B.O. slouching in front of Chabad House.

Even the old lady with the mustache pushing the shopping cart piled high with bottles and rags looked terrific to me. I smiled at her, hoping she would forgive me for rejecting our people for all these years. But she just eyed me suspiciously and clucked her tongue.

Go, ahead, old woman—*be* suspicious! I love you nonetheless, for you are my sister, you splendiferous old bag!

In Canter's deli, ordered a corned beef on rye while basking in the glory of My People.

My God—a roomful of *Jews*. It was truly amazing!

Then, I glanced at the table across from me, where a very obviously non-Jewish couple sat. You know—sort of imitation Brad Pitt/Angelina Jolie types.

I stared at them in horror. Good Lord, how could I have ever wanted to be one of *them?* That girl—with her stupid ski-slope nose and her ugly little flared nostrils. And the guy, with his dumb cheekbones and those ridiculous paper-thin earlobes! Hah! What *pathetic* earlobes!

Go ahead—eat your eggs-over-easy, you disgusting goy dimwits! Go on, talk about how many miles to a gallon you get in your stupid BMW, you repugnant heathens, for nothing you say matters! You are made of corn flakes. White bread. Lime jello. Spam. You are mere fluff! You are but dung for me to step upon and crush with my powerful, thick Jewish heels! You offend me to the depths of my soul—you foul, plastic goyische swine! I curse you! I spit on your graves, for you are already *dead!*

I looked around at the Jews. Those wonderful, noisy, gobbling Jews, *zupping* their soup—*naccccchiing* and *chaccching* to beat the band.

They were *beautiful!*

And *yet*, there was something peculiar about them. A certain quality…

At first, I couldn't put my finger on it. Then the proverbial light bulb went off.

The difference in the Jews was that they appeared somehow to be *waiting*. But waiting for *what*, I wondered?

But of course! How could I be such an ignoramus!

They were waiting for the *Messiah!* Oh, I doubt if they even *knew* that they were waiting for Him, but clearly, that's what they were doing. There was absolutely no doubt about it!

Sure, many Christians were waiting too—but the difference was that the Christians *knew* He was coming, so they waited with a sense of joy. The Jews, however, waited *suspiciously!*

Right then, for some reason, I thought of The I-Don't-Know Man. And then, quite suddenly, I had this—*realization*. In a flash, I knew who he really was!

Yep, you guessed it. The I-Don't-Know Man was really *Jesus*—the Messiah Himself—come back to save mankind!

What a clever disguise! What wonderful irony! It was absolutely, incredibly, fantastically *perfect!*

Tears flooded my eyes. I wanted to jump up, waving my corned beef and shout it out loud—

Hey, everybody! He's *back!* No more *waiting!* No more shame! No more guilt! No more self-loathing! No more suffering! Oh *please*, people! If you'd just stop *chaccching* and *kvetching* for one second, you'd *see!*

But I didn't say anything. I knew they'd just think I was nuts. And you probably do, too. But stop and consider for a moment. Who says that God's got to come back with all that thunder and lightning and stuff? No way! I say He'd come back incognito! Hey, if they'd killed *you* the first time, you'd wanna check out the turf before making the Grand Entrance again, wouldn't you?

As I walked back to my car, I felt like I was floating. It was as if a great weight had been lifted from my shoulders. Yes, my dear friend, Mitzi—*"Jews Like Us,"* indeed! Those wonderful words—words that had once seemed nothing less than the taunting of the devil—had been transformed into words of Divine Inspiration!

As I drove home, my mind was going a million miles an hour. I already had the first act finished by the time I got over Laurel Canyon. I could see it now. Yep, definitely high-concept. It would have a $60 million dollar budget at bottom. Spielberg would direct. Ron Howard would produce! It'd star Tom Hanks as the I-Don't-Know Man, Whoopi Goldberg as The Woman With the Mustache, and Sean Penn as the men's room attendant who finally convinces the world that the Messiah has returned.

Hey, I know what you're thinking, you sneaky sons-of-bitches. Well, *forget* it!

I've already registered it with the Writer's Guild. And my agent has four meetings set up for this coming Monday!

NOIR

NOIR

A STUPID NIGHT

It was Saturday night. A Saturday night not unlike many others. I was down at the Big Shot, your typical neighborhood bar, full of the typical pathetic people who frequented such places. On this night, I was one of them.

I looked down the bar at the gallery of faces. They were a sorry lot—that was for sure. They were men who'd given up—men who the world had beaten. They looked like a bunch of whipped dogs.

I knew if I sat there much longer I'd get depressed, so I looked around to see if there were any girls in the place. Finally I spotted two sitting alone at a table near the back.

I headed over. As I got closer I got a good look at them. Neither of them was particularly good looking. One was extremely skinny, with mousy brown hair and these big, horn-rimmed glasses. The other was this fat porker with a mass of curly blonde hair. When I reached the table I stood there, but neither of them would acknowledge me.

"You ladies mind if I sit down?" I said.

"Suit yourself," the fat one snorted.

I sat down. Neither one of them said a thing. They were trying to act extremely casual. Finally the skinny one said, "I'm C.C."

She looked down when she talked. "This here's my friend Jackie," she said, indicating the fat pig.

Jackie pulled out a pack of Salem lights and lit one up, inhaling through her nose.

I already hated her.

I didn't feel like just sitting there, so I asked C.C. if she wanted to dance. She buried her head further into her chest. "Kay," she said, getting up from her chair.

Her fat friend just sat there, sucking on her cig. She was trying to act as if she didn't care, but you could tell that it had hurt her feelings that I hadn't asked her to dance.

I didn't give a shit.

Out on the floor, I put my arms around C.C. There was nothing to her. No tits, no ass—nothing. Just a stick of a girl. As we danced, she pressed her pelvis tight against mine, which kind of surprised me. I immediately got a hard on, which surprised me even more.

Somehow everything seemed okay. Nice even. I could feel C.C.'s warm breath on my neck. It smelled good. What's more, she was really a very good dancer. She could follow every move I made with no trouble at all.

"What do you do, anyhow?" I asked.

"What?" she said.

"I said…WHAT DO YOU DO?"

I had to practically yell it in her ear, the goddamn band was playing so loud.

When the song ended, C.C. kept her face pressed into my neck.

"I didn't really get what you did—for a living I mean."

She looked up at me then.

"I make monster masks."

The band started into another song.

"Did you say you made monster masks?" I asked, but she didn't answer. I guess she couldn't hear me.

When the song was over, we went back to the table. C.C.'s fat friend wasn't there. Then I spotted her. She was out on the dance floor, necking like crazy with some greaseball who was wearing this very cheap seersucker suit. They had their arms wrapped around each other, and she looked like she was trying to suck the guys face off. It was truly disgusting.

All of a sudden, I started getting very nervous. There was no reason for it, really. I guess C.C. saw it, because she was looking at me kind of funny.

"Listen," I said. "could we—you know—get out of here?"

C.C. looked perplexed. "But my friend..." she said.

I looked out on the floor. The fat pig and her newfound friend were still sucking on each other's faces.

"She'll be fine," I said. "Please...let's just go."

C.C. stood up and put on her coat. It was this red shiny thing with some kind of fake fur lining. It looked like it had come from Woolworth's or someplace like that.

For one second I felt horribly, unendurably sad. But the next second I pushed the feeling away. You didn't have room to feel sad when you were playing out cheesy little melodramas like this.

I followed C.C. to her car—a beat-up, green Mustang. The thing was filthy inside, littered with thrown away Peanut Butter Cup and Abba Zabba wrappers, empty Coke cans, and old newspapers.

We drove through the streets of L.A.

I felt as if I were in some kind of dream. I didn't know where I was, and I didn't care. We passed apartment building after apartment building. Inside them I could see lights on... sometimes a TV flickering. I wondered who lived behind all those windows. What were their lives like? What did they think about? But I didn't wonder hard enough to try to get any answers.

We kept on driving. I thought maybe we were in East L.A., but I couldn't tell for certain. All I knew was that the people on the streets had begun to look more desperate. Finally we pulled up in front of an aging brick building. The sign out front read:

CARLTON APARTMENTS
DAILY. WEEKLY. MONTHLY

I followed C.C. up a musty stairwell carpeted with uriney smelling burgundy carpeting. She got to number 3C and inserted her key in the door.

As the lights went on, I was hit by a wave of shock. The walls were entirely covered with horrible faces—ugly rubbery creatures of every variety. Demons, witches, ghouls, Frankensteins, vampires and werewolves surrounded me.

It was really quite a sight.

The only other things in the room besides the masks, were a small black and white TV, a horrible lime green sofa, and a small twin bed.

I went over to get a closer look at one of the masks.

"Did you really make all these?" I asked.

C.C. didn't answer. When I turned around I saw that she'd taken off her shirt. Then, very quickly, she stepped out of her jeans. She did it so fast that it sort of scared me—though looking at her—there really wasn't much to be scared of. She almost looked like a little boy, standing there like that.

"Let's, go, hey," she said.

Frankly, I didn't really feel much like doing anything, but it looked like I didn't have much choice.

C.C. got under the covers. I followed. She reached over and flicked out the light.

As soon as I touched her, she began to moan. Not just little moans either, but real loud ones.

"OH! OH! OH!" she went.

She grabbed me tight and raked her nails across my back. She was really quite strong for such a skinny nothing of a girl.

I just sort of went through the motions, but it didn't seem to matter.

C.C. was lost to the world...to me...to everything.

When she came, she screamed so loud that she practically shattered my eardrum.

Almost immediately afterward, she fell asleep.

And there I lay in the darkness of her room.

Soon my eyes adjusted to the dark.

I looked around at the strange gallery of faces that lined the walls.

Oddly, they didn't look scary.

Then somehow, instinctively, I realized that these were C.C.'s friends. Her *family*, in a way.

Other than that, I knew nothing about the Monster Mask girl. Whether she had a real family...what she wondered about...what her dreams were. No—of these things I knew nothing. And yet I could smell her cunt on my fingers. It was really quite odd.

Just then I had this strange thought. It was more than a thought, actually. It was this sort of…realization.

What I realized was that everything in the world was going on at once.

Like right this second, someone was having a baby. Somebody else was crying because their boyfriend had just left them. Somebody was picking up a hooker. Somebody was visiting a graveyard. Somebody was planning a wedding. Somebody was jacking off. Somebody was drinking Dr. Pepper. Somebody was taking a shit. Somebody was reading Dostoevsky. Somebody else was reading *The Catcher in the Rye*.

Oh, what a delicious thought! All over the world things were taking place *simultaneously!* People were eating, sleeping, farting, fucking, and standing in supermarket lines. People were laughing, crying, praying, singing and vomiting. People were playing symphonies, being killed in car crashes, watching Jay Leno and mailing away for ads in the back of *Hustler*. People were learning speed reading, going to fat farms, conjuring up Satan, being baptized, doing crossword puzzles, picking their faces, embezzling money, taking antidepressants, being bar mitzvahed, robbing liquor stores, falling down manholes, running for governor, going to traffic school, playing pool, pounding their puds, soaking their feet, doing the bop, and shooting the curl.

People were at shopping malls, magazine racks, racetracks, fish markets, pawn shops, boxing matches, whorehouses, all-night diners, airports, police stations, drive-ins, churches, mental hospitals, used car lots, porn theatres, circuses, dermatologists' offices, taxi dance halls, massage parlors, drugstores, karate studios and Greyhound bus stations.

Somewhere—right this very second—somebody was falling in love. Somebody else was having their heart broken. Somebody was stuffing their face. Somebody was wiping their ass.

Somebody was playing old Junior Parker records. Somebody was clipping the long hairs out of their nostrils. Somebody was squeezing a boil on their tuchus. Somebody was saying their rosary. Somebody was dreaming of dancing witches. Somebody else was dreaming of a fat lady flying up to the moon with a flag sticking out of her ass.

It was *amazing!* Absolutely fucking amazing! And what was most amazing of all, was that while all of this was going on, I was in this strange apartment with the Monster Mask girl—a girl about whom I knew absolutely nothing.

Well, I don't know. Maybe it wasn't such a big revelation—but it seemed like it at the time.

I knew I wouldn't be able to sleep. So I quietly got out of bed and slipped into my clothes. I kissed C.C. on the cheek—then I opened the front door and stepped outside.

It was cold and foggy. I glanced at my watch. 1:30 a.m.

There would probably still be some buses running.

I zipped up my jacket and began to walk.

The streets were empty.

Clip clop, clip clop. My heels echoed against the cold pavement.

I headed down an alley and came out on what looked like more of a main street.

I walked faster now. Little electric sounds were in the air.

Then, at the far end of the street, I saw three figures coming in my direction. I suppose I should have felt scared, but for some reason I didn't.

As they got closer, I could make them out—three black dudes, stroking along in that curious way that blacks have.

They kept walking.

So did I.

I was outside of myself again, and I watched the scene with vague curiosity.

Now I could see them better.

They were fairly young—maybe 17 or so.

Despite the fact that it was cold outside, they were outfitted only in thin, sleeveless T-shirts.

As we got closer we both slowed down.

We all knew what was coming.

Finally when we were within a few feet from another, we stopped. Nobody said anything. Then the guy in the middle—a muscular kid with a red t-shirt and a blue neckerchief wrapped loosely around his neck—stepped forward.

"The money, man," was all he said.

I slipped my hand inside my shoulder bag and moved it around until I felt the butt of my .38.

The kid seemed very nervous.

I didn't even look at his buddies.

Somehow this was between us.

"I said, let's have the money, bro."

"I don't think so," I said.

The kid looked at his friends.

Inside, I felt a tiny bubble of fear erupt, but I willed it away. It shot off into the blackness of my stomach.

Now I was just blank.

Empty.

The kid took another step towards me.

I heard the *click* before I saw the blade flash under the lone streetlamp.

"Give it up, man," he said," or I'll haveta cut you."

I pulled the gun out and aimed it at his chest. I felt nothing—just dead inside. I could see every detail of the kid's face, as if it were in close-up. The smooth cheeks with just a few wispy hairs sprouting out, the wide nose, the long dark lashes, the flecks of green in his pupils.

A tiny vein near the iris of the kid's eye twitched for an instant and then he came at me.

I lowered the gun and shot him just above the kneecap.

He went down screaming.

Immediately one of his friends turned and ran.

I felt no desire to stop him.

The other guy just stood there, as if he didn't know what to do.

I turned on him, pointed the gun, and shot him in the face. A neat, black hole opened just above the cheekbone. His teeth drew back in a rictus of pain, and he went down on his knees.

I stepped forward and shot him in the temple.

This time he toppled over sideways—blood pouring from his ears.

I stood over him, looking down.

He looked curious. Nice, in a way.

The blood was so black.

One of his hands twitched. I thought about shooting him again, but I knew there was no need.

"You're one dead punk," I said.

I turned back to the first kid, who was writhing all over the ground and screaming.

I approached him and pointed the gun at his head.

"Yew one motherfucking crazy sumbitch!" he screamed.

"Yew *crazy*, man—*fuckin' crazy!*

I watched him rolling around for another second.

"What's your name, man?" I asked.

"Fuck you, you goddamn crazy sumbitch!" he yelped.

I bent down and put the gun between his lips, shoving it down his throat until he gagged.

"*I said*...what's your name?"

The kid's eyes were rolling around like crazy.

I withdrew the gun until the barrel was barely touching his lips.

He was crying now.

"Jesus Christ—please don't shoot me again, mister. Please don't shoot..."

"Your *name*," I said again.

He could hardly stop crying now.

"Jesus Christ, man...my name's Maurice. My goddamn fucking name is *Maurice!*"

I removed the gun from his mouth and stood up.

I stayed like that for a full 20 seconds.

Then I put the gun back in my bag.

I looked around.

The streets were empty.

The kid who was holding his knee had stopped rolling around now.

He just lay there sort of whimpering.

I zipped up my bag.

Zip! it went.

Then I turned and began walking down the street.

I thought I'd remembered that we'd passed a 7-Eleven just before we'd gotten to C.C.'s place.

I hoped I could find it. I really needed some coffee, and 7-Elevens have excellent coffee. They really do.

After that, I figured I'd see if I could find a bus that would take me back home.

NOIR

A TERMINAL CASE

His eyes snapped open with a start. He looked around the room in a panic.

Where the hell am I?

Then he remembered. Austria—Salzburg, Austria. *That's* where I am.

He lay back in the bed. He was drenched with sweat. Then, before he could stop it, he remembered it all—the strange series of "accidents" that had caused him to run—the car crash, falling over the side of the cliff, the ear operation which had left him unable to maintain his balance. While he was still recuperating, his wife had informed him that she was leaving him.

The nightmares started almost immediately—followed by the spells...those terrible black spells.

His doctor had told him he was severely depressed.

He wrote out a prescription.

But he knew it would take more than a few pills. He knew if he didn't do something drastic, he'd either crack up or kill himself. So he did what he always did—called the travel agency and ordered a plane ticket.

He looked over at the sleeping figure next to him.

One breast was exposed, lying free of the sheet.

He reached out and touched the tip of the brown nipple. It immediately hardened.

He lay there and watched her, regarding in particular the muscularity of her arms and shoulders.

She had a fine body, no doubt about it.

Yet somehow she did not attract him. She looked rather like a man when she slept.

It must be very early, he thought. So quiet.

But just as the thought occurred to him, he heard a distinct *pop!* from somewhere outside.

Then it was still once again.

He slipped from beneath the covers and naked, ran to the bathroom.

Damn—the fucking house was freezing.

Once inside, he let go a strong stream of piss into the toilet. As he was pissing, he saw the bowl on the floor. It had his name written on it in bright red lettering. *Martin*.

When he'd finished, he picked up the bowl and looked at it. There was a happy face drawn under the name.

Cute. Real cute. This was Gitte's way of reminding him that he always left a drop or two of urine on the floor before zipping up.

"You men are all the same…" she had scoffed in her guttural German voice. "Big *bay*bees."

She had a way of holding onto her *esses* just a little too long, which infuriated him.

After slipping on a sweatshirt and a pair of jeans, he went out the front door.

Outside, the air was crisp and cold.

He looked down the street at the rows of houses.

Each one was perfect, with its little square-cut lawn and perfectly tended garden.

A few people were already out watering their lawns.

Well, he thought to himself—it's what you wanted. No jerks, no street people, no gangs of punks cruising up and down the streets with idiot grins on their faces, looking to rob you or shoot your face off. No, this was as far away from all that as could be.

He walked down the street, fascinated by the *clip-clop* of his heels on the cobblestone street.

Even the quality of the sound here was different.

More separation between the sounds.

More space.

A beautiful girl on a bicycle wheeled towards him. When she got close, he saw that she looked exactly like his wife—so much so that he was tempted to call after her.

But he knew it was only his imagination.

No—he'd be seeing ghosts for a long while—that was for sure.

Soon, he noticed one house that stood out from the rest. Unlike the rest, it was not well cared for. Inside the fenced-in yard, all sorts of junk was piled up—old tires, bottles and cans, boards and bricks.

In the yard, he could make out the figure of an old man puttering around amongst the garbage.

Gitte had told him about the man. Everyone in the neighborhood knew him. He collected junk. Sometimes he made things out of it. Moreover, he kept swarms of bumblebees in hives behind the house. He didn't collect the honey or anything, Gitte had told him. He just liked bees.

As he approached the house, he saw the Bee Man fiddling around with a pile of tin cans.

"*Guten morgen*," he said.

The Bee Man didn't reply. He just stared at him, sort of goggle-eyed.

There was a trickle of spittle running from the corner of his mouth.

He was clearly quite insane.

"*Blork*," the Bee Man said (or something like that). *"Blork, blork, blork!"*

The Bee Man had inserted a finger into a nostril and was digging around pretty good. Then he turned and scurried off, mumbling to himself, into his piles of junk.

A few houses down, a group of people were gathered.

A white ambulance was out front, its lights flashing.

A moment later, two men bearing a stretcher came out of the house.

He approached a woman who was watering her garden.

"Was machts?" he asked.

She gave him a quick once over.

"*Der selbstmord*," she said.

She saw that he didn't understand.

"Suicide," she said. "Vun shot—in der brains. Early dis mornink."

At once, he remembered the popping sound he'd heard.

He wanted to ask the woman more, but she had returned to watering her garden.

When he got back, Gitte was in the kitchen drinking coffee.

She was attired in a peach-colored bathrobe.

A Schubert sonata was on the stereo.

"I think the man a few doors down killed himself," he told her. "They were taking the body away when I walked by."

To his surprise, Gitte's only reaction was to raise her eyebrows. Which was rather curious, since she had almost no eyebrows to speak of.

She continued to sip noisily at her coffee.

"It's quite common here, you know," she finally said.

"Here?"

"Austria—ve haf a very high suicide rate. Vun of da highest in da vorld."

Gitte got up and began washing her cup.

She was a very clean person.

Well, it makes sense, he thought. All those neat, perfect little houses. So clean, so tidy. Too regimented, too constricted. There had to be some price paid for all that perfection.

Gitte was toweling off the table now. She had let her robe fall open so that he could see her small, tight breasts. For a moment there was a dark flash of pubis.

He pretended not to notice.

When she was done rinsing her cup, Gitte walked outside to get the paper. She made no attempt to close her robe.

She always seemed to be exposing herself like this—taking off her top around the public pool or something. She sort of forced her nakedness upon you—thrust it about. Somehow, it wasn't sexy or even attractive. In fact, it was kind of obscene—this aggressive nakedness of hers.

Just as he thought this, she walked by and managed to rub a breast against his arm on her way to the bathroom.

The next instant he heard the shower running.

A moment later she stuck her head out the door.

"You did it again," she said.

"Did what?" he asked.

She held up the little pee bowl for him to see.

"You must learn to shake your ting—odervise you vill alvays leave da drippy-drop."

She was smiling crookedly now.

"I'm sorry—really I am."

Gitte clucked her tongue, then said, "You vill learn—I haf confidence in you. Oh, now don't forget—ve are going to da play tonight in town. Eight promptly—so you must be ready. And please—vear sometink besides dose blue jeans of yours."

"Okay," he replied.

He wished she would hurry up and close the door. He could feel one of the spells coming over him—feel it pulling the edges of his face down—especially around the mouth.

When she finally shut the bathroom door, he sat at the kitchen table, buried his face in his hands and wept bitterly.

In the shower, he could hear Gitte singing a Joni Mitchell song.

When the play was over that night, he, Gitte, and her friend Hans—a bearded student-type who chain smoked Gauloises and had extremely bad teeth—sat at an outdoor cafe.

He had hated the play.

In fact, the only thing he liked about it was one line, which was spoken by a character called The Negerboxer (the nigger boxer). He thought he'd heard the line before, but he liked it anyhow.

It said simply, *"In this life... we are all terminal cases."*

Gitte and Hans were talking in English, but he had difficulty understanding what they were saying. Their words kept getting interrupted in his mind by the popping sound he'd heard that morning.

"Martin, vat's da matter? "Gitte said. She was looking at him sort of funny.

"Oh, I'm just a little dizzy is all. Think I'll walk back home."

He got up and left the restaurant.

As he walked back along the river, he began feeling better.

All the little houses looked so pretty at night.

Inside each one there were lights on. And in each one, he knew, there were people—people with thoughts and ideas and dreams.

People with *lives*.

It was so curious.

For somehow he *had* no life.

For some reason, he had been relegated to the status of a permanent observer.

It had always been like this.

When he reached Gitte's house, his bladder was bursting.

He made straight for the bathroom.

As he unzipped, he saw the bowl on the floor with his name on it.

He looked at it for a long while.

Then he aimed at the bowl and let go.

Soon the bowl overflowed onto the bathroom floor.

He continued pissing on the floor, then proceeded to make a nice little design up and down the walls, soaking the towels and the roll of toilet paper in the process.

Still, the bladder wasn't empty.

He continued pissing in the sink, and finished off by soaking Gitte's brand new Waterpik toothbrush.

Then he went to the bedroom, packed his bag and called a cab.

When the driver arrived, he told him to take him to the train station.

Two days later he arrived in the town of Lille. He gave the taxi driver directions to the hospital.

Twenty minutes later, they arrived at an old, greying brick building located at the edge of the sea.

He walked up and down the ugly grey corridors, past people in white smocks who sat silently, staring at nothing.

Soon he found room 200-C, and went in.

She was sitting in her wheelchair, her head down on her chest—just like the people in the hallways.

"Laurence?" he said. *"Laurence?"*

She looked up, and at once her face brightened.

"Oh, Martin…oh, it's *you!* God—I didn't think you would come."

"I talked to your parents last week. As soon as they told me about…it, I told them I'd be here. Didn't they tell you?"

She didn't answer. She just opened her arms for him to come to her.

He went over and embraced her.

"I've lost weight," she said, embarrassed.

Oh, God, my poor baby, he thought. *You're so thin.*

She couldn't have weighed more than 80 pounds.

"I start physical therapy next week," she told him. "They can do things now...with computers. Perhaps I will be able to walk again. They said maybe a year..."

Her voice trailed off...

"Hey," he said, "You want to go look at the ocean?"

"Oh yes—that would be wonderful."

"Good. C'mon—let's get the hell out of here."

He put a blanket over her legs—God, they were so terribly thin—and wheeled her out through the stark, grey corridors—outside into the warm sunlight.

"It's nice, no?" she said.

"It's nice…yes," he smiled.

On the way to the beach, they passed other people pushing family members or friends in wheelchairs.

People smiled or nodded silent hellos as they passed one another.

When they reached the edge of the sand, they found a wooden ramp that led down to the sea.

The sky was beginning to turn grey, and the ocean was billowing up in little tufts.

Something seemed slightly ominous about the setting...but he didn't say that to her.

She looked so happy.

"Too windy for you?" he asked.

"Oh, no, it's wonderful—please, let's go out some more. I want to watch the waves."

Finally they found a spot and stopped.

They sat there, saying nothing.

A few feet away a pretty little girl wearing leg braces was playing with her mother.

"Come to Mamma—come on, baby," the mother said, holding her arms out.

The little girl giggled and then went *hippety hop, hippety hop* to her mother, who shook her hair and laughed.

He noticed that he had a lump in his throat.

It was such a pretty sight; one simply couldn't bear to look at it for too long.

He and Laurence sat in silence.

He looked at the profile of her face. So classically French—the long nose, the high forehead, the wide mouth—lips slightly pursed.

She looked rather like a Gauguin, he thought. Not at all pretty in the dull American way.

No, she was truly beautiful.

He put his hand in her lap and she covered it with her own.

Then he began speaking very softly—almost as if he were talking to himself.

"You remember the winter we slept in the attic of that old house—how we stayed up all night telling each other stories? God—remember how *scared* you were of that one I told you—the one about Peter And The Wolf?

"Jesus, it was *cold*...remember? We had that big Eiderdown quilt, but we still had to sleep all scrunched together so we wouldn't freeze to death. God—those sure were good times, weren't they?"

But Laurence didn't answer.

She was looking at him now, with the strangest expression on her face.

"My God," she said, "your eyes! Martin—what's the matter with your *eyes?*"

"My *eyes?*" he said. "I don't know what you mean—"

Laurence looked very frightened.

She started to reach over to touch his face—but just then something began to happen.

There was a commotion on the surface of the sea, as if something were bubbling underneath the water.

Then, suddenly, a gull shot straight out of the ocean and fell up at the sky.

It was going hideously fast.

They both watched it in horror.

When the gull finally hit the top of the sky, there was a loud *popping* sound—then it burst into a million pieces.

NOIR

PRIVATE DANCERS

In downtown Los Angeles, there is a time and a place where you have never been. But once you go there, you may never quite be able to leave.

Downtown L.A. The jungle.

It's dark now, and the daytime folk—the crazies, Jesus freaks, bums and bag ladies—are all tucked away somewhere for the night. Now, only the hardcore low-lifes are out. Winos, alkies, junkies, and lonelies. Tough-as-nails hookers, dudes in skirts, tall skinny pimps outfitted in lime greens and emergency yellows. Dirty young stud hustlers jiggling their pockets and staring down old men in front of movie theaters. Oh, yeah. They're all here.

At Sixth and Broadway, a glassy-eyed Mexican—a huge machete tucked into the back of his chinos—fades into the darkness of an abandoned storefront. There's a racket from inside the bar next door. A second later, an old black guy—blood streaming from his nose and mouth—runs outside and down the street. On his heels is a maddened transvestite screaming, "Gimme my hundred, motherfucker! Gimme my hundred, man!"

Bad scene. Not cool to be down here alone. Uh-uh.

But wait. Over there—a flashing sign. Maybe a place to go—get out of it all.

Outside the red and green neon sign blinks off and on: GIRLS! GIRLS! GIRLS! FIFTY BEAUTIFUL DANCE HOSTESSES!

You make it inside, head up the stairs toward a red light that glows from around the corner. The burgundy carpeting smells like piss. But what the hell—might as well check it out. Past the sloe-eyed Mexican cat with the spider tattooed on his wrist, guarding the door.

Bob Seger music wafts from the room.

There—you're inside now and...Jesus—what the hell is *this?*

Instant time warp. Flashing Christmas tree bulbs and a tattered old HAPPY NEW YEAR sign that looks like it's been here since 1943. A funky old juke sits in a corner.

And over there on the couch sit the girls.

Waiting to dance.

God, will you get a load of the outfits they're wearing! Gaudy red crinoline, snaky black gowns—low cut to the max. Bright, chintzy blouses dripping with sparkles and spangles. Stiletto heels. Pedal pushers and pumps. Everything looks like it comes from Woolworth's.

Dime-store cheap. Trashy but sexy.

Across from the girls—seated on folding wooden chairs—are the men. A handful of Mexicans and Orientals...a few stone perverts—but mostly just a lot of desperate, shabby old guys. They're seated maybe 15 feet from the girls, arms folded across their chests—and, y'know—just staring.

Some of the girls stare back. Others—not liking the sizing-up process—avert their glances. A redhead with a ton of caked-on undertaker makeup gives one of the perverts a salacious wink, but gets no response.

"Awwright, *fellas*," barks a guy over the microphone, "Ten free minutes of dancing with the girl of your choice. Attsright guys—*ten free minutes!*"

Nobody budges. Finally, a tiny Japanese man goes over and asks a black girl—whose breasts are practically spilling out of her dress—to dance. She glares at him sullenly, then goes over and sticks her card into the time clock. He follows her out on to the dance floor.

The music comes on...

You're my private dancer, a dancer for money...

Back in the twenties they were called "stag dances," "nickel hops," and "monkey hops," but the name that stuck was the most appropriate one: *taxi dancing* (customers are on a time clock, just like a taxicab). And just like the old Rogers and Hart song says, it really *was* ten cents a dance. Out of that, the club got seven cents; the girl got three.

By the early '30s, there were over a hundred taxi dance halls operating in New York alone, and more were springing up throughout the country. Customers danced the Lindy Hop, the Puppy's Tail, and the Chicken Scratch to the sound of live bands. On weekends there were rhumba and tango contests. There was a dress code for the women—dresses cut "no lower than the top of the sternum in front and the uppermost lumbar vertebra in back." The men were required to wear neckties, which they could buy at the door for a dime.

In 1929, due to a violation of the Police Commission rules, the dance halls were temporarily closed in Los Angeles. The County Welfare Department opposed the ruling, issuing a statement that said that "girl instructors in the taxi dance halls are not as bad as they are painted." Nevertheless, it was fairly well documented that dance halls were places where prostitution, if not openly marketed, was readily available. Moreover, the clubs seemed to attract the dregs of society.

In 1925, Paul Cressey—a special agent for the Juvenile Protective Agency—along with a team of investigators—conducted an investigation of the dance halls located on Chicago's South Side. In his report, Cressey noted that *"the taxi dance halls are organized to exploit, for a profit, a situation of promiscuity. It is a mercenary and silent world. Feminine society is for sale, and at a neat price. The dwarfed, the maimed, even the pockmarked, all find social acceptance there. Together with the other variegated types, they make, of the institution a picturesque and rather pathetic revelation of human nature and city life."*

Today, taxi dance halls can still be found in Chicago, Los Angeles, and New York. In L.A., there are some 12 clubs, all located within a one-square mile radius of the downtown Convention Center. The clubs range from sleazy (Danceland, the Latin Lady) to so-so (the Savoy, Club Flamingo, the Paradise) to semi-swank (Club Mikado, the Starlight). The customers are everyone from street people to wealthy businessmen.

Of course, it's no longer ten cents a dance. Most of the dance halls charge the same price—30 cents a minute, or $18 an hour. Of this money, the girls make from 11 to 20 cents per minute, depending on how many minutes a night they dance.

No alcohol is served. Coffee costs a dollar. Cokes are $2.50. In addition to the dance floors, which vary in size, all of the clubs have little tables for couples to sit at, and TV rooms, where the action gets a little heavier.

But the most interesting feature of the taxi dance halls is that, despite the price hike, nothing has really changed since the '20s. The world outside may have become modernized, computerized—but the world inside the dance halls has remained somehow timeless.

Inside the Flamingo, located at Twelfth and Figueroa, the atmosphere is late-'60s tacky. Christmas tree lights illuminate the dance floor, and music wafts from an ancient jukebox. The girls—mostly white, a few blacks—sit on the red Naugahyde couches, play video games, or sip coffee at the bar. On Wednesday nights, the club features beauty contests, during which the girls pose in everything from bikinis to lingerie.

Sleepy, a goateed Mexican, takes tickets at the door. Occasionally, he'll walk downstairs and patrol the parking lot. Janet, a tough little brunette, sits behind a counter, selling dance tickets. Willie, the security guard—a stone killer if ever there was one—leans against a back wall checking out the action. GiGi, a chubby waitress whose ratty brown hair looks like it'd make a good home for a family of lice, hops between tables, hawking coffee and Cokes. Every so often she'll yell at the top of her lungs for no apparent reason, "Hey *cut loose* now! Yeah! You guys *cuttin' loose?"*

Dee, a baby-faced girl of 19, looks up from the paperback she's reading. She says it's her second night back after a two-month layoff. "I came back 'cause my boyfriend [Willie, the security guard] is workin' here," she says.

But tonight Dee looks glum. Apparently Willie has jilted her for Victoria, a raven-haired lass with an absolutely incredible body. But Dee is resolute: "She's a bitch. He'll figure it out sooner or later."

"The only way to survive here is to ignore your feelings," Dee continues. "You gotta make the guys think you're gonna go to bed with them. You gotta string 'em along. The men here? If they don't speak English, they're pigs. Believe me—I get quite a workout on the dance floor. It's fucked. See, I've got this thing about strange men touching me. Maybe it's a hangup, I dunno. Anyhow, after Christmas, I'm gonna get me a regular job...maybe a waitress or a domestic. They make pretty good money, y'know."

"This place isn't really for normal people," says Sissy, a wan-looking brunette who drives over a hundred miles from her apartment in Anaheim to come to work each night. "You try not to hurt their feelings, because these men are very lonely, and they can't go to places where normal people go.

"I feel rented—that's the only way to put it. A lot of times you're sitting on that couch with guys staring at you and you just feel like a piece of meat. That's what they call it, you know—The Meat Rack. Yeah, it's pretty terrible, but I don't know what else to do. My boyfriend's real mad at me 'cause I'm working here, but he doesn't have a job, and I've got three kids to support. I'm gonna quit as soon as I save enough money. My oldest daughter keeps buggin' me sayin', 'Mom, when are you gonna get a *normal* job?"

Inside the club's office, Victoria sits, her head in her hands. She looks up, red-eyed. "Ya got an aspirin? Man, I've got this *splitting headache*.

"I wanted to go home," she continues, "but we're not allowed to leave until 2:00 a.m. I don't know if I can take it any more—I really don't. I mean, how would *you* like it if some guy with the most horrible body odor in the world was slobbering in your hair and grinding you all over the goddamn dance floor? This place *sucks!* When you come to work, they tell you everything—everything except what to do when one of those creeps gets a hard-on and starts jamming it between your legs."

In the four months Victoria has been working at the Flamingo, her highest paycheck has been $112.56 for a week's work—a far cry from the $650-a-week-plus-tips that the club advertises. When asked why she doesn't quit, she looks perplexed. "I don't really have any skills. I mean—what would I *do?* I'm not gonna go be a stripper. Anyhow, it's not *that* bad. I mean, my boyfriend works here, and my sister too, so it's kinda nice sometimes, I guess."

Bluejay, a sleepy-eyed redhead attired in a slinky black gown smiles and lights a Camel. "Hey, this is an ego trip—don't let 'em tell you any different. Even if the guys are dogs, it still makes you feel good...the attention, I mean."

Bluejay's worked at nearly all the L.A. dance halls. She knows the score. "Most of the guys that come in this place have a real bad reputation. So they try and look for new girls who don't know 'em yet. Then they think they can get away with whatever they want.

"A lot of the clubs are really bad. They had a VD epidemic over at one club a while back. Lotta pimps workin' the room, lookin' for new meat.

"The way it works is, a guy comes in and says, 'where can I get a girl to do what I want?' Then the floor manager sets up the deal. The guy'll take the girl out after the place closes, but by then he's already dropped maybe $200 on the dance floor. In the end, the guy *always* pays. What the girls try to do is find a guy with lotsa money, then they'll *bleed* him to death. I know one girl who got $1,400 from this guy, and she didn't even sleep with him. She just played a mind trip on him."

As we're talking, GiGi prances by with a tray full of coffee mugs. "Hey, you guys *cuttin' looooose* now?!" she yelps.

Bluejay rolls her eyes. "Real ditzy, that broad," she snorts. "Yeah, we got all kinds here."

She nods her head towards a mousy little brunette with a bad case of acne who's sitting alone on the couch. "A real space case," Bluejay says. "She never dances. All she does is sit on the couch all night taking her raincoat on and off. Too much angel dust probably.

"See that one out on the dance floor?" she says, indicating a skinny Oriental woman doing a slow bump 'n' grind with a man of about 70. "She's wearin' a wig. Doesn't want anybody to know who she is during the daytime." Bluejay stubs out her smoke. "Like I said, we got all kinds. Some of 'em live in hotels, some work day jobs, lots of 'em have husbands, families. Some are here lookin' for drugs, or even for a husband. Yeah, honey, like I said—you name it, we got it."

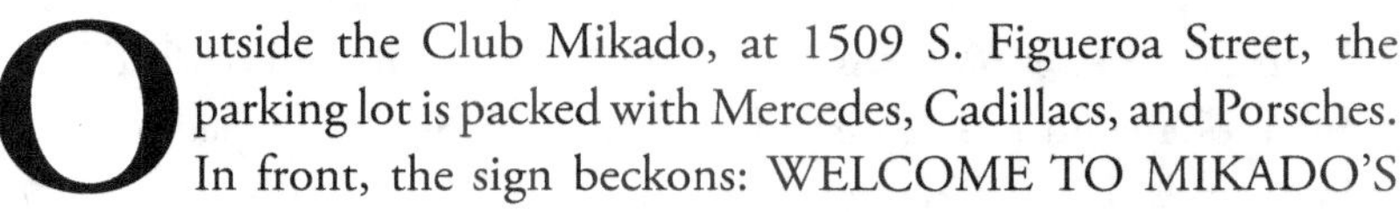

Outside the Club Mikado, at 1509 S. Figueroa Street, the parking lot is packed with Mercedes, Cadillacs, and Porsches. In front, the sign beckons: WELCOME TO MIKADO'S

WORLD. There are a few photos of the girls attired in Playboy Bunny-like costumes, and a neon backlit South Sea Islands panorama.

Inside the club, the décor is phony plush, and the customers are mostly well-heeled Oriental businessmen. Like the other clubs, the girls sit on the couch, but here the men observe them from behind a glass partition. After the customer selects a girl, the couple is introduced by the floor manager or "mammasan."

Out on the dance floor, couples boogaloo as unbearably loud music—everything from disco to Japanese rock 'n' roll—makes conversation all but impossible.

Mary, 20, a pretty blonde from Toronto, came to California four months ago with her girlfriend. When they found themselves broke, they answered the ad in the *Los Angeles Times* for dance hostesses. "Yeah, you meet some nice girls," Mary says. "In fact I've made quite a few friends since I've been working here. Some of the customers are okay too...but a lot of 'em are real sickos."

Mary nods her head toward a big, hulking guy wearing pop-bottle thick bifocals, who's peering intently at the girls through the glass partition. "He's a real case. His whole trip is to check a girl out, go into the TV room with her, and then tell her how he likes to rape 12-year-old girls. He gets off on watching your reaction.

"Then, of course, there's the foot fetishist. He hits all the clubs. He'll pay for a girl, and all he wants to do all night is to sit on the couch and rub her feet. Pretty sad, huh?"

Elke, a busty German girl, is one of the old timers at the Mikado. Two years ago she married the club's manager, LeRoy Holmes. "When he first came in, he was just a customer," Elke remembers, "but I had my eye on him right away. Finally, he gave me a ride home, but he never touched me. I told my roommate, 'It didn't work again.' But after a month or so, I got him up in the apartment, gave him a little cognac, and he asked me to marry him. Yeah, I guess it's kinda romantic."

Jane, 22, works during the day as a schoolteacher, and dances at the Mikado four nights a week. An extremely plain girl with mousy brown hair and big sad eyes, she looks as if Laura had just stepped out of a production of *The Glass Menagerie*. "The first night I worked here, a guy took me into the TV room and had his pants unzipped in about two seconds. I didn't know what to do, so I clocked him out. No, it's no fun, but I'm in a bad financial situation...I'm two months behind on my rent. I feel degraded sitting out there on that couch. That's the worst part, actually. In a way, this is still better than just going out to a regular nightclub. I mean, the guys treat you terrible there, too. Here, at least you're getting paid."

Twyla, a skinny 19-year-old with a smear of red lipstick on her mouth, moved out to California from her hometown of Gary, Indiana in order to become a model. She worked at the Starlight before she got started dancing at the Mikado. "Hey, ya gotta go where the business is," she says cheerily. "This place works two ways...either you become cold and bitter, or else you become smart. Me, I'm havin' a ball. I only dance with who I want to. I never dance with Americans—they're the *worst*. Their greatest hobby is beating their wives three times a day an' sayin' 'hey, baby, I've got 12 inches.' But I *love* Orientals. Oh, yeah. I just go *crazy* every time I see one on the freeway! Those guys really know how to spend the money. I've gotten jewelry, my rent paid, trips to Las Vegas, furs...lotsa stuff. Hey, if I like them an' I wanna sleep with them—who cares? I don't look on it as prostitution. I think of it as being with someone you like for money."

By 11:00 p.m. on a Friday night, all of the girls are with customers. The couch is empty, save for one stoic Vietnamese girl. "Her problem is, every time a guy gets fresh with her, she'll clock him out," says the security guard. "I don't know if she makes any money. I asked her one time, an' she told me she didn't care about the money. Said she's just here looking to find a guy who'll marry her." He casts a sidelong glance at the girl. "Yeah, well—good luck, honey."

Built in the forties, the Roseland Roof, located on the fourth floor of the Fenton Building at 833 Spring Street, is L.A.'s oldest taxi dance hall. The once elegant club has now gone to seed, but the marble floor and art deco archways hint of grander days.

Roseland is one of five clubs owned by Bill Tate. With the exception of the Paradise, all of Tate's clubs (the Galaxy, Las Palmas, and the Chicago Club) cater to the large influx of Latinos that have moved into the downtown area. "It's kind of a Latin USO," says Ron Saminsky, a bulky ex-cop who manages the hall. "Guatemalans, El Salvadorans, Mexicans—they all come here to meet girls from their own countries."

Saminsky leads me upstairs and down a musty, darkened corridor. As we walk, he shines his flashlight on old, framed photos of dancers from the past—beautiful, bobbed-haired women attired in evening gowns—which line the walls.

Inside Saminsky's office sits the original "BEAUTIFUL GIRLS! 10¢ A DANCE" sign from the club's heyday. "The dance halls get to be a way of life," he says. "When I first started coming here, I thought it was crazy…people paying this much just to dance with somebody. But I had to try it for myself." Saminsky clocked out a girl and wound up marrying her. "I know it's kinda corny," he says, "but that's the way it happened.

"This is a really tough grind for some of these girls. They work all day in the downtown sweat shops, go home and sleep for a couple of hours, then come down here and dance all night. A lot of them send the money back home to their families."

When Saminsky first began working at the Roseland, there were problems with violence. "We had to deal with a lot of the local gangs… the Playboys, the Temple Street gang, and the 18th Avenue Crips—but now we've got it pretty well cleaned up. The gang members can't really afford to come in here, and when they do, they know they've gotta behave themselves. It's pretty peaceful now. In fact, this place is kind of a neutral zone. People from countries that are at war with each other come in here and get along fine."

LeRoy Dorfman, 72, the janitor at Roseland, has been working and dancing there since 1952. He lives down in the basement of the club, where he's kept company by his dog, Brenda. Occasionally, he still comes upstairs and clocks out a girl. "Yep," he grins, "I useta dance with lots of 'em. Now, I don't really get out that much anymore. Sometimes I'll go up there an' just sit around."

LeRoy emerges from his room—a tiny cubbyhole filled mostly by an ancient mattress—with a fistful of crumpled old photographs of the girls from bygone days. "Back in them ol' days, it was lotsa fun. Sometimes the girls'd give me free tickets, 'cause they liked me an' all."

LeRoy points out a pretty Mexican girl in one of the photos. "That's Lisha. Her and me started goin' together when she was 18. She's 24 now. I took her an' her mother to Knott's Berry Farm, an' to Catalina Island. They asked me if I wanted to move down to Tijuana an' live with them. But then Lisha, she got into some trouble. She's in jail now over in San Berdoo.

LeRoy's hands shake as he points out another girl. "This one, I took care of her. She had a lotta boyfriends, but then she got crippled, an' I was the only one to go see her. I took care of her for nine years. Yeh, it was tough. She got t'drinkin'. Then she got cancer. It was pretty bad."

LeRoy fingers a huge dent on the left side of his head. "Some nigger stomped on my face over in the alley behind the Paradise. All I had on me was four dollars. Yeah, these clubs can get pretty bad. One guy took some of the girls home an' got killed in his own backyard. A few years back, the owner of Danceland got shot dead, right over there on Figueroa. Sure, it gets kinda scary—but usually Brenda here'll take care of me."

LeRoy runs his fingers over the photos, remembering. "What I need now is to find me a girl who'll take care of me. I'm kinda sick, you know. Lisha, she told me that when she gets out, her an' me is gonna get an apartment together, but…I dunno. I'm afraid she's gonna go an' get started on the dope again."

LeRoy drifts off for a moment. "Yessir, them old days was real good, but now it's different. I dunno…I mean, I don't really get out that much anymore."

"There's three things you've gotta remember about women. They hate us, we hate them. They're stronger than us. They're smarter than us. And most important...they don't play fair."

That quote—perhaps the most succinct summing-up of present-day male/female relationships—was uttered by none other than that master of the sneer, Mr. Jack Nicholson. Nowhere is the spirit of Nicholson's statement played out so clearly as in the taxi dance halls.

In her novel, *Dry Hustle*, Sarah Kernochan wrote about her experience working in a New York taxi dance hall. The work began as an undercover assignment for *Cosmopolitan* magazine, but Kernochan became so obsessed with the milieu and the lifestyle that she wound up working for over a year. Along with another girl she met in the dance hall, Kernochan embarked upon a cross-country hustling spree, at the end of which she'd become the consummate con artist.

Sitting in an L.A. coffee shop, Kernochan explained the mentality necessary to be a successful taxi dancer. "Most men and women have a natural antipathy towards one another. Whether it's a teaspoon or a gallon. In order to be in this kind of profession, you have to reach down and focus on your anger and turn it into cunning. You have to have a touch of larceny, a touch of revenge. After I finished my book, it took me practically a year to stop sizing men up to see what they're worth. It warps you. You've gotta see men in a certain way—any hooker will tell you that."

Kernochan even found herself falling in love with one of her customers, who appeared as the character Cody in her novel. "The guy was a real lowlife. He was actually a murderer. But he was a good hustler himself. That's the kind of guy I wanted…a macho guy who couldn't be fooled—whereas if anyone had treated me nicely or showered me with gifts, I would've had total contempt for them."

Peg, a 21-year-old Led Zeppelin groupie, is a prime example of Kernochan's theory. After Peg's boyfriend beat her up one too many times, she moved out and began working at the Starlight, where she danced under the name Angel. Peg got her friend Staci a job at the club as well. But Staci, who couldn't get past her natural innocence, soon quit. "It was really terrible," she recalls. "It got to where I'd start crying before I went to work."

Peg, on the other hand, learned the art of survival in the dance halls quickly. "You've gotta play it smart, she says. "In the beginning, I was getting all kinds of business, but then it stopped, on account of I wasn't putting out. Only the girls who turned tricks were getting lots of minutes. I mean, like this fat Mexican chick—really an ugly mutt—she'd be clocked out all the time. Hey, I'm not conceited or anything, but c'mon—gimme a break!

"I don't wanna sleep with these guys, so what I'll do is, I'll tell them I'll go out with them. That gets 'em tipping. But I tell 'em I want 'em to come in five or six times before I'll, y'know…*do* anything. Then on the seventh time I'll just say 'sorry, I changed my mind.' But, by then I've already got hundreds of dollars from them.

"If they don't tip me I make this big scene…just insult the hell out of 'em, y'know? Like I chased this one guy out of the club. I told him he was a loser for coming into a place like this and having to pay for a girl.

"Hey, most of these girls are really airheaded out. Like that one over there?" she says, indicating a chubby blond. "A class A-1 bimbo. All she talks about is the orgies she's gone to and stuff. Me, I'm smart. I don't sleep with anybody. I just get their money. Yeah, it's a crack-up. I mean, they're so stupid—they *deserve* it!"

When a girl starts work in a dance hall she goes through a cycle with definite and fixed stages. At the outset, a new girl will get a lot of customers, until she is—so to speak—used up. Then she'll either have to move to another club to become "fresh" again, or she'll have to find new tactics to keep her customers interested. This can involve anything from wearing sexier outfits to turning tricks. In any case, for a girl to make sufficient minutes, she must engage in a type of dancing commonly referred to as "grinding."

"If you don't dance that way you might as well forget it," says Pinki, who's worked several of the clubs. "I sat on the couch for a long time, but now I'm out there humpin' it like the worst of 'em. Some of my friends won't talk to me, but I don't care. It's the money I'm interested in."

After a while, a seasoned dancer will learn the art of sizing up a customer quickly. The men are either "one night stands," "fish" (somebody who'll pay the rent) or "sugar daddies" (a long-term fish). According to seasoned taxi dancers, the best fish are Chinese, Japanese or Filipino, referred to by the girls as "Flips." "I'd never have a Flip for a boyfriend," says Janet. "They're too damn possessive. But they're okay to keep around...and if you know how to work it, they'll spend a lot of money on you."

If a girl finds herself an easy touch, her fellow dancers would be best advised to keep their hands off. Friendships go out the window when it comes to hanging on to a big spender. "I found me a real good one," says Dorothy, who works at the Flamingo. "This other chick started to go after him the other night, but I told her I'd cut her fucking throat if she didn't cool it."

Like Bluejay says, in the end the guy always pays. "There's always another sucker just waiting to be taken. I used to have a steady boyfriend, but no more. Uh-uh. I'll never get tied up with another jerk. All they wanna do is keep their eye on you. They take your money, an' never buy you nothin'. But now I've got a different attitude. What

I have is mine…and what *they* have is mine too, if I'm smart enough to get it."

Lucy, who works as a dancer on her off nights from her regular job as a dominatrix, put it most succinctly. "Of *course* I hate men," she smirks. "Why else would I be working here?"

Most of the customers at the taxi dance halls don't want to talk. Of those who do consent, most are either regulars, or older men who've been coming for a number of years. Interestingly, though most of them say they don't really like the dance halls, they keep coming back.

"It's better'n sitting in your room watching TV," says Benny Goslin, who lives in downtown in the Hotel Rosslyn. "Ya know, the nights get sorta lonely, so I come down here, I dunno, maybe a coupla nights a week. Sometimes I dance, sometimes I maybe have a coffee with one a' the girls, or else I just sit and watch. Nah, I'm not lookin' to get involved. It's just a way of passing the time."

"All dese girls are after is yer money," says Sam De Wald, 46. "But dey don' get far wid me, nossir! Know why? Cause I'm onto dem—dat's why! I know the score, an' y'know what? Before, I wuz just tryin' t'keep dem from puttin' one over on me… Now *I'm* tryin' t'put one over on dem! Yeah! I know what I'm after—an' I'm gonna *get* it!"

Rick Schwartz, 34, is an ex-policeman who now works part-time as a bodyguard. Rick spends his nights off in the dance halls, mostly watching from the sidelines. He generally goes from one club to another, sometimes hitting as many as six per night. "I used to dance," Rick recalls, "but it just got to be too expensive, in more ways than one. The thing is, see, you kinda get addicted to these places after awhile. It's weird. I can't really explain it. But it's no good. Sometimes you fall in love with one of the girls, sometimes they'll fall in love with you…but it never works."

Rick points to a picture of a pretty dark haired girl on the wall. "That's Chiquita. Pretty, huh? Her an' me was goin' together for awhile, but she found some guy with a lotta dough an' ran off with him. No, I don't know where she is." Rick lights a smoke and looks out at the couples on the dance floor. "Yeah, there's a lotta stories in these places. Problem is, they're all sad."

Sonny Kiplinger, 31, is at the Paradise tonight where his girlfriend Diane dances four nights a week. "Yeah," Sonny says, "I been comin' down here for a long time. I keep sayin' I ain't comin' back, but hey!—I can't stay away. Like tonight, I got all showered an' shaved an' stuff to go out...but I wound up down here instead. Hey! I don' wanna go to no regular nightclub anyhow. Last night I spent all my money on this chick, then find out she's only 17. *Sheeessshh!*

"Hey! These places are gyp joins! All of 'em! But you learn fast. I ain't dancin' tonight anyway. I only got about ten bucks on me.

"See that's my girl over there...the blonde. I came down here tonight to get on her case, but she promised me she ain't gonna dance with no other guys. Y'know, it's funny...I don't like to see her dancin' with nobody else, but I can't quit her, ya know what I mean? An' she gets crazy jealous if I dance with any of the other girls. Ah, but what the hell...Women, they're all crazy—right?"

Leo Kowalski, 63, has been coming to the dance halls for the past three years, ever since his wife died. "It's funny why I like these girls," he says. "I'm not really interested in them, 'cept maybe to dance with. Sometimes I take somebody out to breakfast. But it's better not to get involved with women anyhow, 'cause they'll try and hook you if they can. Me, I just like bein' around pretty little girls. Who wants to date old women, anyhow? There's something about old women that makes me tired before I even get started. People are always inviting me to parties and dragging some old woman in for me, but I just take off and come down here instead! They've got some nice little girls here. Good girls. None of them are prostitutes, either...I don't care *what* they tell you."

Sergeant Bill Alvin of the LAPD Central Vice Division disagrees. "Most of the taxi dance halls have prostitutes working in them. Sometimes the management is encouraging this—sometimes not. It all depends on how well the club is doing. What happens is, a customer comes in, pays for a girl's time, and then leaves with her. That way the club is making money—as if she's dancing—while she leaves and turns a trick. Sometimes, the floor manager will supply a girl for a price, and they'll get a kickback on the prostitution.

"It's really hard for us to control it. If we sent an undercover operative in, he might spend $200 dancing and never get a violation. Meanwhile, we could get nine or ten streetwalkers in that amount of time. Look, we may make an occasional bust, but the fact is, these clubs aren't going to go out of business. They're simply too profitable."

Jon Fen Fong, owner of the Club Mikado (as well as the motel around the corner on Olympic) concurs. "Business velly good...velly good indeed," he smiles, revealing a gold tooth. "You got pretty girls... you got customers. No problem."

At 3:00 in the afternoon, the lobby of the Hotel Frontier at Fifth and Main streets looks like Grand Central Station. A group of old women are huddled around a TV set watching the afternoon soaps. A noisy bunch of men are arguing over the outcome of Larry Holmes' latest fight, gesturing wildly and passing a bottle of Thunderbird between them. A few old men sleep on benches.

Rooms at the Frontier go for $15 a day, $22—if you want a black and white television set. There is no heat.

I ask the guy at the desk what room Lori Velasquez is in. He asks me what for, and I tell him I'm here to interview her for a story on taxi dancing. He says he doesn't know what taxi dancing is, but anyway I can't go upstairs. Guests only. A $10 bill takes care of that.

On the eighth floor, I knock on Lori's door for five minutes. A skinny black guy standing in the hall watches me. Finally, Lori opens the door a crack. I show her my press card and she lets me in.

The tiny room is filled by a bed, which Lori flops back into. She's wearing red bikini underwear and a tie dyed T-shirt. Her five-year old daughter, Jesse, is happily drawing and watching *Road Runner* cartoons on TV.

"I was 14 when I started dancin'," Lori recalls. "got me a fake ID. It's no problem. Most of the club owners will get one for you. Yeah, used to turn a few tricks back then. Not a lot—mebbe one or two a week. Pick up an extra couple hundred dollars. I dunno. But I quit all that when I got married. Then last week my ol' man left me, an' I didn't know what to do. So I moved into this place an' got me a job dancing at the Savoy. I don't like it...makes me feel kinda old, y'know. When I go to work I have to leave my kid with my mom. She lives in the hotel across the street; she's on Social Security. I don't really like leavin' Jesse with her, 'cause she's kinda crazy. Tried to slash her wrists a coupla times. I hope I don't haveta keep dancin' long, but it's all the money I got right now."

Jesse comes over, sits in my lap and shows me her drawing. I ask her what it is, and she tells me that it's a fat man laughing up in the sky.

Lori says that she doesn't really have much more to say and that she needs some more sleep before going to work tonight. I thank her and leave.

Out in the hall I press the elevator button. The skinny black guy is still standing there. He rubs his chin for a moment, as if making an important decision. "You widda newspaper?" he finally asks. I tell him yes.

"I used to be on Bugs Bunny," he says, then turns and disappears down the hallway.

Janet looks ten years older than her twenty-four years. Even when she smiles, her eyes remain hard, suspicious. Well, it's no wonder. Janet's life hasn't exactly been a piece of cake.

As a teenager, she was raped by her stepfather and bore him a child. Later the child was killed. Four years ago, Janet left her hometown of Duluth, Minnesota—leaving two children behind—and came out to California where she began dancing at the Paradise.

Today, though, she works only part time as a cashier at the Flamingo. Janet's entire world revolves around the taxi dance halls. Her present boyfriend, a Filipino, is a former customer. In fact, Janet has never dated a man that she hasn't met at the dance halls. "I think about it sometimes," she says, "but it's just never happened."

Though Janet's basic attitude is one of mistrust ("you can't trust the men *or* the women; it's dog eat dog") she's become a mother figure to some of the newer girls who haven't yet learned the ropes. Presently, she shares her $440 a month apartment—a tiny two-room affair located a mile from the clubs—with GiGi and Rhonda, both of whom work at the Flamingo.

At 4:00 in the afternoon, Janet is just waking up. She was out until 5:00 a.m. hanging out in the coffee shop at the Olympian Hotel, the after-hours spot for the girls from the various clubs. "It's my favorite time," Janet says. "That's when you get to hear all the good stories."

As Janet lights her first cigarette of the day, Rhonda, a pretty, 21-year-old Sally Struthers lookalike—is trying on different outfits for a late afternoon date. "Ooooh, ain't *this one* pretty?" she coos, twirling around in a tight fitting getup that outlines her sumptuous body.

Though Rhonda's face doesn't bear the scars of her past like Janet's, her life hasn't been easy either. At 13, she ran away from home with a biker, later marrying him. But Rhonda's new beau jilted her for her older sister, with whom he had a child. Last year, Rhonda left her home in Lake Tahoe and came down to L.A. where she hopes to get work as a model or an actress. Right now, though, she's thoroughly enjoying her work at the Flamingo, where for the past several weeks she's won the Wednesday night beauty contest.

"It's such a kick-back job," Rhonda says. "You get to take as many breaks as you want. In fact, you don't even have to show up if you don't want to. You get to wear what you want...like I can be a beauty queen, or a total sleaze. All depends on how I feel. Sure, a lotta the men are creeps. But then there's always the possibility that Mr. Wonderful's gonna come in, and you're gonna pay *him* to sleep with *you*."

When Rhonda leaves, Janet looks troubled. "I dunno about that girl. All she thinks about is men, men, men. I keep tellin' her she'd better watch her ass, but I guess she's just gonna have to learn the hard way."

There's a knock on the door. It's Bridgette, a tough-looking brunette who lives upstairs. She's here to borrow a dress before going to work tonight at the Club Mikado.

"Got anything that's gonna fit over these boobs?" Bridgette asks, wandering into Janet's large walk-in closet. A moment later she emerges, half in and half out of a shiny red outfit, which she's having trouble squeezing over a pair of football-player shoulders. Bridgette raises her arms, exposing a pair of unfashionably hairy armpits. "I don't like ta shave," she offers. "My legs neither. Gives me a rash."

Unlike Rhonda, Bridgette isn't interested in getting involved with men. "Last time I put a man first in my life, honey, I wound up stone-cold broke. Couldn't even buy my own kid a damn Christmas present. Hey, my boyfriend was a used car salesman. I mean, that sucker could *talk*. Like ta meet up with him now, though. I've learned a few tricks of my own. Hell, bet I'm a better hustler than he is.

"'Sides," Bridgette says, "I've got this little, uh, problem with men. See, I've got a way of makin' any man I'm with so mad that he'll hit me. So I keep on gettin' beat up. It's sort of an illness, I guess. Anyhow, I've got a pretty mean temper myself."

"You're not kidding!" Janet chimes in. "The last time this girl lost that temper of hers, she wound up smashing Willie, [the Flamingo's security guard] in the face. It took four of us to pull her off him."

"Ah, I was just a little drunk," Bridgette offers. "Anyhow, what about the time you punched out that chick right in the club?"

"Hey, the bitch threw hot coffee in my face!" Janet counters. "No way anybody is going to get away with that!"

"It's not that I don't like men," Bridgette explains. "It's just that, well—I don't think I know how to accept love. I just don't believe in it anymore…not since my husband attacked me, an' started stabbin' me with a kitchen knife."

"This job is hell on your relationships," Janet says. "I mean, after you've had creeps pawing at you all night, you don't even really want a man around when you get home."

At precisely 10:00 p.m. I pull up across the street from the Club Starlight at 1224 S. Broadway. I sit in my car for a few moments, watching customers walk inside.

Moments later, passing a storefront window, I catch a glimpse of myself. Hmmmm. Not bad. I'm wearing grey slacks, a black linen Harris tweed sportscoat, and have on a fake pair of horn-rimmed glasses. I'm hoping that the management—who've refused to allow me entry after I'd identified myself as a journalist—won't recognize me.

At the door, I pay the $2 entry fee to the cashier, and seat myself at the table. Before I've even had a chance to check things out, the floor manager—a smiling moon-faced Chinese fellow—approaches me. "Hello, sir. You like I bling you a girl?"

"Girl? Well, uh…yeah, I guess so."

"We got a lotta pretty girls here." He points to the couch. "You pick one."

I peer through the glass at the girls outside, but it's difficult making up my mind.

"What kinda girl you like, sir? Maybe I help you."

"Well, let's see. I was thinking, maybe...ah, an Oriental."

"Ahhhh." He smiles. "You wait. I bling."

Moments later he returns with a tiny Korean girl whose name (I'm told) is Lee. The manager quickly departs. Lee sits still for a moment, her eyes downcast. Then she looks up at me, unblinking. "What name you?" she asks.

"Name? Ah…Otis. Otis Bingenheimer."

Lee doesn't respond. She simply reaches out and feels the sleeve of my jacket, as if testing the material. "Nice," she says. "I like."

I'm just thinking to myself how pretty she is—such a tiny little thing—when Lee smiles, revealing a mouthful of crooked, discolored teeth. What's more, only half of her lip seems to move upward, while the other half remains stationary.

"What kinda work you do?" Lee asks, still smiling.

"Work? Well, I ah…I own a chain of bowling alleys."

"Bowingawweys?"

"Yeah, you know—you throw the little balls down the lane and knock the pins down."

Lee looks nonplussed. "You make lotta money?"

"Well, yeah, sure. Yeah, I do okay."

"How much money you make?"

"Ah, I guess mebbe $200,000 a year…give or take a little."

Again the smile. "I *like* money." Then she takes my hand. "You wanna dance wid me?"

"Well, I don't really dance much…" But Lee is tugging me out onto the floor, where we slow dance to a lilting Japanese song. She has a wonderful young body that, I dare say, seems to actually be throbbing beneath the thin cotton of her dress. Her hair smells nice. I can almost forget that set of choppers.

When the song ends, Lee asks me if I want to go into the TV room. Well, why not? Might as well play this little scene out.

Inside the dimly lit room, a few couples sit on couches. A black girl sits, holding hands with an old man of about 70. They're watching Merv Griffin. The old man appears to be smiling. Over in a corner, another couple is locked in a fierce embrace.

Lee and I sit on a couch. Much to my dismay, she is smiling at me again. "You vewwy handsome man," she says.

"Uh, well…thank you very much."

"You like Lee?"

"Well…sure. You seem very, ah…nice."

The next second I feel a hand on my crotch. It begins doing a little dance.

"Maybe you take Lee shopping! Lee look vewwy nice in expensive dwess!"

The dancing hand quickens its pace.

"Maybe you take Lee Las Vegas! Lee *like* Las Vegas!"

Ah-ha. So *that's* the game. Well, sorry, sister, but you picked the wrong guy to dry hustle. This is one cat that knows the score.

I glance at my wristwatch. "Uh, I think I'd better get going. I just remembered that I have to go home to feed my cat."

The dancing hand retreats. Lee looks sad, and for a moment I feel sorry for her. She gets up and leads me to the cashier, where she turns in her time card. The bill for approximately an hour and a half comes to $27.50, plus $10 for the Cokes we've been drinking. After I've paid, Lee stands, gazing at me with those big, unblinking eyes. "You come back? Dance wid Lee?"

"Sure," I tell her, and hand her a $10 tip before depositing her back on the couch.

Outside, the night is pitch black. Sirens are wailing in the distance. An old guy lurches drunkenly down Broadway. I get into my car and sit for a second, watching customers go into the club. Then I gun the engine and split.

I make it back home in time to catch *Viva Las Vegas* on the late night movie.

The taxi dance halls raise a number of issues, which I'll have to leave for someone more sociologically inclined than myself. Still, it would seem that the most important question is—are the dance halls a world unto themselves, or are they simply a microcosm of the world outside? And is there really any separation?

According to Janet, there isn't.

"Listen," she says matter-of-factly. "The other day I went to this restaurant in Beverly Hills to have lunch, and the first thing you know some guy comes up and starts hustling me." Janet emits a harsh laugh. "It's *all* a gigantic hustle—inside the clubs or out of them. It doesn't make any difference."

Well, maybe. But if that is, in fact, the case, then is Bridgette's point of view inevitable? "I used to have all these fantasies...these dreams of how life would be," she says. "But no more. They're just gone. This is reality...*this* is how it is. Sure, I wish I could feel young again and have the dreams I used to...but I guess I've just seen too much. It's shitty, but what the hell. That's life, I guess."

Of course, there'll be those who will argue the point. But Bridgette and Janet aren't listening. Too many miles down the road. Where will they wind up? It's hard to say. But one thing's for sure; no matter where they go after they get too old for the dance halls, there'll be new girls to take their place on the red Naugahyde couch, and to take part—for a few years anyhow—in the endless one-night-stand of the taxi dance world.

Inside the Flamingo, Dee sits in the dressing room fixing her makeup before going out onto the dance floor. She's quit for the second time this month, and this is her first night back. Though it's only been two weeks since I've seen her, she looks somehow older.

It's raining outside. Dee lights a smoke and looks out the window. The red and green from the club's neon sign blinks off and on in the oil-slicked street.

"Much as I hate this place, I keep coming back," Dee says flatly. "I hate to admit it, but I guess I'm addicted. I dunno, maybe it's because…well I don't really have any friends on the outside. At least here I'm not alone.

"The thing is, the longer you stay here, the harder it is to quit. I guess maybe I'm stuck. It's not something I'd recommend to any friend of mine. I mean, this place'll make you crazy. Any girl that comes in here, she's got a problem. If she don't have one when she comes, she's got one when she leaves. See, in a funny way, the club keeps you hoping. People work here 'cause they need money...they need friends...they need an old man. They need *something*…and they think they're gonna find it here."

Dee flips her cigarette out the window, poofs her hair, and gets up. "One thing's for sure," she says before going out the door, "there ain't nobody that's here just for kicks."

NOIR

SLEEPWALKER

I can still remember the day. It was one of those hideously hot, Valley days that I hated—the kind of day that made everyone look even more desperate than they actually were. Somehow the heat exposed people—made them transparent. It made them look miserable and silly and unbearably sad all at once. Most of all, the heat uncovered the flimsiness of their lives—the thin little string of tasks that made up their day, giving it the illusion of permanence.

On this day, I was driving along when I saw this girl walking through the parking lot of a shopping center. Actually, to say she was walking isn't quite correct. It was more like she was *floating*—though her feet were decidedly on the ground.

At first I thought to myself, My God—that person has the worst posture I've ever seen! The poor girl looked as if she had a sway back. Her hips were thrust way forward, and she seemed to walk from her pelvis, almost as if an invisible string were pulling her along. Besides that, there was an odd, somnambulistic quality to her—almost as if she were walking in her sleep.

I stopped my car and watched her. She was incredibly filthy. There was paint splattered all over her arms and legs and face. Also, she had all these little strands of string or something hanging from her hair. The overall effect was that she'd just walked away from some sort of disaster—an earthquake, or perhaps a tornado.

Despite her ragtag appearance, I could see that underneath the disheveled look, she was quite beautiful. She was wearing only a thin halter top, a pair of stained, brown Bermuda shorts, and thongs. She had a wonderful body. I figured her for maybe seventeen or eighteen.

I watched the girl as she sat on a bench and lit a cigarette. I got out of my car. I was feeling fairly brazen—not like my usual cowardly self—so I went over and sat down next to her.

She barely even turned her head when I sat down. She just kept sitting there, smoking her cigarette.

Soon, I began to feel self-conscious.

"What's your name?" I finally said.

It was the only thing I could think of.

"Sissy," she replied, still not looking at me.

So there we sat. She made no move either to be friendly or to leave. It didn't seem to matter to her whether I was there or not.

I noticed that Sissy had a book in her purse.

"What're you reading?" I asked.

I was just trying to make conversation.

She pulled out the book and handed it to me. It was *Swann's Way.*

"Do you like Proust?" she inquired, looking at me for the first time.

I didn't really remember if I liked Proust or not, but I said yes anyhow.

Sissy took in this information and regarded me coolly.

"Sometimes, me an' my sister read him out loud to each other. We like to do that."

I couldn't think of anything to say, so I didn't say anything.

After she'd finished her smoke, Sissy got up from the bench. She seemed disturbed about something. "I have to go home and make dinner for my father," she said. "He can't cook for himself."

She regarded me for a moment.

"You wanna come?"

It seemed kind of abrupt, but I figured why not? I had nothing else to do.

Ten minutes later, we pulled up in front of a seedy apartment complex in Canoga Park. Out front, a multitude of aging, wrecked automobiles sat. There were kid's toys and shopping carts scattered all over the lawn.

"This is it," Sissy said.

As we went up the walkway, I noticed a bald person sitting on the curb. I say *person*—because it was impossible to tell his age. He could have been 16 or he could have been 40. There was a long string of drool coming out of the side of his mouth.

As we got closer to him, it was obvious that he was retarded.

"Hi Jason," Sissy said to the guy as we walked past him.

Jason looked up at Sissy and drooled some more onto his bare chest.

"Gnrrrrkk," he replied.

I followed Sissy up the stairs and into the apartment.

Inside, the place was filthy, not to mention unbelievably hot. There was an air conditioner—one of those cheap window kinds—but for some reason it wasn't on. Clothing was strewn all over the floor, and the place smelled of sickness.

Seated in a yellowing, stuffed chair was a man clad in gray slacks and a dirty undershirt. A half-empty bottle of vodka was clutched in his hand.

The man was watching a baseball game on a small black-and-white television set, but the sound was so low you could barely hear it. It was strange watching all those little men running around with no sound—but the man didn't seem to mind this.

"You hungry, daddy?" Sissy asked the man.

The man just grunted, not looking up from the TV set.

"Daddy likes baseball games," Sissy informed me.

Sissy went into the kitchen and I sat on the couch watching the baseball game. I didn't particularly like baseball, but there wasn't much choice.

Pretty soon I began to feel dizzy. I didn't know if it was because the place was so hot, or if it was something else, but suddenly I didn't want to be there any longer.

I walked into the kitchen where Sissy was cutting up some vegetables on the counter top.

"I have to go now," I said. "Maybe I'll see you later."

"OK," said Sissy, not looking up at me.

I got in my car and drove back home. Once there, I tried to do some work, but I couldn't stop thinking about Sissy. I didn't know exactly why—but somehow she had gotten to me. I thought about what she had told me about herself—which hadn't been much.

All I knew was that she'd recently moved to California from Atlanta, where she'd lived with her mother and her stepfather. Her mother was an actress who'd done mostly plays. Her only film was a bit part as a nurse in *One Flew Over The Cuckoo's Nest.* As for her stepfather—a man named William Boggs Fitzsimmons—he was a writer whose sole claim to fame was a book about pigs, aptly entitled "The Hog Book."

By seven o'clock that night it was still hot as hell. I couldn't concentrate on my work, so I decided to walk over to Sissy's place. She only lived about a mile from me. I figured I could use the exercise.

When I got there, I walked upstairs and knocked on the door. There was no reply.

I knocked again.

A moment later, a fat girl answered the door. She was eating what looked to be a ham sandwich, half of which was hanging out of the side of her mouth.

"Is Sissy here?" I inquired.

The fat girl stared at me as if she hated me. She took another bite of her sandwich.

"It's for you!" she yelled over her shoulder, still glaring at me.

A moment later Sissy came to the door. She looked completely different than she had earlier in the day. She'd changed into an orange summer dress, which outlined her lithe, young body. Her blond hair—now pulled back into a ponytail—was clean and shiny.

Oh man, I'm telling you, she looked terrific!

Sissy seemed very happy to see me.

"Oh, it's such a nice warm night," she said. "Let's go for a walk."

Before I could say anything she was bounding down the stairs.

We walked along the side of the freeway and up over the hill—the one where, as a kid, I used to hide and throw dirt clods at passing cars. At the bottom of the hill was the Rocket Bowling Alley—one of my old teenage hangouts.

The sun was just beginning to set, and the crickets were already chirping.

It was a magical time of day. Even ugly old Canoga Park looked pretty OK.

Every few moments I'd glance over at Sissy.

She was truly beautiful. What's more, she constantly seemed to change, even as I looked at her.

"Who was that girl that answered the door?" I asked her.

"Oh, that's Boom Boom. She's my sister. Well, *half*-sister actually."

"I don't think she liked me very much," I said.

"Boom Boom doesn't like anybody hardly," Sissy replied. "Don't take it personally." She smiled at me when she said this. She had a wonderful smile. And right then—just for a second—I sort of thought I might be in love with her. It seemed pretty crazy, but what could I do?

"How old are you anyhow?" I asked her.

Sissy didn't miss a beat. "Sixteen" she grinned. "But I can look lots older. Mostly I don't even get asked for my ID!" she said proudly.

After we'd walked for awhile, Sissy and I went back to the bowling alley. Once inside, we bought Cokes and a bunch of candy bars out of the machine. We sat at a table, eating the candy and drinking Cokes and watching the bowlers. It was nice.

Sissy lit up a smoke. So did I. I didn't actually smoke, but somehow, being around Sissy, I just felt like doing it.

Then she started talking. To tell you the truth, I didn't really listen all that much to what she was saying. I just loved looking at her across the table from me. I loved the sound of her voice with its soft, Southern drawl. I thought she could say anything, and I'd be able to listen to her forever.

What I did hear of Sissy's conversation was fascinating. When she'd lived in Atlanta, she'd had this boyfriend named Mouse who was a biker. Mouse used to hit Sissy a lot, and one time he even knocked a couple of her teeth out.

"See?" she said.

And with that, she popped out her two front teeth.

It was funny. Even without her teeth, Sissy was beautiful. But it wasn't so much her physical good looks—which were considerable—

that had gotten to me, but rather this chameleon-like quality that she had. She seemed to be able to change almost at will. One moment she could look like a little girl, the next second her face would grow hard and cold—like a woman twice her age.

Oh, Sissy had been around the block a few times, I had no illusions about that.

She told me that Mouse had made her sell her body when they couldn't get the rent money up. The first time she'd been only twelve.

"You mean you were a prostitute when you were twelve?" I exclaimed.

"It wasn't so bad," Sissy mused, munching on a Snickers bar. "In fact, it was sorta fun."

I must've given her a funny look.

"Don't worry," she smiled. "I don't do it with anybody now unless I really like them."

Later, Sissy told me about this one time when she and Mouse had been real down on their luck and Mouse had decided to rob this liquor store. Sissy didn't actually do any robbing, but she'd driven the car. As she sat waiting in the car outside the store, she'd heard a shot. Then Mouse had come running out.

"I don't know for sure," she said, "but I think he mighta killed the guy. He never would tell me for sure, but I really think he did."

Her eyes went foggy for a minute, and then—*bingo!*—she became a little girl again.

"This is fun sittin' here now, isn't it?" she beamed.

"Yes," I said. "Yes it is."

Inside, I could feel my heart go *pitter pat, pitter pat.*

God, she was so beautiful!

I was really pretty crazy about her.

I didn't care if she'd robbed a million liquor stores!

The next morning, Sissy came over to my place. We decided to walk up to the delicatessen in the shopping mall and have some breakfast.

That day I was in a pretty black mood.

"My father is dying," I told her. "He has cancer. The doctors said he only has six months to live."

Sissy just looked at me.

"We all have to die," she said.

I thought that was a pretty strange response, but I didn't tell her this.

When we got to the deli, Sissy kept asking me nonstop questions about all the Jewish words on the menu. She seemed to be getting a big kick out of the fact that I was Jewish.

"You're my first one!" she chirped, running her tongue over her large teeth.

She seemed so happy, that pretty soon I began to feel not quite so depressed.

I watched her as she spread cream cheese on a bagel and slurped noisily on her glass of orange juice.

Then, while she munched her bagel, Sissy did something that I thought was absolutely wonderful. Underneath the table, she reached across and put her hand in my crotch—right there in the deli and all.

The next second I had the biggest hard on I've ever had in my entire life.

"Let's go to my place and fuck," she said.

"But what about your dad, and, er...Boom Boom?" I asked.

"Daddy's down at welfare pickin' up his check, an' Boom Boom's at work," she said, squeezing my crotch.

"Come on—let's go!"

"Alright," I said, trying to sound casual.

We went to Sissy's apartment and fucked. We fucked for hours and hours and hours.

Sissy was absolutely tireless. Long after I'd worn myself out, she still wanted more. In fact, she seemed to gather energy with each subsequent fuck, which I thought was rather nice. Still, there was no way I could keep up with her.

Finally, I lay on my back, staring up at the stucco ceiling.

I was drenched in sweat.

The apartment was a million degrees, but I didn't mind. Somehow it added to the atmosphere.

I imagined that Sissy and I were in Atlanta—or at least some Southern town like that—and soon I fell into this Tennessee Williams-ish kind of fantasy.

Sissy and I were Elizabeth Taylor and Paul Newman in *Cat On A Hot Tin Roof.*

All we'd do all day is lie around in our underwear. We'd clink our iced teas and smoke cigarettes and blow the smoke out real smooth like they do in the movies.

Outside the house, I could hear the low murmur of Southern people talking out on the front porch and the sound of the gardener sweeping up piles of leaves.

Tsshhhh, tssshhhhh went his rake.

Pretty soon I drifted off to sleep.

I awoke to find Sissy sucking greedily on my prick. She didn't notice that I'd woken up, so I just watched her as she went about her business.

Most girls look fairly stupid with a prick in their mouth, but not Sissy.

On the contrary, she remained quite lovely. She really did.

When she finally noticed that I'd awoken, Sissy let my prick slip out of her mouth.

"Hello!" she said.

"Hi," I answered.

Then, just like a little kid with a new toy, she began to pretend my penis was a gearshift knob on an automobile.

"Rrrrnnnnn, rnnnnnnn, rnnnnnn," she went, shifting into second.

"Please don't shift my penis," I asked politely.

Instantly Sissy began to pout.

Oh, she was such an actress, this one!

But then she seemed to get a bright idea. You could see it on her face.

The next second she climbed on top of me and sat right down on my rigid cock.

"I like to be on top!" she said, bouncing up and down. "It's *fun!"*

Sissy looked down at her blond cunt, which was dripping juices all over my crotch.

This seemed to delight her.

Everything seemed to delight her.

"I like it when it gets all wet and sticky," she said, scooting up and down on top of me.

"Yunnhhhhhh," I replied.

When we'd finished our lovemaking, Sissy said she wanted to go over to the Thrifty Drugstore to get an ice cream cone. This was fine with me. I really didn't care where we went, to tell you the truth.

Inside the drugstore, Sissy was like a little kid. She wanted to touch everything. She kept stopping to handle the perfumes, the greeting cards, the hairbrushes and combs. She seemed particularly fascinated with all the different colored bottles of shampoo.

As we walked through the store, I noticed that Sissy was wearing this really horrible old pair of tennis shoes. They were practically falling apart. I told her she should pick out some new ones.

"Really?" she said. "Are you sure?" She couldn't believe that anyone would want to buy her anything.

"Go on," I said. "Really—it's all right."

Sissy looked and looked, finally deciding on a pair of blue deck shoes. They only cost $3.50, so I told her to get another pair, but she said no—one was enough, thank you. For a girl that was basically poor white trash, she really had very good manners.

When we got outside, it was dark.

We walked down a side street, past all the little houses with their lights on inside.

Sometimes you could see people gathered around a TV set, or perhaps a man in a chair reading a novel.

Everything seemed very still and peaceful.

For the moment the world seemed a good, safe place to be.

I wondered what it would be like if Sissy and I got married.

Would we be in one of those little houses, watching TV or reading?

Would she come up behind me, and put her hand on my shoulder, just lightly?

Then the next second, the other part of my brain jumped in and said, "What the hell are you talking about, man! She's just a *kid*. A goddamn 16-year-old kid, for God's sake! A 16 year-old ex-hooker who's robbed liquor stores and maybe even participated in a murder! Come *on* man—wake up!"

Just as I thought this, Sissy took hold of my hand, and all the thoughts went away—*poof*—just like that.

We walked along, not saying anything—just holding hands.

She was a great hand-holder. She didn't grasp too much, or not enough. No, she did it just right. And her hand never got all sweaty either.

Man, she was really something!

The next day Sissy and I drove up the coast highway to Santa Barbara.

We stopped at this one beach in Ventura where a long rock jetty ran for several miles along the sand.

Then we noticed something peculiar about the place. Inside the rocks that made up the jetty, there were all these cats. Hundreds of cats—maybe more. They were obviously wild—you could tell from the look of them. Most of them were very skinny, as if they hadn't been fed for a long time. It was really a very strange sight, seeing hundreds of cats climbing all over the rocks like that.

Sissy seemed very excited by this. She went over and tried to pick up one of the cats, but it arched its back and hissed at her.

"Be careful," I said. "They might have some kind of disease or something."

But Sissy kept on running after the cats—climbing in and out of the rocks—talking to them and chasing them all over the place. She kept it up for the next couple of hours.

Late that night, we drove back to Los Angeles along the coast. The lights on the ships out at sea made the scene look like some kind of magical fairyland.

Sissy was very quiet during the ride. Ever since the cats she'd been quiet.

Finally we got to my house.

"Do you want to come in and watch TV?" I asked.

Sissy looked at me blankly.

"I don't care," she said, real pouty like.

We went inside. Sissy plumped down on the couch and sulked silently while I watched a rerun of *The Fugitive*.

I've always been a very big David Janssen fan.

"Are you all right?" I asked after awhile.

But she wouldn't even look at me.

"What's wrong?" I finally asked. "Is something bothering you?"

"You people make me sick," she spat.

"*What* people?"

"All you people—you're all exactly the same," Sissy hissed.

She was glaring at me now. There was real hatred in her eyes.

"And *you're* just like all the rest! You and your cancer and your death and your talk, talk talk. God, is that all you ever do is *talk?"*

"What the hell are you talking about?"

"FUCK YOU!" Sissy yelled, jumping up off the couch.

"FUCK YOU TO DEATH!"

And with that, she stormed outside.

When she came back inside the house, Sissy was friendly and sweet again.

She kissed me on the cheek, then headed for the door.

"I gotta get home and make sure daddy's eaten some dinner. He'd sit in front of that dang TV all day and just not eat a thing if I let him get away with it."

I found Sissy's concern for her father to be quite admirable.

"OK," I said. "See you tomorrow..."

"Bye sweetie," she said, kissing me again before she left.

Normally I couldn't stand it if someone called me *sweetie* or *honey*, but when Sissy said it, it sounded wonderful.

I *told* you I had it bad.

The next morning I drove over to Sissy's house. When I got there, I ran up the stairs and knocked on the door. A moment later her fat sister answered.

"Hi Boom Boom," I said. "Is Sissy here?"

Boom Boom still looked like she wanted to kill me. "Sissy ain't here right now," she spat.

"Do you know when she'll be back?" I asked.

"Come back later," Boom Boom said. Then she slammed the door in my face.

When I got home, I tried to get some writing done, but nothing would come. I simply couldn't stop thinking about Sissy. Every time I thought about her my heart seemed to hurt. Oh man—it was awful.

At around 4:00 p.m. I went back over to Sissy's place.

Out front, Jason was sitting on the curb watching cars and drooling on himself.

"Hi Jason," I said.

Jason looked up. *"Fnnnggg gwanngh,"* he said.

"Have you seen Sissy?" I queried.

Jason looked at me rather quizzically, inserting a finger into his left nostril.

"Phhhgggggghh," he said, taking a good healthy pick at his nose.

I went back upstairs and knocked on Sissy's door, but this time nobody answered.

Finally I gave up and left.

When I got home it was around 5:00 p.m.—the time of day I hated most.

Nothing seemed to make any sense at this time of day. Everything was in limbo. Nothing was firm.

It made me feel very weak and scared.

This happened to me every day at this time—but on this day it was particularly bad.

My doctor had told me that if I felt the depression coming on, I should immediately do something physical—but I just didn't have enough energy. It was like something had sucked all the life out of me, and I was just this dead thing—this blob.

Finally, I decided that the best thing to do would be to go to sleep, so I went and lay down on the couch.

Soon I fell into a strange dream.

In the dream I was back at the Cat Beach—only this time, something was wrong there. The entire beach was littered with the bodies of dead cats. A few stray cats hobbled along, poking around amongst the bodies of their mates. They were obviously very sick, and would soon die too. In some of the rocks along the jetty, mother cats were eating the bodies of their sick and dying babies. The hot sun glared down on them. Something horrible and ominous was in the air—a strange sound—or maybe even a kind of demonic presence of some sort. Whatever it was, it was terrible.

I awoke in a sweat, and before I knew what I was doing, I was driving like a madman over to Sissy's house.

When I got there I bounded up the stairs two at a time.

My heart was beating a mile a minute.

Knock, knock knock.

Nothing.

Bang! Bang! Bang!

A moment later, Sissy's father answered the door.

He was still attired in the same dirty white undershirt he'd been wearing that first day I'd met him.

He stood there blinking up at me, unrecognizing.

"Is Sissy here?" I asked.

He just stood there, sort of weaving around. "I said—*is Sissy here?*"

"Nuh," he finally said.

"Well, ah—where is she?"

"Sissy won't be back," her father said.

"You mean she won't be back today or..."

"Sissy won't be back—*ever*."

"But...I mean..."

"She's gone!" he repeated. *"Gone..."*

The poor guy looked like he was about to cry.

I didn't know what to say, so I just turned and walked back down the stairs.

Behind me I could hear something that sounded either like coughing or crying—I couldn't tell which.

I didn't feel much like going home so I walked back over the hill to the bowling alley.

It was really crowded when I got inside.

I went and sat at the table where Sissy and I had sat a week ago.

I just sat there, letting the sounds of the clattering balls and voices fill me up.

Then I noticed that there was something peculiar about the bowlers—but I couldn't figure out what it was.

Then suddenly it was clear—they were all deformed in one way or another.

There were paraplegics, hunchbacks, quadriplegics, guys with no arms and legs—cripples of every possible shape, size and variety.

I sat and watched the crippled bowlers.

They were having a grand time—laughing and shouting, drinking beer, and being rowdy—just like regular people.

I watched a guy with no arms wheel his chair down the lane and throw the ball with some contraption he'd rigged to his teeth. His buddies all cheered him on, laughing and snorting madly.

It was really something.

As I watched, I tried to feel sorry for the crippled bowlers, but I couldn't pull it off.

After that didn't work, I tried to thank God that I had my health and all that, but I couldn't do that either.

I was just so damn sad and lonely that I couldn't feel much of anything.

After about an hour, I left the bowling alley and went home.

On the way, I went by Sissy's place again. I was sort of hoping Jason might be out front on the curb. I thought maybe I'd try to strike up a conversation with him or something. But when I got to the curb where he usually sat, it was empty. This made me feel even worse than ever.

When I got home, I lay down on the couch and flipped the TV on with no sound. My face felt all numb, and my mouth didn't seem to be working very well.

I wanted to cry or something, but nothing would come.

There were little things clicking and popping in my brain—but I did my best to ignore them.

After awhile, I fell into a dull, gray sleep.

About a month later, I was at home watching a cooking program on afternoon TV. Watching cooking programs is one of my favorite ways to pass the time. The only thing I don't like is if the person on the show sticks his arm up some old chicken's rectal cavity or something. Things like that can be pretty disgusting. Fortunately, this doesn't happen very often.

Anyhow, I was watching this cooking show, when I heard the mail clank in the little slot. I went and got it. It was the usual garbage—bills and stuff. Then I spied the postcard. I knew instantly who it was from.

Sure enough, the postmark read Atlanta, Georgia.

The picture on the front of the card was one of those corny old cartoons of a bum hitchhiking in the middle of the desert. The caption underneath the picture read, *"I'll make it...one of these days."*

I'd always loved those old postcards. They reminded me of long stretches of empty highway and little pink motels with green neon signs that shone in the night and ten cent bottles of Dr. Pepper and ladies in flower print dresses. That kind of stuff—*you* know.

On the back of the card was a note. It read simply, "Thanks for the tennis shoes," It was signed, "Love, Sissy."

I noticed the handwriting. It had those large squiggly letters with big, huge dots over the i's. *Very* teenage.

I sat back down on the couch and thought about Sissy.

I wondered what she was doing.

I wondered if she'd gone back to Mouse—to robbing liquor stores and hustling her ass on the streets.

I pictured her face. I wondered if it would grow hard and bitter by the time she reached twenty.

I wondered if she still read Proust aloud. I even wondered who was making lunch for her father, now that she was gone.

I wondered all kinds of things, but I didn't get any answers.

I looked at the postcard again.

I held it under my nose to see if any of Sissy's smell had rubbed off on it, but it just smelled like an ordinary postcard.

The cooking show ended and another program came on.

The show was called *Body Buddies*.

It featured this not-very-in-shape couple doing a bunch of stupid exercises.

The guy had this gigantic gold medallion around his neck and this phony curly hairdo...and the woman had fat, white arms that jiggled whenever she moved.

It was impossible to look at them.

Finally, I flipped off the television.

I sat there, staring at the empty screen. I watched the tiny speck of light in the middle of the screen grow smaller and smaller and smaller.

Finally it disappeared.

I couldn't think of anything to do—so I didn't do anything.

NOIR

FALLEN ANGEL

Richard Sandwich was looking for a job. So far, he'd applied for positions as a librarian, at a Wendy's hamburger stand, a greeting card shop, a delicatessen, a Marie Callender's House Of Pies, a bicycle shop, and a Xerox store.

But he hadn't gotten any of these jobs. That was all right, however, because what Richard Sandwich wanted more than anything else in the world was to work in a furniture store. To be completely factual, what he actually wanted to do was to *live* in a furniture store. Working there would just be a small part of the picture.

What Richard Sandwich imagined, when he dreamt his furniture store dream, was that he'd go through his ordinary workday just like everyone else. But then, after the store closed and the people had left—*that* would be the wonderful part.

Then, Richard Sandwich would have the entire furniture store to himself.

He could leisurely walk amongst the sofas, couches and chairs, tarrying as long as he wished at particular favorites. He could try them out for comfort, and perhaps even snooze for awhile. If he got bored, he could simply move to a different piece of furniture.

Or he could lie on the beds—all the beds of various shapes and sizes. Sometimes he would just lay on top of the blankets, so as not to mess things up. (Neatness enjoyed a very high priority in Richard

Sandwich's life). He could even get *under* the covers if he wished. He could stack as many blankets on top of himself as he wanted to. Ten, twelve, fifteen blankets—oh yes!—just to feel that delicious heaviness that lots of blankets always bring.

And then, if he really wanted a special treat, Richard Sandwich imagined that he would stick one bare foot out from under the covers so as to feel the cool night air on his naked toes.

Ah—*heaven!*

Perhaps, Richard Sandwich thought to himself, the people passing by the store at night would peer in through the window and watch him as he went about his affairs. This would be fine with him. In fact, it wouldn't disturb him one little bit! Let them gawk if they wished. Let them press their faces up against the window glass. It didn't matter a whit, for they were out there—in the world—while Richard Sandwich was in his nice safe, warm furniture store.

His *home*, by damn!

Despite this pleasant scenario, during his job hunt, Richard Sandwich had failed to apply to one single solitary furniture store. This was because he was the type of person who didn't like not getting something he wanted. Especially when it was something as special as this.

So Richard Sandwich simply decided to look for an ordinary job. He'd just keep his furniture store dream as an idea—for now at least. He had *lots* of ideas in his brain, so one more wouldn't really matter.

Today, Richard Sandwich had decided to try finding work at the shopping mall near the tiny downtown apartment he occupied. That way he'd only have to take one bus to work. (Richard Sandwich did not drive).

On this day, he'd been in the mall for perhaps an hour, going from one store to the next—but none of them had any job openings.

Finally, Richard Sandwich went into the Broadway. Once inside the store, he followed the signs that led downstairs to the personnel office.

Richard Sandwich entered the office. The room was pink—but not a very *nice* pink. There was a woman standing behind the desk with her back turned towards him.

"I'd like a job application, please," Richard Sandwich said to the woman's back.

The woman turned around. She had a mottled pinkish face covered with small blond hairs that shone under the harsh light of the room. Somehow, the flesh of her face looked dead.

"We don't have no jobs right now," the woman said, "but you can fill one out if you want. It's strictly up to you," she added.

There was something nasty in the woman's voice. Richard Sandwich decided that he did not like her.

She was dead inside.

For just an instant, Richard Sandwich had a very vivid picture of the woman's insides. This happened to him sometimes. What he saw was that the woman's organs were all eaten away. What was left of them was rotten and putrid. Hosts of maggots fed on the dying organ meat.

Richard Sandwich's head swum.

The dead flesh woman handed Richard Sandwich an application.

"I don't have a pen," he told her.

The woman handed Richard Sandwich a pen, scowling at him as he took his seat.

As he filled in the blanks, Richard Sandwich noticed that there was another woman sitting in the chair across from him. She was apparently filling out an application for work, too.

The woman was bone-thin, and it was difficult to tell her age. She might have been thirty or she might have been fifty. There was decidedly something strange about the woman, Richard Sandwich decided.

None of her parts seemed to go together. Her face didn't work. Her head seemed tiny and meaningless under a huge stack of unkempt brown hair. On the very tippy-top of the hair stack, a yellow ribbon had been affixed.

This struck Richard Sandwich as odd. But the oddest thing of all was the vest the woman wore. It looked like it had been made out of a very cheap tiger skin rug. The kind of tiger skin rug you might buy in Woolworth's.

Actually, the vest looked like something that Raquel Welch might have worn in one of those cave woman movies she'd done early in her career.

The whole effect was very disquieting.

It simply didn't add up.

There was something extremely sad about the senseless woman—something that caused a lump to form in the back of Richard Sandwich's throat. He wondered about the woman's life. Was she married? Who were her friends? What did they *talk* about? What did her house look like?

Richard Sandwich decided that the senseless woman probably lived alone in a small, dingy apartment with a green sofa.

She might have a cat, but Richard Sandwich could not be sure about this.

Suddenly Richard Sandwich felt that he had to get out of the office.

It had become terrible in there.

He folded the application and put it in the black shoulder bag he always carried.

He thought about stealing the pen that he'd borrowed from the dead flesh woman, but he decided not to.

Sometimes little things like that could cause problems later in life.

"I'll bring it back later," Richard Sandwich said.

"Well, ya don't haveta hurry," the dead flesh woman said, "'I tol' ya...we don't have no openings anyways."

Anyways...

How could people *say* things like that? Richard Sandwich wondered.

A maggot crawled out of the woman's nose.

Thank you," Richard Sandwich said.

Then he turned and left the pink waiting room.

Next, Richard Sandwich decided to visit the Book Department. He liked Book Departments, although the ones in department stores generally were not particularly good.

Behind the Book Department counter stood a fat girl. She probably weighed close to three hundred pounds. The fat girl was talking to a woman who appeared to be asking her a question.

"YES, I THINK WE HAVE THAT!" said the fat girl. "YOU'LL FIND IT IN THE HARDBACK NONFICTION SECTION! I SAW A COPY THIS MORNING!"

It was very curious.

The fat girl was standing only a foot away from the woman, yet she was *yelling*.

Her voice was so loud, in fact, that Richard Sandwich actually had to put his fingers in his ears.

He walked several rows away, but he could still hear the fat girl yelling emphatically at the questioning lady.

Richard Sandwich wondered why the overly-emphatic fat girl had to yell like this.

Then it was clear.

This was how the overly-emphatic fat yelling girl made contact with the world.

The problem was that she'd overdone everything. She had grown her armor of blubber to hide from people, and then she yelled at them from inside her fortress of fat to make sure that they heard her. She reached out and touched people with her blub and her overly-emphatic fat yelling voice…but the *problem* was that she touched them whether they *wanted* to be touched or not.

Certainly, Richard Sandwich did not want to be touched by her in this highly aggressive fashion.

Still, he did not want to be too hard on the overly-emphatic fat yelling girl, for obviously this was how she felt love. Oddly though, it was her very fatness and yellingness which kept her from feeling the love she desired.

How *peculiar*. In this sad old world, Richard Sandwich thought, all anybody really wanted was to feel *loved*. Yet they were constantly doing things to keep themselves from feeling it.

Just as Richard Sandwich thought this, he heard a tremendous crash somewhere off to his right.

He looked over to where the noise had come from.

A tiny black man had dumped an entire cartload of books onto the floor. As he picked them up, Richard Sandwich regarded the man.

He was wearing a badge, which signified that he was an employee.

But what struck Richard Sandwich most about the man was how *neat* he was.

Everything about the tiny black man was impeccable. His freshly pressed shirt, his shiny black wingtips, and his neat, short haircut. He even had tiny, neat ears!

"Oh gosh, oh dear," the small, neat black man said as he began picking up the books.

As he was doing this, a stumpy woman with wild, popping hair with a pencil stuck in it came and stood directly over him. This was obviously the manager.

"Is everything all right over here?" the woman asked nasally.

"Oh yes—it's fine—really it is," said the small neat black man, scurrying to pick up the books as fast as he could. "I'll clean it up right away."

But as he bent over to pick up more books, the tiny, neat black man's rather large rear end knocked over several books behind him.

"Oh *my!"* he said, turning around.

The manager just stood watching him, a scowl on her face.

"I'm sorry," the tiny, neat black man said.

He got doen on his knees and began picking up the second pile of books, while the manager stood over him, clucking her tongue.

Richard Sandwich walked several aisles away from the scene, which had made him extremely nervous.

Good God—weren't bookstores supposed to be *peaceful?*

But then, life just wasn't the same anymore.

Not *any*where.

Richard Sandwich picked a book off the shelf.

The title of the book was *Women Who Love Men Who Hate Women.*

The person who'd written the book had lots of letters after her name.

Richard Sandwich read a few lines and then put the book back on the shelf. He felt a small bubble of anger rise inside his stomach.

To *think* of it! Some idiot with letters after her name had written this ridiculous book, and now *more* idiots were going to read it!

And to what purpose?

The world was already full of enough useless information without such foofaraw.

Richard Sandwich looked at the shelves and shelves of books, and wondered how many of them would really change people's lives.

Most of the books, he knew, had no purpose at all. And most of the people who had written them had no business writing books.

But there they were!

Just as Richard Sandwich thought this, he heard a terrible crash. He walked over one aisle.

This time, the tiny, neat black man had fallen off a ladder. He was lying all crumpled up on the ground. A dozen or so books had fallen on top of him.

The tiny black man got up and tried to act like everything was okay, but you could tell he'd hurt his back.

"Oh dear shit," he said to no one in particular.

Richard Sandwich walked away from the scene as quickly as possible.

Good God—the man was a walking catastrophe! *Let him break his own fool skull, if he wants... but I'm getting out of here!*

Once outside the book department, Richard Sandwich quickly headed through Millinery, past Ladies Lingerie, then got on the escalator going upstairs.

Coming down the opposite escalator was a middle-aged couple.

They were both wearing Mickey Mouse T-shirts and smoking cigarettes.

There was nothing particularly remarkable about the couple, except for the fact that the man had his arm around the woman's waist much too tightly.

It wasn't a nice, friendly arm around a waist. It was more like the man was holding the woman captive—though she seemed not to take notice.

The man and the woman were talking to each other in these very monotonous voices.

Richard Sandwich couldn't hear what they were saying. All he heard was the drone of the voices.

It made him very tired just listening to them.

Richard Sandwich also noticed that neither the man nor the woman looked at each other when they talked.

Somehow he knew that they had been talking to each other for years in this fashion.

Richard Sandwich wondered which one of them was going to die first.

It wasn't that Richard Sandwich particularly *enjoyed* engaging in these type of observations. It wasn't even that he *tried* to do it. The fact was, he couldn't *help* it.

Actually, he didn't really *do* anything. It was more that people just told him their stories. They told him with their faces and their bodies and their voices and their cigarettes, and, well—all of themselves.

They couldn't hide a thing.

What's more, they didn't *want* to.

Like the loud yelling fat girl, everyone really craved to tell you their stories.

More than anything else in the world, they wanted someone to *listen* to them.

And so, in their silent, demanding language, they told you things from the deepest recesses of their souls.

The *problem* was, they didn't *ask* your permission before they told you. They just went right ahead and *did* it, which was very rude of them, Richard Sandwich thought.

As Richard Sandwich continued to walk through the department store, he listened to all the stories going on around him. He could actually *hear* them, though there was no sound. Yet the stories had a pitch—a rhythm all their own.

They swirled, and whirled…merged and blended like some great, mad symphony.

A cacophony of people—wailing and crying and pleading.

God, the *things* they said! The *tales* they told!

Awful tales...painful tales…lurid tales…obscene tales.

Tales of anguish and terror—and of a thirst that could never be quenched by anything human.

Some of the people cried out in the midst of their pain. Others actually begged to die—to be released from their suffering—and yet they knew they could not. No, they were trapped forever in an endless living nightmare—like trying to wake up out of a dream and then waking up to find you were in another dream and then another, and another, and another—

Lord, the *hellishness* of this horrid, miserable life!

Richard Sandwich felt the walls of the department store closing in on him.

He began to walk faster now. He tried to scuttle in between people, but he couldn't seem to move fast enough. His legs felt as if they were made of butter. People would bump him or touch against him, sending him awful, agonizing messages of their terrible guilt and emptiness.

They *breathed* on him.

They smashed against his flesh!

They were mad!

Insane!

Crazy as loons—these poor, demented souls!

Richard Sandwich felt weak in the knees, His throat began to constrict.

He felt that he might pass out at any moment.

Faster now—hurry...

God, can't breathe…hurry...keep moving.

Jesus, *more* people—

But they weren't even *people* any longer! For now, with his terrible X-ray vision, Richard Sandwich saw through their skin—clear through to the insides of their bodies. It was horrible.

Most all of the people were empty shells—nothing more than stumbling, wheezing, empty husks.

Pod People—

Still, others had become inhabited by strange, cruel spirits that lived inside them and sucked the life out of them. These inhabited people had a sort of brown, hazy quality about them that you could actually see, if you looked at them out of the corners of your eyes.

They were particularly terrible to look at.

My God! Got to get *out* of here. There, up ahead—the Furniture Department!

If I can only make it. If I just can move my legs a little *faster. Faster, faster...*

Okay, okay—safe now.

Richard Sandwich stood with his toes sweating in his shoes and breathed in the peacefulness of the Furniture Department. The noise was gone. Only the quiet hum of the air conditioning unit could be heard.

He looked around at the vast expanse of couches and chairs and drank in the wonderful sight of them.

There they were! Waiting for people to come and sit in them—

Richard Sandwich let the silence of the room fill his chest. Then he began a slow, leisurely walk through the Furniture Department.

Look there…in that little alcove—a bedroom set. How *wonderful!* Imagine lying in that bed and listening to the darkness. Imagine waking up and turning the bedside light on in the middle of the night.

Click!

In the next alcove was a beautiful old English-styled bedroom set.

Lovely.

Richard Sandwich walked over to the bed.

Hello bed!

He bent down and pressed his nose into the fresh clean sheets.

Ahhhhhhh—

Richard Sandwich looked out over the vast expanse of furniture and for a moment—just a moment—he felt what it would be like to be in this place all by himself. The sensation was so powerful that he could feel it in the pit of his stomach. It made him feel all warm inside…

"Can I help you, sir?" said a voice.

Richard Sandwich turned to find a dark-skinned man attired in a natty camel's hair sports coat. The man had inky black hair and smooth olive skin. Richard Sandwich noted the man's fingernails, which he wore quite long.

"Sir, can I help you vid anything?"

Hmmm. Slight trace of an accent. The rolling of the R's. Must be a Hindu.

The salesman smiled now. Somehow his teeth seemed red.

"No thank you," said Richard Sandwich. "I'm just looking."

"Veddy good, sir," said the man.

Richard Sandwich smelled the man for a moment as he spoke. It was a nice smell…yet there was something at the back of it. Something foul that had been covered up.

At that moment Richard Sandwich knew the man was dying. The man himself did not know this, but it was true nonetheless.

Cancer, yes—that was it. It had already metastasized to the bone.

Soon it would travel through the lymphatic system...then it would then pass to the brain.

After that the man would die quickly.

Richard Sandwich had a powerful vision of the Hindu man lying—gaunt and pale—in a hospital bed.

There seemed to be something around him…a haze of some sort.

Then, to the right of the man, a whitish figure materialized.

It was the figure of a man, yet it was larger than a normal man.

The figure breathed heavily, as if very fatigued.

As Richard Sandwich watched, another figure materialized just to the man's left.

This one was also white, but a bit more transparent than the first figure.

Somehow Richard Sandwich knew that the two figures were angels.

They were there to help the man die.

As he was thinking this, the room seemed to grow dim.

And then, at the foot of the bed, a third figure emerged.

The figure was illuminated from the inside as if lit by an inner fire.

There was a tiny point of light at the back of the eyes.

This was another angel, Richard Sandwich knew—but he was somehow different from the other two.

For one thing, his color was darker. Not exactly black… simply darker.

This must be a fallen angel, Richard Sandwich thought.

And as he thought this, a terrible chill went through him.

The dark angel just stood there, breathing in and out.

He seemed to expand in size with each intake of air, then shrink back as he expelled his breath.

There was a hum of sound around the dark angel—the sound of a song. The song was neither in a major key nor a minor key. It wasn't in any key at all, and yet it was a song that drove on and on, soundlessly—

Upon hearing the song, the dying Hindu opened his eyes very wide.

The man seemed to want to keep his eyes open. There was a battle going on in him. Even though he wanted to let go—yet he struggled to live.

Now the dark angel began to move closer to the man. But as he did, the other two angels seemed to grow larger.

At the sight of this, the dark angel took a step backwards.

His song grew fainter, and the fire at the back of his eyes dimmed.

The dying man emitted a soft, high-pitched sound from the back of his throat. He pulled the bed sheets higher around his neck.

Suddenly Richard Sandwich felt very weak. He had to get away from the vision.

He began walking. He wondered if perhaps he should have told the man what he'd seen, but he knew he could not.

Richard Sandwich looked at his watch. It read 3:33 p.m.

The watch was a Timex.

He walked through Men's Wear and towards a back hallway where the men's restroom was. He knew where to find it. He'd been there before, though he could not remember exactly when.

Once inside the restroom, Richard Sandwich breathed a sigh of relief. He went to the urinal, unzipped, and let go a hard stream—regarding it as it splashed against the urinal walls. It was extremely yellow in color, he noticed.

As he watched his yellow pee, Richard Sandwich had a strange memory. It involved a time when he'd been working in this telephone boiler room—one of a myriad of terrible jobs he'd held over the years.

At the job, he'd sat next to a pretty Mexican girl with beautiful dark hair. She was truly lovely. They'd even gone out for coffee upon a couple of occasions.

Soon Richard Sandwich realized that he'd fallen in love with the pretty Mexican girl. He'd even imagined them getting married.

They'd have a small, nice house—with lots of candles and good food smells.

Sometimes the Mexican girl's mother would even come and spend the night and it would be very cozy. The mother would be permanently indebted to Richard Sandwich for rescuing her daughter from the bowels of sin and depravity and for giving her a taste of the good life.

But one day the pretty Mexican girl told Richard Sandwich that she had a boyfriend—and suddenly his dream was over.

This made Richard Sandwich very sad. But not nearly so sad as something the beautiful Mexican girl had told him about herself and her boyfriend.

"His name is Armando," the girl had said, "but you know what I call him? I call him Yellow Bee."

She smiled, exhibiting her fat, white teeth.

"He calls me Yellow Bee, too," she continued.

"We *like* to do that," the girl added.

Richard Sandwich nodded his approval—though inside he had gone far away, where he wouldn't have to feel sad about the Mexican girl not being his wife and living in the house with the candles and the good food smells and her visiting mother.

But later, when Richard Sandwich thought about the girl, he couldn't get out of his head what she had told him about herself and her boyfriend and their terrible nicknames.

Richard Sandwich simply couldn't imagine two people walking around actually calling each other *Yellow Bee*.

It was—quite simply—one of the worst things he'd ever heard in his entire life!

Thinking of it made Richard Sandwich want to laugh or cry—he didn't know which.

After he was done urinating, Richard Sandwich looked at his face in the mirror. It looked strange somehow.

Richard Sandwich took off his glasses. Then he put them back on.

He took them off.

He put them on.

Took them off.

Put them on.

Took them off—

Put them on—

Took them off—

Put them on—

Tookthemoff—

Putthemon—

Tookthemoff—

Putthemon—
Tookthemoff, putthemon—
Tookthemoffputthemon—
Tookthemoffputthemontookthemoffput ...
JESUS!!

No matter what Richard Sandwich did, his face made no sense to him.

Richard Sandwich thought about his face. He realized that he had had this face every day for all of his thirty-six years. And yet it was *not* the same face—

All of the molecules had changed.

Nothing of his old face was left.

It was dead and gone forever.

Yet still, he walked the earth with the same face, and yet it was not the same and yet it was.

This was an amazing truth.

Richard Sandwich looked at his glasses.

He noticed that there was a tiny scratch on one lens.

This upset him.

He felt that if he could *just* get that scratch off the lens, then everything would make sense once more.

Richard Sandwich took a piece of tissue paper and wiped and wiped and wiped—but no matter how hard he wiped, the smudge would not come off the lens.

Suddenly Richard Sandwich felt a thick black bubble of anger rise up in his throat.

He felt like gagging.

It made him want to take his glasses and smash them into a million pieces.

Stupid glasses! How *dare* they be smudged like this?

"You motherfucker!" Richard Sandwich said to the glasses.

The glasses did not reply.

"That's right," said Richard Sandwich. "You'd *better* keep your mouth shut, or I'll grind you to smithereens with my big, thick heels."

Richard Sandwich looked at his watch again. It read 4:44 p.m.

Richard Sandwich couldn't figure out where to go.

He thought of this and he thought of that—but there wasn't enough reason to go any place to give him the energy to move.

Finally, he went into one of the stalls and sat down.

Soon he began to read the graffiti on the wall.

Most of it wasn't very interesting.

The best of the lot was a stick figure of a girl with a gigantic vagina and an arrow pointing to it.

There was something slightly comical about the drawing. Next to it was scrawled—

FOR A HOT FUCK CALL MARCY—347-1827.

Richard Sandwich wondered if there really was a Marcy—and if there was—what she was doing right now. Was she really a bad girl with a big fat vagina—or was she actually a fine, upstanding American who'd had this cruel hoax played on her by some stinking god-damn pervert?

But then, Richard Sandwich stopped wondering these things.

He was starting to feel very bad again.

Soon the dizziness began to overtake him.

This time it was really horrible.

Something pulled at his skull. Harder now.

Soon Richard Sandwich felt as if his brains were being sucked out of his head.

"Oh God, no—" Richard Sandwich begged. "Please—*no more...*"

Richard Sandwich held his head in his hands and began to talk.

It was difficult to make out what he was saying—but if you got very close you could hear.

"Greater is He that is in me, than He that is in the world," Richard Sandwich said. He kept saying it over and over and over again until the words became nothing more than a sound in his throat.

It was 10:10 p.m. when Richard Sandwich got off the toilet seat. He didn't know what he'd done during the last several hours, but something had happened.

Something was clean.

He emerged from the bathroom.

He stood there in the hallway looking into the empty store.

Everything was still lit up, but there were no people now.

The place was silent. So silent.

Only the hum of the neon lights—

As he stood there, Richard Sandwich thought briefly about the Dead Flesh Woman, the Senseless Vest Lady, the Overly-Emphatic Yelling Fat Girl, the Tidy Falling Down black man, the Mickey Mouse Monotone Couple, the Yellow Bee Mexican Girl and the Dying Hindu.

He wondered about each of them.

What was their *purpose* in the world?

How would they end up?

Did any of them ever think about *salvation?*

And as he thought this, Richard Sandwich had the strangest sensation. It was a totally new feeling—one that he'd never had before. What the feeling told him was, that despite all the pain he'd had for all these many years—despite that—somehow he knew that someone was taking care of him.

Richard Sandwich looked out into the empty department store.

Here am I, he thought. *Here am I—*

He bowed his head and said a silent thank you.

He waited another moment—

Then he walked out of the bathroom and headed directly towards the Furniture Department.

NOIR

THE DRY BONES

The hand of the Lord was upon me, and carried me out in the spirit of the Lord, and set me down in the midst of the valley which was full of bones, and caused me to pass by them round about; and behold there were very many in the open valley; and lo, they were very dry.

And He said unto me, Son of man, can these bones live? And I answered, O Lord God, thou knowest.

Again He said unto me, Prophesy upon these bones and say unto them, O ye dry bones, hear the word of the Lord.

Thus saith the Lord God unto these bones, Behold I will cause breath to enter into you, and ye shall live:

And I will lay sinews upon you, and will bring up flesh on you, and cover you with skin, and put breath in you, and ye shall live: and ye shall know that I am the Lord.

So I prophesied as I was commanded: and as I prophesied, there was a noise, and behold a shaking, and the bones came together, bone to his bone.

And when I beheld, lo, the sinews and the flesh came upon them, and the skin covered them above; but there was no breath in them.

Then said he unto me, Prophesy unto the wind, prophesy, Son of man, and say to the wind; Thus saith the Lord God: Come from the four winds, O breath, and breathe upon those slain that they may live.

So I prophesied as he commanded me, and the breath came into them, and they lived, and stood upon their feet, an exceeding great army.

Ezekiel 37:1-10

It was just past midnight and I was stumbling down the hallway. "Come on, feet!" I said. "I'm only trying to go to the bathroom to take a pee..."

But my feet would not obey me, and as I made my way to the bathroom, I stumbled, crashing into the wall.

The house was pitch black because that's the way I liked it. I hate light, so during the day, I have blankets draped over all of my windows. At night, I try not to let any street light leak into the house.

When I got into the bathroom, I thought I was walking towards the toilet, but instead I walked into the wall and smashed my head against the mirror.

After much thrashing about, I found the light switch and flipped it on.

I looked like a casualty from a great war. Blood streamed down my face, staining my lips and teeth.

When I finally located it, it was only a small gash above the eye, but I could see that it was very deep.

I peed and felt somewhat better. I thought maybe I should go get the thing stitched up, but the idea of going to the Emergency Room in the middle of the night was unthinkable.

Then, as I made my way back to bed, I fell again and crashed on the floor. As I tried to stand, the room started spinning, and (as John Lennon said) I fell into a dream.

Now I was scared.

Maybe I've had a stroke, I thought.

As I lay on the floor, I went into a full-blown panic attack.

If I don't do something fast, I'm going to die right here on my stupid floor.

There was no longer any choice. Slipping into some jeans and a T-shirt, I grabbed my bag, stuck a couple of books inside (if you've ever gone to the Emergency Room on a Friday night you know that you'd better bring some books), and headed out the front door to my car.

I made the four miles to Kaiser Permanente in a flash.

I hate Kaiser Permanente with a hatred that is beyond description. But that's another story—

Unfortunately, it was the only medical coverage I had, so there was no choice.

When I got to the counter, the girl behind the desk didn't even look at me. Apparently she didn't notice that there was a human being standing directly in front of her.

After what seemed an eternity, the girl finally looked up from her computer.

"Your membership card," she said, nastily (I don't know why so many of those girls behind hospital counters are so nasty, but they are).

I tossed my Kaiser card down on the counter, doing my best imitation of Clint Eastwood in *Dirty Harry*.

"That'll be $50," she intoned.

I threw two twenties and a ten down on the counter, with an even bigger dose of hostility than I had my membership card.

I wanted her to know how much I hated her.

The waiting room was packed.

A whole bunch of people were squished together onto an ugly yellow couch. Behind them, a few people who had stolen chairs from another room sat silently.

Everybody was watching a tiny TV screen affixed to the wall.

Even though the sound was off, the Waiting Room People watched intently.

Nobody said a word, except for a couple of teenage girls attired in spangly T-shirts.

They were yukking it up about some reality TV show called *Rock of Love.*

I had no intention of joining the group.

I reeled back to the counter with the nasty girl behind it.

"I think I'm having a heart attack!" I croaked, clutching at my chest.

"Oh, my God," I cried, hamming it up, "Please—I've got to see a doctor *right now!*"

"Triage!" said the girl behind the counter, banging on the door behind her.

A moment later, a dark-skinned woman with a turban on her head opened the two metal doors that separated the Emergency Room from the waiting room, and motioned me inside.

Without saying a word, she slapped a blood pressure cuff onto my forearm.

"Vat's wrong?" she said.

"I had this pain right *here*," I said, pointing at my heart. "And then I fainted...*three* times!"

"How you get dis?" she said, dabbing at the cut above my eyebrow.

"Ahhh...I guess I got it when I fell."

The woman reached into a drawer, pulling out something that looked like a staple gun.

Pop! Pop! Pop!

She put an ace bandage over the cut, and gave me a once over.

"Don' vorry," she said. "No scar. Stitches deesappear in about a veek."

She took me by the hand and led me to a dirty brown chair in the hallway.

"You seet heere," she said, then turned and walked away.

The first thing I noticed about the Emergency Room was that it was totally freezing in there. My lips were chattering all over the place, so I zipped up my sweatshirt. Then I pulled the hood up over my head.

I liked having my hood up like that. It felt safe in there.

As I sat on the chair, I saw people being wheeled in and out of the room on stretchers. Some were young, some were old, but none of them looked very happy, except for one old lady who smiled crazily as she was being toted along by two men wearing blue ambulance driver uniforms.

"Wheeeee, wheeeee, wheeeeee," she laughed giddily, as they wheeled her down the hall.

"I looked at my watch. It was 2:00 a.m." I sang, playing imaginary guitar to the Chuck Berry riff that had just popped into my head.

Time seemed to have stopped inside the ER.

I knew I'd been sitting on that chair for a long time, but it didn't bother me.

In a weird way, I was kind of enjoying myself.

Then a pretty girl with her dark hair falling around her shoulders approached me.

"Hi!" she said, much too enthusiastically.

"I'm Tina. I'm your nurse!"

Well, this isn't going to be so bad after all, I thought.

Tina escorted me into a room, gave me the standard hospital gown and told me to take off my clothes. Then she turned and left, not bothering to close the curtain all the way.

I'd always hated those gowns, because no matter how much you try to cover yourself up, invariably your butt or something else is still hanging out.

Suddenly I heard screaming coming from the room across from me.

"Ghaaaaaaa, ghaaaaa, gaahhhhh," it went.

I peeked through the curtain.

A wizened old lady was lying on her side all scrunched up in the fetal position. She looked completely dehydrated. Her skin was dry and brittle. In fact, the skin seemed so thin that you could almost see the bones popping out from beneath her flesh. I was tempted to go and get her a glass of water, except I didn't know where to get one.

"Noooo, no no!" she screamed. *"Gahhhhhhhh..."*

Even though her screaming was really loud, nobody came into the room to help her.

After a while she got quiet again.

Well, what do I do now? I thought.

I tried to walk to the bathroom, but my legs were still wobbling all over the place.

Maybe I really did have a heart attack—or at least a stroke, I thought.

Actually I was kind of hoping I did, because I didn't want to have wasted a trip to the Emergency Room.

After what seemed an eternity, Tina came back in the room. She was accompanied by a crinkle-faced old hag of a nurse wearing a pointed cap that made her look like the witch in *The Wizard of Oz.*

The nurse sat down on the bed next to me, looking at her chart.

"Touch your finger to your nose," she said.

I did as I was told.

"Faster...faster!" she commanded. I did a few more nose touches.

"Now touch your finger to my finger."

"Faster...*faster...faster!*"

Then she made me stand up and walk around the room.

As I did, she took inspection, walking around me like a drill sergeant.

When she was done, I sat back down on the bed.

"Can I get a blanket or something?" I asked. "I'm really cold."

She reached into a closet, and threw what looked like a pile of old rags at me.

"Why do they keep it so cold in here?" I asked.

The nurse looked at me as if I were a moron. "Bugs," she said.

Bugs?

"Do you know how many bugs are in this room right now?" she snorted. "A hospital is one of the dirtiest places in the world...but the Emergency Room is the *dirtiest* place in the whole hospital!"

Then she got up and walked out, leaving me holding the pile of rags (which turned out to be sheets and blankets).

After she left, I started thinking about what she'd said. I'd never considered it before, but actually it made sense.

My God! There probably were really millions of poisonous microbes floating around right this minute, getting into my lungs and chest!

I pulled the blankets over my head, and tried to pinch my nose so that I wouldn't inhale any germs.

But then I was distracted by a loud voice coming from the room adjacent to mine.

I got up and peeked inside.

There was a little old Jewish lady talking in Yiddish to a man who I figured was her husband.

They seemed to be having a fight of some sort, and she kept shaking her finger in his face.

Though she was kvetching at him with great fervor, her husband didn't respond.

He just looked bored by the whole thing.

She'd probably been shaking her finger in his face like that for the last 40 years.

A moment later a doctor came into the room.

"DOCTOR, I CAN'T MAKE A BM!" the woman said. She was talking so loud that everybody in the place could hear her.

"I TRIED AND I TRIED...I TRIED FIVE TIMES. IT STARTED TO COME OUT, BUT THEN IT WOULDN'T COME OUT ALL THE WAY!"

The doctor mumbled something, but I couldn't hear what he was saying because the dry old lady had started screaming again.

"Gahhhhhh, No! No! No! Don't! Don't do it! Ghaaaaa, ghaaaaaa..."

I walked a few steps closer to get a better look.

She seemed to have almost disappeared.

Her skinny little body was all scrunched into a tiny ball at the foot of the bed. Occasionally the ball would wriggle about, but if it hadn't been for all the noise she was making, you'd have never known that there was a person in there.

Nurses and doctors—some young, some old—scurried though the ER. They all looked as if they had something very important to do.

I watched a pretty young nurse and a ponytailed doctor go out into the hallway. I heard the girl laugh. I sneaked a little closer, so I could hear them. I couldn't make out exactly what they were saying, but their talk reeked of sex.

I wondered if working in a hospital would be a fun job. I'd thought about it a few times, but the closest I'd ever come was stealing a white smock and a stethoscope from my doctor's office and walking around the hospital corridors, looking very important. I used to do a lot of stuff like that when I was younger, but now I don't do it so much anymore.

Only recently had I begun to feel my age—which, by the way is none of your business.

Let's just say that it's not a very funny number. Before, when your number was still funny, whenever you'd go to the hospital and see all the dried up little old people shuffling about on their walkers, or waiting (waiting for what?) in their wheelchairs, oxygen masks affixed to their faces, you'd never think of them as human beings—people like *you*. You'd think that they were another species of some sort.

But then one day it dawns on you that sooner or later you're going to *be* one of those people. Maybe you don't have the wheelchair or the oxygen mask yet—but it ain't too far down the road, brother.

And that's when you start thinking about God. You might not think about him much, but brother, I'll tell you, you DO think about him. You'll be going about your business, watching reruns of *I Love Lucy*, or *Twilight Zone* (I only watch black and white TV, and most of the time I do it with the sound off) and all of sudden, God will come and talk directly into your ear. There's no mistaking it. It *is* God. Period. Finito.

And God says... *Will you listen to me now, my son? Will you shed your old life, give up your fleshly ways, and turn to me?* He might not use those exact words, but that's the essence of it.

And of course, you can either listen to those words and say, "Don't bother me," or "Thanks, but not right now..." Or you can say, "Hmmm—maybe I'd better start listening."

And even if you don't want to, sooner or later, you'll realize that you've *got* to listen. In fact, if you really want however many days you've got left to count for anything, you better listen as much and as often as you possibly can. That's the only thing *to* do. Nothing else makes any sense.

Excuse me—I've gone off on a tangent there.

I looked at my watch. It was six a.m., but Chuck Berry was nowhere in sight.

A couple of hours later, a bunch of stuff happened all at once.

A nurse came into my room wheeling a gigantic machine. She stuck it on my chest and took what I assumed was an X-ray. After she left, a doctor came in. He was a Chinese guy in his 40's, with a bad case of acne.

I immediately recognized him. He was the same doctor who'd come into the room to see my mother, who was in the ER after she'd had a stroke. My mother was in really bad shape, and I recalled this guy laughing and patting her on the head.

"Yew gonna be fine!" he chortled, giving her another pat on the head.

I remember having to walk out of the room so that I wouldn't punch his stupid face in.

The doctor told me to stand up and balance on my toes. Then he pushed on my forehead.

He held out his fingers.

"Push fingah," he said.

"Now pull fingah."

I did the push-pull exercise a couple of more times, after which he turned and scurried out of the room.

A few minutes later, a Mexican guy who looked like he'd once been a boxer, came in, put me on a gurney and wheeled me out of the ER. For some reason I liked this guy.

"Why is it so cold in this place?" I asked him, as we wheeled down the hallway.

"I don't know. It's stupid, man...but after awhile you just get used to it."

He didn't say a single thing about bugs.

I was wheeled into a room, where another guy put a bunch of electrodes on my head. I knew they were testing for lesions in my brain or something like that. But in my mind, I thought maybe I was being tested to see if I had demons inside me like that girl in *The Exorcist.*

Sometimes I thought I might really *have* a couple of demons. I mean, you really never know about that kind of stuff, do you?

After the test was finished, the Mexican guy came back and wheeled me back to my room. It was fun looking up at the ceiling and watching the lights go by.

On the way, I saw Tina in the hallway. She was talking and laughing with a bunch of other nurses. I passed right by her but she didn't even look at me.

"I'm really hungry," I said to Tina. "Can I get some Jell-O or something?"

Tina looked up at me, but this time she didn't look so friendly.

"I'll be with you in a minute," she snapped.

I rolled past the room of the brittle old lady.

For a minute I thought she was gone, but when I looked more closely, I could see this lump moving around at the very foot of the bed.

My legs seemed to be working pretty well now. In fact, except for being so hungry, I felt pretty darn good.

Then it struck me that, except for the cut in my forehead, maybe nothing had happened to me at all.

Maybe I'd just had a gigantic panic attack. I'd had panic attacks all my life, but in the last year or so, I had been getting them much more frequently. A lot of days I couldn't even leave my house because I was afraid a gigantic crack was going to open up in the sidewalk and swallow me up! Stuff like that. Frankly, on those days—I was afraid of *everything!*

I sat on my bed for awhile more. Through the curtains, I could see the acne-faced doctor sitting behind a bank of computers. He was yukking it up with two other doctors about the results of the Lakers game.

I got up off my bed, pulled my gown around me, and walked over to him.

"You get any test results yet, doc?"

"Yah," he said, bringing up a screen on his computer. "Yew fine. Nothing wrong wid yew! Yew in good shape, man!" he said, giggling to himself.

"But what about my balance? Is my balance okay?"

"Stand on toes," he ordered me.

I did as I was bade.

"Yah," he giggled. "Yew bawance fine. You dance like a ballewina!"

"So I can go home?"

"Well," he said. "I gottah consult wid another doctah. Maybe yew stay."

I felt my heart sinking. I didn't *want* to stay. All I wanted to do was to get the hell out of that place.

"But, doctor, if nothing is wrong with me, why can't I go home?"

He turned his face and looked up at me for the first time. At first he looked very grim—like a prison guard. The next moment he broke into a smile.

His teeth were yellow.

"Yah," he giggled. "Yew go home."

Back in my room, I found four plastic containers of Jell-O which had been tossed on my bed. I was so hungry that I ate all of them.

Then I took a good pee. and started slipping on my clothes.

The IV was still stuck in the back of my hand, so I began to remove it.

Suddenly Tina appeared in the doorway.

She looked really angry.

"Hey!" she yelped, snatching at my arm. "You can't do that! That's *my* job!"

Then in one swift movement, she grabbed my wrist, ripped off the bandage, and yanked the IV needle out of the back of my hand. Immediately a huge welter of blood shot out, staining my shirt.

Tina looked at me disgustedly.

She reached into a cabinet, pulled out a gigantic hunk of cotton, stuck it over the open wound, then slapped a swatch of tape over it.

Still scowling, she handed me a sheet of paper.

"Give this to the girl at the desk," she snorted.

She turned huffily and stomped away.

I grabbed my bag and literally *ran* to the metal doors that would take me back to the real world.

All I wanted to do now was go to the Denny's around the corner and get a massive breakfast of bacon and eggs, after which I'd drink about 15 cups of coffee.

When I got outside, I had to scrunch up my eyes because the sunlight was so bright.

I looked at my watch. It was almost 3:00 p.m. I couldn't believe it. I'd been in that bloody place for over 14 hours! Yet somehow it seemed as if no time had passed.

Before I went inside the Denny's—which was only about a mile from Kaiser—I bought a newspaper. It was odd, because I hadn't read a newspaper in months. I didn't want to know what was going on in the world. All I wanted to do was to stay in my room with the blankets over the windows and watch TV with the sound off.

But now, I happily read the paper from cover to cover.

I even read the sports section, though I have absolutely no interest whatsoever in sports.

After I'd eaten my breakfast, I ordered another side of bacon and had four more cups of coffee. I felt great.

When I approached the girl at the cash register to pay my tab, she looked at me kind of funny.

"Your hand," she said. "Your hand is bleeding."

I looked at my hand.

Sure enough, the blood had leaked through the bandage and was dripping all over the place.

"Here," she said, reaching down below the counter. "Let me put a new bandage on that for you." She brought out a cloth and dabbed at my hand, pressing on it until the blood stopped. Then she put a fresh bandage over the wound.

As I watched her patch me up, I realized that I'd seen her before. Even though I hadn't been in that particular Denny's for about four years, I remembered her.

She was past 40 and wore no makeup to disguise it. Though she wasn't a knockout or anything, I suddenly thought that she was the most beautiful woman I'd ever seen. She had that odd kind of beauty that women in old Western movies often have.

I felt my heart go *bumpety bump.*

All I wanted to do at that moment was to kiss her sweet, unlipsticked lips.

I wanted to ask her if she'd leave her Denny's job and come and live with me.

We'd get the hell out of L.A.—out of the filth and muck—and go to some place that didn't have any Kaiser Permanente Emergency Rooms and all the poor, sad, brittle old people who were going to die there.

"When you get home, you should change your shirt," she said, breaking my reverie.

"Thank you," I said. Then I turned around and walked out.

Instead of going home, I decided to take a drive over Malibu Canyon and check out the beach.

As I drove over the canyon, I realized I couldn't remember the last time I'd been to the beach. It must have been ten years...maybe more.

When I got to Malibu, it looked practically the same as I remembered it.

I took off my shoes and ran down to the water. The waves were pretty good, and the surfers were getting some nice rides. Inside, where the waves were just waist high, kids were either body surfing, riding boogie boards, or just playing in the water.

I watched the slick bodies of the young boys and girls playing in the sea, laughing and skipping through the white wash of the water.

I knew I'd never be one of them again. Those days were gone forever. But for some reason, I didn't feel sad about that.

I continued watching the body surfers. Someday they might be in the Kaiser Emergency Room with an oxygen mask affixed to their face, but right now, they didn't have to think about that.

I sat there, watching the people play in the water and listening to the sounds of the sea.

As I sat there, suddenly a voice came into my ear. It wasn't loud, but it was definitely a voice I recognized.

It was funny. I'd heard that voice all my life...though I didn't know who or what it was.

Every so often I heard the dry, hellish screams of the brittle old lady in the hospital. There seemed to be a cruel laughter behind it.

But I didn't pay attention to the cackling.

I just sat there, letting the waves and the voice of the Lord wash all the fear and sickness out of my body.

FARCE

FARCE

PENISES

I really don't know what to say about penises. I guess I have mixed feelings about them. I mean, I know they have purpose in life and all...yet somehow they always seem like an extra appendage—you know what I mean? Also, you will have to admit that they are extremely silly looking. I don't understand girls that go on and on about "what a nice cock you have," and all that sort of stuff. I really don't. Penises look too much like wrinkled little old men—kind of like little elves or something. I don't know why, but I've always had the idea that penises should be on wheels. They'd just roll on down the street, stopping occasionally to greet each with glad hellos. That would be nice, don't you think?

FARCE

VAGINAS

Ok, now I'll tell you the truth. I don't really know what to make of these things. They are odd. Sometimes I think they are swell. Other times I think they are foul, evil, ugly and nasty. I'm sorry, but I do. In fact, they scare me. From various angles, they look like a clam, a piece of beef jerky, a sausage pizza, or a wicked Halloween mask. Also, they often smell like codfish. And yet men of courage go absolutely crazy for them. Often they will lose the lives over them! This is obviously quite silly. I think you ought to seriously consider this the next time you go looking for a piece of pussy.

FARCE

MY STUPID DOG

I once had a dog named Kenny Maytag. He was some kind of a wiener dog, I guess. Now I am not a great fan of dogs, but I loved Kenny Maytag dearly. He was a peculiar dog. He seemed to have no purpose in life. In fact, he did nothing. He did not roll over, fetch or play dead. He could not even bark very well. He just sort of *yarfed.* I always thought it was rather odd that I had a dog that did nothing—but that's just the way it was.

Actually, one thing I liked about Kenny Maytag was that he would get very embarrassed if you laughed at him. I think he'd been embarrassed since the time my wife Spatula and I gave him that awful name.

We rather enjoyed this neurosis of his, however. Therefore we would continually make fun of him, which caused him to get even more embarrassed. When he would get embarrassed, he would go around and around in circles and try to bite his own tail. This caused us to laugh gleefully and taunt him. Sometimes he would run around in circles and urinate on himself. This caused us to laugh uproariously and taunt him even more.

Many people requested information as to why we acted in such a cruel fashion to this poor, demented beast. Unfortunately, I have no answer to this question.

FARCE

JAY JEE'S PENIS

When I was just a little snuffer, maybe four or so, we lived in this big old house up in the Hollywood Hills. I don't remember it much, but I know lots of movie stars and people in the "business" used to live up there. I know it because my mom still reminds me of it to this day—dropping names like Kirk Douglas, Tony Curtis, and Burt Lancaster (as if I cared!)

Anyway, I had this little friend next door—a girl named Jay Jee. She was my little buddy. We used to play all day out on the long brick front patio—cowboys and Indians, cops and robbers—all the usual stuff.

Anyway, one day, a kind of funny thing happened. Jay Jee came over to my house completely naked. I mean, we were only five or so, and her parents were probably the kind of parents that let their kid run around naked. Bloody stupid liberals—

Anyhow, there she was, naked as a jaybird. And boy, was I in shock!

"Mommy, Mommy," I called. "Come *quick!*"

My mother, a lovely dark woman, appeared at the door with the Sunday paper in her hand. She seemed to see nothing strange in the scene.

"Look, mommy!" I cried. "Jay Jee has no penis! What happened to Jay Jee's *penis?*"

Poor Jay Jee. She didn't seem to understand that her act of nakedness was causing me the most profound discomfort.

My mother, in that soothing way of hers replied matter-of-factly. "Oh, she probably got it cut off in a sword fight." Knowing that Jay Jee and I often played Robin Hood and other games like this, it was quite a good response. In any event, it seemed to satisfy me.

Jay Jee, for her part, seemed quite removed from the inherent drama of the situation. That is, until her mother came out, hurriedly rushed over, picked her daughter up, and began furiously smacking her bottom as she carried the poor thing home.

Guess I was wrong about those liberal parents.

Anyhow, that afternoon, my lovely mother and I went for a walk, up by the Hollywood dam. We were holding hands, something I liked to do a lot. On the way, we saw a big, hairy tarantula creeping along in the dirt and it scared me. But with my mother along, I was all right.

Everything was always all right with mother.

FARCE

AN UNFORTUNATE SITUATION

When I was in I guess, the sixth grade or so, I had this record album by Harry Belafonte. I don't remember the title of it, but the cover was bright green and it had—among other songs—"Matilda" and "Day-O" on it. I liked "Day-O" the best. I'd go around humming it all the time. The only part I didn't like was this one part about the "ugly black tarantula." In fact, it sort of ruined the whole song for me. I couldn't understand why old Harry would ruin a perfectly good song about banana boats and such by sticking in a part about a goddamned tarantula. But I suppose Harry knew what he was doing, because "Day-O" was a very popular song. It really was.

Anyway, one day, I was playing Harry's record real loud on the old stereo—the cut was "Matilda." It's the one where Harry whistles the beginning part. Harry was quite a good whistler, by the way. Anyhow, it was such a happy song and all, that I felt like doing something special. So what I did was, I took off my pants—well, not all the way off—I just sort of pushed them down around my knees, and then I started dancing all over the house, singing at the top of my lungs.

MA-TILDA, MA-TILDA
MA-TILDA, SHE TAKE ME MONEY
AN' SHE RUN VE-NE-ZUELA

I was getting pretty crazy to tell you the truth—knocking into furniture and stuff. I kept falling on the floor because of my pants being down around my knees and all, but it didn't matter because I was having such a great time. The only problem was that my girlfriend, Renate had come over and was looking at me through the window—only I didn't see her because I was so engaged in my dancing and singing and stuff.

Renate was this very pretty German girl who lived right behind me. Actually, she wasn't all that pretty, but she had managed to get her tits before the rest of the girls in our class. I liked Renate a lot because she let me feel her tits. Not only that—she actually called her tits *tits*, instead of boobies, or whatever it was that girls in the sixth grade usually refer to their tits as.

At any rate, this situation proved to be unfortunate for me, since when Renate saw me dancing around like a madman with my pants down around my knees and singing a Harry Belafonte song, I guess she thought I was kind of strange or something. When I looked up, she was just standing there with her mouth formed into this funny little O shape. Actually I thought *she* looked kind of stupid, but I didn't say this at the time, since I felt even stupider.

Well, sad to say, but old Renate and I never got along too well after that day. In fact, very soon afterwards she got a new boyfriend—this greasy Italian guy named Vic Delpizzo, who years later would wind up in a mental institution for chopping up his mother with a hatchet. Heck, I knew Vic was a crummy guy right from the start. I even told Renate, but she wouldn't believe me. For some reason, girls never know guys are crummy, even when it's quite obvious how crummy they really are! But girls are funny. Everybody knows that.

Just recently, I found a copy of the green Harry Belafonte album. Found it in the bargain bin at Kmart. It made me kind of sad, finding it there. Oh, don't get me wrong—I like Kmart all right. There are lots of interesting people to watch there. Crummy people, I suppose.

But crummy people can be interesting, just the same. Just don't stay at Kmart too long if you ever want to go look at people. It sort of *gets* to you after awhile. You might even start doubting the existence of God and stuff, for making so many crummy-looking people.

Anyhow, I only paid a buck sixty-nine for the Harry album. I took it home and put it on the stereo and it made me remember old Renate and her tits and Vic Delpizzo and all that stuff.

The trouble was, I still hated that part in "Day-O" about the ugly black tarantula. Someday, if I see Harry, I'm gonna ask him how come he went and ruined a perfectly good song like that. Of course if *you* see him, you can ask him for me. Just be sure and let me know what he says, okay?

MUGS AND THUGS

NOTHING PERSONAL: ONE-ON-ONE WITH A HITMAN

It all started with a late afternoon phone call. The voice on the other end of the line immediately got my attention. It sounded like it was coming from the bottom of a well.

"My name is Joey Carbone," the voice rasped. "I think I have a story that might interest you..."

I'd heard the line before. A million times, actually. But on this occasion, the caller had my total attention. It wasn't simply that he identified himself as an ex-Mafia hitman—one who now had a contract out on his own head for turning state's evidence. No, it was something else. Something I couldn't put my finger on. But no matter. Whatever it was, Joey Carbone had me hooked.

Carbone told me that he was looking for someone to write a book about his life as a mob enforcer. He said he didn't figure he was going to be around much longer, and that he wanted whatever proceeds were left to go to his two daughters.

"Nice pitch," I thought to myself. "Play on the old sympathies."

Despite my skepticism, I stayed on the line.

Two hours later I was still listening.

"So, ya innerested, or what?" Carbone finally asked.

I tried to play it cool. “I’m not sure,” I said. “I’ll think about it and get back to you.”

Long silence.

“No, I’ll call *you* back. Day after tomorrow. Same time.”

Before I could respond, the line clicked dead.

I sat there staring at the phone.

The fact is, I’d lied to Carbone. There were no two ways about it. I wanted to write his story. I wanted to write it *bad*.

I phoned my agent in New York. He wasn’t encouraging. “There’ve been lots of books about mob guys,” he said. “Unless this guy can really come up with some juicy stuff, it’s gonna be a tough sell.”

I didn’t care. After all, I figured, how many times in your life did you get the chance to climb inside the brain of a genuine wiseguy...a stone-cold killer? No sir—for me there was no choice—book deal or no book deal. I was going to dance with Joey Carbone.

The entire next day, all I could think about was Carbone. He completely occupied me. *Possessed* would probably be a better word. My mind was filled with old black and white images of a time long gone...of gangsters and gun molls and flat-nosed guys wearing pin striped suits and Borsalino hats.

All Friday afternoon I waited for Carbone’s call.

It never came.

Two days passed.

Three...

Four...

Nothing.

I figured it was all over. Carbone had taken a powder. Hell, maybe I’d dreamed the whole thing up.

A week later I was laying on the couch—the TV flickering soundlessly—when the phone rang. I reached over and picked it up.

“How ya doin’, pal?” the voice on the other end rasped.

“Not bad,” I said, trying my best to sound cool.

Carbone didn’t apologize for being a week late in getting back. He just went on and on—as if we were already in business together. I told him I’d need a minimum of two hours a day with him for the next several weeks. I told him I’d have to tape all of our conversations.

After I transcribed the tapes, I'd write two chapters that I'd send off to my agent. If we landed a book deal, we'd split 50/50.

"Anyway you wanna do it, pal," Carbone said in an overly-friendly tone. "I got faith in you, my man."

Usually compliments didn't get to me, but when Carbone said that, I felt ten feet tall.

"OK," I said. "Where do you want to meet?"

I could feel Carbone thinking hard.

"Meet me tomorrow at Nate 'n' Al's. Twelve sharp."

"How'll I recognize you?" I asked.

"Don't worry, pal. I'll recognize *you*."

Something about the way Carbone said that last bit sent a cold chill up my spine.

At 11:30 a.m. the following morning, I entered Nate 'n' Al's—a prominent Beverly Hills deli. I'd decided to arrive early, then watch the door for Carbone to enter. I figured he'd probably stand out in some way from the rest of the entertainment biz types that frequented the place.

As I was thinking this, I noticed a fiftyish man with a thick mane of snow white hair sitting at a back table.

No doubt about it—the guy was staring at me.

There was something about him—a certain aloofness—a separateness from everyone else in the room.

When the man smiled at me, I knew I was about to meet Joey Carbone in the flesh.

As I approached, Carbone didn't move.

When I sat down he extended his hand.

His grip was solid as a rock.

"How ya doin', pal?" he smiled, revealing a set of pearly white teeth.

After a few brief amenities, I took out my recorder and flipped the On button.

To my delight, Joey Carbone was a born storyteller. Almost immediately, I found myself totally mesmerized by him.

On this day, I heard about his teenage years. It was during this period of his life that Carbone had gotten started in the enforcement game by "beating another kid half to death with a baseball bat." After that, he'd continued climbing the ladder—gradually working himself up through the various levels of some of Chicago's top families, until he'd become a high-ranking hitman for the mob.

At one point, I asked Carbone if he hadn't ever considered a *normal* lifestyle. He emitted a short guffaw, causing pieces of his pastrami sandwich to fly from his mouth.

"I don't think you understand," he said. "I *loved* the lifestyle. I loved wearin' four-inch collared shirts and spit-shined shoes. I loved walking around with a coupla grand in my pocket all time. Hey, pal—I didn't' come down from the mountain with Moses. I wuz up there shootin' dice! I was lookin' to rob somebody! I wuz lookin' to bust somebody's chops! I'm a *hood*, man...an' that's all I've *ever* been."

As Carbone talked, I noticed a napkin sitting on the seat beside his knee. He saw me looking at it. Gingerly, he lifted the napkin to reveal a shiny, steel-blue .38 caliber Smith & Wesson.

He must've seen the shocked look on my face—

"Best place for it," Carbone deadpanned.

"Ya don' haveta waste time pulling it outta yer fuckin' pants."

I nodded nervously, then continued listening, as Carbone continued spinning stories for the next hour-and-a-half.

Joey Carbone and I met every day that week. Each time he would select a different restaurant. Sometimes I'd show up at one he'd designated and he'd phone—have me paged—then tell me to meet him somewhere else.

Joey was one paranoid cat. After listening to his story, I understood why.

Whenever we'd meet, Carbone had a regular ritual. He'd always sit—back to the wall—in a booth from which he could check out his surroundings. As he talked, his eyes never stopped surveying the room.

On this day, I listened as Carbone casually related a story of how he'd cut off a man's finger in order to make him "give up" some money he owed.

Carbone was clearly a sociopath. He had absolutely no conscience whatsoever. This was hard to fathom, because the guy sitting across from me was positively charming. It was only later that I realized it was exactly this quality that had made Carbone so successful in his chosen profession.

But after awhile, the grisly incidents became a bit too much for me.

"Joey," I asked. "Didn't you ever feel bad about all the people you've hurt?"

Carbone fixed me with a look I'll never forget. A look that was a combination of incredulity, pain and, yes—disdain.

"Don't you unnerstan'?" he spat. "It was nothin' personal. It was *never* nothin' personal. It was strictly *business*."

Carbone claimed he only hurt people when all else failed. What he really enjoyed, he said, was conning them. He was so up front about the fact that he was a con, that I barely noticed it when he began conning me.

It started with a simple request.

"Say, pal," he said one day after our meeting, "can you loan me $20? I'm a little short today."

I said "Sure," and forked over.

The next time it was $50.

Soon I was doling out money in increments of hundreds and two hundreds. I knew I was being taken for a ride, but for some reason, I didn't care. In fact, I *liked* the fact that Carbone was screwing me. Somehow in my mind, it made the story I was writing even better.

Interestingly, the more Carbone conned me, the more mistrustful he became of *me*. He kept asking me if I'd played the tapes I'd been making for anyone. When I told him I hadn't...he got ugly and accused me of lying. "Don't *ever* fuck me over," he warned darkly. "You wouldn't like the consequences."

Finally, I thought. Finally—I'm seeing his other side.

Though this side of Carbone's character interested me, I was also getting angry. I'd shelved every other project I was working on for this one—and now he was accusing me of screwing *him*.

"Look," I snapped, after he'd questioned me one too many times, "I'm giving you my time. I'm giving you my dough. What's *with* you? If you can't trust me by now, we might as well just hang this whole thing up."

A whole gamut of expressions traveled across Carbone's face. "Lemme tell you a story pal," he said. "I once had an Uncle Louie, see? I loved the guy. Now, Uncle Louie, what he useta do was—he'd' put me on top of the icebox and tell me to jump. I'd jump and he'd catch me. I'd jump and I'd jump and I'd jump. One day he didn't catch me. I fell on the floor and really hurt myself bad. I says, 'Uncle Louie, why did you *do* that?' And he says, 'Kid I just want you to know something. Don't ever trust *anybody*.'"

Carbone fixed me with that look again. "And I *don't*. I don't trust a livin' motherfucker in this whole fuckin' world."

At precisely 10:00 a.m. the next day, my phone rang. It was Carbone. I could tell by his tone that I was in for another tirade.

"Listen," he said. "I wanna know how long it's gonna take you t'write this goddamn thing."

"But Joey," I pleaded. "I've just barely finished transcribing the tapes."

A nasty edge crept into Carbone's voice: "Well I'm tellin' you, friend—'ya better get it done quick, cause I'm getting' real nervous."

"Listen Joey, I..."

"No—*you* listen. You better get us a fucking book deal within a week. You or that fucking agent of yours. I don't give a shit. I wanna see some action here, pal."

There was a pregnant pause.

"I ain't kiddin' you. Unless I see some dough within a week, you're gonna be one sorry motherfucker!"

When I hung up the phone, I was shaking.

The next time Carbone phoned me, he was back to normal. However, this time it was I who was angry, though I kept my voice in check.

"Listen, Joey," I said. "I think you better get somebody else to write this book. I just can't do it in the time you need."

There was a long pause.

When he spoke again Carbone's voice was ice cold. "Now, listen and listen good, motherfucker. I poured out my guts to you. I don't like somebody runnin' around with my story in their head, you unnerstan'? So just remember one thing. I know where you *live*. I know every single fucking thing about you...and if you're fucking with me, you ain't gonna like the consequences...if you get my meaning."

Carbone was right. I didn't like it one little bit. I scrambled for something to say.

"Look," I said, trying to sound calm. "I just don't think I'm the right person to write your book is all. How about if I give you back all the tapes I've made?"

Another pause. "How do I know you ain't made copies of em?"

"You're just going to have to trust me, Joey," I said, trying my best to sound confident.

The fact is, I was scared shitless.

Another pause. Then, "OK, meet me at four o'clock. Nate 'N' Al's. Make sure you bring em all."

Before I could say anything, the phone clicked dead.

I was working against the clock. As quickly as I could, I gathered the tapes and threw them into a manila envelope. I was shaking like a leaf. What would Carbone do when he saw me? Drag me out to the car and knock me off? I was sure he'd at least walk me to the nearest ATM, where he'd clean me out. As I walked out to my car, my hands and legs wouldn't stop shaking.

I drove over to the Beverly Hills Hotel and left the envelope with the tapes in them at the front desk under the name of Dr. Ruben. Then quickly, I drove over to Nate 'n' Al's. I knew Carbone had a habit of showing up early. This time I had to beat him.

I made it inside of three minutes. Then I parked myself in a phone booth across the street from the restaurant.

A moment later, I saw Carbone's car pull up. As soon as he'd gone inside, I dialed the restaurant phone and had him paged.

A moment later, he answered.

"I don't want you to say anything," I said in my best tough-guy voice. "Just listen to me. The tapes are at the front desk of the Beverly Hills Hotel under the name of Dr. Ruben. You can pick them up anytime. Now I want you to know something, Joey, I know where *you* live too. Don't forget that I make my living *investigating* people. So you need to know that if I *ever* hear from you again, the Feds will show up at your door so fast, your head's gonna swim."

There was a really long pause this time.

I held my breath.

I could feel Carbone thinking hard.

"You think you're a pretty smart motherfucker, don't you?"

"Nothing personal," I replied.

Another pause.

"They better all be there," he said.

"Don't worry, Joey. They're all there."

"If they ain't—"

"Goodbye, Joey."

I hung up the phone.

From my spot across the street, I watched Carbone leave the restaurant and get into his car. I watched it head down the street and disappear around the corner.

Oddly, I noticed that I was feeling kind of sad.

It wasn't just that my book deal had gone down the toilet. No, it was more than that. I knew that in some weird way I was going to miss old Joey.

Well, the hell with it. Only one thing to do now.

I exited the phone booth and headed over to Nate 'n' Al's to have a corned beef sandwich and a cup of coffee.

AN EYE FOR AN EYE: MURDER IN LOUISIANA

Lake Arthur, LA—Six TV sets, stacked one on the other, were found in Michael Perry's hotel room after his arrest in Washington, D.C., in mid-1983. Strange words and markings—*"sleep," "Mi body," "Olivia"*—had been scribbled on the screens in red felt-tip pen. Drawn on some of the screens were gigantic eyeballs.

The desk clerk at the Annex Hotel said that Perry had paid a month in advance for the room, into which he'd quickly disappeared, police would report later. Perry had been very quiet, the clerk said, never coming out except at night, and then only for a trip to the candy machine in the hallway.

Then, according to police, after another tenant accused Perry of stealing a cassette tape player, Perry was arrested. A computer check revealed that he was wanted on five counts of first-degree murder in Louisiana. The victims—killed with a shotgun—included Perry's parents, two cousins and his two-and-a-half year old nephew.

For Michael Owen Perry, 30—who is accused of the biggest mass murder in this part of the country—the TV sets are one of several curious elements in a complex case.

The name Michael Perry is well known to Gavin de Becker, who heads up security for singer Olivia Newton-John, as well as a variety of celebrities. De Becker said that an investigation by him and his staff shows that Perry had become obsessed with Newton-John after seeing her in the 1980 film *Xanadu*, in which she plays a muse who returns to Earth.

Perry wrote Newton-John two letters in 1982, and made five trips to California in an attempt to meet her, de Becker said. The obsession may still exist, according to Perry's lawyer Mark Romero. "Olivia's name just magically appeared the other day on the wall of Michael's jail cell," Romero said.

Perry has been confined to maximum security in the Jennings County Jail for the past 20 months. His trial is scheduled to begin here Monday. More than 50 people from around the country have been subpoenaed for the trial, including employees from the store in Washington where Perry supposedly bought the TV sets found in his hotel room.

In the first newspaper interview since his arrest, Perry told the *Times* emphatically that he was innocent. "They think I murdered five people, my parents, my own nephew—good li'l entertaining guy. But I killed no five people, understand?"

He also denied that he was obsessed with Olivia Newton-John. "The first time I ever saw her," he recalled, "I was with my girlfriend and that movie *Grease* was playing. My girl said, 'Hey, look—there's Olivia Newton-John,' and I said 'Fuck Olivia Newton-John.' That's *exactly* what I said."

Regarding the letters he's sent the singer, Perry stated, "I found out all you had to do to write somebody was to give their name, their city and their ZIP (the letters were addressed to Olivia Newton-John/ singer actor-Australian, Malibu, CA). So I said, 'Well, man, I'm gonna write me a movie star.' That's all there was to it, man."

Perry also denied that he'd traveled to California specifically to see Newton-John in 1982. "I caught myself in Malibu and the thought came to my mind that she lived there, so I asked a couple of people where she lived. They said, 'Oh, right next door,' so I go next door and I knock and I said, 'Hi y'all...I'd like to speak to Olivia,' and some guy said 'What do *you* want?' and I said, 'I'd like to ask her, you know, how she felt about playing a magical muse'...and that was that, really."

Despite these statements, Jeff Davis Parish Chief Detective Ervin Trahan said that Perry has confessed twice to the murders (once to Trahan and once to Perry's Aunt Zula). Trahan said Perry also revealed where the guns were found—in the Broadmoor Ditch (a water-filled gully located south of Jennings, outside of Lake Arthur). Perry told Trahan that the location of the guns came to him "in a dream."

Though the defense was attempting to suppress the evidence, as of pre-trial hearing August 21, the court ruled that the confessions and the finding of the guns were admissible, said co-defense attorney Ricky Arceneaux.

The commonly held opinion in Lake Arthur (pop. 3,200) seems to be that Michael Perry is guilty. At one time he was arrested for threatening the lives of his parents and was confined to a mental institution for his aberrant behavior.

People here are hoping for the trial to end quickly. "It's gonna be a three-ring circus during this trial," said Police Chief Jimmy Boudreaux. "We just want it over with so we can resume our lives." But even if Perry is found innocent, it may make no difference. "His life ain't worth a plugged nickel on the streets here if he gets off," said one local who asked not to be identified.

When told of the comment, Perry's lawyer, Mark Romero, seemed nonplussed. "You've gotta remember," he said, "that these are backwoods people. When something like this happens, well—it's an eye for an eye."

While Perry was growing up here, people regarded him basically as a good kid. Remembered his elementary school teacher, Alice Pearson: "He was very bright and always courteous. He was a good boy."

Perry's boyhood friend, Dale Hahn also had similar memories. "He was a real cute kid," said Hahn. "Always had a little gleam in his eye."

An inveterate music lover, Perry played trumpet in a rock band called the Great Pretenders that worked around the Jeff Davis Parish. "Mike always loved his music," said Hahn.

But after Perry's older brother Ronnie was killed in an oil field accident, some townspeople began noticing changes in Perry's demeanor, including John deLaunay, 30, who'd known both brothers: "He seemed to feel the whole town was against him. He thought people were watching him. Everything got to be secret agent-type stuff."

Perry began spending long hours in the trailer behind his parents' home reading the Bible, say his family and friends. He changed his appearance often. Sometimes he'd be long-haired and bearded; other times he'd cut his hair in a Mohawk or shave his head bald.

Some of Perry's antics were comical. When his father asked him to trim the trees at the side of the house, Perry took a buzz saw and cut them off at the roots, police records relate. He completely stripped the interior from his car, replacing the front seat with a five-gallon bucket and the steering wheel with a pair of Vise Grips. "We'd see him drivin' around town sittin' on that bucket, and we'd just go, 'There goes that ol' crazy Mike!'" laughed Chief Boudreaux.

One day Perry walked into the bank. He was wearing a freshly cleaned all-white suit. He looked sharp—except for the fact that he had cigarettes protruding from both nostrils and both ears. "All of his questions were intelligent and appropriate," recalled a teller at the Calcasieu Bank in Jennings. "It was just odd to be talking to someone with cigarettes in their nose and ears."

Perry went through various name changes. He was alternately known as T-Mike, Crab, Robot, and T-37. Then he went to court to have his name changed to Zewick Ma.

"I did think it was a rather strange name," recalled Vernon Jeansonne, the lawyer who filed for the change, "but legally there was nothing wrong with it. Later he came back and wanted to change his name to God, but the judge told him 'We already have somebody with that name.'"

Perry changed his name once more, finally settling on one that he felt totally comfortable with—*Eye*.

Recalled Alice Pearson, whom Perry had gone back to visit in 1981: "I remember I said, 'It's nice to see you, Mike,' and he said 'My name's not Mike anymore, Mrs. Pearson. It's Eye.' Then he said something very peculiar. He said, 'I'm gonna show all these people around here that I'm another Jesus Christ.'"

As police reconstructed events, one afternoon in 1982 Perry turned on HBO and saw *Xanadu*. Family and friends recalled in interviews with the *Times* that he seemed to become obsessed with Olivia Newton-John. He watched her every chance he could get and played her records and tapes over and over.

Next came the letters, two of them, sent by registered mail. After telling the singer that her photos are "rather haunting," Perry wrote that "either the dead bodies are rising or else there is a listening device under my mother and father's house. The voices I here [*sic*] tell me that you are locked up beneath this town of Lake Arthur and were really a muse who was granted everlasting life."

The second letter was written using four different colors of ink "simply because there are four rivers which ran from Paradise," Perry wrote.

Perry began making trips to California, according to security consultant de Becker. On two occasions he tried to see Newton-John at her Malibu home but was rebuffed by security people, De Becker said. Between these trips, Perry would return home to collect his Social Security disability check (he'd been injured by a shotgun blast in a bar altercation). In July of 1983, he returned home, but had already bought bus tickets to return to California.

On July 19, 1983, Ernest Ashford went to visit his stepson, Brian LeBlanc, 22, who was staying at the home of his cousin, Randall Paul Perry, 19, who was also Michael Perry's cousin. When Ashford entered the house, he found the bloodied bodies of Brian and Randall, still in their beds. Each had been shot in the eyes with a shotgun.

After Chief Detective Ervin Trahan noticed blood on the house two doors away, police discovered the bodies of Michael Perry's parents—Chester, 48, and Grace, 47—as well as their grandson, Anthony Bonin, 2 ½. All three victims had been killed by a shotgun blast to the face.

Police said that in the house they found hand-written lists of people that included all of the dead, as well as the names Olivia, Matt (Newton-John married long-time boyfriend Matt Lattanzi in December of 1984) and a "Judge O'Connor." In the child's crib were found, among other objects, an overturned crucifix and a painting of the Madonna and Child.

The police determined that Michael Perry was the prime suspect. They combed the nearby wooded area for Perry, a practiced survivalist. For 12 days, Perry wasn't to be found. "It was 12 days of horror," recalled Boudreaux. "Everybody here was packing guns," said Trahan. "I'm amazed somebody didn't get killed. You gotta remember, these are Cajuns. Cajuns, they don't liketa live in fear. They'll kill you b'fore they live in fear."

When the Jeff Davis Parish Sheriff's Department got word from Washington that Perry was arrested, they left immediately. Trahan and his men found Perry very cooperative. Perry gave permission for extradition, saying: "If Louisiana is needing me now, I guess I'd better go back and see what's going on."

Perry told a reporter later that he was in the capital "to do Bible study." However, Detective Trahan said that he felt that Perry was trying "to encounter" Supreme Court Justice Sandra Day O'Connor.

Perry said in his interview with the *Times* that O'Connor reminded him of Newton-John, "especially her eyes." Trahan said that during the ride back to Louisiana from Washington, Perry told him that he was angry with the judge "because a woman shouldn't be doing a man's job."

Gavin de Becker is regarded as an expert on the fans who are obsessed by stars. Based in Studio City, he provides security for Newton-John as well as other superstar clients, including Dolly Parton, Cher, Robert Redford, Tina Turner and Brooke Shields.

A two-time Presidential appointee to the National Institute of Justice Advisory Board, de Becker is working on a research project funded by the Department of Justice titled, "Violence and Mental Disorders: The Choice of Public Figures as Victims."

In assessing the relative dangerousness of the 3,000 cases that he's handled, de Becker (who refers to himself as "a threat assessor") puts the various fan delusions into specific categories.

Examples of the categories under which de Becker classified fans include "religious obsession" (the fan thinks he's Jesus Christ), "special powers" (the fan thinks he's a messenger from God), "debt owed" (the fan thinks he wrote Dolly Parton's latest hit and has threatened to kill her unless he's paid), "science fiction" (the fan thinks the world is about to be taken over by alien beings), and "Outcon," short for outside control (the fan thinks he is being directed by a radio transmitter implanted in his brain).

Based on the letters sent to Newton-John, de Becker said he classified Michael Perry under three separate categories: religious, sex/love and science fiction. "We considered him to be especially dangerous to my client," said De Becker, "because he had written her a role in one of his delusions."

De Becker is especially interested in the effect of TV on the obsessive personality. "Today," he said in an interview, "you have an entire sub-population who relates more to television characters—soap opera stars and such—than they do real people in their own lives. Just as historically people focused on Jesus Christ, because the Bible *was* mass media, today you have all this folklore surrounding Marilyn Monroe and Elvis. Our mental hospitals used to be full of Jesus Christs. Today they're full of Luke Skywalkers and Captain Kirks.

"Now when you stop and look at the Michael Perry case and ask yourself, what's the one thing that's wrong with this picture, what doesn't fit?—it's immediately clear. It was his interest with Olivia Newton-John. Everyone else (with the exception of Judge O'Connor) was a real person in his life. Yet his obsession with Olivia was clearly the controlling factor for him. Perry is someone who had no social support system. In effect, TV was his only effective social contact."

In Perry's police file is a report by Dr. Walter Risler, a psychologist who was hired by de Becker to interview Perry while incarcerated in the Jennings County Jail. The report states that Perry was obsessively watching TV and was particularly hooked on *General Hospital* and that he'd become particularly excited by an episode that dealt with "a mystic," and another that dealt with "survivalism and escape to a desert island."

Since his teens, Perry seemed increasingly obsessed with TV and music. Dale Hahn, a boyhood friend of Perry who recently moved to Clute, Tex., said that when Perry visited him shortly before the murders occurred, "Michael watched MTV practically 24 hours a day."

Darlene Gaspard, a local waitress who formerly dated Perry, said, "Whenever you'd see Mike, he'd always have a radio strapped to his belt and them ol' earphones on." Perry even wore a pair of earphones during a recent local TV interview.

In their book *Snapping* (a study of sudden personality change), authors Flo Conway and Jim Siegleman state: "Television may affect the total personality—not simply an individual's actions, but the way he or she perceives the world." Adds de Becker, "What TV does is ruin your ability to edit and discern. But with a psychotic or schizophrenic, whose ability is already eroded, you can see how this can be extremely dangerous.

"The problem with Michael," de Becker said, "Is that he was not just some guy who sat around and fantasized. He got on planes, buses…he hitchhiked. He made the trip to California five times…!"

During his interview with the *Los Angeles Times*, Perry seemed willing, almost eager, to answer questions. Except for an angry outburst at the jailer, whom he accused of stealing batteries from his cassette tape player, he was extremely polite and friendly. He displayed a quick intelligence and a vivid memory for detail, though his conversation tended to go off on tangents.

With a three-day stubble of beard and an added 20 pounds, Perry hardly resembled the skinny kid paling around with his dad, or holding up a freshly-caught fish, who appears in some old family photos shown in the *Times*.

Perry, outfitted in a new pair of jeans, and a Pendleton-style plaid shirt, spoke about a number of subjects, including religious orientation (*"I take the Bible at heart, man."*), his musical tastes (*"I like it all; it's all great."*) and his reason for going through various name changes. *("Hey, I wanted to have the name of God, the creator of the universe, y'know?")* He also flatly denied having anything to do with the murders. (*"They said they thought I was going to California to kill Olivia Newton-John and that I was in D.C. to kill Judge O'Connor, but this is an absolute lie!"*)

Perry seemed to become more animated when the discussion turned to Newton-John and *Xanadu*. He seemed to be especially fascinated by one scene in which Newton-John, attired in a leopard skin outfit, is singing, backed up by a rock 'n' roll band (affixed to the drummer's double-kit of bass drums are two large and very visible eyeballs).

"When she turns around in that scene," Perry recalled, "I immediately notice the appearance she has on her face. It was the *same* face that I saw on my mother in 1961."

On that day, Perry's mother woke him to go to school, he related. But when he looked at her, she had a face that was "completely different. I said, 'Oh my God, what is this?' I said, 'Mother, did you see your face?' She said, 'What face?' and I said, 'Go look in the mirror.' She went to look and came back and said, 'I look normal,' and I said, 'Oh no, you *don't!*' Anyway, in the movie of Olivia Newton-John, that's what my mother looked like."

Perry went on to say that later he saw Judge O'Connor on TV and that she had the same face. "It's a face that's not…smooth. Of course, I'm not calling it a witch or anything, but it could be, you know, considering some of the witches I've seen in Disney movies and such."

Perry was diagnosed as paranoid schizophrenic by psychiatrists at the Feliciana Forensic Facility in 1982, records show. However, a recent court-ordered psychiatric evaluation has ruled that Perry is legally sane and can stand trial.

Some locals dismiss him as insane. But many townsfolk simply refuse to buy it. "I always kind of thought it was an act," said Dale Hahn. "It was like he was playing a game, sort of seeing how far he could take it."

"Crazy? No way, man," scoffed Detective Trahan. "We got a French saying down here, that in English means 'the smart fool.' That's Perry—the guy is plenty smart, but if he can, he'll bluff you all to hell. I think the man is sick, but crazy…well—maybe crazy like a fox."

But there's another dark explanation offered for the violence that took place here two years ago. "Better be careful," warns lifetime local resident June Langley, 21. "You're messin' around with some pretty scary stuff."

When asked what she means, Langley sidles closer and drops her voice a notch. "Michael Perry is possessed by a demon, y'know. People down here don't like to talk about it, but it's true."

Considering that this is the heart of Cajun country, a part of America steeped in voodoo, magic, and mysticism, the talk of Perry's link with Satan worship isn't all that unusual. Many people here are simply too superstitious to discuss their real feelings regarding the murders.

Rita Kershaw, 73, mother of Cajun singer/fiddler Doug Kershaw, has lived in Jennings all her life. Seated in the kitchen of her tiny framed house, she puts her hand on her Bible before consenting to discuss Perry.

"Maybe God's gonna punish me for sayin' dis, but dat boy ain't crazy. Evil, mebbe. He don't have da eyes of a crazy person. Some a dem poor people, dey didn't have no heads left at all. Now if dat ain't da work of da devil, I dunno what is!"

But at four on this Sunday afternoon, all talk of death and demons is washed away by the sound of fiddles, accordions and steel guitars. Half the town is packed into T-George's, a ramshackle beer joint in Lake Arthur that holds weekly dances. Sweaty couples swill beer and two-step around the floor to a Cajun band.

A few miles down the road, at a local wedding, more couples dance to the sounds of E.T. and the Satellites—a country-rock band fronted by Detective Trahan.

For the moment at least, it seems as if Lake Arthur is truly—like the sign at the city limits says—"A Good Place to Live."

Stuart Goldman reported on the Perry case for the *Los Angeles Times.* The Perry article appered in the Calendar Section of The September 8, 1985 issue of *The Times.*

MUGS AND THUGS

KING OF THE BOUNCERS

When liberty verges on license, and gaiety on wanton delirium, the bouncer ejects the gayest of the gay and—bounces him.

—*National Police Gazette,* 1865

They call him Big John, and troublemakers are his business. For the past 25 years, Big John has bounced the troublemakers out of virtually every bar and nightclub in Los Angeles. He has worked them all—straight, gay, and transvestite. Black and Latino. Cowboy and biker bars. Hollywood sleazy and Beverly Hills plush. He has gone up against guns, knives, pool cues, beer bottles, saps, blackjacks, tire irons, and baseball bats. Miraculously, he only has a couple of scars. Ninety-nine percent of the time it was his opponent who wound up on the floor—or in the hospital. Hence Big John's moniker—King Of The Bouncers.

On this recent Sunday afternoon, "Big John" Schulps sits at a back table in the Sagebrush Cantina—a Calabasas watering hole—nursing an iced tea. He takes off his shades and surveys the crowd, an odd assortment of tennis-outfitted locals, surfers, hippies, stuntmen, bikers, and rock 'n' rollers.

John's not working today, not officially at least. "When you've been at it as long as I have," he offers, "you're *always* working. If one of these kids gets in trouble," John says, indicating a couple of guys in "security" T-shirts moving through the crowd, "I'm right there."

Kids. The term isn't meant to be condescending. More like a mother hen overlooking her brood. "A lot of the guys get a little, uh… overanxious. They want to wade in there and duke it out. But you can't do that. This is a life-and-death business, man."

"This place looks peaceful now, but it can erupt at any second. It's weird. *Boom*—all of a sudden it's just *on*. Then it spreads like wildfire. We've had some pretty bad scuffles in here. During the last real nasty one, some football players got into it with some basketball players, who started fighting some mountain men from Agoura. That one lasted around 45 minutes. It was bloody. We had two bouncers hospitalized that night."

Big John takes a pull on his iced tea and puts the shades back on. "It doesn't take long to get to the animal in a man. I learned *that* early on."

Big John's first bouncing gig was at the Club 99 in Bakersfield, a place that catered to cowboys, oil workers, and truckers. "It was a rough joint. That's where I learned the ropes."

The man who taught Big John, Marshall Halsten, was head bouncer at the Club 99 in the late 1950s. He was 43 at the time, Big John's age today. John talks about Marshall in the reverential tones normally reserved for a guru. "He taught me everything I know: how to use a doorway to your advantage, how to block a pool cue, how to use a bar stool. Plus little tricks like…" Big John takes a roll of nickels out of his pocket and wraps a huge, meaty fist around them. "You hit a man in the heart with this, an' he's gonna go *down*. It's dirty—but hell, this is survival. Marshall taught me that…only he used quarters," John laughs.

"But fighting was really the least of it. What I learned from the old man were the rules of the game. The *code*. He said, 'Never beat a man if you can help it.' A lot of those guys just want to talk to you. But if you do have to thump someone, don't beat him past what he deserves. If a guy's down, if he's whipped—that's it.' Cause if you really beat a man bad, he's gonna go home and think about it. Then he's liable to come back after you with a gun. So you've got to be fair. That's why Marshall lasted so long, I think—because he had a code of ethics."

"I used to go over to his house for dinner sometimes...and it was really funny to see this big, old, tough man. He had a little house, a dog, and a garden. A library full of books. He was incredibly well-read. He had class, culture, wisdom, and strength—all the qualities we admire. I came to think of him as kind of a nobleman. Still, if you pushed him…I can still see those old gray eyes. They'd get just like death—and then it was 'spankin' time.' That's what he called it. And when he'd fight, oh, man—it was pretty to watch. A work of art."

Bouncing wasn't a full-time occupation for Big John. He played pro football for the Minnesota Vikings, spent several years as a rodeo rider, and got his master's degree in architectural design from UCLA. But weekends would find him back in the bars.

"I had this weird dual existence," he recalls. "Especially when I was in grad school. By day I'd be in lectures on abstract design, and at night I'd dodge beer bottles. And instead of taking UCLA co-eds to parties, I'd take barmaids. They were my pals—my *buds*. Yeah, bouncers and barmaids," John says, "they're just kind of a natural. Good companions. One thing you don't do, though, is fall in love with 'em."

"Those were good times," he says. "I dunno, today the violence is *different*. More crazies out there. Back then, people liked to drink, party, and fight. It was fun."

In the '60s, John worked clubs like the Whisky, which he refers to as a "babysitting job," and the Palomino, back when it was a hangout for Clint Eastwood and his stuntman buddies—not to mention the Hell's Angels. "That place was *bad*. One of the bouncers got shot with an arrow. I used to come to work with my hands taped up, just to save my knuckles."

Today some of the memories seem downright funny, like the time at the Classic Cat when the bouncers took on a host of drunken employees from the Bank of America. "That one turned into a full-scale donnybrook," John laughs. "Everybody got into it. The waitresses were hitting guys over the head with trays. Even the cook was fighting."

But Big John never gets too lighthearted about his work. "Death is always just around the corner. I was working a place called the Blue Quail one night. These three guys were slapping around this little

Mexican fella. Finally he left, but 15 minutes later, he came back with a big old pump shotgun, and *bwam!*—he splattered one guy all over the wall. I mean, there were pieces of bone everywhere. Messed the other two up pretty bad. Then he set the gun down against the bar, ordered a drink, and waited for the police to come. I remember thinking to myself, 'Man, you just *never* know.'"

Though it's not legal, Big John packs a gun when the situation calls for it. "You've got to. Like I said, it's survival—and you can't count on the police. No *way*."

"Two years ago I was working the Pumpkin Festival (in Calabasas) and 15 bikers grabbed this little girl and just dragged her off. I called the California Highway Patrol and they said 'Sorry—it's too crowded. We can't get in there.' So I went after her. This one punk was raping her, an' I told him, 'I want her, man,' and he said, 'Come on and *take* her.' I stuck a .38 in his chest and said, 'If you move, you're gonna lose it right now, friend.' Then I told her to grab onto my belt and we got out of there. Hid her out in a booth. I told my guys, 'If they come in after her, we're gonna stop them.' It was *scary*. That's *war*—you can't call it anything else."

"Today lots of people are carrying guns, and I don't mean just one gun...but three or four. Sometimes, I'll be working a club, and see guys wearing big overcoats, and I'll rub up against 'em and feel that hard thing. So you've gotta be careful. *Never* come on like the Seventh Cavalry. That's another thing the old man taught me. He said, 'John, don't go charging in there. Kinda *ease* on in. Check things out.' Still, when you know there's a problem, you've got to be ready to back things up—even if the odds are against you."

How does one accomplish that? "You've got to make 'em *believe* you. It's eye contact. I'm 6'4", 260 pounds, but there are guys out there bigger than me, tougher than me. So you've got to let them know that you'll hurt 'em. You've got to make them ask themselves, 'Is it *worth* it?'"

"Sometimes you can't avoid a fight. I can tell by the look in a man's eye if he's gonna go for it. There's this little vein right by the iris, and if I see it start to tighten up, *boom!*—I'm gone. Then I don't care *who* that sucker is—I'm gonna take him out."

"Still, I've *talked* more guys out of fights than anything. It's getting tougher, though. I don't have as much patience as I used to.

I can't take the verbal abuse. Recently there was this guy that I *really* wanted a piece of. He epitomized everything I hate—he was a bully, he was loud, offensive, drunk, foul…I literally *begged* him to take a poke at me. But he must've seen the look in my eyes, because he wouldn't. But see, that's no good. Because a bouncer is supposed to keep the peace, not create more hostility. It's like the movies really. Basically, it comes down to good guys versus bad guys. Bad guys start fights. Good guys finish them."

"Then I've got this…*reputation* to contend with. It's kind of like the law of the old West—the fastest-gunslinger bit. There's always that young guy that's gonna want to have a go at me. The challenge. I can't sit in a bar like a normal person. I've got to have my back up against a wall, and always be on the alert. I really *do* feel like one of those old gunfighters."

Even though the Western film may be passé today, we just may be seeing an updated version of one in the future. Big John was recently approached by a producer who wants to make the film based on his life, to be entitled—what else?—*The Bouncer*. Typically, he sidesteps any talk of ensuing fame and fortune.

"This is Hollywood," he snorts. "Lots of people talk about making movies. Most of the time they don't get made. Still, if it happens, I think people could relate to it. It'd be sort of a modern-day Samurai theme—a one-man-against-the-odds kind of thing."

Meanwhile, Big John's got a budding ceramics/knife-making business to keep him busy. Maybe he'll coach a little Pop Warner football. And there are always the "kids"—the young up-and-comers in the bouncing biz—to teach.

"I want to pass on what Marshall taught me," John says. "There's a whole tradition—an unspoken set of rules. A bouncer is a multifaceted individual. He's a philosopher, a therapist, a priest, a father-confessor, a furniture mover, a sometimes-lover. He must be firm, loyal, parental, and—above all—human. This goes way beyond beating some guy up. It's a way of life."

Well, maybe so. But one gets the impression that when the chips are down, Big John has a certain fondness for the age-old ritual of combat. "Yeah," he says, the green eyes twinkling, "when I know it's inevitable, well—it's the ultimate test. It's a heavy thing, facing down a man and seeing where your courage comes from. It's not about who's the *baddest* dude. It's about who's got the most heart. Because once the bullshit stops and you're gonna go for it, then there's no more words. There's just deeds."

John M. Schulps passed away on July 31, 2010, after a brief illness.

ABOUT THE AUTHOR

George Orwell once stated that every honest writer is motivated by two things: the desire to show off, and the habit of noticing unpleasant facts. There is simply no better description than this for the work of Stuart Goldman.

Goldman's irreverent, no-holds-barred commentary has caused him to be labeled a muckraker, a misanthrope and a curmudgeon.

Goldman eschews labels. But the undeniable fact is that, however you choose to regard him, Stuart Goldman's witty, wickedly brilliant style sets him apart from the rest of the pack.

"Most columnists today are trying to be safe," Goldman says. "They're afraid of offending people. These guys shouldn't be called critics. They should be called what they are—PR shills."

H.L. Mencken, Mark Twain and G.K. Chesterton are clearly Goldman's mentors—both in style and theme. "If there's one thing I intend to do," Goldman says, "it's to revive the kind of criticism that made the work of the original muckrakers so fresh and vital."

Goldman's essays, columns and critical reviews have appeared in the *Los Angeles Times, the San Francisco Chronicle, The Herald-Examiner, The L.A. Weekly, The Cleveland Plain Dealer, Paris Match, Oui, Chic, Penthouse, High Times, National Lampoon, Esquire, and National Review.*

For two years he wrote the "Final Cut" column for the *Los Angeles Reader*. In that column, Goldman drew a bead on a wide range of targets and fired at full auto. Amongst those under the gun were vegetarians, Scientologists, rock critics, Elvis imitators, trance channelers, the ACLU, aerobics instructors, New Agers, street mimes, films about teenagers, and humorless people.

"I don't dislike humanity," Goldman smiles. "Just humanity's excesses."

Those excesses include pomposity, maudlinism, conformity, greed, incompetence and hypocrisy. "What irks me most about the time we're living in is this pretense of friendliness," Goldman says. "I'd prefer it if people just said, 'Look, I really don't give a good goddamn about you.'"

Goldman's weapons against the oppressive, stultifying aspects of life as led by the Me Generation are irony, satire—and a frequently savage sense of humor. But Goldman is not only a muckraker. One day his column is hard and tough. The next day it may cause fits of uncontrollable laughter. Next time it might bring you to tears. "There's no formula," Goldman says. "I just try to tell the truth, and to be entertaining. I'm more interested in the heart than the head."

After leaving the University of California at Santa Barbara, Goldman took up the life of a professional musician, touring with Doug Kershaw ("The Rajun Cajun") and John Stewart (formerly of the Kingston Trio). He's been a sideman for a host of name recording artists including Leon Russell, Tanya Tucker, Steve Goodman, Thumbs Carllile, Garth Hudson (of the Band), Dolly Parton and Albert Lee, amongst others.

"The gig I remember most fondly was playing with Kinky Friedman and The Texas Jewboys," Goldman grins. Kinky and I have a lot in common—we're both big boxing fans, as well as being dyed-in-the-wool True Crime addicts.

In 1976, Goldman entered the field of writing as a music critic. At the outset, Goldman served as the Music Editor at the *L.A. Free Press*. He had a weekly Country Music column at the *Los Angeles Daily News* and was the first Entertainment Editor at the *L.A. Weekly*. He was a pop music critic at the *Los Angeles Times*, but he eventually grew weary of going out and "hearing terrible bands that couldn't even tune their instruments." Thereafter, Goldman took a side-step into the field of investigative journalism.

Over the years, Goldman has covered some of the country's major criminal cases, including The O.J. Simpson Murder Case, the Menendez Murder case, the Natalee Holloway Case—to name a few. But what Goldman enjoys most is finding small, "unusual," stories—ones that aren't getting any print because they don't fall within the run-of-the-mill guidelines.

One such piece was "An Eye For An Eye: Murder In Louisiana," during which Goldman reported on Louisiana's most prolific (if one can put it that way) serial killer, Michael Perry. (Perry planned his killing sprees in groups of ten—which was a result of his obsession with The Ten Commandments).

In interviewing Michael Perry, a bright, witty—and clearly psychotic murderer of a number of people in his hometown of Lake Arthur, LA—Goldman got to know Perry quite well.

"I can't say that I "liked" Perry, Goldman explained, "but I wasn't about to write him off—as other writers did—as 'a monster.' We had some very compelling off-the-record talks during the time I spent interviewing him," Goldman recalls. "At the end of it all, he asked me if I'd mind mailing him some CD's. Let's just say that he had very diverse musical tastes." Goldman recalls.

The Perry story ("An Eye For An Eye: Murder In Louisiana,") is one of the more compelling pieces in Goldman's book. But what's remarkable, is that Goldman can turn around and write a piece about his life-long crush on former Mousekeeter, Annette Funicello.

Goldman and Funicello became friends after he interviewed her for *Sh-Boom* magazine in1989. The two hit it off, and they wound up going out together (accompanied by Funicello's husband, Glenn) to dine at some of Annette's favorite Italian eateries. Goldman and Annette solidified their mutual love of country music, by heading out to Ryan's Roundup—one of the oldest "honky tonks" in the Valley.

"I wanted her to hear 'the real stuff.'" Goldman says. "And she loved it."

"We had a lot in common," Goldman says of his friendship with Funicello. "It was kind of weird, because though—as adults—we became friends, I never gave up the childhood crush that I'd had on her, ever since first seeing her on The Mickey Mouse Club back in the '50s.

"It was a terrible loss," Goldman says, of Annette's recent passing. "That's one that I'm never going to recover from."

In 1984, Goldman was offered a regular column by the *L.A. Reader*, a subsidiary of the *Chicago Reader*. During the time Goldman wrote "Final Cut," the circulation of the *Reader* boomed. Goldman amassed sacks full of mail each week and soon gained a national following—even though the *Reader* was published locally in Los

Angeles. By the time Goldman left the *Reader* in 1987, his column had been picked up by newspapers around the country.

In the late 80's Goldman's writing began to evidence a growing conservatism. In fact, Goldman was ultimately given the thumbs up by the maestro of the conservative movement, William F. Buckley, Jr., who published Goldman's "Confessions of a Poison Pen Artist," (a chronicle of Goldman's battles with the liberal press) in *National Review* magazine.

Goldman entered the film industry in 1986 after optioning his first screenplay, "The Bouncer," (based upon an assignment to find the toughest bouncer in L.A.). The film ultimately got made—but not Goldman's version.What began as a down 'n' dirty profile of a true renaissance man, ultimately appeared on the big screen as yet one more "embarrassingly inspid martial arts piece of dogshit." Goldman (who had brought his attorney with him to the film's opening at Grauman's Chinese Theatre) sat and wept through the film that he had spent two years writing. "We had become like brothers, Goldman says about "Big John" Schulps, who inspired the film's lead character. "I had promised him that I would tell his story onscreen—and now I had to explain to him how his life had been turned into a fucking comic book."

"Sure, I thought about suing," Goldman said, but his attorney told him that he should feel proud that he had now joined the ranks of screenwriters who had been ripped off by Hollywood.

In 1996, Goldman sold his *Spy* magazine article, "Spy Vs. Spies" (based upon Goldman's investigation of the tabloid industry) to Phoenix Pictures. Phoenix attached Oliver Stone to direct the film. As of this date, the film hasn't yet been produced, but seventeen years after the initial sale, Goldman and Phoenix have been discussing the project again.

As for where his writing career is heading, Goldman says that journalism is where his heart lies. And though a "kinder, gentler," Goldman has emerged as of late, Goldman insists that when push comes to shove, he has no intention of backing off the the hard-edged reportorial style that he has left him with the moniker, "The Journalistic Hitman."

Whatever tone he takes, whatever subject he tackles, you can bet on one thing—Goldman's witty, insightful, dead-on-target commentary keeps readers coming back for more. Recently, one fan summed it up. "I'm an often lonely writer and sometimes I feel ready to throw in the towel. But when I read Goldman, I want to get up and write my ass off. I want to scream for the rights of normal individuals and antiquated belief systems where men are men, women are women, and the role reversals haven't become so terribly suffocating."

One piece of Goldman fan mail said it all. "Hemingway isn't dead. He's still living in Stuart Goldman—a man with enough guts and talent to fill every empty beer can I've ever tossed."

SOURCE NOTES

Not having all of the sources readily available from which these articles were culled, I'll do my level best here to identify as many of them as possible. A good portion of the articles which appear in this book were taken from my bi-weekly column, "Final Cut," which ran in the *Los Angeles Reader*, 1985–1988. ©Permission to reprint granted by the *L.A. Reader*, and *Voice Media Group*. Many pieces were taken from original articles published in the *L.A. Weekly*, 1983–1990. © Permission to reprint granted by the *L.A. Weekly* and *Voice Media Group*. Other articles were originally published in the *Los Angeles Times*, 1975-1990. ©Permission to reprint granted by the *L.A. Times*. "The Baddest Dude In The World" originally appeared the in the March, 1979 issue of *Hustler* magazine. © Permission to reprint granted by LFP Publishing Group, LLC. "One Tough Mother," was originally published in the May,1980 issue of *Chic* magazine. ©Permission to reprint granted by LFP Publishing Group, LLC. "My Date With Annette" was initially published in the 1989 issue of *Sh-Boom* magazine. ©Permission to reprint granted by LFP Publications LLC. "Cauliflower Alley," was originally published under the title of "Fight Club," in the Sept 23, 1983 issue of the *L.A. Reader*. ©Reprinted by permission. "Murder As Therapy," was originally published in *National Review*, Nov. 29, 1993. ©Reprinted by permission. " An Eye For An Eye: Murder In Louisiana," originally appeared as "TV Addict's Grim Legend On The Bayou," in the Sept 8, 1985 issue of the *L.A. Times*. © Reprinted by permission. "A Word About Stuart Goldman," was written by Jane Getz.

ACKNOWLEDGEMENTS

I want to pay homage to the following people—each of whom has had a major impact on my life. They are not listed in order of importance or by any other methodology. They just happened to be floating through my mind when I sat down to write this:

"Big John" Schulps, "Little Leslie" Pineda, Aaron Copeland, Adam Parfrey, Al Bruno, Al Stricklin, Alan Funt, Alan Hooker, Alana Pierce, Alanna Nash, Albert Glasier, Albert Lee, Alex Lee, Alfonso Barnhart, Alfred E. Neuman, Alice Mathiez, all pedal steel guitar players everywhere, all people named Otis, all the greasy lying pastors who made me realize you didn't have to go to church to be a real Christian, all the people who reject you so you can get stronger, all the Warner Brothers TV shows from the 60s, Althea Flynt, Amos Garrett, Amy Garland, Andy Devine, Andy Griffith, Anita Rudolf, Anne Chabrol, Anne Frenoy, Anne Leighton, Annette Funicello, Arlene Sullivan, Arlo Guthrie, Arnold Urquidez, Art Buchwald, Art Kunkin, Art's Deli, Arthur Guy, Arthur Lee, Arthur Miller, Aunt Adeline, Aunt Charlotte, Auntie Flo, Baby Catt Garland, Baby Wazoo, Barbara Gibello, Barbara Pierce, Barbara Tobin Hill, Barbie Jones, Barney Fife, Barney Hoskyns, Basil Rathbone, Bela Lugosi, Bella Zane, Benjamin Semach, Benny "The Jet" Urquidez, Bernice Goldman, Bert Jansch, Bertrand Chabrol, Beverly Eckert, Biff Rose, Big Jay McNeely, Bill Bentley, Bill Elder, Bill Jones, Bill Nauman, Bill Nowlin, Bill Ryusaki, Billy Barty, Billy Cole, Billy Garland, Blackula, Blind Boy Grunt, Blinky Rodriguez, Bob Dylan, Bob Parsons, Bob Sunseri, Bob Tucker, Bob Wills, Bobby Black, Bobby Darin, Bobby Driscoll, Bobby Jordan, Bobby Rydell, Bolo, Brandon Lee, Brenda Lee, Brien Chapman, Bruce Bass Bassett, Bruce Jay Friedman, Bruce Lee, Buckwheat Zydeco, Bucky Beaver, Buddy Emmons, Buddy Holly, Buddy Knox, Buffalo Bob Smith, Buffy Ford Stewart, Buster Crabbe, Cal Worthington, Camille L'Italien, Captain Penny, Carel Gage Luck, Carmen Sanchez, Carol Gondon Lax, Carolyn Hester, Carrie

Schubert, Chad Watson, Chalet Rosegg, Charles Crews, Charlie Chan, Charlie Falcone, Charlie Parker, Charlotte Chabrol, Cheri Goldman, Cheryl Holdridge, Cheryl White, Chloe Mathiez, Chris Darrow, Chris Hillman, Chris Hinshaw, Chris Reagan, Chris Reagan, Christopher Reeves, Chubby Checker, Chuck Berry, Chuck Connors, Chuck E. Weiss, Cindy Davidson, Clara Odri, Clarabell, Clarence "Gatemouth" Brown, Clayton Moore, Clint Eastwood, Clint Walker, Coleman Luck, Coleman Luck Jr. 111, Connie Stevens, Cord Fisher, Craig Sheibal (the first guy to give me a black eye which prompted me into studying martial arts), Cranium Head, Crusader Rabbit, Cubby O' Brien, Cynthia Rosas, Dale Arden, Dale Fielder, Dan Inosanto, Dan Tyack, Danielle Hishaw, Danny O'Keefe, Danny Timms, Darleen Wilkerson, Darlene Gillespie, Daryl Shack, Dave Alvin, Dave Flanagan, Dave Kirkpatrick, Dave Pearlman, Dave Potter, Davey Graham, Davey Jones, David Alkire, David Dubler, David Hinds, David Janssen, David Lindley, David Nelson, David Weaver, Davy Crockett, Deborah Van Valkenburgh, Deborah Walley, Dee Bleek Hodges, Deems Taylor, Del and Sue Smart, Del Smart, Dennis Lustig, Dennis Mendenhall, Dennis Wilson, Denny Bruce, Denny Lustig, Diane Lewis, Dick Clark, Dick Dale, Dick Lane, Dinah Shore, Domonique Odri, Don Bredes, Don Conka, Donna Greene, Doris Day, Dorothy Pierce, Doug Kershaw, Doug Kershaw Jr., Dougie (the first kid I ever beat the shit out of), Dr. David Boyer, Dr. George Fishbeck, Dr. John, Dr. Jonathan Wong, Dr. Lewis Engel, Dr. No, Dr. Sidney Gold, Dr. Simon Wu, Dr. Walter Martin, Dr. William F. Brewster, Drew Friedman, Du-Pars and all the cool coffee shops in the world, Duane Eddy, Duffy Wenz, Dumbo, Duncan Renaldo, Dyle's, E.C. comic books, Edd (Kookie) Byrnes, Eddie Barnhart, Eddie Cochran, Eddie Haskell, Eddie Ponder, Eddie Tduri, Eddie's Corner, Eddie's duck, Eddie's goat, Edgar Bergen, Edmund Carpenter, Edsel Ford Wong, Eileen Apoe, Elliot Pachulski, Elvis Presley, Emmanuelle Mathiez-Frenoy, Eric Apoe, Eve-Marie Frenoy, Eve-Marie Mathiez, Fabian Forte, Faith Domergue, Fart Man, Fats Domino, Fats Waller, Fatty Patty Farm Girl, Fay Hamilton, Fayssoux McLean, Flash Gordon, Frank Prentice, Frank Sinatra, Frank Weimann, Frank Zumo, Franki Ward, Frankie Avalon, Frankie Lyman and the

Teenagers, Fred Sokolow, Fred Tackett, Fred Walecki, Frederick Exley, Fritz Perls, Gale Storm, Garth Hudson, Gary Credle, Gavin de Becker, GD Walker, Gene Fullmer, Gene Krupa, Gene Sculatti, Gene Vincent, George Jones, George Reeves, Georges Frenoy, Gerry Soffen, Gorgeous George, Grandma Sophie, Grandpa Jake, Greg Brennan, Greg Harris, Gregory Segal, Guy Madison, H.L. Mencken, Hank Garland, Hank Williams, Harriet Nelson, Harvey Kurtzman, Haystack Calhoun, Helen Hooker, Henri Preiss, Herb Steiner, Hersh Farborough, Holly Bryant, Hopalong Cassidy, Howdy Doody, Hoyt Axton, Huey-Dewy-and-Louie, *Humbug* Magazine, Hunter S. Thompson, Huntz Hall, Ian and Sylvia, Irene LaFond, Iris Schneider, Irving Zane, Irwin Blacker, Isaac Pachulski, J.D. Salinger, Jack Davis, Jack Johnson, Jack Webb, Jackie Presslor, Jacob Mann, Jake LaMotta, James Arness, James Darren, James Dean, James Ellroy, James McCool, James Nelson, James S. Thomas, James Stewart, James Taylor, Jamie Garbacik, Jamie Storm, Jan and Arnie, Jan and Dean, Jane Brosius Riggio, Janet Mulford, Jason Para Smith, Jay North, Jay Silverheels, JayDee Maness, Jean-Francois L'Italian, Jean-Louis Mathiez, Jeanie Rackle, Jeff Bridges, Jeff Davidson, Jeff Lee, Jeff Maurer, Jeff Pierce, Jennifer the Mystery Girl, Jenny Pachulski, Jeri Mulford, Jerri Fusch, Jerry Donahue, Jerry Jeff Walker, Jerry Kindela, Jerry Lee Lewis, Jerry Mathers, Jerry Pierce, Jerry Sebransky, Jerry Thurgood, Jerry Williams, Jesse Ed Davis, Jessica Getz, Jim McGuinn, Jim Palenscar, Jim Pfaff, Jimmie Ditzel, Jimmy Bryant, Jimmy Cain, Jimmy Clanton, Jimmy McLarnin, Jimmy Rogers, Jimmy Zane, Jo-El Sonnier, Joaquin de Luis, Jock Mahoney, Joe Frazier, Joe Goldmark, Joe Karbo, Joe Louis, Joe Medwick, Joe Naylor, Joe Pass, Joey Dee, John Agar, John Arbaces, John Barth, John Fahey, John Fante, John Hobbs, John Irving, John Renbourn, John Stewart, John Stone, John Ware, Johnette Naponitalo, Johnny Cash, Johnny Crawford, Johnny Echols, Johnny Legend, Johnny McKnight, Johnny Otis, Johnny Weissmuller, Johnny Winter, Jon Kurnick, Jonathan Edwards, Jonathan Winters, Jonny Murray, Jordan Buck, Joseph Farah, Joseph Heller, Joshua Karp, Joshua Weisser, Josie Tomlison, JT Steiny, Judge Richard Neidorf, Judy Garland, Judy Goslin, Judy Haas, Judy Ritter, Julius La Rosa, Karel Luck, Karen Lee, Karlene Gallegly, Kathy Beaudine, Kathy Faircloth,

Kathy Sobel, Keith Richards, Ken Heyman, Kenny Forsi, Kerry Hotchkiss, Kete Bowman, Kim Fowley, Kim Winn, Kinky Friedman, Kirby Schwennsen Taylor, Kittra Moore, Kobe Bryant, Kolbe Wenz, Kory Goetzman, Krishnamurti, Larry "Ratso" Sloman, Larry Black, Larry De Wald, Larry Flynt, Larry Holmes, Larry Williams, Larry Yurdin, Laurel and Hardy, Laurence Frenoy, Laurie Masters, Laurie Stratford, LaVon Spencer Case, Lawrence Welk, Lazar Saminsky, Lea L'Italian, Leadbelly, Lee Anne Qualls, Lee Quarnstrom, Lenny Breau, Leo G. Carroll, Leo Gorcey, Leo Rosten, Leon Russell, Leonard Bernstein, Leone Lee, Lerina Apoe, Leslie Pineda, Levon Helm, Lillian Roth, Lilly Urquidez-Rodriguez, Linda Hull, Linda Ronstadt, Linda Scifo, Linda Webb, Little Lulu, Little Richard, Lloyd Thaxton, Lon Chaney, Loops, Loren Newkirk, Lori Rochat, Louis Chabrol, Lucille Ball, Ludlow Elementary School, Lynn French, Lynn Stafford, Lynne Cheryl Bush, Madeline Burke, Manny Perlman, Marcel Proust, Margie Mulford, Margo Rofe, Maria McKee, Mario de Laval, Mario Lanza, Mark Helprin, Mark Linn, Mark Pachulski, Mark Shapiro, Mark Stein, Marsha Maurer, Martin Lee, Martine L'Italien, Marv Landfield, Mary Meacham, Mary Mendenhall, Mary Snowdeal, Mary Weed, Maryanne Jones, Matt Connelly, Matt Damon, Maureen McCormick, Max Schwenssen, Maxie, Mel and Dorothy Perry, Mel Bay, Melvena Kaye, Melvin, Melvin Cofsnofski, Merle Haggard, Michael Dare, Michael McCall, Michelly Cordova, Mick Jagger, Mickey Cohen, Mickey Dolenz, Mickey Raphael, Mighty Joe Young, Mike Adelson, Mike Bloomfield, Mike Mazurki, Mike Medavoy, Mike Nesmith, Mike Perlowin, Mike Tomlinson, Miles Davis, Ming, Ming The Merciless, Miss Harper, Moby Grape, Mort Sahl, Mortimer Snerd, Morton Able, Mr. Moto, Mrs. Brockmier, Mrs. Esquer, Ms. Harper, Muhammad Ali, my first 78 which my mom made me break after Chris Hinshaw's mother finked on me, Nancy Edwards, Nancy Gerbault, Nancy Guy, Ned Rorem, Neil With The Deal ("did you know nine out of ten people need a new mattress?"), New Orleans, Nic du Toit, Nick Van Valkenburgh, Nilan Ritter, Nivlem The Great, Norman Mailer, Norton Buffalo, Ohio, Ozzie Nelson, Pam Kaye, Pam Kershaw, Pancho, Pat Boone, Patti Haas (my hair stylist), Patty ("The Bad Seed") McCormack, Patty Hall, Paul Butterfield, Pauline

Barnhart, Pee Wee Kershaw, Penis Man, Peter Alsop, Peter Stampfel, Peter Tork, Phillip Roth, Phineas T. Bluster, Phoenix Justice Arjuna, Pin Man, Pinky Lee, Poco Rusty Young, Pohlian Tan, Pop Tart, Porter Wagoner, Princess Summer-Fall-Winter-Spring, Professor Longhair, Quasimodo, Rags, Raj Rathor, Ralph Policek, Ralph Steadman, Randy Zacuto, Red Rhodes, Red Skelton, Red West, Reina Carerra, Renate Lemn, Renee Czakjowksi, Reverend Ike, Richard Boone, Richard Kip, Richard Price, Rick Danko, Rick Grosvenor, Rick Shea, Rick Utter, Ricky Nelson, Ritchie Valens, Roald Dahl, Robben Ford, Robbie Robertson, Robby Turnner, Robert de Niro, Robert Hilburn, Robert Schmidlkofer, Robert Shank and family, Rocky Marciano, Roger Price, Rolene Brumley, Ron Evrey, Ron Floyd, Ron McQueen, Rootie Kazootie, Rosalie Sorrels, Rosie Flores, Ross Sluyter, Roz Larman, Ruby Rob Fitzsimmons (white boxer with the longest reach in history), Rusty Hamer, Rusty Kershaw, Rusty Young, Sal Guitarez, Sal Mineo, Sal Sunseri, Sam Bush, Sam Lee, Sampson, Sandra Tomlinson, Sandra Tracey, Scott B. Hall, Scott Thomas (my beautiful friend...my first death), Serena Westhead, Sergei Prokofiev, Shaker Heights, Shaker Square, Sharon Tomaney, Sharon Warner Broughton, Sheila Soltes, Sheriff John, Sid Caesar, Simone Bailey, Slavek Hanzlik, Sneaky Pete Kleinow, Snoopy, SnowJewel White, Snyder's Magic Shop, Solange Frenoy, Sonny Liston, Sophia Mann, Sophie Tucker, Spade Cooley, Speedy Otis, Speedy West, Spin and Marty, Stanley Beherens, Stanley Strosser, Steamboat Ed Haas, Steve Blauner, Steve Diamond, Steve Hunter, Steven Peeples, Steven Toombs, Stevie Kaufman, Stevie Ray Vaughn, Stuart Schulman, Sue Marks Shenfield, Sue Rosenberg, Sue Smart, Sue Tait, Sugar Ray Robinson, Susan Collison, Susan Dawn Scott, Susan Toney, Susie Nicholas, Susie O'Hayer, Susie Pineda, Suzy Simmons, Sy and Dorothy Pierce, Sy Devore, Tab Hunter, Taj Mahal, Tameron Greene, Tauni Taber, Taylor Caldwell, Ted Greene, Ted Post, Than Wyenn, The Shaker Square Bum, The Baby Wazoo, The Bailey twins, The Big Bad Wolf, The Buffalo Springfield, The Byrds, The Cisco Kid, the city of Cleveland, The Coasters, The Colony Theatre in Shaker Square, The Creature From The Black Lagoon, The Del Vikings, The Diamonds, the entire Frenoy family (including all the wives, husbands and children with different last names), The Everly Brothers, The Farting Match, The Hardy Boys, The House Of Wax, the kid who did my tattoo, The Little Rascals, The Oh No No's, The Rapid Transit Stop at Shaker Square, The Reverend Wing F. Fing, The Road Runner, The Royal Teens, The Shank Family, The Surfaris, The Terminal Tower, The Three Mesquiteers, The Troggs, The Ventures, The Wicked Witch Of The West, The Wolf (from Peter and the Wolf), Thelonious Monk, Thumbs Carllile, Tim Hall, Timothy Carey, Tom Faciano, Tom Mix, Tommy Jones, Tommy Sands, Toni Gripp Brink, Tony Dow, Trey Thompson, Truck Hannah, *Trump* Magazine, Tubby, Tuck Andress, Ty Hardin, Umberto Eco, Uncle Norm, Uncle Remus, Uncle Scrooge, Vince Barbi, Vladimir Greenberg, Wahee Troger, Wallace Wood, Wally Guse, Walt Disney, Wendy Bergman, Wendy Kaufman, Will (Sugarfoot) Hutchins, Will Elder, Willard Huyck, William F. Buckley, William Howard Taft High School, William Travers Holben, Willie Abrams, Winky Dink, Woody Woodpecker, Xavier Cugat, Yehudi Menuhen, Zaskia Carerra, Zorro, Zumbo, all the people who take tickets and sweep up in movie theatres—especially in the afternoon when I love to go to the movies alone—and of course Jesus Christ—who made all this possible (I think).

Many, many wonderful (and terrible) people have been left out... thousands of them. My apologies—dear friends and colleagues. You will continue to populate my dreams and shape my life in countless, mysterious ways...and I will continue to add you to my prayer list which grows longer day by day. I love you, one and all....

THANK YOU

I wish to thank the following people and companies, without whom the publishing of this book would not have been possible: Althea Goldman-Pachulski, Andy Van De Voorde, Arthur J. Harris, *Billboard* Magazine, *Black Belt* Magazine, *Chic* Magazine, Craig Haller, Cynthia Gallagher, Deb Milius, Donna Hahner, Dylan Stewart, Elizabeth Cooper, Eric Varela, *G.L.O.W.* (Gorgeous Ladies of Wrestling), Heather Anne Cheney, *Hustler* Magazine, Inanna Arthen, Indigo Love, *Inside Kung Fu* Magazine, Jaimee Garbacik, Jane Getz, Jason Mueller, Jill Bailin, Jim Dawson, Johnny Whiteside, Jonathan Killebrew, Joni Landfield, Laurence Frenoy, Linda LaFond, Lindsay Little, *Los Angeles* Magazine, Lucy Zepeda, Matt Katzenberger, Medical Center Pharmacy, Michael H. Klein, Mike Lenehan, *National Review* Magazine, *Oui* Magazine, *Paris Match* Magazine, Pat Godinez, Patrick Piciarelli, Ray Troll, Richard Bashara, Richie Suarez, Sven Kamm, The *Hollywood Reporter*, The *Los Angeles Free Press*, The *Los Angeles Herald-Examiner*, The *Los Angeles Reader*, The *Los Angeles Times*, The *Los Angeles Weekly*, The *San Francisco Chronicle*, *Voice Media Group*, *World Net Daily*.

www.ingramcontent.com/pod-product-compliance
Lightning Source LLC
Chambersburg PA
CBHW071219250626
47163CB00001B/48

* 9 7 8 0 9 8 9 9 1 7 4 1 4 *